"HOW COULD YOU POSSIBLY DREAM MY DREAM?" AN ASTONISHED ERCY ASKED.

"It wasn't a dream," said the Gypsy girl. "It was a memory of a past life—and we are all bound by it. I have an obligation. You are a seer. Halimer Grant is a magician."

Ercy gritted her teeth in exasperation. "I am a scientist, and scientific inquiry will find an explanation for what is happening here—and how Halimer Grant fits into all this."

"Science is the opposite of magic," said the Gypsy girl. "In Zeor, while I learn science, you will learn that magic is real. I just hope you learn to respect its power before you learn how real it is."

Berkley Books by Jacqueline Lichtenberg

CITY OF A MILLION LEGENDS
FIRST CHANNEL (with Jean Lorrah)
HOUSE OF ZEOR
MAHOGANY TRINROSE
MOLT BROTHER
UNTO ZEOR, FOREVER

MAHOGANY TRINROSE
JACQUELINE LICHTENBERG

BERKLEY BOOKS, NEW YORK

All of the characters in this book are fictitious,
and any resemblance to actual persons, living or dead, is
purely coincidental.

MAHOGANY TRINROSE

A Berkley Book / published by arrangement with
Doubleday & Company, Inc.

PRINTING HISTORY
Playboy Paperbacks edition / August 1982
Berkley edition / July 1986

All rights reserved.
Copyright © 1981 by Jacqueline Lichtenberg.
This book may not be reproduced in whole or in part,
by mimeograph or any other means, without permission.
For information address: The Berkley Publishing Group,
200 Madison Avenue, New York, NY 10016.

ISBN: 0-425-09309-3

A BERKLEY BOOK ® TM 757,375
Berkley Books are published by The Berkley Publishing Group,
200 Madison Avenue, New York, NY 10016.
The name "BERKLEY" and the stylized "B" with design
are trademarks belonging to Berkley Publishing Corporation.

PRINTED IN THE UNITED STATES OF AMERICA

To my daughters, Naomi and Deborah
because they will soon be teenagers themselves
To Jean Lorrah
because she invented the Tigue mutation
And to the *Ambrov Zeor* and *Companion in Zeor* staffs
because they supply the series with so much enthusiasm

Acknowledgments

In this book, you will meet Joeslee Teel Tigue, a character who has arisen through the interaction of two Sime/Gen fans.

Jan McCrossen Mike, who served a stint as editor of *Ambrov Zeor,* is a student of the Ancient's gypsy tribes. She helped flesh out the culture of the Sime/Gen gypsies even though they are not descended from the Romany tribes but are simply wanderers or nomads with their own culture and customs.

Jean Lorrah, a professor of English at Murray State University in Kentucky, who earned fame as a *Star Trek* fan writer and is now a professional science-fiction writer, added the Tigue mutation to the Sime/Gen universe. Tigue women are channels; Tigue men are talented Donors.

It seemed to me perfectly natural that Joeslee Teel would turn out to be a Tigue channel, and so she is also partly inspired by Jean Lorrah.

Others whose aid I must acknowledge include Marion Zimmer Bradley for her terse commentary, Christine Bunt, Pat Gribben, Judy Segal, Lisa Waters, Katie Filipowicz, who is now editor of *Zeor Forum: Transfer for Ancients,* and Karen McCleod Litman, editor of *Companion in Zeor,* all of whom read and criticized the manuscript. Anne Pinzow Golar, managing editor of *Ambrov Zeor,* also provided much inspiration and the impetus to get this book finished.

All three of the above-named Sime/Gen fanzines can be contacted by sending a self-addressed stamped envelope (SASE) to:

Ambrov Zeor
P.O. Box 290
Monsey, N.Y. 10952

Jacqueline Lichtenberg
Spring Valley, N.Y.

Prolog

Below them the town rioted.

Digen Farris sat behind the chopper pilot where he could see the instruments as well as get a full view through the windshield. Dark clouds formed a low ceiling over the sprawling valley town surging with angry humanity. In the town square, three bright columns of flame leaped skyward. He couldn't escape even by closing his eyes.

His Sime senses painted the lurid picture for him. Not for the first time, he cursed his innate sensitivity. The dying happening below reached up to claw at his nerves. From the rioters rose a miasma of anger, terror, and killust which sang through every cell of his body, touching off responses he had to choke back.

He inched closer to Im'ran, who observed quietly beside him. The Gen's nager, the field surrounding his body, was a welcome shield.

"Wellway Central to overhead choppers. Respond." The radio crackled with the static of the storm that had drenched the desert hills for the last three days.

Digen's pilot activated his microphone. "This is Rialite Rescue Service with four choppers over Wellway Town responding to your emergency call. We request further information."

The three rescue choppers flew a tight formation around them, visible as bright green and white forms through the mist and rain. Digen could barely make out the Central operator's words over the noise.

". . . afraid you're too late. An hour ago, they broke into the jail and took the prisoners."

Digen leaned forward and snagged the copilot's microphone. "This is the Rialite Controller. May I speak to your Mayor?" He knew now what those pillars of flame meant. The eighteen gypsies, Simes and Gens mixed, had been held in protective custody when the Mayor had called the nearest Sime Territory

10 JACQUELINE LICHTENBERG

authority—namely, Rialite and Digen—but it had taken them three and a half hours to get here.

Several minutes later, the radio spoke. "This is Mayor Treldies of Wellway Township, Gartin Territory."

"Digen Farris, here, Mr. Mayor. Is there any way to reason with that mob?"

"If there was, I'd have done it by now. We did our best to protect your Simes, Mr. Controller, but they're all gypsies."

"What did they do?" asked Digen. Normally he wouldn't consider gypsy Simes as under his jurisdiction. However, when a band of mixed Sime and Gen gypsies traveled out into Gen Territory, the resident Gens held the Sime government responsible—and here, that meant Digen.

"Townsfolk figure they're causing the rain," the Mayor responded. "They're planning to burn them at the stake to stop the rain before it washes the whole town away."

"The charge, then, is—witchcraft?" It was a statute on the books in some Gen Territories.

"What else would you call it?"

"Have they been legally convicted?"

"Hell—no! That's a lynch mob out there. If you can get your people out, you're welcome to them. You can take them to Carlston, where they can get a fair trial."

But, Digen realized, he wasn't going to get any further help from the Gen authorities. "Thank you, Mr. Mayor. We'll do our best."

Digen thought fast. "Number Two!" he called on his command frequency. "Drop down over the square, moving fast. Find out if they have guns. Number One and Number Three, unlimber your ladders and stand by to deploy on target. Fil," he ended to his own pilot, "we'll circle the edges of the crowd using our downdraft to scatter them."

When the Number Two unit was not shot at, Digen ordered it to follow the others into the center of the square and drop ladders to the prisoner gypsies awaiting execution. The ones on the pyres were already dead.

The maneuver was working, a Sime dangling on the end of each chopper's ladder to cut the gypsies free, attach harnesses, and lift them out, when a multi-branched flash of lightning lit up the hillside above the town. It was only then that Digen caught sight of the wall of water rolling down upon them all.

He grabbed for his exterior microphone and jumped the gain

MAHOGANY TRINROSE 11

up to maximum. His voice boomed out over the whole valley. "Your dam has broken. Repeat. Your dam has broken. You have approximately ten minutes to reach high ground. Our choppers will assist those stranded. We are calling for outside assistance."

He flipped to his command channel. "Two, keep broadcasting that warning. Three, get those Simes *out* of here! Number One, as soon as you've secured your gear, get some height and try to punch a signal through to Baker. I'm going to Emergency Channel Three to try to reach any in-Territory help I can. There are over twenty thousand people down there."

By the time he turned his attention once more to the mob below, it had dissolved into hundreds of individuals streaming for the elevated sides of the valley. At the farther edges, heavily loaded farm vehicles worked their way to high ground. He was glad he'd brought the large choppers with full equipment. Each could take on twenty or thirty passengers if they had to.

For the next few minutes, he was busy directing the rescue efforts. He only had time to notice the swarm of cars leaving the Wellway Central building, the Mayor and company abandoning the town. And then he saw the train, heading for Rialite.

It came speeding out of the pass toward the trestle over the river. Clearly, the wall of water which had swept through the center of the town would hit the trestle even while the train was on it.

He pulled his choppers away from the now empty town, broadcasting to all below that two more rescue teams were on the way, and sped downstream. He landed all the choppers on solid ground above the flood waters, and as the rain began sheeting down once more, he directed his crews to use the gypsy Simes who were uninjured to help locate and rescue any survivors.

He hadn't had time to watch the water sweep away the trestle. Already corpses were floating by their position. His Number Two and Three choppers rose, rescuers dangling beneath, hauling panic-stricken forms out of the dark waters onto rescue platforms.

Off on the far side of the raging river, Digen sensed a peculiarly resigned Gen nager. It was impossible to see that far through the torrential rain. But by zlinning with Sime senses, he could discern that one lone Gen had been overlooked.

Turning to the knot of gypsies huddled beside him on the bank, he picked two healthy Simes and said, "You—and you—come on!" He led the way back to his own chopper, where Im'ran was down in the passenger compartment unlimbering first-aid supplies.

12 JACQUELINE LICHTENBERG

He climbed into the pilot's seat, directing the two Simes to man the rescue platform that had been rigged under his chopper, then he lifted straight up and over the other working teams. Im'ran poked his head through the back hatch. "What—Digen!"

Over his shoulder, Digen yelled, "Stray Gen! Man the ladder!" And then they were in position. The wind was picking up, driving the rain sideways until it was a solid sheet covering his windshield. By Sime senses alone, he held the chopper steady over the victim, who was riding a swift current that would soon dash him into some rocks at the edge of the torrent.

And then the Gen was on the rescue platform, clinging to the Sime who was securing a harness around him, not shocked but bemused. Digen lifted and set down again on his well-chosen spot of high ground, cutting his motors. *Whew! I'm glad I can still do that!*

When he got to the compartment where the nearly drowned Gen was being given first aid by Im'ran while the two gypsies hovered warily at the far end, he had to stop.

The entire compartment was lit up to his Sime senses by this new Gen's field. It had a clear, disciplined quality and a power never seen in an out-Territory Gen. *No wonder I spotted him way over there!*

He went over to the cot on which the Gen was lying, breathing deeply now with only an occasional cough. Im'ran was saying impatiently, "Well, aren't you even going to thank your rescuers over there? Or don't you talk to gypsy Simes?" The gypsy rescuers shrank into the corner.

"Im'!" said Digen sharply. "This man is at least your equal as a Donor!" He turned to the Gen. "I'm Sectuib Digen Farris, Rialite Controller—and I presume you are the new Donor they've been promising to send me all winter. No, don't try to talk yet. You're not hurt, but you could go into shock, so I want you to stay in that bed under those blankets and keep warm."

"No argument, Sectuib," said the Gen. "I am grateful." He eyed the gypsies. "Would you please tell them so for me?"

Digen shrugged. Obviously, the two gypsies wanted no part of this Gen. He went to the two who had helped him. "You did that like professionals. We all thank you."

Eyeing the Gen, one of them said, "Can we go now?"

"You're going to have to ride back to Rialite with us . . ."

The second objected. "No! We can't—I mean, can't we ride

with the rest of our people?'' But his eyes were also on the strange Gen, who was now steadfastly ignoring them.

Digen couldn't make out what was spooking them, but he conceded and went to end off the rescue operation and get the injured to proper medical facilities at Rialite, where they were also struggling with the flood tonight. It was going to be a long night.

Chapter 1

The moment she laid eyes on the man, the future changed.

As long as she could remember, she had accepted that she would die in changeover. But now, with every step closer he came, first the hope and then the irrational conviction came over her—*I'm going to live*.

She knelt in the rich loam of her garden, her trinroses all around her, and watched the two men approaching. The Sime was her father, Digen Farris, Sectuib in Zeor, Controller of Rialite. He was tall, rangy, looking older than he really was. With him was a Gen, not as tall but oddly just as imposing a figure, with brilliant blue eyes and shocking white hair, though he could hardly be much over twenty.

As he came nearer, the searing intensity of her conviction faded, and in its wake came a shuddering fear, just as irrational, that she would—because of this man—be able to grow a mahogany-colored trinrose that would do exactly what the legends said it would. For the future had changed.

Using every scrap of her Zeor discipline, Ercy shoved the hope and the fear way down inside where no Sime, not even her father, could detect it. Then she got to her feet, suddenly conscious of her dirty coveralls and unkempt hair. The men stopped by the neat row of smooth river stones that edged her plot, and Digen said, "Ercy, I present Halimer Grant, Donor First, our newest staff member."

Ercy smiled at the Gen, her mouth dry and her mind without a word in it.

"Halimer Grant, this is Aild Ercy Farris, my daughter, and Sectuib Apparent in Zeor."

For a moment, the Gen seemed confused, noting her smooth forearms without even the trace of tentacles. She was a child, not an adult Sime, not a channel like her father; certainly it was premature to name her ready to take her father's place as head of

MAHOGANY TRINROSE 15

the prestigious and sprawling company known the world over as Householding Zeor.

Ercy felt an almost irresistible urge to squirm under the Gen's gaze, but her father's flashing eyes told her clearly that a future Sectuib does not squirm. Then in his maddeningly clinical way, her father said to Grant, "Ercy turns sixteen next week, but there's still no sign of changeover. Nevertheless, we're preparing carefully. Her birth characteristics indicated she'll be the most sensitive channel in the family since my brother Wyner Liu died."

Slowly—he seemed to do everything slowly, even his blink was slow—Halimer Grant smiled. It was as if the smile started peeping at last out through his blue eyes and warming her through and through, evaporating her nervousness.

Grant proffered his hand, bowing. "I am honored indeed to be permitted within the presence of such an accomplished gardener."

She let him take her fingers. He had the smoothest skin she had ever touched in her life. He let her remain locked in that silent communication until her father said, "I'll be briefing Halimer on his duties for the rest of the morning. If you see Im'ran or Mora, send them up to the office."

"Yes, Father," Ercy responded automatically. As she watched the Gen make his way back down the flagstone path, she could not quite remember how she had lost touch with his fingers.

"Ercy!" snapped her father. "You haven't been paying attention! I said, when you've had lunch, I want to see you in the clinic again."

"Again? Oh, Father . . ."

"From today on, until—this is over for you—I want to check you three times a day at least."

All the infuriating clinical detachment he could don like a cloak dropped away, and she could see his love for her, his fear for her life. "All right, Father, whatever you say."

Digen turned away. His long stride brought him up beside Grant before the Gen had started up the broad front steps of the Controller's Residence. Together, they walked to Digen's office.

"Hajene Farris," said Grant, using Digen's official Tecton title, "isn't such a late changeover a dreadful pathology in a Farris?"

Digen nodded. "Ordinarily, one would expect a Farris channel to change over at around age ten, eleven at the latest. There's absolutely no record of any Farris surviving changeover as late as sixteen years. But Ercy will. She has the same birth characteris-

16 JACQUELINE LICHTENBERG

tics as my brother Wyner Liu. I'm now sure his problems stemmed from premature changeover and Ercy is a healthy specimen of Wyner's substrain of the Farris mutation.''

"That's an interesting theory—"

"Don't get me started on it—we'll never get any work done. We've been terribly short-handed. I'm expecting thirty new admissions to the College of Channels today—every one of them a special problem—and the Senior Class is graduating today.''

Inside the office, Digen began pulling files and ledgers from the shelves, outlining the new Donor's responsibilities. Rialite's main business was the training of newly matured Simes, freshly through changeover. These young Simes spent their first year in a state of adaptability which gave them a learning rate often up to ten times normal. During that first year, they were expected to absorb a normal six-year college education.

Digen briefly reviewed the organizational structure of the Muir College of Channeling, and then outlined the medical histories of the new admissions. Rialite always got the tough ones.

The training of a channel was not to be entrusted to just anyone. The channels were the only Simes who could take selyn, the energy of life itself, directly from volunteer Gen donors without killing them and then channel it to Simes in need. Channels were the backbone of the Tecton, the organization that supervised the selyn delivery system, preventing Simes from killing Gens for selyn. And the Donors—the specially trained Gens like Halimer Grant—were the only ones who could serve a channel's personal need for selyn and survive the experience.

As he ran through the routine indoctrination for a new staff Gen, Digen watched Grant closely, trying to form a judgment.

Something about Grant bothered him. It was, Digen decided, the Gen's energy field, his nager, that puzzled him most. It had a kind of shimmering, organized clarity that couldn't be natural. It had to have been schooled into the man from his day of establishment. But by what method, what school, what House?

Flipping the books closed and stacking them before Grant, Digen asked, "You connected with any of the Householdings?''

There was a pause as a whispery shadow flicked through that strange nager. *If I couldn't see him visually,* thought Digen, *I'd think he was a ghost.*

"Not—not officially," answered Grant. "But I've spent a lot of time around Householder types. I respect Zeor.''

"I didn't mean that. Obviously, you're not prejudiced. I was just wondering where you were trained.''

MAHOGANY TRINROSE 17

In genuine startlement, Grant said, "Does it matter?"

"No, of course not," Digen reassured him hastily. "A Tecton Donor is a Tecton Donor. That's what you obviously are. I suppose your papers will arrive eventually. I heard the World Controller's office was eight months behind in their paperwork and I suppose it's the same everywhere with these new regulations. And the way you arrived—" Digen shrugged helplessly.

"I'm sorry I lost all my things in the storm, but when that bridge went out, I was lucky to get away with my life."

"It's no problem. I'll request duplicates tomorrow—when I get around to it. The important thing now is to get today's admissions processed before we have tomorrow's admissions standing around wondering what to do with themselves."

Digen began stacking books onto Grant's outstretched arms. "Here's the campus map. You should be able to find your office. Take a couple of hours to get settled before the train arrives. I'll meet you then on the platform."

Grant nodded and left. Digen, seeing that he had a few minutes yet, raced through some of the work that had piled up since the previous afternoon. Then he glanced through yesterday's newspaper. There was an item about the extradition of a convicted witch who had taken asylum in-Territory. If the Sime government forced her to go back, the Gens were planning to burn her alive—before witnesses. Digustedly, Digen threw the paper aside and left his office.

Ercy was waiting patiently for her father, putting the finishing touches on a problem-set for her trigonometry class. She thought she was finally beginning to understand cosines. With a sense of triumph, she looked up as her father walked in carrying the thick chart that detailed her whole medical history, right down to the amount of selyn she'd drawn from her mother at birth.

Digen set up the testing scopes and instruments around his daughter, adjusting the darkfield backdrop against which he'd view her body fields as he played various influences over her.

Ercy watched her father painstakingly making notes, glancing at her from various angles, adjusting his instruments. She was so used to it after all these years that she could anticipate his moves.

After a time, her father said, "Fine, now just for the record I want to do a full lateral contact probe this afternoon."

"The record!" she said glumly. "That's all I am, a specimen, an experiment. When are you going to write me up for the Journal?"

18 JACQUELINE LICHTENBERG

He set his chart aside and took her hands. "It's not like that, Baby. I have to be sure . . ."

"That's just it, I'm not a baby!" said Ercy with a vehemence she had not intended. And suddenly there were tears in her eyes. "You know what your trouble is? You want me to grow up, but when I act grown-up it scares you, and you want me to be your little baby again. You just don't know what you want, that's all!"

"Who told you that?"

"You see? You can't credit me with any brains. Nobody told me. I saw it when you introduced that Gen—Grant."

Digen, refusing to be baited, said, "What did you think of Halimer Grant?"

Suddenly thoughtful, she replied, "I don't know. He's—different. Is he going to stay long?"

"As long as I can hold on to him. Grant's—*very* good."

She received this in silence, and Digen took the opportunity to slide into lateral contact position. The internal examination took only a moment. He had merely to extend his four delicate, nerve-rich lateral tentacles that were normally used only in transfer, make a solid contact with the skin of her forearms, and a fifth contact, lip to lip for maximum sensitivity to her internal fields, and withdraw.

She was accustomed to the channel's examining technique, and didn't flinch. But as he withdrew, she touched a finger to one of his lateral sheaths, where the ronaplin gland bulged slightly, and met his eyes. "I didn't realize you hadn't taken transfer yet. I guess I was a little nasty just then. I'm really sorry, Dad."

And worried, too, thought Digen.

"Oh, don't look at me like that!" she snapped. "I'm beginning to feel like a bomb everybody expects to explode!"

He caught her eyes with a steady gaze, trying to sound positive. "Ercy, you're going to have a perfectly normal changeover. We've been over this a thousand times; know it and hold on to that knowledge. Hold on hard, because it can't be much longer. Honest."

"But there's no sign! You've told me a hundred times, a channel always knows months—even a year or more beforehand—exactly when he'll hit changeover. I've never felt that!"

"Well—Wyner didn't know beforehand. Everybody always thought that was because he was so young, but . . . ."

"Wyner! I'm so sick of hearing about Wyner."

She was near to tears. *No! I won't cry like a baby!* Her father shouldn't have to deal with her hysteria when he was in need. She jumped down from the examining table and began putting her schoolwork away. "Dad? Remember I said I wanted to go away for my channel's training? I've changed my mind. I want to stay home—I want to train here." Silently, she added the brutal honest truth to herself, *under Halimer Grant.*

Taken aback for a moment at his daughter's sudden capitulation to a long-standing argument, Digen said, "Why?"

"I just realized today. It could be very nice."

"You're not scared of the outside world, are you?"

"No—I don't think so, anyway. I mean, after all, if I can face changeover, what's a little thing like a world? I'll go anywhere the Tecton sends me, afterward, but I'd like to stay here for my training. Besides, this way, I won't have to leave my garden."

So that's it, thought Digen. *That garden!* But at least she had given up the grim notion that she was going to die in changeover if she was already making plans for her garden afterward.

Ercy said, "You'd better hurry, Father, or you'll be late for graduation."

Chapter 2

Ercy heard the train whistle just as she was leaving her trigonometry class. She cut through a shaded glade and around the senior students' housing, intent on being the first in line for the mail. She had some special fertilizer on order which she had to get into the ground the moment it arrived. With luck, it might make the new trinrose buds come out mahogany.

The three graduating classes, Channels, renSimes, and Gens, were drawn up in crisp rows on the train platform, neatly intermingled with one another to give the arriving students a concrete impression of the goals of their education. The brand-new Tecton crest rings shone brightly on the hands of the channels and Donors who were going to work for the Tecton.

As she drew near, she heard her father addressing them, talking about how they'd all worked together to avert real disaster in last night's flood here. He made the whole annoying mess into a kind of glowing symbol of their new lives, and she admired him for his art in this, knowing that his transfer had been delayed because of the flood, so he was still in need.

Need was the periodic nightmare of every adult Sime, especially channels. What could it possibly be like to live with it? Some people said it was like starving to death. Sme people said it was more like suffocating or drowning. *If Halimer Grant stays, I'm going to find out what need is like after all*.

As the train coasted into the station, her father ended his speech and turned to Grant. From where she stood, Ercy couldn't hear their words, but she knew from his gestures that he was explaining how they would get the arriving students sorted out. Suddenly, she felt acutely uncomfortable watching them—her father's tentacles gesturing; Grant's untentacled arms bare to the shoulder, smooth and deeply tanned. She turned to walk around the station house to the post window to wait for her mail.

Leaning against the wall, soaking in the late-afternoon sun, she

MAHOGANY TRINROSE   21

closed her eyes, wondering how it would feel to be grown-up and able to zlin, to see by selyn refraction, not by light.

"Hi, Ercy!"

She came to with a start. "Oh, Im'ran!"

The slender, gaunt-faced Gen coming toward her was as much her father as Digen was. He was married to her mother and served her father as a permanent Donor because of the locked transfer dependency, the orhuen, that they shared.

"Where's Digen?" asked the Gen.

"Showing our new Co-Dean how to get a class of channels started. He just finished his speech." Seeing how worried Im'ran looked, she added, "Dad doesn't seem under much strain yet."

"He shouldn't be—yet—but—" He broke off, his attention going to the scene on the platform. The ceremony broke up and Digen came toward them, Grant at his side.

Im'ran moved to take his place at her father's shoulder, and Ercy knew that he was now bringing her father's selyn fields into his own steady bodily rhythms, alleviating a great part of the strain of need for her father. But she wondered what it would be like to be able to zlin the fields meshing between them.

Pulling her thoughts together, she turned toward the window, where the mail clerk already had the mailbag open. They were exceptionally efficient today, she thought, probably because her father was nearby.

"Ercy," said the clerk, "here's your *Gardener's Tips* copy for the month. That what you're waiting for?"

She took the magazine. "Yes, thank you," she said, concealing her disappointment.

She did all her chores, spent two hours on classwork, showered, read her magazine, presided over supper in the absence of her parents, who were still sorting things out after the flood, and then she went to the lab to wait for her father's last check of the day. She felt she could run all of Rialite by herself if she had to. After all, she was turning sixteen.

She was sitting on the examining table, swinging her legs and contemplating her accomplishments, when Halimer Grant came in.

"Ercy! What are you doing here?"

"Waiting for my father."

Grant came all the way into the room, setting aside some papers he was carrying. "I have to find the supply room and put through these requisitions," he said, "but I'm glad to see you."

"This is my father's personal lab," she offered, wishing vio-

22 JACQUELINE LICHTENBERG

lently that there wasn't such a lump in her chest where her heart should be. "The supply clerk works way at the other end of the building and around the corner."

"Oh," he said, looking over his shoulder at the papers. "They said the east corner of the building."

"Right. This is the west corner." And then before she could stop the words, she said, "That's fairly typical of a lost Gen." Before the words were out, her hand started to fly to her mouth to stop them, but she aborted the gesture, feeling impossibly childish.

Grant chuckled merrily. "It seems I got lost in that storm and haven't found myself yet. Can you tell me something?"

She nodded, her larynx frozen.

"What were you doing with the trin bushes this morning? Those grafts interest me. Do you grow your own trin tea here? In this sandy soil?"

She shook her head, swallowing hard until she could speak. "I've worked the garden into a good loam, mostly using kitchen scraps and manure, but the climate is wrong for good tea—at least that's what the Simes said about my efforts and I suspect they were being charitable."

"Then why cultivate the bushes? Your garden is spectacular enough without them."

"For the flowers I want—" She broke off. *What if he laughs at me?* She met his eyes again, and a brilliant white calm wakened within her body. The words came tumbling out. "My parents think I gave up long ago, and I let them think that because—well, because the daily fights about it just wore me out. I know how absurd it sounds to them—my trying to grow a mahogany trinrose."

She looked at him defiantly, but oddly enough, he was regarding her without a trace of the usual ridicule. "Have you—have you succeeded yet?"

"No," Ercy admitted. "But this spring, I've made up some new genetic charts and I'm going to start cross-pollinating again. I've got a theory the real key is both chemical and—and—" *I can't tell him that!*

"And?"

"Ah, well, it's all very complicated, researching a legend, but Dad always says science is an inherently slow procedure."

She thought she detected an air of relief in him, and wished forlornly that she could zlin his nager. On a sudden leap of

MAHOGANY TRINROSE 23

intuition, she said, "You know something about the mahogany trinrose, don't you?"

"Oh," he answered in his slow manner, "no, I once had a friend who tried growing them."

She wondered if he spoke slowly to give himself time to choose his words, or if he chose his words because he spoke slowly. "Did your friend ever succeed? Maybe we could compare notes? I keep a thorough scientific journal even though I'm just researching a superstition . . ."

"No—no, I don't think that's possible. I've lost touch with him. But what would you do with such a bush if you got one?"

"Take pictures. Publish an article. Try to get some pharmaceutical house to test it. Wouldn't it be something if the legends turn out to be true?"

Slowly, as always, he said, "What—which legend?"

"That even a Sime addicted to the kill—a real junct Sime who's killed for years—the kind you only read about in history books—can survive disjunction and never have to kill again, by using an extract made from the mahogany trinrose."

"There might," said Grant thoughtfully, "be some truth to that legend—but I wouldn't—" He broke off as she met his eyes, hoping he wouldn't scoff as all the others did. "Ercy—have you already chosen to specialize in disjunction?"

"Well—I hadn't really thought about it, but I suppose so. With *my* father—it seems only natural."

"Your father?"

"He's only technically junct, you know. He could never actually kill any Gen because the scar on his lateral would kill him first. But every so often he does have to take junct-style transfers from Im'ran. They both hate it. Dad wants to disjunct so bad he's willing to risk his life. The only thing preventing him is that he has no heir until I change over. He's Sectuib—he can't risk his life unless Zeor is safe. But he wants to."

"Why?"

Words failed at that strange question. "I'm only a child and even I can imagine what it must be like for him being legally barred from functioning as a channel! I'd expect any Donor to understand. Why, the only thing keeping him from dying of entran is his orhuen with Im'."

"I have," said Grant even more slowly than usual, "seen what happens to a Tecton channel who cannot work. Entran is such a sterile word for that—agony." He seemed to pull himself away from a vision and focused on her. "Even though his

24 JACQUELINE LICHTENBERG

transfer dependency on Im'ran controls the entran symptoms, he must suffer simply because he's a talented healer barred from healing. But, Ercy—why is it up to you to disrupt the situation? And why in this particular fashion?''

"You remember how he became junct in the first place. It's in all the history books—only half the time they quote the superstitition that his junctedness happened simply from transfer with a Distect Gen. Really, it happened because that particular Gen, Distect or not, was his matchmate and was suffering from underdraw. Why not fight superstition with superstition? The mahogany trinrose is just a legend, a fairy story, but if science can find a way to grow one and extract a drug which will ease transfers—then science triumphs over stupidity. People will realize that there's no such thing as 'magic,' only natural laws we don't yet understand. Then they'll stop burning people and rioting against so-called magicians.''

"You feel very strongly about that, don't you?''

"Was I shouting? I'm sorry, I get carried away.''

"I didn't intend criticism of your behavior.''

"Well,'' answered Ercy without thinking, "I'm supposed to be Sectuib-Apparent in Zeor.'' And then it hit her. "I mean, I'm going to be Sectuib in Zeor.'' After a moment or two she realized she was staring wide-eyed at Grant. *Sectuib-Apparent in Zeor trying to grow an impossible flower. And if he knew about the moon, what would he think?*

But all he said was: "Yes—the future—changed.''

"You changed it.''

"I—did.''

"Why? Why did you come here?'' The words seemed to come out of their own volition, though her voice was choked to a whisper by a fear she couldn't name.

"I—had to. I had to come—here.''

She found his hands resting on her wrists, her eyes almost level with his as he leaned closer to say very quietly, "We can deal with a changing future. We can and will deal with the future we have chosen.''

If he took his hands away, she thought she'd faint.

There was a sound at the door. Without startlement, Grant turned. He disentangled his hands slowly, placing hers in her lap.

At the door, Im'ran had moved in beside Digen, watching them. Ercy wondered how long they'd been there. Digen came into the room, his overly quick, jerky stride betraying his need.

"No,'' said Digen as he advanced, "don't move apart. I want

MAHOGANY TRINROSE 25

to get a good reading on this. Hal, give her a full transfer position, would you?" As he moved, Digen picked up Ercy's chart and began observing them from every angle, as Halimer slid his hands almost up to her elbows. "That's right," said Digen, jotting down some notations. "Lip contact, too."

Grant leaned in to make the lip-lip contact. Ercy shied back. No Gen had ever done that with her before.

Vexed, Digen said, "Ercy, you'll have to get used to it sometime."

"But not yet," she objected. She was sweating in sudden embarrassment. Grant watched Digen.

"That's very interesting," muttered Digen. "Im'ran, you try it. Hal's only mid-field. You're much higher now . . ."

Businesslike, unruffled, Grant relinquished his place to Im'ran.

Im'ran said, "You know I wouldn't hurt you, Ercy. Come on, cooperate. It's for your own good." He slid his smooth, untentacled Gen arms up along hers and held her loosely as he bent to make lip contact.

He was thin and hard, built almost like a Sime. His smooth arms had never seemed Gen to her. Or, they hadn't before today. Now, for the first time, she had to force herself to permit Im'ran to touch her, to make the hard, impersonal lip contact, like a channel's examination, very, very far from a kiss. Im'ran held it for just a second longer than a channel would, then broke, sliding his hands down her arms. The skin of his hands felt rough after Grant's, and she wondered what they would feel like after her changeover.

Im'ran asked, "What are you getting, Digen?"

"Not sure. Hal, let's see you again. Ercy, let him make contact."

Again, as he touched her, she broke out in a cold sweat, embarrassed by the tremendous inner response she couldn't name. But it was no stronger when he made lip contact, and she managed to hold still this time, pleased with her self-control.

Digen finished his notation, smiling. "Thank you, Hal. There's a response factor that wasn't there a couple days ago. What I can't figure out is why it's the lower field that's getting through to her. Ercy, what are you feeling?"

"Embarrassed, that's what."

"I apologize if I've discomfited you, Ercy. But don't you realize what I've just said? This is it. The inflection point I've been searching for these last six years; the very first sign of changeover, before any nerve cell accretions have even built up.

26 JACQUELINE LICHTENBERG

There's a subliminal awareness, a sensitivity you didn't have before. Isn't there?"

She shook her head. "I don't think so." But she had to force herself not to squirm under his gaze.

Digen put the chart aside and came to her. "Ercy, you're entering a new world now, the world of the Tecton where the channel has no private parts. If I'm hard on you, it's because I want you to adjust to it quickly."

"I'll try, Dad." She gave herself full credit for sitting still when she wanted to run screaming from the room. She'd been taught that in changeover people always sought solitude, as a cat would go off to give birth. She could understand why now. *If this is really it*. "I don't feel anything, though, just embarrassment."

Her father gave a tight little smile. "I know. We'll keep testing you until we can pin down a date. It will be at least six months, maybe more. I think this is the earliest detection of changeover on record, and we have it only because of the careful observations we've kept on you—and because of Hal here."

Putting away his record books, Digen watched as Ercy left, followed closely by Hal. "Im', if I didn't know it was impossible, I'd almost say that Hal has somehow triggered Ercy's changeover."

Im'ran looked at him sharply, then laughed.

Chapter 3

It was six weeks before Ercy began to believe it was really happening. All this time, preparations were going on around her, but somehow without actually convincing her it was real. She was given a refresher course in changeover physiology. To do the work, she had to drop her trigonometry course, and seldom made it to her garden at dawn.

When she finally did manage to get out at first light, she often saw Halimer Grant walking in the distance—a silhouette against the rising sun. Once she saw him standing perfectly still during the prolonged moment when the sun cleared the horizon, and for the rest of that day she echoed inside with a quietude she had never experienced before. She began to make a special effort to be out at dawn, watching and waiting for him. And when she made her diary entries at night, often the only item worth noting was whether or not she had seen him that day.

Her fertilizer came and she began her new experiments. As the days lengthened into spring, her whole garden wakened into new growth, and there was much work to keep her busy. Yet before sleep came at night, there were always thoughts about what Halimer Grant had said—that one time they talked. Why did she want to grow the mahogany trinrose?

It was the only goal of her life. She had long been convinced that she would succeed in presenting her father with the mythical kerduvon drug made from the dark flower, and then die in changeover. Her death wouldn't matter because her father would be disjunct and able to take care of Zeor. When once she had mentioned her knowledge of her fate, it had so upset her parents that she had decided it was better not to talk about it. But the conviction had never faded. Until now.

Now the future had changed. Grant had changed it. Why? And how did she know? She had audited some psychology courses, and learned to accept apparently sourceless knowledge as the function of her subconscious.

28 JACQUELINE LICHTENBERG

But now she began to wonder what facts her mind could possibly have based this knowledge on. When had she made the choices that had led to a new future?

During these weeks, she found herself dreaming more often than she had since she'd gotten over childish nightmares. One dream in particular haunted her for days.

She was standing in shadow, surrounded by dark figures. The sky lightened and the sun edged over a craggy mountain peak. She woke with the conviction that her life had just begun, and all choices lay before her. An odd conviction lingered when she woke that Halimer Grant had stood in that company greeting the sunrise. She realized that it was just another wish-fulfillment dream. She had no time for such nonsense.

Her father was trying to get enough data to calculate her changeover day, since she still had no feeling for it at all. He put her back on the strict regimen of diet and exercise, concentration and coordination drills, tedious memory exercises and self-control tests that constituted much of Zeor's own pre-changeover training. It was designed to develop her personal will to the point where she was strong enough to deal with transfer deprivation.

Day by day, he raised the standard of performance he required of her. Even her rest was regimented into four periods of deep relaxation every day, until she could snap from total alertness to total relaxation on command, and she was required to remain wholly alert without any tension.

The increasing standards, more than anything, convinced her that they were serious about her approaching changeover, though she still felt nothing within herself.

One time, after finishing his late-night examination of her, Digen said, "Don't go, Ercy. Im' should be here in a minute."

She ran a comb through her short, dark hair and waited patiently. A few weeks ago, she would have protested that she was already late for her evening relaxation drill, feeling that if he was going to assign a regimen, she had a right to expect him to be consistent. But now her father had a right to command every detail of her life because she was a Zeor channel in training, and he was Sectuib in Zeor.

As Im'ran came in, her father turned, putting aside his charts and graphs. "All right, Ercy. You've been showing signs of fatigue and you haven't been doing well on your concentration. I'm going to start you . . ."

MAHOGANY TRINROSE 29

Ercy gasped, deeply offended. "I have met every standard requirement! I've been scoring at Rialite's top rank on everything."

"At, yes, but not above. You've spent the last six years waiting for changeover, lazing around. You've forgotten everything you ever knew about how to work. You do what comes easily to you and stop there. Well, you can run your life that way, Ercy, and the world will still worship at your feet because you are better than average without trying. But I will not accept the pledge of anyone who will not give Zeor—and the world—their very best."

That stung. Not to be allowed to pledge Zeor? "I'm sorry! I'll do anything you say, Father—Sectuib Farris."

Her father took a deep breath and beckoned to Im'ran.

"We haven't talked much about this," said her father, "not for years. But it's always been assumed in this family that Im'ran would provide your First Transfer. That poses certain problems."

She looked at Im'ran and saw not a second father but a Gen—a professional Donor of the highest order, almost an alien being.

". . . an orhuen of twenty years' standing such as Im' and I have," her father was saying, "is not an easy kind of dependency to break into. If the break is not done right, it could be fatal."

"Is it really worth it, Dad?"

The two men traded dark glances, and as one, answered, "Yes." "Yes, it's worth it."

Im'ran said, "Digen and I worked this out a long time ago. We know how to manage it."

Her father nodded. "What I want to do now is build a relationship between you and Im' so that it will be easier for him—and for you."

"All right," she replied reluctantly, "what do I do first?"

"I want you to begin using the channel's transfer rooms for your drill sessions. You're working now, Ercy. Im's time will be debited to your account. I'll expect you to fill out all the appropriate forms."

Just like that, without fuss or fanfare, she made the transition from child—a legal nonentity—to adult. She would be receiving a Donor's services and be held responsible for the accounting, months before she would even go through changeover.

She went with Im'ran up to the top floor of the lab building where the channels who worked at the Controller's Residence had their transfer suite. Having never been allowed up here

30 JACQUELINE LICHTENBERG

before, she had to stare about her wide-eyed. The suite itself consisted of a large sitting room appointed in bright green and white with clear yellow draperies around the heavily insulated walls and windows. It was an intensely quiet room with something of the air of a library. All around the large room, doors opened into the small transfer rooms, which were equipped to handle any transfer emergency.

As they came in, a channel was sitting with her Donor in the far corner, sipping trin tea. The channel noticed Im'ran's field and, spotting Ercy, raised one tentacle in question.

Im'ran gave a signal in return, and guided Ercy into one of the transfer cubicles. She went with tender steps, hardly daring to identify with her future-self who would come here as a right.

Closing the door behind them, Im'ran dimmed the lights, then absently ran through a routine check of the medicine cabinets as if he were going to do some real work. She stood in the middle of the floor, feeling like an intruder in the adult world.

She forced herself to turn and examine the rest of the room. It was decorated in an opalescent gray and vibrant blue though the furniture was ordinary Tecton standard. There was a reclining contour lounge on either side of her, a couple of high stools in the corners. Equipment was rigged over each lounge on swingout arms. In the little hall leading into the room, one side held a sink and counter with a tiny hot plate. A narrow door led into a shower room, and she could just make out a commode. The walls were lined with glass-fronted cabinets filled with neat rows of jars and bottles, and a little desk jutted from the wall.

Seeing the forms there, she laughed. It came out a little strained. "How in the world can I sign those forms Dad wants me to fill out? I don't even have a designation yet!"

Pushing the swinging arms out of the way, Im'ran said, "You put 'Ercy Farris, pre-changeover therapy.' That's the standard charge in a case like this."

He sat down on one of the contour lounges and looked up at her.

She sat down opposite him, keeping her eyes on him with strict discipline even though she wanted to inspect everything in the room.

Im'ran said, "I hate to say it, Ercy, but Digen's right. I remember your attitude when you were a kid. You used to really put your back into your work. You've got to recapture that attitude."

MAHOGANY TRINROSE 31

"It used to be just a game, a challenge and a lot of fun. Remember how we used to bet desserts over whether I could do a thing the first time? Maybe I'm just too old for games."

"It's no game now. This is for real. Not merely to get you through changeover, Ercy, but the sum and substance of the channel's basic skills. The better you master this, the further you'll be able to go with your inherited talents."

"Relaxation drill? Learning to do nothing?"

"Just what do you think transfer is all about? Do you know the hardest thing a channel has to do? The one thing which saves more channels' lives every year than any other skill I know of?"

"I have a crawling suspicion it's relaxation."

Im'ran nodded. "It's based on that elementary drill you've been not-learning. The ability to relinquish control of a transfer to your Donor on signal, without warning—instantly. Or, conversely, to pick up that control if your Donor loses it. The same basic skill lets you control your secondary system to collect selyn from untrained Gens."

"All right," she sighed. "Just tell me what to do."

"Lie down," said Im'ran, going through a smooth sequence of motions which somehow caused the lounge she was sitting on to go flat as a board while the lights dimmed even further and the lounge's heater came on. Im'ran pulled a blanket up over her despite her protest that it was too warm already.

"As long as I'm about it, I may as well teach you right," he said as Ercy closed her eyes. He took her arms, sliding his hands about halfway up to her elbows in what would become, when she had tentacles, the transfer position. Im'ran tapped out a code, saying, "This is the signal to relinquish all control to me. Now, you depend on me to protect you from all painful influences. You are safe. You can relax."

Ercy took a long abdominal breath, flicking her mental awareness once around the inside of her body, commanding a quick tense-and-release to each muscle, and let herself go limp. She was rather proud of how quickly she could do it. It hadn't been an easy technique to learn.

"Good, but slow."

Im'ran's voice had changed, slipped almost an octave deeper, and she could hear the separate thrumming of each vocal cord. She had to open her eyes to see that it was still Im'. She took another deep breath and relaxed purposely.

"Control," said Im'ran, "creates strain; strain creates tension;

32 JACQUELINE LICHTENBERG

and tension creates the necessity to release. You're trying to control tension—a contradiction in terms."

Frustrated, Ercy wanted to wail: *What do I do then?*

"Let's try something else," said Im'ran, still in that low tone that gave her shivers. She was very conscious of his Gen-ness again. "Ercy, I want you to tense your right leg but keep every other muscle in your body relaxed."

She tensed her right leg, then found the small of her back arching away from the lounge. She relaxed her back and found a little puff of air escaping her lips, barely a grunt, but still an effort. Once she had been able to do it.

"You're very tense, Ercy, the kind of tension that gets Gens killed. I think Digen was right," said Im'ran. "You've been practicing these things alone too long. I'm inhibiting you, aren't I?"

"I guess I am nervous. I'll work on it, all right, Im'?"

He nodded. "Digen says you're responding to fields, but you aren't allowing yourself to be aware of the responses. Roll over and let me try something else."

She did, asking, "What?"

His huge Gen hands came onto her back, lightly at first and then more firmly. "Close your eyes and concentrate on my touch—my full attention is on you now, focused on this point—now this—follow the touch with your mind."

She did as he instructed, following the light and then firm touch all over her back, vertebra by vertebra, rib by rib; he worked with an uncanny talent for chasing the ripple of resisting tension in her neck, her knee joints, ankles, toes, her arms and hands, until she thought she could feel the warm sweep of his attention even after he had stopped.

She was almost asleep, yet more aware than she'd been in a long time. Her mind drifted into such an uncritical state that when she saw Halimer Grant walk through the wall and stand looking down at her, she accepted his presence without wonder. He wore an emerald-green robe with the hood thrown back. On his breast hung a flashing jewel in the shape of a starred cross.

Suddenly, she realized that her eyes were closed, that she must in fact be dreaming, and instantly the Gen's presence evaporated. She pushed up on her elbows, only now aware that the lights had come up in the room and Im'ran was puttering around the hot plate producing the delightful aroma of trin tea.

"Did I fall asleep? I'm sorry—I guess it's just so late . . ."

MAHOGANY TRINROSE 33

"No, you weren't asleep. But I think you got down a little deeper than you usually do. Tea?"

She sat up, folding the blanket back into its compartment at the end of the lounge. "Yes, I think I'd like some tea. I got cold." When he gave her the glass in its plastic holder, she said, "But I think I was asleep. At least I had a dream, and I only do that when I'm sleeping."

Im'ran sat on the other lounge, stirring his tea, saying, "I wouldn't worry about it if you did doze for a moment. We'll start our real work in the morning—eight o'clock all right with you?"

His manner was completely different now. She nodded, though, saying, "That's my usual time. And I have color-memory drill with Mom at nine, so eight is fine." As she drank her tea, she filled out the accounting form, laboriously reading the instructions for each box and filling most of them with "not applicable." As she came to the signature line, she paused, realizing that this was a turning point in her life, her first official, legal signature. And she made a decision.

Her mother had given her the first name, Aild, usually a man's name, to honor a promise she'd made to her own father. But Ercy had never used the name and thought she never would. Now, however, she signed the form boldly: A. Ercy Farris.

Im'ran said as he turned to leave, "Oh, two weeks from tomorrow, hold that evening open. I've arranged with Mora for you to observe her transfer."

Ercy dropped the accounting form into its out box, staring at Im'ran. "Observe—Mom's—does Dad know?"

"I haven't told him yet." Seeing her utter confusion, Im'ran came back into the room and closed the door again. "Ercy, it's never been Digen who's refused to let you observe his transfers. It's me. I wouldn't let him. He's still unstable, and I'm afraid I couldn't handle it. But Mora's transfer should be fairly routine, and by Zeor custom it's long past time you should have observed a transfer."

Ercy took a deep breath, her first excitement abating. She couldn't count how many times she had asked for this privilege and been denied. "Dad won't permit it."

"I'll convince him, don't worry." Then he smiled. "There have to be some advantages to being orhuen to a Controller! Besides, Mora and I may be only adopted into Zeor, but we know a good custom when we see one. Digen has often said how important the experience was for him—and, forgive me, I know you don't want to hear it, but it was an important experience for

Wyner, too. And Mora says she has learned to regret not having had the experience herself. So there's no way you're going to get cheated out of it.''

Ercy smiled her most acquiescent smile. "I'll reserve the evening, then." But as Im'ran left, she promised herself cynically to save a few horticulture journals in case she was left with nothing to do that night.

Chapter 4

"But Mora's not a Farris!" Digen objected. "It's not going to do Ercy any good to observe her transfer."

"I think you're wrong," said Im'ran.

Digen rocked back in his chair, shoving the charts and papers away across his desk. "This isn't like you, Im'."

"You handed me the responsibility for teaching Ercy relaxation."

"Yes, I did, didn't I?" Digen got up and went around the desk, standing in the sun by the window. "It's hard for me to delegate any responsibility where Ercy is concerned."

"You know," said Im'ran, "that's a great part of the trouble between you two. She hasn't the faintest idea how much you love her. All she ever sees—all you have ever let her see—of yourself is Sectuib Farris training the next Sectuib in Zeor. And, Digen, sometimes I think you don't even realize how much you love that kid, because all you think day and night is how crucial it is everything be done correctly for her. Maybe, sometimes, something should be done incorrectly simply because you love her."

For a long time, Digen stared silently at the rolling green lawns under the spring sun. As always, Im'ran's observations were too painfully right. "Can I—yet—allow myself the luxury of loving my daughter?"

"I didn't mean indulging her every whim and fancy. She's ready, Digen. But you've failed to sense it because you're so intent on not making any mistake with her."

Digen shook his head. "It should be a Farris transfer. I've been trying to arrange it, but—"

"Is there really that much difference, from Ercy's point of view? She can't zlin the fields."

"She's already getting much more than you realize. I'm afraid it's the wrong thing to do."

"Which is more important, that her first vision of a channel's personal transfer be of a Farris transfer—or that she master the basic states of relaxation?"

36 JACQUELINE LICHTENBERG

"That's the choice? Is it really that bad?"

Im'ran nodded.

Bleakly, Digen considered a Tecton channel was a thing, not a person. And the better the channel, the more of a thing he became to the Tecton bureaucracy. He was, unconsciously perhaps, training Ercy to withstand the kind of pressure that had broken him twenty years ago. But maybe Im'ran was right again. Maybe the strength not to break under that pressure came from a sense of self that could be obtained only by being loved as a child, for oneself and not for one's future talents. His brother Wyner had given some of that to him where his own father had failed, so he knew how precious it could be.

"All right, Im', I'll trust your intuition. Keep me from being too hard on her. You know how I feel."

No sooner was Im'ran gone than Digen's secretary showed in his next appointment, Halimer Grant.

"Hal! It's been weeks. How's it going?"

"Under control. At least my Co-Dean calls this under control, and I'm willing to take his word for it."

Digen grinned. He knew that they had been struggling with a space problem since they'd lost one of their buildings to the flood. "You should have your new building before summer," said Digen, patting one of the construction contracts on his desk. "But that's not what I called you about."

Rummaging in his desk drawer, he came up with a little jeweler's box, and handed it to the Gen. "This came yesterday."

Grant took it, opening it with great puzzlement. Then his nager showed one of those slow reactions he had become famous for at Rialite. But this time it was tinged with some sort of reservation Digen couldn't quite name. The man was an utter enigma.

"Go on," said Digen, "try it on."

Obediently, the Gen took the Tecton-crest Donor's identification ring out of its box, all gleaming gold and sparkling gems, and slipped it on his finger, shaking his head. Digen said, "I noticed you lost yours along with everything else in the flood. So I had one made for you. Not that you require identification. Anybody can zlin what you are from halfway across Rialite."

At last the reaction within the Gen surfaced as a smile, and there was genuine gratitude clearly suffused through his nager. "Thank you, Hajene Farris. I will wear it with honor. You have given me a moment worth telling my grandchildren about—one day . . ."

Yes, thought Digen, any time the Sectuib in Zeor did anything

MAHOGANY TRINROSE   37

for anybody, it was a story to awe grandchildren with. Would Ercy ever learn to live with that? He knew he hadn't.

"Pleasantries aside," said Digen, "you are posing us quite a problem. I just got this letter." Digen slid the official stationery across the desk to the Gen. "It says they can't find any trace of your records. They claim you don't exist. I, being an empiricist at heart, prefer to accept the evidence of my own senses."

"Bureaucracies often resemble nothing so much as a kitten tangled up in a ball of twine."

"I told them to hire some clerks who can read and have them look again. But in the meantime, I think it would be a good idea to put through a request for replacement papers—start a new file for them to lose. Here."

Digen pushed a set of forms across to Grant, and the Gen took them. Digen said, "This is the third time in the last five years that this exact same thing has happened to me. But the last time was just two years ago. I think things are getting worse."

"I wonder what would happen if they lost your file?"

"Headline news around the world, that's what," answered Digen. "*The Sectuib in Zeor Does Not Exist!* You know, you might have something there. It would take something like that to cure these papermen of their multiple copies. Whatever—see if you can find time to get those forms filled out. I've got to go ship those gypsies off to Carlston for trial."

Digen got up, closing Grant's file, and his eyes fell on a green transfer appointment card on his rack. "Oh, here's your appointment card." He started to hand it over, then he saw the name of the channel Grant was to be serving. He stopped, staring at the name in complete shock. *Mora ambrov Zeor.*

He had completely forgotten about that decision.

Ercy had a tremendous affinity for Grant. He thought hard with all his forty years of experience as a channel and decided that Grant might—just might—make up for its not being a Farris transfer. The man was indeed that good.

He handed the card over to Grant, saying, "I've also authorized my daughter to observe Mora's transfer this time—that is, of course, if you don't object. Donor always has veto."

Looking at the card, Grant radiated confusion. Digen added, heading briskly for the door, "I don't have time right now, but Mora would be glad to explain the Zeor custom."

For Ercy the next two weeks passed in a blur. She completely lost her sense of confidence in her intuitions, and could find no trace in herself of an awareness of her changeover. While she

38 JACQUELINE LICHTENBERG

continued to watch hungrily for Grant every morning, she also felt her emotions becoming far more complex than they had ever been. She was gradually becoming a stranger to herself. *It must be just that I'm growing up, at last.*

On the evening she was to witness her mother's transfer, Ercy met Im'ran at the lab and they went upstairs to the transfer suite together. Her mother was already there, sitting in the lounge area, sipping a glass of cold tea.

Just since the morning, she seemed to have aged ten years. Her hair, sprinkled with gray, was wound into a braid across the top of her head, but after a day under a construction worker's hard hat, wisps stuck out in every direction, unheeded. Her deep tan seemed to have paled. She had the thin, wiry Sime build, but now Ercy noticed how the skin of her cheeks sagged.

She's old.

She walked across the lounge beside Im'ran, pausing only when he stopped to say, "Ercy, I won't leave until Hal arrives. You've never seen her in this condition. Don't let it bother you. It's normal. Just remember, she's a good channel."

Sitting down beside Mora, Im'ran took her glass and handed it to Ercy. "Make us some hot tea, would you?"

Ercy took the glass, steadfastly casual. Inwardly, she was shaking. Mothers are impervious, omnipotent. But now Ercy knew better. Mothers are human, too.

Does growing up mean losing your mother? Or is it only the illusion of mother that has to be lost? Could I ever give that illusion to a child?

As she went to the hot plate on the sideboard, she saw out of the corner of her eye how Im'ran turned to her mother, sitting carefully apart from her but concentrating his Donor's attention on her. She couldn't zlin the fields yet, wouldn't be able to until after changeover, but she could see the nervous strain relaxing its grip on her mother, and she felt herself relax, too.

She brought the tea glasses on a tray, handed them around, and sat on a wide bench opposite them.

Her mother met her eyes then, and Ercy could sense the effort to put up a brave front. But it was a ragged front, full of gaping holes. It was as if the whole dynamic essence of her mother had disintegrated right before her eyes. Her gaze fixed on the tightly sheathed tentacles along her mother's forearms. The skin on the tops of her forearms was deeply freckled, and now Ercy could see the network of dry wrinkles under the freckles.

MAHOGANY TRINROSE   39

Im'ran said, in that low-pitched, professional voice, "He should be here by now. Want me to call and check for you?"

"No," Mora said, "no, he'll be here. Digen said he handed him the green card personally." She met Ercy's eyes with a helpless little gesture, her hands shaking, her laterals licking out of their wrist orifices.

"Mom, if you don't want me here . . ."

Mora shook her head. "It's all right, Ercy. It isn't as bad as it looks, Baby."

Ercy looked to Im'ran, afraid to appeal to him to do something.

Im'ran had been working from a distance, careful not to act as if he were going to serve transfer. But now, biting his lower lip, he moved in to take her hands, well clear of the restless laterals. Under a deep frown, he said, "Let me."

Mora gave an open-throated, trembling sigh. "Careful, Im'."

"I've got it. Lean a little; I'll just belay for you."

Five minutes before the appointed time, Halimer Grant came in, threading his way across the sitting room. He stopped, surprised to see Im'ran working. Ercy saw their eyes meet in silent communication, and then, almost like a ballet, Im'ran relinquished his position to Grant.

Her mother slumped in the curve of her Donor's shoulder, still in hard need but comfortable now that all doubt was gone.

Im'ran asked Grant, "Where have you been?"

"Surely you didn't think I'd be late!"

Coldly, Im'ran said, "It is custom, is it not, to show at least half an hour before appointment?"

Mora shuddered under the impact of Im'ran's anger. Grant tightened his grip on her hands, and said to both of them, "Please don't be angry with me. I didn't mean to cause anxiety." Then he helped Mora to her feet, turning her toward the appointed room. "Mora, do you want Ercy to come with us?"

"Yes," said her mother, in the barest whisper, as if forcing the word out.

Im'ran stiffened as if suffering with her. Ercy knew that he tried not to be anywhere near Mora when she was in need because at that time he was always high-field and ready to give transfer to Digen. Yet Mora was Im'ran's wife. They'd loved each other since before her father came into their lives. *How he must yearn to give her transfer—and he never can because of the orhuen with Father.* It was a strange new thought.

"Go on with them, Ercy," said Im'ran, turning her after Grant and her mother. And then he hurried away.

40 JACQUELINE LICHTENBERG

Inside the tiny chamber, Ercy took the stool in the farthest corner, curling up as inconspicuously as possible, wishing she'd never asked for this and certain at the same time that it would have come, whether she asked or not.

But no sooner had she settled down than Halimer had her mother installed on the contour lounge, speaking in that softly professional tone she'd come to associate with a working Donor. Hal's voice made Im'ran's sound colorless and distant by comparison. In moments, her mother was breathing deeply and calmly, and she said, "I want to control this one. I have no particular problems this time."

"As you like." He let her take his arms, winding tentacles about his well-muscled arms with a lashing force that made Ercy wince. But Grant hardly seemed to notice. A peculiar neutrality came over his face, as if he'd turned his personality off somehow. Her mother's face assumed an expression she had never seen before, but it was quickly blocked from her view as Grant leaned over for the necessary fifth contact, lip to lip.

There was a momentary blue flash, gone so fast Ercy wasn't sure she'd even seen it. Then her mother slowly dismantled the contact and melted back onto the lounge in profound relief. Her face was once again *Mother. And what does Dad look like when that happens to him? He's junct.*

"You are very powerful, Hal," said her mother quietly. "For a moment, I suspected you were going to snatch control from me."

"I felt you falter just after commitment, but then I realized it was only your style."

"You're twice the Donor I'll ever need," she replied, shaking her head. "You have a style I've never encountered before."

"If it discomforts you—"

"Not at all! That was—excellent." She tilted her head back toward Ercy. "I'm sorry, Baby, that it wasn't much of a show. I'm not usually in such a hurry."

Grant frowned. "I should have spent more time with you. Next time I will. Is there anything else I can do for you?"

He seemed to expect her to say yes, but she replied, sitting up, "No." Ercy felt as if her mother were embarrassed. "I'm fine. Sorry I snapped at you. Hal—I've got to go. They'll be waiting for me by now." At the door, she turned to Ercy. "You'd better get to bed. It's late."

"Yes, Mother." Ercy unwound her legs from the chair, only now realizing she was very cramped. "I'm coming."

MAHOGANY TRINROSE 41

But as her mother went off, Halimer stopped Ercy. "I hope you weren't disappointed. But that's really all there is to it."

Ercy smiled up at him. "What would you say if I told you I've dreamed about you?"

"Dreamed . . . ? Often?"

"Oh—only once."

"When was this?"

Suddenly shy, Ercy replied, "Weeks ago. Does it matter? It was just a dream—of you walking through a wall wearing a bright green robe and some antique jewelry."

"Really? That's—interesting. Where was it? Here?"

"How did you know!"

"Do you often remember your dreams?"

"No, not too often, but this one was so vivid. That's been happening a lot, lately—I guess it's all part of growing up." Suddenly anxious, she blurted, "Oh, it was just a silly dream. I shouldn't have mentioned it. I just thought—" She had no idea what she'd been thinking, her mind suddenly a blank. She grabbed the first words that came. "You were good—with Mother. Maybe—maybe someday I'll get a chance to find out how good."

And then she was embarrassed and had to clench her fist to keep it from flying to her mouth.

Pausing—it seemed he was always in the middle of a pause—Grant said, "I—would—like that, I think."

With several backward glances, Ercy hurried herself off to her room. There would be no session with Im'ran, as he was busy with her father. And, though her body was immature, she was not ignorant. She knew that after transfer, channels and Donors would be more interested in sex than anything else.

Her mother had Im'ran. But who did her father have? As far as she knew, her father had never held any interest in any woman other than her mother—at least not since she was old enough to notice. Intensely curious in a strange new way, Ercy lay awake long into the night, trying to imagine what must be going on all about her that she—because she was still a child—was excluded from.

Unable to sleep, she got up and went out into the family's private sitting room to find a newspaper. The newest one on the stack hadn't been touched. She took it into her room to read, but tossed it aside in disgust when her eye fell on a story about efforts to ban her favorite fairy-tale book about the mahogany trinrose because it was about magic. Under that was an item on proposals to make burning alive the mandatory sentence for

42 JACQUELINE LICHTENBERG

convicted practitioners of magic. The back page carried three city riots, and she didn't want to know what they were rioting over.

She crawled back into bed and was amazed to discover herself slipping easily over the blurred edge of sleep.

The moon flooded down on her garden, and she looked up and saw Halimer Grant walk through a tree. His bright emerald robe was ashen green in the strange light, and she could just see an occasional flash of jewels on his chest.

"How can we live in a world where they burn people alive?"

She didn't realize she had spoken until he answered her in his slow, grave manner. "Science is the process of collecting and organizing facts to reach an understanding of their significance. Magic is the process of using an understanding of the significance of things to reach a harmony of facts and occurrences."

"I don't believe in magic; I don't believe in witches."

"Note that those who are against the practice of magic are using magic, saying that burning a magician magically undoes all the magic he has done in his lifetime."

Ercy giggled at the absurdity and woke up coughing. For a few moments, she recalled the dream vividly. "That'll teach me to read the newspaper before going to sleep!" she muttered, and went back to sleep.

She woke with a start to find dawn brightening the windows. She barely recalled her dream. Dressed in her overalls, she went out to do some early gardening, taking the kitchen scraps to her compost pit.

The exercise relaxed her, and the garden itself always seemed to heal her ills better than any medicine. Here, among living beauty, she often reached something akin to the intoxication of the post-transfer state, all her senses wide open and fed on purest pleasure.

In those rare moments, she often felt that all she had to do was present the world with a mahogany trinrose—or better yet, kerduvon, the drug derived from it—and people would instantly drop their superstitious terrors and make the whole world into a garden. *Well, maybe not instantly. It might take a few days,* she chided herself.

She was working compost into the soil around the nasturtiums that kept the bugs off her trinroses when Grant came into view and the sun peeped over the horizon. Suddenly, everything in her yearned searingly for him to come over—just the once—and talk to her.

He stood as he always did, facing the sunrise, pausing as if it

MAHOGANY TRINROSE   43

had caught him by surprise, and then he turned and came through the arch in the hedgerow that separated her plot from the clinic. Absently, she noted he wasn't wearing his green robe. She hadn't trimmed the archway in weeks, and he ran into some twigs, getting wet with a shower of dew.

He mopped his face with a handkerchief, and seemed to catch sight of her for the first time. He came toward her purposefully. And once again, she was taken with the certainty that she could indeed survive changeover—with Halimer Grant giving her First Transfer. *Is that what I've known all along and have been afraid to acknowledge to myself?*

"Good morning," he said, stuffing his handkerchief back into a pocket and squatting down beside her.

"Morning, yourself. Can I ask you a personal question?"

"I don't consider personal questions impolite."

"Why do you greet the sunrise every day?"

"It is important to remember the beauty of nature, the cycle of beginnings—and endings—to acknowledge your partnership with them—to love all of life and embrace it without fear. And you, Ercy—why are you out so early?"

"Oh, I always work in the garden an hour or so before dawn. Then I have my session with Im'ran, breakfast, chores, and a couple of hours of study—I have to repeat the whole pre-changeover thing because it's been so long. Then Im'ran again, lunch, study, chores, and Im'ran again. Not to mention the lab sessions with Dad."

"Busy girl. I'd no idea . . ."

"It's all work, work, work, and I'm never good enough to please anybody." Ercy was startled at herself. She hadn't even known she felt that way, let alone that it would all come spilling out like that.

But Grant just smiled. "What, pre-changeover depression already?"

"Yeah, for six years. I'm used to it by now." She was turning the spade steadily. He took it away from her, grasping both her delicate hands in his huge ones.

"Look, Ercy, last night, your behavior pleased me—and I think your mother was very pleased, too. All over Rialite, I've never heard a word spoken against you. In spite of your position, you've won respect and even admiration here."

"I wish—" She wrenched her hands away from him and let them fly up to hide the way her face crumpled as she began to

44 JACQUELINE LICHTENBERG

fight off a crying fit. "I wish I could feel changeover coming, the way I'm supposed to!"

She was suddenly flooded with an anguish she hadn't known was there at all. *I wish I knew if I was going to live or die.*

His arm came around her shoulders then, and she let herself cry against his chest. She felt his forearm across her backbone as he held her—just as her father had held her so many times. Only Grant's arm was smooth. Gen. And with that awareness, she also thought she felt the warm searchlight of his attention on her—or was she just imagining that?

Self-consciously, she pulled back, sniffing away the tears.

"You know, Ercy, sometimes wishing can make things come true, but you have to be careful not to wish any harm or to interfere with anyone's free will."

She looked up at him sharply, remembering how she had wished he would come over to talk. She'd never wished it before—*but he can't know that! I didn't mean any harm.*

"Oh," she laughed, "making wishes come true is for fairy stories!"

He thought about that for a moment, toying with the spade. "If you could scientifically construct a theory of reality in which a natural law would operate to manifest the wish, then you would put wishing into the realm of science, right?"

"Ye-es, I guess so."

"In other words, magic is just science we don't understand."

"Yes, of course." Her father had said that many times, and she had seen how it often could be so. "But *wishes?* Wishes *don't* work!"

"Oh? Have you run experiments to ascertain that?"

Was he laughing at her—because she'd been crying like a baby? "Don't be ridiculous."

"I'm serious, Ercy. Let's experiment right now, together. All right?"

"Three wishes, right?" she asked, unable to keep the cynical ring out of her voice.

"If you like. You don't have to tell me what yours are. I'll just wish that your wishes come true, provided they harm no one and tend toward harmony with nature. Number one, now."

And he closed his eyes, so she applied herself to wishing that she would come to the awareness of impending changeover the way all channels did. As she wished it, she found tears squeezing out of the corners of her eyes. *I really want it.*

"There," said Hal, as if he'd just finished a big job.

MAHOGANY TRINROSE 45

She opened her eyes, and felt happy. The sun had risen slightly, the edge of shadow receding until her knees were warmed.

"Well, ready for number two?"

"All right," she agreed, and closed her eyes. *I want Hal for First Transfer, but I don't want Im'ran to feel abandoned.*

Again, she felt it with all the power of the emotions she had not been letting herself know were there. And when it was over, she felt lightened of an enormous burden.

"Ready for number three?" asked Grant.

"Yes, this is fun!" *One last childish fling!*

"Here goes."

She closed her eyes and visualized a mahogany-colored trinrose growing on the plant before her—and then the whole garden blooming in the rich red-brown flowers. Her own hand came out toward the flowers, holding a small bottle full of brown liquid— kerduvon. *Oh, I wish, I wish.*

When it was over, she wiped the tears from her eyes with the back of her hand, wishing for tentacles so she wouldn't get her face dirty.

"Thank you," she said. "I do feel better—or maybe just exhausted."

He nodded. "Part of the trick is to get in touch with your real feelings. You can never be satisfied with yourself until you know exactly how much you are capable of, and precisely how close you've come to your own flat-out maximum. You will learn to be satisfied with nine-tenths of that maximum most of the time. And once in a while, like just now, you'll know the special perfection of achieving ten-tenths of your own personal maximum. But, Ercy, you can't live ten-tenths all the time, and you shouldn't expect it of yourself. No mortal can sustain ecstasy and live."

"You sound like my father." Then, before her good sense could halt the inspiration, she said, "Have you ever thought of pledging Zeor?"

He turned to her. "No. I haven't."

"Why not? I thought everybody in the world had."

Sighing in a very uncharacteristic manner, he said, "I—well— I've taken on enough—obligations for one lifetime."

Obligation? thought Ercy. If Grant saw pledging a Householding as an obligation, then surely he would be a good candidate for Zeor. Most people only saw what a House could do for them— the prestige, the financial security, the fosterage homes where their kids could be brought up in a Householding morality, the retirement homes; they saw the benefits but never the obligations.

46   JACQUELINE LICHTENBERG

"Actually," said Ercy, "there aren't that many obligations, and there are some benefits, especially in a big House like Zeor. You ought to think about it. Seriously."

"Maybe I will," said Grant. "But right now, I've got to go. It's almost time for the first classes of the day."

"Is it? Sh-shit." She threw the trowel into the tool box and ran toward the house. "See you later!"

"I'm afraid I disappointed her, Digen. By the time Hal got there, I was in such a state that I took him instead of demonstrating relinquishment as Im' wanted. Am I a failure as a mother?"

Digen shook his head, clasping her fluctuating fields with his own even though they were sitting across the wide dining table from each other. "No, Mora, not at all. As I understand, Im' had to belay for you. With him being high-field and attuned to me, small wonder you lost yourself."

Mora smiled, responding to the firmness of Digen's nager. "You're still post yourself. I don't know how you can be so calm. I'm riding some kind of emotional roller coaster."

Digen frowned. "Hal should have been good enough to avoid instability for you, anyway."

"I suppose he is. He seemed to want to work through it with me, but I couldn't—not with Ercy watching. And really all I wanted was to get home—to Im'."

Im'ran was coming in from the kitchen, carrying a tray of orange juice. One of the kitchen workers, a renSime man with a limp, came after him with a tray of steaming cereal.

Im'ran said, "Well, Mora, all I could think about by that time was you."

"Im'!" said Mora. "Ercy might hear!"

A rude snap of Im'ran's precisely quantized, fanir's nager expressed exactly what he thought of such prudishness. But, because he was a fanir, his nager was strangely dominant, dragging any nearby Sime into his own rhythms.

Digen said to the renSime, "Thank you, Fil. And my apologies on Im's behalf."

Im'ran apologized for disturbing the fields, saying, "I just forgot you're not a channel, Fil."

"Then I take it as a compliment. Excuse me." Fil left, swinging his now empty tray, and they all began breakfast.

"I'm starving," said Mora. "I guess it wasn't such a bad transfer after all!"

They all laughed as she dug in, and Im'ran asked, "Where's

MAHOGANY TRINROSE 47

Ercy? She late again? Are we working her too hard, do you think?'' He helped himself to a generous portion of the hot cereal and poured on the honey. Being Gen, he had to eat for the calories to run his body. The two Simes, claiming to be ravenous, took portions scarcely fit for a mouse. But this morning, they ate with obvious relish.

"Maybe," answered Digen. "But it'll keep her mind off her problems." And then, sensing the slight nageric shift as Ercy came through the hall door, he said, "Here she is now."

Im'ran, seated beside Mora, turned to look at Ercy. Mora, looking only with her Sime senses but not turning to see with her eyes, said, "Aild Ercy Farris, you can't come to the table covered with grime like that."

Ercy stopped in the doorway. Digen said, "If you're going to work in the garden, you should budget your time so you can change before breakfast."

Im'ran added, "Look at her, Digen, she's grown right out of those coveralls, and they're practically new."

Ercy looked down and noticed the cuffs of her pants were almost at the middle of her calves. She felt like crying, but held herself in a kind of stasis, waiting for them to make up their minds what she should do. Digen, utterly intrigued by the change in her nager since the previous night, said, "At least you washed your hands. Come and eat, and later you can go down to Supplies and get some new coveralls."

Mora nodded, eating her own cereal and spreading fruit on her bread. "Growing the way you are, your diet is very important. Four meals a day wouldn't be bad for you at this point."

Ercy, seating herself gingerly beside her father, said, "I can't imagine when I'd have time."

"Then grab a candy bar," said Digen. "You require the calories so your body can use the other nutrients for growth."

Ercy helped herself to an apple from the bowl on the table and began peeling it, munching the peel as she went.

"You should eat some hot cereal," said Mora. "You require the proteins."

"I'm really not very hungry this morning," she said.

Digen scrutinized her minutely. He'd seen a similar effect on her before, but where?

"Digen?" asked Mora. "How tall do you think Ercy will be by changeover? I want to order her a nice dress. She's a very pretty girl under all that grime."

"I haven't been able to get a good estimate of her changeover

48 JACQUELINE LICHTENBERG

date yet. But it's safe to say she'll be my height before First Year is out. Only a bit shorter at changeover, I expect. But it's no problem. She'll wear a yawal, of course."

"A yawal!" said Mora. "How disgusting. I won't have it. Not my daughter."

Digen put down his spoon, deliberately reaching for the teapot. The yawal—the garment once used to dress captive Gens to be presented to juncted Simes for their pleasure in the kill—was customary in Zeor as a clear object lesson. Digen said as much, adding, "And that lesson is our oath—Out of Death Was I Born, Unto Zeor, Forever."

Mora met his eyes, their nageric link solidifying. "I wouldn't think of defying a House custom. It's just that—a *yawal?* Is it really necessary in this day and age?"

Im'ran said, "The yawal is customary in Imil, too, Mora, if only for the heir to the House. But in Zeor, every healthy Sime wears the yawal at his changeover party, the heir not distinguished from anyone under the oath of the House. The Householding can be no stronger than the oath that binds its members."

Mora looked from one to the other. She had not been a member of any Householding before she pledged Zeor and married Im'ran, and Digen knew that sometimes she felt as if she were living in a foreign country.

Mora said, "At least it can be a satin yawal, say with some nice trim in Zeor blue?"

Digen shook his head. "Cotton. Plain."

"She looks awful in white, Digen. She should wear yellow."

Digen shook his head.

"It's all right, Mother, really. It's kind of a proud thing, you know. It's not done the old way in many Houses any more. Besides, this way you can leave the hemming to the last minute. And then I'll be decently covered, anyway."

"And," said Digen, "most Farrises are not allergic to cotton. Wyner was allergic to satin and almost all the synthetic fibers."

Im'ran shoved back his chair. "Ercy, I think it's time we got to work."

Ercy got up. "I hope it's not going to be one of those days when I'm late to everything."

"Wait," said Mora. "Digen, can't you give us a date for her? For the invitations? Members in Zeor from all over the world have been writing to ask."

Digen got up, facing Ercy. "Come here, let me get a look at you this morning. Maybe we'll skip our morning examination so

MAHOGANY TRINROSE   49

you can catch up with yourself.'' He took her into transfer position, scanning her deeply, then disengaging in smooth sequence.

"You've been with Halimer Grant again!'' said Digen, recognizing the syndrome. "And this morning, too—or—last night, after Mora left?"

Mora said, "Ercy! You said you'd go right up to sleep.''

"Every time Hal lays a hand on her,'' said Digen, "her rate of change soars by measurable factors, and I can't explain that. As it stands now, I'd estimate sixteen weeks from today, plus or minus three days—probably minus with Hal around.''

Sixteen weeks! thought Ercy. Four months. It was both too far in the misty future to be real and altogether too soon. Her trin annuals would be in bloom—her last chance at a mahogany trinrose.

Her mother was saying, ". . . but how can we put up four hundred people for a week? If she's late . . .''

Digen shook his head. "I don't know.'' He glanced at Ercy, who was trembling once again on the brink of hysterics. "I don't want to move into town and take the hotel. All my facilities are here, and I want to be sure Ercy has the best available. I can't deal with this today. There's graduation this afternoon, and a meeting with building contractors. And, Ercy, don't you dare be late for your noon exam. I can't wait for you.''

"Fair enough; you're letting me off the hook this morning.''

"Actually, I'm letting myself off the hook. It always seems I'm over-scheduled the day after transfer, because I can't keep up before transfer.''

As they all scattered about their business, Ercy walked with her father toward his office, where some people were already waiting for him. "Dad? Have you ever thought of inviting Halimer Grant to pledge Zeor?''

"Why should I do that?''

Ercy knew that the honor of giving her First Transfer would go to one of the best Donors in Zeor, not an outsider. If Grant didn't pledge, there was no chance . . . "Well, he's good enough, isn't he?''

"Being 'good' isn't enough, Ercy. Zeor is a certain attitude toward life.''

"I think Hal would fit into Zeor.''

"Ercy, what's really on your mind? I haven't got a minute but I'm not going to dash off with you left hanging in the middle of an important thought.''

"I don't know how to put it,'' she fretted. "Dad, you know I

50 JACQUELINE LICHTENBERG

wouldn't hurt Im'ran for the world. But is there any reason why he has to serve my First Transfer?''

Digen stopped. They were outside the glass front of his receptionist's office, but for the moment the hall was empty. ''You want Hal.'' Why hadn't he seen this coming?

''Let's put it this way, Ercy. There's no reason you shouldn't want Hal. His nager has a salutary effect on your system, even now. I'd be a bit worried if you weren't wanting him—I just didn't expect it quite so soon. Mora says, just a few weeks ago you were wondering if you could be in love with him! So, I'm surprised you've come to perceive him as a Gen and to react to him, consciously, to the point where you'd abandon Im'.''

''I'm not abandoning . . .''

Digen snapped, ''What else would you call it?'' Then, regretting the sharpness of his tone, he said, ''I'm oversensitive where Im's feelings are concerned. Orhuen does that to people. You'll have to forgive that and learn to live with it.''

''I'm sorry, Dad. I know. I wouldn't hurt Im'. I couldn't bear to hurt him.'' *Even Hal knows that.*

''Ercy, I've got to tell you something.'' It was painful to think of it, but Digen told himself she had to know—now. ''Years ago, Ercy, before you were born, Im' saved my life when he became orhuen to me. To stay with me, he gave up something that was important to him—a lifelong dream, the privilege of giving First Transfer to a channel of his own level. Because he's been serving as my exclusive Donor, his level has become so high there's hardly a channel in the world anywhere near him—except you and me. I promised you to him before you were born, Ercy, because—because I owe him that, and more.''

He had no right— ''I—had no idea it meant that much to him. But—isn't it traditionally my choice?''

''Usually, it would be. But in this case, it's a medical decision, which makes it my decision as your Controller, your Sectuib, and your physician. If Hal were best for you, medically speaking, I'd arrange it.'' Digen added grimly, ''It's not going to be easy to breakstep this orhuen. It's a really tight relationship as such things go.''

''Then why go to all that trouble?''

Several people were in the corridors now, giving Digen and Ercy a wide berth to afford them a measure of privacy. ''It's a good Zeor discipline. And this breakstep, if we time it right, may complete my disjunction, at last.'' Digen turned away from Ercy

MAHOGANY TRINROSE 51

to pace up the corridor. *Ilyana!* Transfer with her had left him junct. But, twenty years after her death, he still loved her.

Shocked by the fleeting glimpse of her father's intensity, Ercy came a few steps after him, her voice a choked whisper. "Dad— at risk of your life! I don't want you to—"

"Ercy," said Digen, turning to cut her off. "This isn't the place to discuss it. It isn't a—personal—decision I'm making. A Sectuib can't afford—not ever—to put himself above his House. You are the heir to Zeor, and we will do what is best for you. From Wyner's records, it's clear that if his First Donor hadn't been a fanir, he'd have died right then, so Im' is the only Donor in the world I would trust to you—and with you. That's a Controller's judgment; nothing personal."

"Ercy!" called Im'ran, coming around the corner and spotting them. As he approached, he said to Digen, "Am I interrupting? I've got to finish with Ercy before my meeting with the new Donor Staff Committee."

Im'ran was serving a term as Chief Donor of Rialite, supervising the Gen staff of the whole coalition of colleges that formed Rialite. In many ways, he was Digen's opposite number, with an agenda almost as full.

Her father nodded. "We'll talk about it later, Ercy. For now, all arrangements stay as is. Understand?"

Ercy nodded. She understood she wasn't to mention her wild ideas to Im'ran. But she'd never seen her father manipulating other people's lives before. *But that's a Controller's job—isn't it?* And after all, if Im'ran became emotionally upset, he wouldn't be able to keep her father steady through post-syndrome, and all Rialite would suffer.

As she went with the Gen, she sighed hugely and resigned herself to it all. Last year, life had seemed so very simple— before the future had changed.

Chapter 5

In the days that followed, Ercy put the matter of First Transfer out of her mind and concentrated on her garden.

She had three distinct varieties of trinrose—annual, biennial, and perennial. The perennials, trimmed back for the winter, looked like gnarled old grapevines sprouting tender new shoots which would soon be covered with white flowers. The biennials were just coming into bloom, some with delicate pink flowers and some with deep crimson blooms, such a dark red that she had hoped they would turn mahogany with her new fertilizer. But they hadn't. Now it seemed she'd have time for one more annual generation to experiment on—if she lived.

During these days, an old dream resurfaced. And it was also a memory. She had been about four years old, just learning to read her first picture books, when her father had made one last attempt to complete his disjunction and had been deathly ill for weeks while Tecton therapists came and went, shaking their heads and sympathizing helplessly with Im'ran.

One day, she had been reading her favorite picture book with her mother, and in the story, the wizard had produced a mahogany trinrose and—waving it under the princess's nose—had instantly endowed the renSime princess with the ability to take transfer from her terrified Gen lover without killing him, as if she were indeed a channel, and not a junct renSime.

To this day, Ercy could remember the picture of the mahogany trinrose in that book, now threatened with a legal ban because of its emphasis on magic. Her own copy fell open automatically to the heavily laminated illustration of a graceful dewy brown flower held in two ventral tentacles while the tips of the fingers caressed the velvet petals cupping that flower like a beloved treasure. The background had been rippling yellow satin, giving the whole the air of a photograph.

She had stared at that picture for hours on end. It had engraved

MAHOGANY TRINROSE 53

itself on her mind with a living vibrancy that bespoke deep and hidden truths made concrete and obvious.

Looking at that picture, she had known things that she, a mere baby, had no way of knowing or expressing. Yet the overflowing urgency to make everyone understand had driven her for years to study and read beyond her age level. The only other memory she had from that time was of standing before Im'ran, clutching her picture book and sobbing uncontrollably because she couldn't force him to look at the picture and understand the answer to all their problems from it the way she did.

Whenever she thought of it, even to this day, she was overwhelmed with tears of anguished frustration at her inability to force people to *understand*.

She still held the irrational conviction that a real mahogany trinrose was the key to saving her father's life, which was in terrible danger.

And it was certainly possible to grow a mahogany trinrose, given enough time and meticulous effort.

For many years, Ercy had been hand-pollinating and selecting her annual varieties of trin plants for one strain that smelled too strongly of licorice to make good tea but had dark-colored flowers, and another strain that had reddish flowers and the scent of mint.

After a brief exposure to astronomy in a science class, she had hit on the idea that the phase and position of the moon affected the abundance, hardiness, or maybe even color of all plants. Testing this idea on her kitchen garden, she had grown cantaloupes bigger than some watermelons and parsnips she couldn't get both hands around.

For the last two years, she had tried planting her trin annuals by the phases of the moon, with control groups planted at other times. Now she was ready to try replanting the seeds produced by crossing her two main strains. If she planted with the moon just right, she theorized, the flowers should turn out mahogany— provided the soil wasn't wrong.

So, late one night, Ercy took her carefully stored bag of seeds and crept quietly out to her garden. As she took out her tools, trying to keep them from clinking in the hush of the night, she looked up to see the sliver of the new moon over the train-station roof.

The moon, the pulse, the very rhythm of life. In the deep, velvet darkness in which she could barely see the hand in front of her face, she felt an almost unbearable brightness inside her

54   JACQUELINE LICHTENBERG

mind. Her whole body tingled with an exquisite awareness. She understood what Grant had meant—nobody could sustain this ecstasy and live.

Borne on that tide, she turned to the already prepared soil and, measuring with the handle of the trowel, carefully and reverently placed her seeds and covered them, marking the rows systematically as she went. She worked with her eyes closed, as if she were already Sime. There was an energy in her fingertips, a vibrancy in her whole body, and every movement she made seemed infinitely special.

"Ercy?!" The barest of whispers, but she knew it was Halimer Grant standing over her, incredulous that she should be out gardening at midnight.

"Yes," she answered, also in a whisper.

He knelt beside her, heedless of his clothing. He cast a glance at the moon, then back to her work. "What have you planted?"

His whisper, his presence, wasn't an intrusion but a completion of the special moment. "My experimental annual trinroses." She glanced at the moon, now moving beyond the position she'd chosen for this experiment—this last chance. "I almost didn't make it."

He followed her glance, thoughtfully. Then he touched the mounded dirt, pausing almost in reverence. "Trin annuals. Morning wouldn't be soon enough?"

Compelled not to spoil the moment with misdirected truths, she said, "No—" And suddenly, she was spilling out all the details of her moon-gardening theory and her selection and cross-breeding experiment.

There was no trace of ridicule as he said, "I—see."

During his long pause, Ercy said, "People think—would think—it's magic, but it's *not*. It's all in the rhythm and patterns. If you can sense them, pick them up and work with them rather than against them, you always get higher yields and healthier plants—and people, too, I'll bet. That's my theory, anyhow. Living in this world is like living inside a huge, beating heart."

Ercy stopped, sure that now Grant really would think she was crazy.

"I've never heard quite—that—description before, but I think I take your meaning. To me, the universe is an exquisite work of art. The tiniest glimpse of its perfection is all any mortal can bear. Yet we all live for one thing only—to gain such a glimpse. And once gained, to repeat the experience again and again until it kills us."

MAHOGANY TRINROSE 55

Ercy understood that yearning and wondered if she'd ever know such a moment again. "Have you ever had such a glimpse?"

Grant's hands were clasped tightly in his lap, his head bowed so that the faint moonlight barely touched his features. "Yes."

Something in his whisper tightened her throat and made tears start to her eyes. She couldn't breathe until he added, "But I have forsworn the search to repeat it. I don't know, now, whether I'll be able to keep that vow."

I've changed his future, just like he's changed mine.

She became aware that she was staring at him, when he glanced again at the moon. "It's getting late." He rose, helping her to her feet. He smiled, all Rialite instructor again, and only then was Ercy aware that the armor usually worn between people had dissolved for a moment between them. Her training had sensitized her to the presence of this daily armor both in herself and in others, and she now knew that its absence was what caused Im'ran's voice to change so when he was working.

Grant was striding down the path to the faculty residence before she realized that in this technological age, few Gens could tell time by the moon, rising and setting at different times every night—unless they deliberately kept track.

This is my time. I have no obligations, no responsibilities. Whatever happens after this time, I'll be able to respond appropriately, effortlessly. Meanwhile, nothing is demanded of me, not even to remain conscious.

The sessions with Im'ran, rhythmically punctuating Ercy's day, gradually built up a deep, inward trust that these few moments were hers alone. And one evening, she was finally able to let go on signal, falling, into total relaxation. She had felt it once, seven years ago, but lately she had given up ever achieving it again. And so it came over her, as if she were diving, slicing cleanly into tingling fresh water, and she could feel in slow motion the surface of the sun-warmed water parting to engulf her, slicing sensuously up her limbs, over her body, her face, scalp, deep into her brain as if the structure of her brain had become like the open cells of a sponge and could breathe.

She felt light, floating as if should she move to get up, she would forget to bring her heavy body with her, and would stand looking back at it. Though her eyes were closed, she seemed to see every detail of the room, including Im'ran lying beside her on the lounge, holding her hands but deep into his own relaxation state.

56 JACQUELINE LICHTENBERG

Surely she wasn't actually zlinning the room? She wanted to hold on to the phenomenon, examine it closely, but the moment it came to her attention she found herself bobbing up toward full consciousness, and her eyes opened themselves, leaving her only the memory of an odd form of vision, a memory she wasn't certain of—and yet, she *was* certain . . .

Im'ran also surfaced when she did. As she sat up, she watched his face, startlingly younger in repose, resuming its familiar lined, craggy appearance. He smiled. "That's it, Ercy. You did it at last."

"You, too?"

"Yes."

"Then how did you know I did it?"

He rubbed his fingers together. "I could feel it, as much as a Gen can," he added ruefully.

"It was very strange," said Ercy. "I seemed to be seeing with my eyes closed—but I don't think I was zlinning."

She inspected her arms, and Im'ran laughed. "No, certainly not zlinning, not for a few more weeks anyway." He got up and went to put water on for the tea they always shared after their last late session of the day.

"Yes, I know," she replied, "but everything does seem to be changing." She looked down at the spare contours of her long, slender body. Could she detect a slight, new rounding and softening? She had grown again, right out of her clothes. "I've had a lot of—strange experiences lately."

"Oh? Like?"

"Well, like one day"—*night actually*—"I was working in the garden and I was overcome with the most incredible ecstasy, like I was alive for the first time in my life. And the next morning I woke up crying in such a wretched misery as I'd never known before. I couldn't even remember any dream. I just felt that I had had something wonderful and had made myself give it up."

"Well, you have in a way, Ercy—childhood, a childhood long enough to let you grow up in ways most of us—me, and Mora and Digen, too—never really did. Maybe that's it."

"Maybe," answered Ercy doubtfully.

Im'ran came to sit in his place opposite her. "Or you have studied the hormonal changes of puberty. It's a little early for you yet, but it could just be the normal emotional instability of growth. By your fourth transfer, you won't have that problem any more, I guarantee it."

MAHOGANY TRINROSE 57

Ercy sighed. No, it was more than just hormones, she was sure. She had touched something that night in the garden. Hal had understood because once he had touched it, too. Had they both lost it, forever? Her eyes filled with tears, but she blinked them angrily away as Im'ran went to pour water into the teapot.

"If it's just growing pains," he said, "the relaxation practice will help. Eventually, you'll have to master it to the point where in the midst of an attack of pure, irrational hysteria you can snap into the total relinquishment state. That ability is the only thing that's kept Digen alive all these years."

"I know it's important. And now I've done it, I'm not sure I can ever do it again."

"Hasn't Digen ever told you my special talent is patience with the skittish Farris thoroughbreds?" Im'ran was chuckling wryly as he came back with the tea glasses, handing her one and resuming his seat.

Ercy inhaled the tangy scent. "Did I ever mention you make the best tea I've ever tasted?"

"Thank you," said Im'ran, "but that was an abrupt change of subject. I've noticed that adolescents do that when they're embarrassed. Embarrassment usually comes from an acute, new—raw—awareness of self. Perhaps as a 'skittish Farris thoroughbred'?"

"I think when I become World Controller, the first thing I'll do is take the newspaperman who coined that term and lock him away in the deepest, darkest dungeon I can find," said Ercy, without a trace of malice but without much humor, either.

"Digen hates it, too. But you have to learn to live with these things when you're born a public figure."

"Dad's spent his whole life learning to live with things he hates. That's a pretty bleak way to live. It makes you wonder if the whole thing is worth the bother."

"Ercy, you mustn't talk like—" Im'ran started in automatic rebuke. But he paused, then, setting his tea aside, and took her hands in a firm but gentle grip. "Now, wait a minute. There are grim moments in life, true, but there are things that make life worth living. Surely, Ercy, we haven't taken all those moments away from you?"

Uncomfortable at his intensity, Ercy inched away, folding her hands around her tea glass and sipping it slowly. "I wasn't thinking about the past. I was looking into the future. People make a lot of jokes about Farris thoroughbreds and Zeor customs. There's even a lot of resentment that we take pride in holding to a higher standard than the world considers adequate. But if Dad

58 JACQUELINE LICHTENBERG

tries to call a small news conference, five hundred top reporters will show up three hours early. If I wanted to be World Controller, I could have the job four years from now. Is there any other pre-changeover channel who could say that?

"People seem to think that power like that gives you a lot of choices in life. Why don't they realize that a channel's life consists of having the power to get what you want, but having to give it up because other things are more important? Oh, Im', does every worthwhile moment have to be bought at the price of agony? If so, there are no worthwhile moments."

Ercy was appalled at what was coming out of her mouth. But she felt better, having said it.

Im'ran asked, "What have you had to give up lately?"

Halimer Grant. But no, she couldn't say that. Her father had made it clear how much it would hurt Im'ran if she asked for someone else.

"Well," she said, draining her tea glass, searching for true words that didn't say too much, "It's just a general pattern of life. Take my changeover party, for example. Has anyone consulted me about any of the details—even one?"

Mulling over what she'd said, Im'ran took her in a close hug.

"Oh, Im', I didn't mean it like that. It's just—just I wonder if it's worth the bother."

"Well, Ercy, I'm telling you, and you can ask Digen and Mora, too. It's worth the bother, Ercy. Growing up is hard. This is probably the hardest thing you'll ever have to do in your life, especially since you're not getting the usual channel's warning of changeover. But it will happen, and you'll find out that on balance, life is worth the bother. Store up the memories of the good times, because they can carry you so far over the bad times."

Ercy pulled away, suddenly aware that she was being comforted as a child—and liking it. "It's late. I have to take a shower and get to bed."

"Digen, I didn't know what to say to her. I haven't seen depression like that since—since—"

"—since I broke down," finished Digen. It didn't take a channel or an orhuen mate to see how disturbed Im'ran was. And for a change, the matter had come up in their private suite at the end of the day when it could be given some real attention. The family had a large penthouse consisting of five spacious rooms arranged around a central living room. Ercy had one of the large

MAHOGANY TRINROSE 59

side rooms adjoining the kitchenette, from which patio doors led onto the roof. Next to the kitchen was a library-office in which Digen and Mora, being Sime and requiring less sleep, often worked while Ercy and Im'ran slept. Then came Digen's private bedroom, and on the far side of the suite adjoining Digen's room, Im'ran and Mora shared the other large room, well away from Ercy's.

Mora was taking a shower in her bathroom, and Digen and Im'ran had the privacy of Digen's room.

"No," said Im'ran, "not quite as bad as you've been. But you should have heard her. She complained of not being consulted about her changeover party. That wasn't just a random example she chose, but it's not decoration or invitations bothering her. Digen, I think she doesn't *want* me to be her Donor."

Digen knew how oversensitive Im'ran was about the alteration in his selyn field frequency brought about by shaking plague. He felt that channels ought to be repelled by his almost imperceptible deviation from the dead-true Tecton standard rhythm he'd been born with because, as a fanir, he drew them into his rhythms.

"She can't zlin yet," said Digen. "She has no Sime sense awareness at all. There's just no way she could be detecting that very slight off-true increment in your field. Im'ran, *I* can only detect it when I concentrate."

"If she fulfills herself, she'll make you look like a Third Order Channel."

"Very likely," answered Digen. "But, Im', she told me, some time ago, what was bothering her. It's not that she doesn't want you—it's that she does want Halimer Grant."

"Ah!" said Im'ran, the gloom in his nager lightening. "That would explain it. But why?"

"You wouldn't ask if you could zlin his nager. He's in our range, Im', though I don't know why he doesn't carry the rating, or why I haven't heard of him before."

"Well, you haven't been in circulation for a long time. There could be a lot of things going on that we haven't heard of."

"True," Digen sighed. "I'm not surprised she wants him— every Sime who gets within zlinning distance does. But during her First Year, she'll certainly get him often enough. I'll have to have another talk with her."

"About what?" asked Mora, coming in as she tied a wrap around herself. Im'ran explained quickly, and Mora said, "Maybe you'd better leave that to me. You concentrate on getting us a staff of Donors who can handle her."

60 JACQUELINE LICHTENBERG

Im'ran said, "It looks like you'll have to fight for them."

"She'll have to learn to work with the Donors the Tecton sends her." Digen tried to keep bitterness out of his voice. It was the lesson he had failed to learn himself.

Digen paced restlessly, then tried to shake off the awareness of failure. He extended his tentacles, first the pairs that lay along the top of each arm, the dorsals, sliding along the back of each hand, then the pairs of ventrals that lay sheathed along the bottom of each arm and touched the palms of his hands, and then the tips of his fingers. At the peak of his stretch, he extended the four lateral tentacles, one along each side of his arms, and then, relaxing, he let them all dance back into their sheaths, as he let out a sigh.

Mora, also a sensitive channel, stretched with him and shared his relaxation. Im'ran yawned with them and went to sit between them on the bed. "Twenty years," said Digen. "Maybe I'm too old to fight the Tecton any more."

"I don't think we're too old," said Im'ran. "But we're getting soft sitting out here in the wilderness."

"I thought you liked it out here," said Mora. "I do. Where else could a First Order Channel spend most of her time bossing a construction gang, playing architect and contractor, and actually watching dream buildings become reality?"

"And," said Im'ran, "you know why I prefer not to have to deal with strangers every day the way I would if I worked in the city at a Sime Center."

"I've told you," said Digen, "you shouldn't be so self-conscious about being off-true. It's not like body odor."

Im'ran winced, and Digen realized he'd expressed too truly just the way Im'ran felt about it. He put one arm around the Gen's shoulders, letting his tentacles grasp the Gen's finely developed biceps. "Look, if you weren't just that increment off-true, you and I wouldn't be matchmates and I wouldn't be alive to tell the tale."

"I wouldn't trade anything for what we've got, the three of us," said Im'ran. "Even so, I still don't like to go off Rialite."

"I was thinking about that, the other day," said Digen. "Whatever happens, we will be leaving Rialite."

"Well," said Mora, "I've had fun building this place, and my buildings will be here long after I'm dead. But, Digen, I don't really want to go back to the Sime Centers."

Digen sighed and stretched out on the bed, hands behind his neck, tentacles massaging his scalp. "There was so much I

MAHOGANY TRINROSE 61

intended to do with my life. And here I sit, nearly fifty years old, and none of it's done—not one thing—and the world is going to pieces because of it. This hysterical revival of the Church of the Purity—witch burnings, and last week a full-scale riot that almost burned the Controller's Registry building because somewhere a mob got the notion that witchcraft practices are actually causing an increase in the mutation rate."·

Im'ran said, "And just look at this snarl-up over Hal's papers, or—the very idea of having to fight to get training Donors for Ercy!"

Digen asked, "Im', what happened to our youth?"

Im' and Mora were looking down at him, the consternation in their collective nager almost seeming to form into words—*you know very well what happened to these twenty years*.

"I haven't lost my memory," said Digen, "I've suddenly regained something that's been sitting on a high shelf inside me, getting dusty." He sat up, looking from one to the other. "I feel as if I'm waking up to find I've been buried alive—and I want *out* of this coffin!"

Now that he'd put words to it, Digen realized it was more true than he'd known. The mere hint that this period might come to an end stirred him in ways he'd thought long since beaten out of him.

When Im'ran had brought him back from the Distect House of Rior, he'd spent four years in a vague limbo of convalescence. *Ilyana*. Her name still hurt immeasurably just to think it. Her basal selyn production rate had exactly matched his basal selyn consumption rate. She had been a closer matchmate to him than Im'ran was, and he had been touched and opened by her along selyn transport paths that, before her touch, he hadn't even known were there, the paths that were active only in the junct, the killer Sime. With her, he'd had a junct-style lortuen relationship, so satisfying that he'd never had the urge to kill.

At the very moment when she died, in an explosion of her own making, Im'ran had picked up the broken threads of his lortuen with Ilyana and sealed those unspeakable inner wounds with the bonds of orhuen, the transfer dependency between Sime and Gen of the same sex, which—lacking the sexual dimensions—was only slightly less powerful than lortuen. Im'ran had saved his life, and to this day had prevented him from ever feeling the impulse to attack a lesser Gen and strip him of selyn in the kill. But still his junctedness disqualified him from ever touching a

62 JACQUELINE LICHTENBERG

Sime or Gen in a Tecton channel's function for fear he would waken killust in Simes, or terror in Gens.

The thought, as always, brought his frustration to peak intensity, only this time, with a hope for an end in sight, it was more than he could bear.

Tensely, Mora said, "Digen, you're going to try it again, aren't you?"

Im'ran, dismayed as he caught the meaning that had passed nagerically between the two channels, said, "Digen, let's take this one step at a time. If you can't make it through the disjunction crisis, then we can back off and try again."

"And draw out the agony?" He gripped his Donor's hand. "I don't know if I have the strength to go through another long, tedious, exhausting illness."

"But," said Mora, "you're well now . . ."

"No, I'm *not!*" Regretting the peevish tone, he added, "I'm not really well. I'm just alive on a delicately balanced knife edge thanks to Im's skills. Mora, do you think you could live in secondary dormancy, never even using your channeling abilities— with the prospect of nothing more for maybe another fifty or seventy years?"

"That's a strange thing for somebody to say whose physician gives him six months to live," answered Mora.

Digen laughed. "Thirty-five years ago, they took one look at this lateral scar and only gave me six weeks to live. Now I've got six months to live—I'm improving! And I'm impatient to be completely well."

"Impatient enough to die trying?" asked Im'ran.

"Yes," said Digen, "if it comes to that."

Mora frowned. "That's a cruel thing to say to your orhuen mate."

How often had Im'ran sat with him through the extremities of his illnesses, saying grimly: *If you die, on that day, I die too*. It was an awareness they shared. It was the definition of orhuen.

"I'm sorry, Im', I didn't mean it like that. I was twenty-seven or -eight when I first met you. I'd already spent fifteen years battling for my life against this lateral scar." He held up his left arm and extended the left, outer lateral tentacle, one of the nerve-rich members usually exposed only during transfer or channel's functionals. The scar was an angry mark going nearly all the way around the tentacle. It blocked the orderly flow of selyn in Digen's internal systems and caused him no end of problems— especially when he had been working channel's functions regularly.

MAHOGANY TRINROSE 63

Im'ran put the inside of his wrist against the delicate member, managing the field balance for Digen with the expertise of years. "That battle is over."

Digen took the Gen into the Tecton standard transfer grip, omitting only the lip-to-lip contact point that would initiate selyn flow. "I want to get back to *work*. I want my licenses back—and since I've never"—*killed*—"hurt anyone, Gen or Sime, because of my condition, if I can attain disjunction, I can make them give me at least my in-Territory licenses back so that I won't just vegetate until I die."

The two men looked each other in the eye and Digen felt a sleeping lion waken in the other man, and stand up to roar glorious defiance at the world. It was as if in Im'ran, too, a stream of energies dammed up by the flotsam of decades had suddenly sprung free. Digen felt his lips stretching into a strange, almost feral grin matching that on Im'ran's face. Mora took a hesitant step and stopped, bewildered. "What—what do you two have in mind? You aren't going to risk—"

"Oh, yes, we are," said Digen. "Aren't we?"

"We can do it, Digen! We really can! Only—Digen—"

Digen and Mora both could feel the sudden apprehension amounting to fear in the Gen, but what Digen could understand and Mora couldn't was that, for both men, the danger of what they planned was a delicious and enticing part of their plan.

Digen said, "I once came to the conclusion that to have something to live for, you have to have something you'd die for. Ercy's grown—or will be in a matter of weeks—and I'm going to be free—to live dangerously, for the highest stakes I can find. I've suddenly discovered that's the only way to live!"

When they looked to Mora, it was obvious what they were saying violated everything she based her life on. And yet—yet— deep down beneath the horror and confusion, there was an answering spark, a delightful tingle which reminded them both of a younger Mora who might be reawakened to join them.

Then she shook her head in disgust. "You're a couple of incorrigible *boys!* You can't turn Zeor over to Ercy at her changeover!"

"Why not?" asked Digen. "It would be good for her—nothing less would be any real challenge to her potential ability. Besides, she'll be three times the channel I am. I can't be Sectuib of a House with her in it." Then he relented. "Oh, I couldn't dump the whole administrative job in her lap. I suppose I'd be regent

64 JACQUELINE LICHTENBERG

for a year or so. Or you could, Mora, if you had to. You're a good administrator.''

"I'm a better engineer. Digen, I never realized until I got out in the sunshine how much I hated working in a Center.''

"She has a point,'' said Im'ran unexpectedly. "I liked healing while I was a Therapist. But I think that's because I never knew anything else. I'm having a ball as Chief Donor here.''

But Digen had a sudden idea. "How would you two like to move into Solar House and take over the World Controller's office? Mora, you could be in charge of building and modernizing all the Sime Centers. And, Im', you can orchestrate the Donors' organizations. We tried shaking things up from the bottom twenty years ago. But I've never served a whole term as World Controller. There are things you can do from that seat that can't be done anywhere else.''

"Turn politician?'' said Im'ran with a wry expression.

"*All* the Sime Centers?'' said Mora thoughtfully.

"Why not? Zeor has a certain—undefined—power in this world. Why not use it to get things done that are long overdue. If they're left undone much longer, the world will surely fall apart at the seams—and, Im', you and I know just how weak those seams are.''

Im'ran met Digen's eyes, and Digen didn't have to hear the words to interpret his nager. "Solar House? It might be fun. But, Digen, you've got a long way to go before you can qualify for public office.''

Disjunction. All the way through.

"We've taken the first few steps,'' said Digen. "They haven't hurt—much.'' Their last two transfers had been delayed a week, and then two weeks, respectively, so that their next transfer would be a regular one and the following transfer would be their breakstep where Digen would take Halimer Grant and Im'ran would serve Ercy.

Im'ran nodded. "But we've got it timed now so that I would be giving you your full transfer on Ercy's changeover day.'' "Full transfer'' was their euphemism for a procedure Im'ran hated because it violated his Tecton and Householding oaths, the transfer which fed selyn through the juncted pathways to prevent the crisis which had, when Ercy was barely four, sent Digen into convulsions, nearly killing him.

"Have you told Hal about this yet?'' asked Mora.

"No, but I will soon. He'll have to agree, formally, you know.''

MAHOGANY TRINROSE 65

"You'll have to work with him, more closely than I am with Ercy." There was a thread of pain in the Gen's nager which knifed Digen deeply. He took Im'ran's arms again, tentacles lightly twined about Gen muscles.

"Im', it's only for one transfer. This will strengthen us, you know."

Im'ran, who had been practicing the demanding Zeor disciplines for all these years, picked up Digen's reassurance from his touch and fed it back to him, nagerically. "I know." He added, "Sectuib."

Digen went to Mora. "You're in this with us. If you don't help, neither of us will have the strength to see it through."

Mora slid her tentacles up to twine about Digen's. Digen could feel the fine trembling of fear in her. But she said, "Yes, Sectuib, I'm—in it with you."

Digen grinned. "All the way to Solar House!"

Chapter 6

"Ah, come in, Hal!" Digen called from his position on the sofa, charts and papers spread on his lap.

Halimer Grant came into the sitting room, closing the hall door quietly behind him. Digen had chosen to broach the matter in this informal setting lest it seem he was using his official powers to back his request.

"Come sit down," said Digen, indicating Im'ran's favorite chair to Digen's left. "I don't suppose you have much time, so I'll get right down to it. I believe you must have noticed that Im'ran has been working with Er—"

Digen broke off as Grant's eyes focused on a photograph of Digen's long-dead brother Wyner which was displayed on the end table between the sofa and chair. The elegantly framed picture had been a gift from his sister Bett.

There was a flash of shock in the Gen's nager, cut off in mid-surge as Grant's fields froze in a way Digen had only seen in sudden death. He reached out toward Grant, sending files cascading to the floor, certain the man's heart must have stopped beating.

But just before Digen's hands and tentacles would have closed on Gen flesh, Grant reached—nager still frozen, eyes glassy— toward the photograph and picked it up. Then the entire whirling complex of fields that always surrounded every Gen seemed to collapse in on themselves, sucked into an invisible point, and disappeared.

Digen, suspended in pure disbelief of his senses, fought to control his own fields, and momentarily Grant reappeared nagerically, his face resuming the *inhabited* look of a living person.

Digen observed warily for a moment, and then, convinced that the Gen's body functions were perfectly normal, he knelt to gather the loose papers entrapping his feet.

MAHOGANY TRINROSE 67

Grant laid the photograph aside and bent to help Digen. "I'm afraid this mess is my fault. I was startled."

"I've never seen a startle-reaction quite like that," said Digen, sitting down to organize the files. "What caused it?"

Grant picked the frame up again, gazing distractedly at it. "Who is this?"

Digen told him. "You've heard me mention Wyner—or if not, then surely Ercy has mentioned him to you."

"The resemblance is—exceptional."

"Yes," said Digen. "Birth characteristics match, too. Remind me to show you the files sometime. Which brings us to what I wanted to talk to you about."

"Hmmm?" asked Grant, still fingering the photograph.

"Ercy's changeover."

Grant looked up, full attention on Digen but not a trace of expectancy in his nager. The man was an impossible enigma. Suddenly Digen wasn't sure he really wanted to breakstep with Grant.

"Shu-*ven!* Hal, I do not understand you or your crazy nager! Look, I've got the medical and performance files that we've started here for you—your documents still haven't been found— and I've given you a tacit four-plus rating. You're operational at my level even though there's no trace of underdraw from not being assigned a four-plus channel—you've never claimed to be four-plus, but—"

Digen trailed into frustrated silence, unable to ask the question that was really on his mind—what had that startle reaction actually been?

"Controller Farris," said Grant into the silence, "I have no doubt that I could match the capacity of any Tecton channel, including yourself. But the Tecton has never called upon my skills to the fullest."

Digen went hyperconscious for a moment, zlinning the Gen deeply. There was nothing but the tranquil statement of a fact. Yet the man wasn't cut off from his emotions in any way.

"Hal, that wasn't startlement. Your nager just closed up and disappeared for nearly thirty seconds. As if you'd died."

"I'm sorry if I disturbed your field balances, Hajene. Though I wouldn't have expected a channel to be disturbed by such a reaction."

"My field balances weren't disturbed—which just makes it worse. With a nager as powerful as yours, I don't see how any

68 JACQUELINE LICHTENBERG

reaction you have could fail to disturb every channel within zlinning distance."

"Carrying such a nager entails a certain responsibility to prevent harmful disturbances."

"It's my mind you've disturbed, and that may be harmful."

"How so?"

"What I called you here to talk about, Hal. I've had Im'ran working with Ercy, preparing to serve her First Transfer. Im'ran is my orhuen partner." Digen's eyes locked with the Gen's, and there was no further necessity for words.

"Hajene Farris—*Digen*—I can't be other than—what I am. If you call upon me, I shall serve with the best of my skills. But if my skills—disturb you—"

"It's just that they're so—*strange*."

"Do I not satisfy all Tecton specifications?"

"Oh, yes, of course, absolutely. It's just that nobody ever specified that a Gen's nager had to be zlinnable at all times!"

There was one of those drawn-out pauses that so characterized Grant's speech patterns. "I was taught that the Gen who aspires to serve the most sensitive Simes is obligated never to use their sensitivity as a weapon against them, even inadvertently."

"So you startle by disappearing instead of slapping every Sime in the neighborhood with the force of your nager?"

Grant was silent, and Digen added, "What I'd like to know is how you were trained to do that."

"It is a total discipline. Very few would be capable of benefiting from it. And I am not qualified to teach."

"No?"

Again Grant was silent, staring at the picture he held in his lap. Digen made his decision.

"I asked you up here, rather than down to the office, because I can't make this a Controller's assignment, and since you're not a member of my House, I can't make it a Sectuib's order. There's only one passable, perhaps somewhat shady, legal sanction for this—as First to First, under the Oath of Firsts. You have to volunteer to do this breakstep transfer." Grant looked up, giving the vague impression he hadn't heard. Digen repeated, "I'm asking you to volunteer."

"I am very reluctant to break into an orhuen."

"Who wouldn't be?" Digen described his plan to precipitate his disjunction crisis by using the breakstep transfer. "All I'm asking of you is to serve me in a perfectly routine Tecton sanctioned transfer. No matter what happens, I will not expose

MAHOGANY TRINROSE 69

you to any aberration or side effect of my quasi-junct condition—you understand that condition, don't you?''

"Since I've been here, I've read through your library of Farris biographies, and even some of Rindaleo Hayashi's papers on your condition, though I have to admit the math was beyond me. I'm very far from the expert that Im'ran is.''

"I don't expect you to take Im's place—this is just one transfer. One *routine* transfer. You'll never even know you're dealing with—a junct.''

"Don't say—Digen, you're not *junct*.''

Now there was emotion in the Gen, pure as the driven sands and as dazzlingly bright. For the first time in years, Digen felt drawn to another Donor. Then it was gone, Grant's nager wholly neutral again. It was as if he'd spoken one word and left it echoing in Digen's systems—*Safe*.

"I'm not asking this just for myself or Im'ran. Ercy's involved, too. As I've watched Ercy developing, I've become convinced her changeover will be perfectly routine up until First Transfer—and then she's going to qualify four-plus with speed and sensitivity way off all existing graphing systems. In my medical judgment, Im'ran is the best Donor for her—with you coming in a close second. Because I've got two possibles here at Rialite, the Tecton won't send me a third even if I asked. I'm not asking. I'm giving her Im'. If you refuse, I'll have to cancel that plan and assign you to her.''

"Isn't it still Householding custom for a Sectuib-Apparent to take a First Donor from within the House?''

"Yes—but it's also custom to attempt to survive.''

"Wyner Liu Farris,'' said Grant, toying with the picture again. "Digen, I volunteer.''

Digen found himself almost unable to speak as he handed over the legal waiver forms and all the other papers and made Grant read them before signing. When Im'ran came in, it was all Digen could do to keep from reaching out to him. And when it was all done, and Grant had gone, he sat with Im'ran, saying numbly, over and over, "Why am I shaking like this?''

The next weeks flew by all too swiftly. Digen and Ercy both watched Rialite's preparations with some dismay, but with a certain pride. The House of Zeor was not only the founder of Rialite, but still its major financial supporter, and the whole place was getting ready to stand inspection, as well as to host one of the most historic events of the decade, the assumption of a new Sectuib in Zeor.

70 JACQUELINE LICHTENBERG

The Rialite staff residence was repainted, and schedules reworked so that many of the instructors bunked in with their students, making space for over four hundred guests. All over Rialite, there was the sound of sawing and hammering, the smell of paint, and often the sound of amateur—very amateur—orchestras practicing for the big party.

They had wanted to build the bandstand over Ercy's garden plot, but Ercy vetoed that, claiming she'd go to Camp Hitchson for her changeover if they did. Since Digen believed she'd do it, too, if her garden were threatened, they decided to rip out the big fountain on the rotunda to build the pavilion which would house Zeor's private proceedings.

Meanwhile, Ercy continued her work with Im'ran and her sessions with her father. But the high point of her day was at dawn, when Halimer Grant would come through the archway in the hedge and settle to talk for a while.

From the day her father had begun working with Grant, preparing the breakstep sequence, Ercy noticed that the Gen no longer seemed so critical of her determination to find a way to help her father disjunct.

When she asked about this, he merely said, "Digen has explained to me why he is so set on altering his situation. And—I'd underestimated you, Ercy, drastically."

One day she found the courage to ask, "It always seems to me that you know more about mahogany trinroses than you're letting on. Why won't you help me—even a little?"

She could tell that she had hit him where it hurt, though she couldn't imagine why. "Ercy, I don't have any knowledge that I can share with you." He rose and left so fast she would have said he was fleeing from her—but Halimer Grant would never flee from anything or anyone.

That was the day the dreams began again.

Halimer Grant walking through walls in his green-cowled robe. Halimer Grant turning into a tree that grew all the way up to the sky. Halimer Grant tromping joyfully through a whole field of trinroses—mahogany-colored trinroses.

She dismissed them all, except one that had a different, vivid texture. Halimer Grant stood on a white cube between two pillars that supported nothing, dressed in his green robe, the cowl shading his face, the jewel flashing brightly on his chest, while all about the edges of a rectangular room shadowy figures stood as if transfixed in the act of lunging toward him, fingers and tentacles outstretched in shimmering rejection.

MAHOGANY TRINROSE 71

"I tell you in truth," Grant was saying, "she is alive now because of me. And so I am responsible. When I looked at the photograph, I saw her previous life, and death. I know why she must grow the mahogany trinrose—and working with Digen, I know he can't survive without kerduvon. We must—you must help her, or let me help her."

"The time for initiative has not yet come. We hold you to your Oath. You know the penalties. Go now, and invade us not again."

And every figure in the room retreated to an upright stance.

Ercy woke with a horrible feeling of falling, and nearly screamed aloud with the shock of impact before she realized she was sitting bolt upright in bed with the half-moon shining in the window. She breathed deeply, trying to calm herself, but the memory of the dream refused to fade as nightmares should.

Photograph? What photograph? Previous life? Death? It was such utter nonsense she knew it was merely another wish-fulfillment dream—Halimer Grant knows all about mahogany trinroses and kerduvon and would tell me if "they" would let him. Wish-fulfillment dream or paranoid nightmare? *God, I wish change-over were over already!*

Several times she started to tell Hal about the dream since her parents were all too preoccupied with their own problems to appreciate her nonsense. But Grant seemed to be steadfastly avoiding the subject of her garden and her legends. Often, he reiterated that she had to establish her own identity, and not to let her father's obsession with Wyner's characteristics hang too heavily upon her.

She applied herself to her studies and training routines until she barely had time for her garden. Thus every moment spent there became tremendously precious to her. Early one morning, during her short talk with Grant, she said, "You know, the first time I ever saw you—it was as if you were the first Gen I'd ever seen."

"And I suddenly knew I'd come to the right place."

"The right place for what?"

"I don't know. To learn, perhaps. I never expected to find such a garden as this—out here in the desert."

Ercy reached around Grant and chose a young carrot, pulling it up with a gentle, circular motion. She hosed off the dirt and offered it to Grant. "This is one of my best carrots. It should be sweet and tender. Here—for you, because the growing things of the earth mean as much to you as they do to me."

72 JACQUELINE LICHTENBERG

Their hands touched, and she felt herself tensing as she always did in contact with him. On a long, exhaled breath, she gave herself the mental command to relax. All at once, the world stilled and she could feel her whole body *living*. In one brief flash, she knew the change working in her, slowly but steadily, pushing upward toward manifestation.

"Hal, I got it! I knew it for a minute—changeover!"

His slow smile surfaced from deep within, as if he were revealing a portion of the sunshine he carried within himself.

Am I zlinning? No.

She never could remember what he'd said then, and the rest of the day passed in a fog as she tried to grasp that awareness once more. It was only late that night as she was trying to fall asleep that it suddenly hit her. The wish had come true.

She laughed over that, and fell asleep with tears of laughter in her eyes.

Over the next few days, life became very difficult for her. She didn't tell her father about her new awareness because she'd only had it once, with no clue as to her changeover date. Her behavior had already become so erratic that her parents had taken to simply tolerating her, which embarrassed her terribly. Even Im'ran treated her as if she were a channel suffering a severe case of post-syndrome. Half-baked reports of a new perception would only be taken as another symptom of hysteria.

One thing her parents did, though, pleased her very much. Dinner at the Controller's Residence was traditionally the big event of the day. The heads of departments, newly arrived or departing scholars, lecturers, instructors and researchers, visiting businessmen or Zeor officers, Tecton representatives, and even out-Territory Inspectors would be invited to dine with the administration.

Over the last few weeks, however, dinner had become more of an ordeal for Ercy since people came to see if she were showing any signs of changeover yet. Then Digen decreed the dinner meal would become, for a short time, a private family affair. But the night before the first of the changeover party guests would arrive, Digen came into the large dining room with Grant at his side.

Im'ran and Ercy's mother were rolling in a serving cart while Ercy set four places. Im'ran turned, saying, "Digen— Hello, Hal."

"Ercy," said Digen, "set another place, would you, please?"

She glanced at her mother, and then brought another place setting from the sideboard. She sensed there was something—not

MAHOGANY TRINROSE 73

right—between Im'ran and Hal. But she didn't know whether it was just that Hal would be serving her father in transfer. As she helped her mother put the piping-hot dishes on the table, she listened with one ear as Im'ran took her father aside for a moment.

". . . no, I don't think her emotional instability is hormonal," said her father. "I suspect it's just psychological pressure, and will abate spontaneously when this is over."

She knew that Im'ran had told him of her latest crying jag. She was becoming more ashamed of herself every day. How could she meet the people of her House if she kept behaving like this? Tears started to her eyes again.

"Let me help you with that," said Grant.

Ercy turned to look up into the Gen's face as he bent over the table beside her. His hand came to rest just brushing her fingers as she placed the soup tureen on the table next to the fruit salad. All of a sudden, she couldn't breathe and she thought she was going to faint.

She sent the command of relaxation down her nerves and was gratified when her muscles melted. Once again, she was suddenly aware of her impending changeover—a clock ticking away inside herself, and under Grant's touch, the clock seemed to change tempo.

Grant released her hand, murmured something she didn't catch, and then they were all seated about the table. Digen took his usual place at the head of the table, with Im'ran and Mora at his right, Grant and then Ercy at his left. Suddenly discovering that her flighty appetite had returned, Ercy reached directly for the steaming casserole. As she helped herself, she saw her father glancing in her direction, then zlinning her.

She schooled herself to her best table manners, determined to prove she could behave if she had to. But inside, she was flying high—*I feel it, I feel it, I know it's happening*. If she could stay calm, she could feel it whenever she wanted to.

Digen and Mora took small portions of soup and filled their plates with a dab of salad and a thin slice of bread. They were both approaching transfer, need leaching away their Sime appetites even in the presence of two hungry Gens.

Over the soup, Digen said, "I am glad you could dine with us, Hal."

"My pleasure," said Grant. "This soup is delicious. And I did understand you had something you wanted to talk about."

"Compliments on the soup go to Im'ran," said Digen, smiling

74 JACQUELINE LICHTENBERG

at his orhuen mate. "He's the master chef who engineers the Controller's Residence specialties."

Im'ran chuckled. "Yes—it's called throwing all the best leftovers together. A fine art."

They appreciated the soup in silence for a while, and then Digen said, "You've never said much about your family, Hal. That's one thing people who work for the Tecton usually do talk about—because, traveling as we do, we don't have much in the way of family life."

"Yes—but—" Hal looked about the table. "People manage somehow to hold on to the people who matter most."

Mora said, "We've been very lucky."

Wondering how to move on to the subject he wanted to discuss, Digen busied himself collecting the soup plates and setting them on the sideboard. He brought back the teapot, pouring some automatically for Mora. "Anyone else?" he asked.

Grant said, reaching for the casserole dish, "I'd like some of this . . ."

But as his hands closed on the serving dish, so did Im'ran's. Their eyes met, and then Im'ran surrendered the dish to their guest—but his gesture—too stiff, too formal—spoke volumes.

Digen, standing behind Im'ran with the teapot, put one hand on Im'ran's shoulder and met Grant's eyes solemnly. "Don't pretend it didn't happen and put up a polite wall," he said to Grant. "You're here as family, Hal, because we have a family problem to work out. All right?"

Im'ran lowered his eyes, and Digen could feel him trembling though his nager was the forever steady fanir's beat. "I'm trying, Digen," said Im'ran tensely.

Digen wanted to forget all about breakstepping and disjuncting if it was going to cause this much pain for Im'ran. He calmed himself and poured tea, setting the pot gently on the table as he resumed his place.

"I know you're trying, Im'. I'm trying, too. But time is running out. Some things have to be resolved now. In a few days, we'll have—other things to worry about." As he spoke, he could feel Grant tightening up, ever so faintly. "We're putting you on the spot, aren't we, Hal?"

Grant took a helping of the casserole, saying, "It—is—a difficult role you have given me. But I did accept it. Yet, it's Im'ran's role that is the most difficult. It is his pain I feel."

At last, Im'ran looked up at Grant, once again in possession of

MAHOGANY TRINROSE 75

himself. "I must apologize. It is we who have asked you to do this for us. I am behaving badly."

"Only honestly," said Grant.

"Honestly?" asked Im'ran. "I don't think so. I—can work with Ercy. She's family and—I guess over the years I've lost the ability to work with—others."

"That's why I brought Hal here tonight," said Digen. "It's been a long, long time since either of us has worked Tecton style. I'm finding it difficult, too. So I wanted you to see how well Hal fits into this family. And I wanted Hal to see what we have as a family."

Ercy's heart raced. Was her father going to ask Hal to pledge Zeor?

Digen paused, noting Ercy's sudden emotional spasm, but the girl was eating her dinner steadily and hadn't said a word. He let it pass, loath to interrupt her eating since she so seldom had much appetite.

He turned to Hal. "You never did answer my question. What does family mean to you—personally, Hal?"

As Hal reached for the teapot, Digen had no impulse to take it from his large Gen hands and pour for him. He had the precision of a Sime in his movements. Digen couldn't recall ever seeing him fall over his feet, or do any of the clumsy, Gen things that always alarmed Simes so much. "And come to think of it," added Digen, "you never did mention where you were trained."

"I consider my family to be those who trained me. Family— those are the people who share your unconscious assumptions about right and wrong, real and unreal, important and unimportant. As a result, you can communicate with those people on a level that—outsiders—can't reach."

As he spoke, his gaze fixed on Ercy and she met his eyes. *They're both philosophers*, thought Digen. *Yeah, he fits into the family all right. But should I be so sure where?*

Aloud, Digen said, "You know, what you've described isn't so much family, to me, as Householding. I believe you once said you weren't formally pledged to any House?"

"No. I am not."

"Informally associated," asked Im'ran, "by marriage perhaps?"

"No. I come from a very small town—much smaller than Rialite, and just as isolated. I think, long ago, when the Householdings were indeed living groups farming and supporting themselves—they were just that, small towns. Perhaps that's why I strike you as something—odd? There really aren't that many

76 JACQUELINE LICHTENBERG

isolated, small towns left anymore, with the slideroad train and telegraph reaching beyond the big cities. The world is changing. And in spots, it hurts.''

"So," said Digen, leaning back with his tea glass cradled in two tentacles, "you come from a rural community where technology isn't worshipped for its own sake. That," he added, locking gazes with Mora, "makes sense.''

She nodded. "Digen has long had a dislike of the modern methods of training Donors by using feedback machines rather than channels. You have the kind of nageric structure that can come only from that—personal—training.''

Digen nodded. "Im' has it, too. He was trained in Imil and pledged Zeor at the time we formed orhuen.''

"That was about twenty years ago," added Im'ran. "Habits can become pretty firmly set in twenty years—and I guess that's why I'm so afraid of trusting Digen to you. *I* know what his requirements are, sometimes even before he does. I know what could happen—with someone who doesn't share our basic understandings.''

"Im'," said Digen, "you're rationalizing. The orhuen bond is the second-strongest known. The very idea of breakstepping an orhuen would send most couples into screaming hysterics.''

"The breakstep is a Zeor concept," said Im'ran to Hal. "Imil has very high standards, but this kind of discipline is utterly foreign to them.''

"I can understand how that could be," said Grant.

For the rest of the meal, Digen sat back and listened as the two Gens began to converse more easily with each other. He admired the way Grant was making it very clear to Im'ran that he shared some of their basic, unconscious assumptions—enough to get Im'ran through the coming test.

At last he stood, saying, "It's late, and Hal and I have some work to do before I do the clinic rounds. Ercy, I'll see you the usual time in the lab, and then your session with Im', and early to bed. Tomorrow you must be at your best to greet the guests.''

"Yes, Sectuib," she said obediently, marveling at how obedience no longer hurt her.

As Digen and Hal left the dining room, Hal pacing along at Digen's left shoulder in Im'ran's accustomed position, Ercy watched Im'ran's face. She could feel his pain despite his new confidence in Grant.

When she went up to her room, expecting to shower and change before her appointment with her father, she found her new party dress spread out on her reading chair, with accessories to match. There was a note from her mother: "Your schedule is canceled for tomorrow. Take the day to yourself until the banquet. Just be sure to budget enough time for good grooming; we all want you to look your very best. We're so proud of you. Mother."

She just stood there staring at the clothing and the note, and it all came crashing in on her. *Tomorrow*.

Chapter 7

Ercy spent her last day of childhood in her garden, getting it ready to be neglected for a few days—maybe a week or so. Reveling in permission to get good and dirty, she even went and collected a couple of wheelbarrow loads of manure from the barns, turning it into the earth at strategic points around the garden and burying the rest with her compost, figuring the odor might keep fastidious visitors at a distance. It was heavy work, but she ignored the nagging ache in her wrist and the rest of her body.

She spent the afternoon writing up her experiment log books, and became so lost in them that it was time to dress for the banquet before she knew it. Leaving them piled on her study desk, she showered and dressed, meticulously checking off each step on a list her mother had left. When she finally looked at herself in the mirror, she hardly recognized A. Ercy Farris, Sectuib-Apparent in Zeor. It simply wasn't her.

When she got to the dining room, her mother was there arranging flowers on the table, which had been spread with a blue-fringed white tablecloth and set with the white dishes with black and gold borders.

"Wow," said Ercy. "I thought the formal banquet was tomorrow night, when everybody will be here."

"It is, it is," replied her mother distractedly. "We only have seven guests tonight—" She broke off as her eyes focused on Ercy. "Aild Ercy Farris, you look—magnificent! Your father's in the kitchen with Fil. Go see what you can do to help—but don't get messed up. I want Im' to see this!"

In the kitchen she found Fil alone. "Where's Dad?"

"Went off with one of the guests, I think. Oh, Ercy! You have grown up, haven't you?" He beamed at her, limping around the central work counter. "No, don't come in here. You'll get all stained. Say, it was you who put these cucumbers on the sink this afternoon, wasn't it? I've used them and some of your sweet

MAHOGANY TRINROSE   79

lettuce and slicing tomatoes for the salads, and there were four left over I'm putting in the centerpiece so you can brag a little.''

"I don't want to brag," said Ercy, walking to the back door of the kitchen to look out. "Did Dad go out this way?''

"Don't go out there! You'll get your shoes muddy.''

"I knew there was a reason I didn't want to dress up! I'm glad changeover only comes once in a lifetime. I don't think I could stand this a second time!'' She went out to the dining room, wondering if she'd ever dare to announce that she was getting married. The thought startled her. It was as if something deep inside her had finally accepted the idea that she was going to survive, that there was a future to plan for.

"Ercy, there you are!'' said her mother. "They're on the front porch. Come, stand right here to receive your guests. I want them to see you first against the background of the table and . . . Here they come.'' Digen led the crowd into the dining room, assuming his place on Ercy's other side. And then the introductions began.

First the visitor would trade oaths formally with Digen as Sectuib of Zeor, the one to whom each member of the House was pledged in life, fortune, and honor. The complicated hand/tentacle clasp and: "Out of Death Was I Born, Unto Zeor, Forever!'' Digen then introduced each person to Ercy, citing his Tecton ranking: QN for a channel and TN for a Donor.

"Sarton ambrov Zeor, QN-1,'' presented Digen.

"Yniss ambrov Zeor, QN-2,'' *Sarton's wife*, added Ercy mentally.

"Jyo ambrov Zeor, QN-2,'' *and this lady is Sarton's daughter*.

"Kfarlin ambrov Zeor, TN-2,'' *Sarton's—um—brother? Uncle? Uh-oh*.

"Jolaine Farris ambrov Zeor, RN—you remember Jolaine, Ercy. Your Uncle Sels's cousin.''

Father's sister's husband's cousin. What's she to me then? Cousin?

There weren't many Farris renSimes or RN's around the world, so Ercy inspected Jolaine while making polite responses.

Then her father was introducing a little girl. "Kadi Farris, and would you believe here she is almost ten years old already?''

"My, Kadi, how you've grown!'' said Ercy, unable to remember ever meeting a Kadi Farris. *Kfarlin's daughter? Or Jolaine's by somebody else?*

"May I present Rellow Farris ambrov Zeor, QN-1.''

Her infamous cousin Rellow, son of Sels and her father's sister

80 JACQUELINE LICHTENBERG

Bett. "Congratulations, Rellow," she said, hoping her politeness wasn't as stiff as it felt.

Rellow smiled, seeming as vicious as he'd ever been. "I never thought this day would come, Ercy."

Without thinking, she retorted acidly, "So you finally made First Order officially—or did Dad mean that only in Zeor?"

"Oh, it's Tecton official now. How many mere Second Order channels have you heard of in the Farris line, let alone in the Zeor Farrises?"

Ercy glanced at the Farris renSime, Jolaine. But she hadn't heard, or if she had, she ignored it. In an undertone, she said, "Rellow, you may be First Order as a channel, but you're surely not ranking when it comes to manners!"

"Yours could use some work, too. Maybe it's a good thing I'm to be assigned as one of your instructors."

Ercy had to swallow hard at a sudden panic. *No, Dad would never do that to me!* And suddenly she knew Rellow was up to his old game of prodding her into earning a reprimand from her father.

She lowered her eyes, and quietly said, "I'm sorry, Rellow. I doubt whether either of us would enjoy it."

And then dinner was brought in with formal flourishes. Right at the outset, Fil brought everyone's attention to the gorgeous emerald cucumbers and other spectacular fruits of Ercy's garden. That set everyone murmuring praise and marveling over her achievements.

She kept her eyes on her plate and refused to let herself say that the produce was only an unimportant side effect of her main program. The one time she looked up in the midst of this ordeal, she saw Rellow holding one of the centerpiece cucumbers and eyeing a large red tomato from her early patch. He glanced at her, frowning, and she lowered her gaze firmly to her plate and kept it there. He knew about her interest in trinroses, and she wished fervently that he wouldn't bring it up now.

Before long, the conversation was flowing smoothly, catching up on family gossip, until eventually it came around to the topic of how dangerous Digen's breakstep was. Her father pointed out that Zeor would now have Ercy for Sectuib and he would only be Regent. From there the channels somehow got into a very technical discussion which Ercy strained to follow, though she scarcely understood one word in five.

Rellow leaned across her place to insert his comments into the conversation of Digen and Sarton, flaunting his expertise for her

MAHOGANY TRINROSE 81

edification. She was irritated in her old pattern, wondering bitterly how she had ended up seated next to Rellow. *Probably because nobody else would sit with him.*

She watched how they handled his comments for a while, and all at once it occurred to her that he was pathetic, and her parents knew it, as did everyone else except Rellow himself.

Im'ran, seated at her right, turned during a lull in his conversation with Kfarlin, and said, "Ercy, you're only picking at your salad. Don't you want some of the potatoes and onion sauce you like so much?"

"No, thank you. I'm not too hungry. Besides, they're better in the scrap soup you make with them than they are fresh."

Im'ran started to say something, but was called back into the technical argument by Sarton. The conversational cross-talk around the table was becoming a din, an almost painful pressure against her head, and though most of it was about her, none of it seemed to include her.

Fil served the carrot cake and the teapot was passed again. The conversation raged louder, and her head ached more, fewer and fewer of the words making sense. Her shoes were pinching and she itched under the tight waistband of her dress. At last she thought to try her relaxation drill and was astonished at how quickly the headache abated and the room came back into focus, the itch and pinch fading from her consciousness. Outwardly she displayed a lively interest in the proceedings while in her mind she built plant genetics charts for growing a mahogany trinrose.

She found a rare amusement in the idea of sitting among such an august gathering, counted practically as one of them, while she thought thoughts they would all classify as pure insanity.

What if I had a bunch of real mahogany trinroses up in my room? How would I tell them about it? If I merely presented the vase full of gorgeous red-brown flowers, they'd have to believe me then.

She was jarred out of her reverie by a sudden pain in her left arm. Rellow pulled back as her tea glass tumbled over onto the table, and a rich brown stain spread across the white cloth. "Oh, Ercy, you've spilled your tea!" said Rellow.

Digen was on his feet and in back of her chair in a single augmented move. "Don't try to get away with that, Rellow. I felt you hit Ercy's arm clear over there." Bending over her, he asked, "Is there something the matter with that arm, Ercy? Little bump like that shouldn't—oh!" His tentacles flashed expertly along her lower forearm to her wrist.

82 JACQUELINE LICHTENBERG

"I just sprained it a little this afternoon, hauling—"

"Rellow!" Digen barked, his sudden outrage apparent to everyone in the room. "You were sitting right next to her and you didn't even *notice*—what kind of a channel are— Or—did you do that on purpose?"

"I wouldn't . . ."

"Stand up, turn around, and face me!" snapped Digen.

Rellow didn't move, and Digen as well as every other Sime there could read the sullen resentment in his nager.

Across the table, Jolaine said, "That's your Sectuib talking to you, Rellow Farris. On your feet."

"You are not my mother! You're only a renSime . . ."

The shocked silence stretched.

There was such pain in Digen for his sister, who'd had to rear this child, that when Digen spoke again, his voice was soft, wholly uncontesting. "Get up, Rellow, and face me like a channel."

As if strings were pulling him, Rellow jerked to his feet and faced Digen.

"Sitting right next to her like that, you couldn't have missed the signs of development Ercy is now displaying. Must I conclude you did that on purpose?"

Rellow evaded his gaze, his nager hard and unreadable in the nageric ambiance of the room full of channels, Donors, children, and even a renSime whom all the channels were striving to protect from the nageric uproar.

"Look at me," said Digen, "and before Zeor, answer truthfully."

Rellow brought his gaze back to Digen's eyes, and said, "No. I did not."

He knows I can't read him here, thought Digen. He looked about the table, his eyes finally resting on Kfarlin, a Gen with a fairly low rating, accustomed to depending on everything but the nager to determine other people's meanings. Kfarlin shook his head. The boy was lying, as Digen suspected.

"Rellow, swear it to me, ambrov Zeor, and I will accept that."

For a while Digen thought the boy was going to forswear his oath to the House and that frightened him. Rellow was heir after Ercy. Though he'd not turned out to be heirship material, his children might be.

Ercy thought: *I'll bet he never even noticed, but now he'd rather lie than admit that he's a lousy channel.*

MAHOGANY TRINROSE **83**

But in the end, Rellow dropped his gaze. "I didn't mean to hurt her. I just wanted to embarrass her because she was being so high and mighty."

"Your objective was to embarrass the Sectuib-Apparent in front of her House?" Digen turned to Ercy. "If you had spilled your tea—or if we had thought you spilled your tea—would you have been embarrassed?"

Ercy had spilled quite a lot of tea over the years, even at formal dinners. "No, Sectuib."

Digen let his gaze roam over the others around the table, sensing their approval of Ercy. He was sure that Rellow noticed it, too.

"Rellow Farris, you will kneel before your future Sectuib and beg her to forgive you. And when she completes changeover, you will pledge to her and through her to Zeor—or you will leave Zeor forever."

Digen was being incredibly harsh, he knew, but Rellow wasn't just any member of the House. He would be second under Ercy, and what he'd just done amounted to attempted murder. The slightest injury to those tender, developing nerves—Digen shuddered—

Conceding stiffly, Rellow sank to his knees. "Aild Ercy Farris, Sectuib-Apparent of my House, I beg and entreat you to forgive my error in judgment that could have resulted in serious injury. In future, I will leave my sense of humor at the doorstep of your abode. Zlin my sincerity and forgive me; that is my plea."

Well, thought Digen, *at least he's learned the proper forms!* And he *was* sincere, too. Sincerely sarcastic.

Ercy said, "I wish you no harm and hold no malice for you, Rellow. Let it be as if it had not happened."

Rellow rose and whipped out of the room, leaving everyone stirring back to life from frozen fascination. Sarton came around the table to Digen, offering his hands. "Unto Zeor, forever, my Sectuib. And am I glad I don't have your job! If that—that—*boy* should ever succeed to Zeor—God alone could help us—if there is a God. Ercy, are you injured?"

Digen frowned as Ercy stretched her throbbing arm. He detected no serious injury, but in this ambient field . . .

"Honestly," said Ercy, "I don't think it's anything to fuss about."

Digen said, "I'm going to take her to the lab for a thorough scanning. The development should be recorded. Please, everyone, finish your meal."

84 JACQUELINE LICHTENBERG

In the lab, they went through the familiar routine together. Digen watched as Ercy sat patiently suspended between emotions, waiting. Ordinarily, that would be good, but at this point—no. Digen made a decision.

"Ercy, you definitely have some nerve fibers and glands forming now. It's so faint, though, I doubt if you'll enter stage one before, oh, thirty, maybe forty hours at the earliest. Right now, I want you to come with me."

He took her down into the deep old basement and at the end of a long, damp corridor, they entered Rialite's Memorial to the One Billion. Here were inscribed the names of those who had given their lives for the principles of the Tecton and the cause of unity between Simes and Gens.

The vaulted room was lit by one selyn lamp under the waters of the fountain and one combustion lamp above in the air. It was cool here, well insulated from the ambient nager of Rialite.

"Since the days of Rimon Farris, every Householding has kept a memorial to those Gens who were killed by our ancestors, Simes who had no choice but to kill Gens in order to live. Since the days of Rimon Farris, we have added to the roll of martyrs, Sime and Gen alike, who have given their lives to abolish the junct transfer."

Ercy wondered what her father was leading up to, but she had a creeping intuition that she knew.

"Every House had its own roll inscribed in its memorial. And then, when Klyd Farris founded the modern Tecton, he brought the custom to the public with the establishment of this very Memorial in which we stand, dedicating it with his own hand. Though the names inscribed here are those of the martyrs to the Tecton, this is very much Zeor's own Memorial. Ercy, come here."

Ercy stepped across the floor, which was inlaid with metal plates on which names were inscribed, and stood beside her father.

"Ercy, together with me, place your hands and arms deep into the water."

She was, Digen noted, still altogether too calm. She had to come to grips with the fact of changeover. With utter trust, she plunged her arms deep into the chill water just as he did.

One of his tentacles guided the fingers of her left hand to touch the selyn lamp's glowing tip. A shock thrilled up her arms and into her body. A terrible—bright—awareness made her feel transparent.

MAHOGANY TRINROSE 85

Then it was over, her father handing her a towel. She looked at her arms, feeling the vague soreness he had named "a slight development there." *It's really happening! Right now, this very moment. The waiting is over.*

All about her, the names of the martyrs leaped into high relief. . . . *who have given their lives to abolish the junct transfer*. The kill. It was real to her in a way it never had been before. *I could go junct. I could kill*. There would be so few Donors who could face her need and survive that she was seized with a cold, prickling horror—the true knowledge of what she had become: Sime.

Digen followed the stages of his daughter's realization as they swept through her, and knew a moment of such pride as to make all the years of struggle worthwhile. No matter how much preparation a child had, that moment of coming face to face with adult identity inevitably shattered the mind and forced a total reorientation. He let it run its course, waiting until she was breathing normally again. "Aild Ercy Farris, step forward."

Ercy took a small step forward, knowing that now she was about to receive Zeor, whatever that meant. She knew only that it was a necessary requisite to becoming Sectuib.

Digen took Zeor's Book of Martyrs from its place and handed it to Ercy. "Read the names of those who have placed the meaning of their lives in your hands for fulfillment."

The list was familiar to Ercy. It started with names of people whose stories were long lost, not even a legend remaining.

"Billy Kell. Drust Fenell. Vee Lassiter. Jon Forester." She read on and on, unaware that the passage of time had altered accents so that the owners of the names would barely have recognized them. As she read, the legends, the stories, and the dry, factual histories of these people as she had learned them became real to her in a new way. It was almost as if, as she called off each name of the roll, the ghost of that person stood forth to answer, "Yo!"

As she came to the end, her throat constricted, tears stung her eyes and she had to blink them away. When she came to the names her father had inscribed, she broke helplessly into open sobs as she read, "Skip Ozik. Joel Hogan. Ilyana Dumas Farris-Farris, Sosectu in Rior. The entire House of Rior."

Digen had braced himself, but even so it was several minutes before he could find his voice.

He took the book from her and set it on the rim of the

86 JACQUELINE LICHTENBERG

fountain, where the light from below cast the shadow of the book onto the ceiling high above.

"All of these have died for Zeor," said Digen, "but the power of their lives burns brightly still. Aild Ercy Farris, daughter of Mora ambrov Zeor and Digen Ryan Farris, Sectuib in Zeor, reach out now and become the vessel through which the power of death will brighten and grace the world of men."

He stretched out his hands to her, tentacles extended to secure contact, and she unerringly offered her grip to him.

"Answer me now from the depths of yourself where life and meaning coexist. What is Zeor?"

Ercy was taken aback. It wasn't the kind of question one went around asking oneself. Zeor—just—*was*. "Zeor," she said out of the compulsion to say something, "Zeor is humanity, individually and together, striving for excellence. Zeor means the striving for excellence. But even more than that, Zeor is a deep knowledge of the gulf between what we are and what we can be, and the inner feeling of what it will be like when we become all we can be that makes the striving seem worthwhile. That's why Zeor is so widely acknowledged as the greatest of the Householdings— because we dedicate ourselves to the broadest of all life principles— it's so broad and so abstract and so basic that it can't really be defined in any usual sense. You just have to feel it in your bones, so to speak."

Ercy had no idea where the words had come from. They spilled out from some deep inner conviction—and in that moment she was flooded with such a warmth of love for her father she could barely breathe. She would do anything for her father—and for Zeor. Anything.

Digen was stunned. He had no idea what he'd expected her to say—anything at all except *that*. For his brother Wyner had often explained Zeor in almost exactly those words, and that was one Wyner quote he had been very careful never to aim at Ercy. Shaken more than he wanted her to see, he gripped her arms carefully but firmly.

"Close your eyes and find that feeling for Zeor within yourself. If you can touch it, Ercy, it will change you even as death never could. *You* will never return from this journey. A new person will emerge who is you—and yet not you. Come now— into Zeor."

Digen settled into deep relaxation, easy to achieve in the isolated quiet of the Memorial. When he had stilled all the random sparks within himself, he could sense on the periphery of

MAHOGANY TRINROSE 87

his awareness the tiny thread of Ercy's developing nerves, the ghost of a selyn current flickering faintly along one arm near his fingers.

He summoned his own perception of Zeor as a ring, the Zeor crest ring of the Sectuib which he now wore. He saw it nestled in a dark, velvet-lined, jewel-encrusted box. He entered the box and placed his miniature hands on the ring and on everything Zeor meant to him.

Ercy felt herself slipping effortlessly into her relaxation drill. As she wondered what was supposed to happen next, she came to an awareness again of the Memorial dark around her. She could almost hear the combustion flame burning—or was that some new sense of the selyn lamp radiation? The dark, eerie vaulted hall was filled with luminous ghosts while the flickering shadow of the Book of Zeor's Martyrs danced on the ceiling.

Incuriously, she felt herself growing larger than her body, extending beyond her skin. Feeling odd, she moved aside, and vaguely noted that her body did not move with her. She looked back at it with the oddest feeling—an awareness that her body wasn't *her*. It was the most reassuring sensation she had ever known.

She could see about her now the faces and forms of men and women, Sime and Gen, whom she somehow recognized, putting name to face with ease. That, too, didn't surprise her.

What is Zeor? They are Zeor. Zeor is a dream. Their dream.

They came nearer to her, smiling, as if greeting a long-lost friend. Not knowing why, Ercy was frightened and stepped back into the shelter of her body.

They came after her, love on their faces, love for her, and suddenly she wasn't frightened. She held out her arms—her family, her friends—and they all came together into her arms, somehow merging into her, within her, becoming part of her.

We are Zeor.

She found herself sheltered within her father's strong arms, shielded by his body, and by Zeor itself. They stood locked together by the grip of their mutual experience, unable to speak or move until Ercy felt her feet numb with the cold of the living rock floor.

"Dad," said Ercy, "did you do that to me on purpose?"

"Do what?"

She started to tell of her vision, but found she had no words. Besides, wasn't it patent insanity—*possessed by ghosts indeed!* No, it hadn't been like that at all. She had become part of some

88   JACQUELINE LICHTENBERG

larger whole, and the whole had become her. She *was* Zeor. But there was no way to say that in words.

"No, don't try to explain it," said Digen. "There aren't any words, Ercy. For each Sectuib, the actual experience is different. Whatever happened, Ercy, it was real in a way nothing else in life can be real."

He found himself smiling, and turned it into a grin before it could become too indulgent. "We'd better be getting back to the house, or people are going to start search parties."

The fresh air revived her sense of reality, and as they came through the archway in the hedge, Ercy threw back her head, breathing the living perfume of growing things, so very different from the air in the Memorial. She felt as if she could smell ten thousand times more keenly than ever before.

Off in the distance, she caught sight of a tall, Gen figure striding along the walkway to the faculty residence and knew it was Halimer Grant on his midnight stroll—one ghost who hadn't possessed her, one ghost to whom she owed nothing. And yet— he was more to her than she could say.

She looked at her father, walking beside her in the darkness, and wondered how she could ever stand as Sectuib to him.

Digen, noticing Grant's field in the distance without thinking about it, turned toward the front door of the Controller's Residence. "Ercy, I'm going to ask Im'ran to sleep in your room tonight. I honestly don't think anything is going to happen so soon. Your field hasn't begun its downplunge yet. But I'll rest a lot easier with Im' beside you."

"I don't mind. I suppose I'll have to get used to that sort of thing, too."

Later, when she and Im'ran went into her room, Ercy helped make up a bed for him on her sofa, shoving some old magazines out of the way underneath it. It never occurred to her to wonder why there seemed to be so much extra room under the sofa. She was overwrought and exhausted, and nothing seemed the same to her anymore.

Over the next twenty-four hours, the few hundred members of Zeor who could make the trip arrived at Rialite by train, chartered bus, and even helicopter, with an occasional party on horseback making a vacation camping trip out of the occasion. With them arrived the press with cameras and recorders aplenty. Soon they had cables laid out to be tripped over by Gens, and they were endlessly posing questions to any passerby.

The pavilion came to life, decked out in fresh flowers and

MAHOGANY TRINROSE 89

brightly colored streamers. Ercy greeted each and every member of her House standing at Digen's side, saying over and over again that she felt only as if she were coming down with a mild flu. The headache came not from incipient changeover, she told herself, but from trying to keep the faces together with the names she had learned from the family tree her mother had given her to memorize.

At the formal banquet in the pavilion, Digen overheard some members talking about Rellow's recent behavior toward Ercy and asking each other who they would put up to challenge Rellow if for some reason Ercy didn't make it.

It gave him a renewed chill to realize just how thin a thread Zeor's future depended on. But there were flashes of uplifting conversation, too, such as the botany professor, Ramirze, marveling over Ercy's tomatoes and cucumbers. The whole Farris family of Zeor was seated at one long table facing the many small tables filled with over four hundred of the members of the House. Digen had made sure that Halimer Grant was seated beside him.

The place of honor at the center went to Ercy, with Im'ran on one side and Digen on the other. Next to Im'ran was Mora, and next to her, her son and Im'ran's, Shirus, who was Ercy's renSime half brother though not a Farris. Beside him sat Rellow. On the other side of Grant was Digen's sister Bett and her husband, Sels Farris. The only Farrises missing from the gathering were Landar, Bett's other son, and Sceneta, the distant cousin Digen was still struggling to have assigned to Rialite. But so it ever was in the Tecton—Digen could not remember the last time the whole family had been together.

Throughout the meal, Ercy sat with her hands curled around her tea glass, the smell of food killing every shred of appetite she might have had. From time to time, Digen attempted to zlin her more closely through the chaotic ambient nager. He was very much aware that Grant's presence upset his previous time estimates because of the peculiar interaction between his daughter and the Gen.

As the meal came to an end, Digen rose to address Zeor. First he introduced Halimer Grant, saying, "Hal is not pledged to Zeor. Yet for technical reasons, which I'll be glad to explain to anyone interested, I have chosen to attempt this breakstep with him." And then he launched into an explanation of why he was timing the breakstep and disjunction completion with Ercy's changeover. "I will accept Ercy's pledge, if feasible, after her

90 JACQUELINE LICHTENBERG

breakout but before her First Transfer—the Sectuib's Pledge which hasn't been seen in Zeor since my father's pledge well over fifty years ago.

"I will then offer my pledge to her, relinquishing my position in Zeor to her." There was a rising murmur of dismay and Digen held up his hands, tentacles spread in a plea for attention.

"With Ercy's permission, I will continue as Regent. However, any competent administrator could handle the business in the event of my sudden death."

There was a sense of shock in the pavilion, but no real surprise. Everyone knew how precarious Digen's life had always been, but precarious situations which endure for over thirty years are perceived as stable.

"This," said Digen, "concludes—"

"No, it does not conclude this discussion!" Rellow was on his feet at the end of the long banquet table.

Digen and Ercy both turned to see him holding three notebooks which Ercy instantly recognized. Digen said, "I believe we have concluded our discussion, Hajene Rellow Farris." He wanted to get Ercy out of there quickly, for her field had begun to plunge as she used selyn in changeover.

"You believe incorrectly, Sectuib Digen Farris," answered Rellow. He turned to the members. "I have here three note-books, all carefully dated, in Ercy Farris's handwriting, pertaining to the use of the stars and phases of the *moon!*—in a serious attempt to grow a *mahogany trinrose!*"

In the stunned silence, Rellow added, in dramatically softened tones, "We are about to pledge to a Sectuib who is practicing magic."

Everyone began talking at once. Ercy, however, was suddenly overwhelmed by a terrible weakness that swept out from the pit of her stomach. In the moment she knew she was going to be sick, she tried to rise, and managed just to turn away from the table when she collapsed, retching.

Only one thought possessed her. *This is it. Changeover for real.*

Chapter 8

Outside the pavilion, the members of Zeor were milling about. Inside, workmen removed the tables and set up for the party. Ercy had been taken away by Im'ran to dress for the occasion. Digen had appointed a committee to examine the notebooks and listen to Rellow's charges, and they had retired to deliberate. Digen himself was caught between the discussion of Rellow's charges against Ercy and demands for the "technical explanation" of his choice of Halimer Grant rather than one of Zeor's own Donors.

At one point, he became separated from Grant, and the Gen was set upon by reporters. Working his way back to his Donor, Digen overheard the tail end of the questioning Grant was fending off.

"And is it true Sectuib Digen Farris intends to resign in favor of his daughter on this very occasion?"

"I am not pledged to Zeor, but I do regard the proceedings of a House as privileged to that House—" He broke off as Digen arrived and the reporters all turned toward him with a babble of questions. Digen gestured for silence, and said into waiting microphones, "The press is welcome to Rialite. Guides have been assigned to show you around. Press kits have been provided. You're welcome to report on the changeover party as it is taking place all over Rialite, and in various cities around the world where Zeor has convened and where other Houses have joined our festivities. Thank you."

Digen ended off, scooping Grant after him as he worked his way toward the Controller's Residence. The twilight was fading, the stars paled by the blazing lights of Rialite, and here and there over the grounds, musicians could be heard warming up for the party.

As they went upstairs, Grant said, "You are a master of temporizing. I couldn't seem to find words that satisfied them."

At any other time, Digen would have laughed in amazement at

92 JACQUELINE LICHTENBERG

such a compliment coming from Grant, of all people. At the moment, though, he was in need. He said, "A lifetime in the public eye teaches one when to *leave* because no words can possibly satisfy the reporters. Of course, I have the status to get away with that and you don't. They would have followed you wherever you went."

"I did get that impression."

On the top landing, Digen let them into Mora's room by the hall door. "Before we go over to Ercy's room . . ." said Digen, dropping onto the bed with a deep sigh. Grant picked up the cue, seating himself beside Digen and going to work on him.

"Of course. You can't talk to her while you're in this condition."

The Gen's hands barely skimmed over the inner corona of Digen's nager at first, and then Digen worked with his Donor to banish the more emphatic symptoms of need. He turned over, sprawling over the pillows and just letting the Gen unravel the kinks for him. When he had taught Grant how to work around his lateral scar, there had been a tangible thrill to professional interaction with a strange Gen, which left Digen feeling young again. *This breakstep may not be easy, but it will work.*

But first—Ercy, and this new problem. He got to his feet, straightened his clothes, thanking Grant as he looked in the mirror to brush back the stubborn cowlick at the point of his receding hairline, streaked with gray but as wild as ever.

Across the sitting room, Ercy's door stood ajar. Digen swung it slowly open to find Ercy, still damp-haired from the shower, pulling on her yawal. Her mother was helping her.

Im'ran said, from his chair in the corner, "Digen, you'll be wanting another reading on her . . ."

"No," answered Digen, waving that aside, "she's fine, aren't you, Ercy?"

"I think so. It just lasted for a few minutes."

Digen nodded. "I don't think you'll have any more problems—physical ones, anyway." She turned from the mirror, biting her lip.

"I have to ask you, Ercy. Were those your notebooks?"

"Yes, Sectuib."

"Do they say what Rellow alleged?"

"Yes, Sectuib."

Mora shook her head, tears in her eyes. "Why, Ercy? We thought you'd given up that nonsense with your dolls."

"Mora," said Im'ran, "let's you and me stay out of this. It's

MAHOGANY TRINROSE   93

Sectuib to Sectuib now, and the succession in the House is at stake."

Digen gave Im'ran a grateful smile, and concentrated on Ercy. "I thought I'd brought you up to understand science, ours and the Ancients'. Science and reality, Ercy, not fairy tales."

"I was using every tool of science you had taught me, only I was using it to research a wild hypothesis I hit on while auditing an astronomy course.

"The earth's motion sets up rhythms. If you go with them, you succeed; if you go against them, you struggle and usually fail—just as in changeover, you have to cooperate with the rhythms of change. So I applied that to the garden, and found that through the waxing moon, there is a real measurable increase in the growth rates of all kinds of plants. So I was running experiments to determine if coloring was also affected. Science, not magic, Dad." She amended, "Sectuib."

Digen was relieved, and then felt silly for having doubted Ercy, even a little. Yet, he had to ask, "Why did you let us think you'd given up these ideas?"

"I—had nothing to convince you with unless I could actually grow a mahogany trinrose. I was running experiments on the trinrose's genetics and chemistry. But it's still inconclusive. You've always said what a big part intuition has played in every major scientific breakthrough. Wouldn't it be criminal for me to abandon my convictions just because they're unpopular and unproved yet? Is that the way a Sectuib behaves?"

Digen smiled, warmed all over with such parental pride he could barely breathe. "No, Ercy, that's not the way a Sectuib behaves. But now you're going to have to go down there with me and prove yourself to them beyond all doubt."

And that may not be enough, thought Digen, hugging his daughter in a mutual affection that was so unaccustomed it was painful.

In the pavilion, the lights were softened and a band was playing. In the middle of the floor, a group was exhibiting a traditional dance, and all around people conversed with a sense of strain Digen had never seen at a changeover party. As he entered beside Ercy, there was a stir of expectancy that subsided into guarded waiting.

"Ercy," whispered Digen, "when the committee reports on Rellow's evidence, we'll deal with the accusations. In the meantime, go ahead and serve the members but do it without all the exchange of pledges."

94 JACQUELINE LICHTENBERG

Digen motioned, and one of the members brought them a large tray of glasses filled with bright amber lantria, a spiced drink traditional at changeover parties. Ercy took the tray, surprised at how heavy it seemed—or, she amended, how weak she'd grown. Im'ran at her side, she went among the guests, offering drinks, calling each by name, and trading politenesses. At first she was afraid of running into hostility, but as the shock of Rellow's accusation died away, the members were willing to await their committee's verdict before condemning her.

The first tray was emptied and she picked up a second. Where a flap of the tenting had been pulled up to let the cool night air into the overheated tent, a knot of Gens had gathered in intense conversation.

As she approached, she heard a few snatches of comments, quickly cut off as they saw her: "Don't see how Digen could have raised her like . . ." "Sectuib certainly wouldn't vouch for her if she were a—" ". . . genetically weak strain, look at Rellow. You know Digen's father was a double Farris . . ."

She held the tray out to them, feeling half naked in the plain white cotton yawal. From the center of the knot of Gens, one woman emerged to take a glass from the tray, saying, "As far as I'm concerned, Aild Ercy Farris will be my Sectuib—if she'll have me."

It was her Aunt Bett, Rellow's mother. The other Gens in the group took glasses, some of them proclaiming clearly, "And mine, too." Im'ran stood behind her, ready to support her, but she knew she had to do this with her own strength.

"I ask only that you inspect and judge me tonight, and give your allegiance to me if you find me worthy."

"I think," said her Aunt Bett, "I speak for all of us when I say we could choose no better, Ercy. You have distinguished yourself this night, carrying on so calmly."

"Thank you, Aunt Bett." As she turned to move to the next group, she saw out of the corner of one eye that one of the Gens dumped his drink angrily into the elaborate floral arrangement, covertly refusing to acknowledge her.

After that, the tray seemed heavier than ever. Her head ached dully, and the room seemed more stuffy than she could bear. Every so often, she would stop and take a deep breath and do her relaxation drill. In those moments, Im'ran, by some uncanny Companion's instinct, would step closer and lay one hand on her shoulder, in firm quiet support.

MAHOGANY TRINROSE   95

It was only as she surrendered the last tray to the member who had supplied it that she felt her knees give way alarmingly, and then Im'ran was holding her up by one shoulder and her father by the other. Aside to her, her father said, "Easy, Ercy, stage two transition, that's all it is. You're moving along quickly. It's only been a couple of hours. Stage two should go pretty quickly as well."

Im'ran whispered in her ear, "We're all very proud of you, Ercy."

She smiled to the crowd, who gradually seemed to be accepting her. The music picked up again, and a talented group of dancers began performing an old folk dance complete with traditional costumes festooned with colored streamers.

After the transition eased, she played with the children before they were finally packed off to bed. Then she chatted with adults who skirted politely around the only issue on their minds.

When she suddenly found she couldn't breathe and began to make for the exit to get some fresh air, Im'ran at her side said knowingly, "Stage three transition. Good, Ercy, good." And he held her while she panted against the resistance of her diaphragm, reciting to herself all the things that began happening with stage three.

She sat on a stone bench with Im'ran, counting seconds until the transition would pass. The sky was dark overhead, the pavilion lights spilling over onto the rotunda where several camera crews were working. Eventually, as she leaned against Im'ran, she found herself breathing normally and feeling fine except for a queasy little flutter somewhere under her stomach. She had energy enough to watch the lighted window of the conference room where the committee was still examining Rellow and his evidence.

"Here she is, Digen!" called Grant as he came out of the pavilion. Behind him, her father paused, zlinning her critically. Grant sat down beside her, and Ercy took one last deep breath, pulling herself together. The nervous flutter settled down as Grant turned his attention to her. "Well, how do you feel, Ercy?"

"Not exactly fine, I have to admit. The hardest part's over, anyway. Those trays are heavy!"

Her father came up behind her, running sensitive fingers and tentacles over the back of her neck and her lower arms. "How was the transition, Im'?"

96 JACQUELINE LICHTENBERG

"Normal as could be. I've rarely seen easier."

If this is easy, I'd hate to know how others suffer, thought Ercy.

"Good," said Digen, "lets get back to the party."

"Digen," said Grant, "it's awfully stuffy in there. I'd like to take a walk. Just half an hour."

"All right," said her father. "We'll be inside."

As Grant left, Ercy glanced at the sky, noting that it was a few minutes before midnight and wondering where Hal went every night and what he did—at midnight. The same thing he did at dawn—greet the beginning of a new day? She realized that was not a bad idea. Her whole life was about to begin; there were new choices to be made.

Her father said, "Im', what about you? Tired?"

"Probably," said Im', "but I won't notice it until this is over. Ercy is making a work of art out of what is usually a messy business. And—hey, didn't the light just go out in the conference room?"

"Yes, I saw it. Let's go inside and get this over with."

It wasn't until that moment that Ercy really began to feel the impact of what Rellow had done. Snooping in her private room, he had stolen what amounted to her diary and was making it public so that, if he couldn't have Zeor, she wouldn't either. She remembered she had left the books on her desk before the dinner that night, and when she'd returned with Im'ran they'd been gone, but she'd been so distracted she hadn't noticed.

As she followed her father back into the pavilion, she found she was holding herself tensed for a blow. Knowing she couldn't survive changeover like that, she made a special effort to summon again the relaxation she had so patiently learned.

On the dais, her father stopped the musicians and had them strike a loud chord for attention. Just as silence fell throughout the pavilion, the committee, five Simes and five Gens, came in with Rellow, filing directly up to where Digen stood.

One of the Simes, a channel so ancient Ercy couldn't begin to guess his age, limped up to Digen at the microphone. Digen said, "Hajene Rindaleo ambrov Zeor will present the report of the examining committee."

That's the legendary Rindaleo Hayashi! thought Ercy. He was a scientist, and he knew what it felt like to be kicked out of Zeor by mistake.

". . . and so," Hayashi was saying, "we do not pretend to understand all that is written in these notebooks. However, one

MAHOGANY TRINROSE 97

thing is clear. Ercy Farris was indeed investigating the effect of the phase of the moon on plant yields and hybridization. It also seems that her main objective was to grow a mahogany trinrose.''

The uproar of conversation forced him to stop until Digen again called them all to order.

''This was the substance,'' continued Rindaleo, ''of Hajene Rellow Farris's accusation, and this committee finds the accusation to be accurate as far as it goes. However, we wish to place before Zeor two thoughts. First, we have all enjoyed the fruits of Ercy's garden, and Professor Ramirze has remarked on the unusual vitality of her plants. Such a discovery, he told me, would certainly win any scientist the Platard Award for Human Service.

''Secondly, we must also point out that Ercy has not boasted or in any way attracted premature attention to her work. Rellow stole the notebooks from her private quarters, and this committee has found his action to be unethical and his motivations to be unworthy of Zeor.

''A third point which I, personally, wish to make on Ercy's behalf is that, as a scientist, I found her notebooks to be kept in the most strict and thorough manner. She was doing *science*—not magic. If she attacks her duties as a channel in this same scientific manner, she will certainly be the best of us all, and my Sectuib.''

When Hayashi had finished, one of the Gens on the committee, Sortine ambrov Zeor, a short, stout woman in her mid-forties with the most benefic smile Ercy had ever seen, came to the microphone.

''Hajene Rindaleo ambrov Zeor has spoken for us all. But I want to add a fourth observation. My credentials are in psychology, as most of you know. In her notebooks, Ercy takes great care to distinguish between hypothesis, theory, and proven fact. I found nothing to indicate that she was calling on supernatural powers to do her bidding. The origins of her theory in the study of astronomy—at her age! astronomy!—was clearly indicated.''

Thanking the committee, Digen took the microphone and called for comments from the floor. Several people spoke, not saying much of anything, and then Jyo ambrov Zeor, Sarton's daughter, got up to speak. ''*If* Ercy performs her duties in the same manner as she has conducted her research, then she'll certainly deserve to be Sectuib. But if she doesn't—? The ambrov Zeor dare not make a mistake in this. I suggest we postpone Ercy's pledge until after First Year, when we can see her in her adult form.''

98 JACQUELINE LICHTENBERG

There was a buzz of agreement until finally one of the younger channels took the floor. "I agree with Jyo. We can't afford to make a mistake. People fear and hate anything which seems to have power over their lives, and no group has more real power than the channels and the Householdings—among Householdings, Zeor is the most symbolic of all, and among channels our Sectuib is acknowledged as the best in the world. How easily all that respect could turn against us—if they thought our Sectuib was dealing with powers they fear. I suggest that we demand Ercy's promise to abandon this research, and that we burn those notebooks here before us. Then this House can unite around Ercy Farris—our Sectuib."

There was a stunned silence, and then an appreciative mutter of agreement. Out in the crowd, Ercy saw Rellow seeming terribly satisfied with himself.

"You've got to answer that one, Ercy," said her father quietly. With a gesture, he presented the microphone to her.

"Thank you, Sectuib Farris," said Ercy, without the least idea of what she could say to convince them. "Members of Zeor. For the sake of the unity of Zeor, what I stand for must be unmistakable. Our responsibility is to fight superstition with knowledge. And so I cannot and will not abandon my research—and when, and only when, I have proof, I will publish my results. When you're armed with knowledge, the dark is not so frightening."

As she finished, she suddenly realized that she had been making a speech—before over four hundred members of her House. Petrified, she gazed out over the crowd silently while her mind went blank.

Digen felt Ercy's nerve break. Aside to Im'ran, he said, "Get her off the stage."

Then he took the microphone and said, "Is there any further discussion?"

When someone rose to speak, Digen heard only a few words, enough to determine the speaker had nothing to say, and his eyes met Rindaleo Hayashi's. The years peeled away, and he remembered himself as a brash young intern burning up to change the world in one swift stroke—*just demonstrate that it is possible to do surgery on Simes, and the world will change its attitudes overnight*.

Well, he'd demonstrated it, doing surgery on Rindaleo Hayashi, then the world's most prominent scientist. Rin had lived to produce more scientific miracles. But not one world attitude had

MAHOGANY TRINROSE 99

been changed—except that the target of all the fear had shifted from medical science to witchcraft.

Hayashi smiled, and Digen returned it, bringing his attention back to the speeches. He let them talk themselves out, and then gave the floor to Hayashi, who proposed the vote: Accept Ercy's pledge now and give the House to her—or wait until she finishes First Year and take the matter up again.

After that, there was some discussion whether Digen should be allowed to risk his life in the breakstep disjunction if the vote was to wait out the year. Ercy began to realize that if her father didn't attempt the breakstep, he would have to take Im'ran in full transfer and that would leave her with Hal. A part of her was insanely delighted, hoping the vote would go against her, but in the midst of it a cold chill spread through her. *Is my second wish about to come true? Wishes don't make things happen.*

Eventually, they voted to declare a balloting hour, and while that was being set up, the debate broke into small groups arguing heatedly. As Digen came down from the stage, Grant met him, his nager like a refreshing breeze. Ercy, standing nearby, found the strange queasy flutter in the pit of her stomach again quieting. It did not reappear until sometime later, after Im'ran had eased her through another transition and they sought Digen out again.

"Digen," said Im'ran, "when can I vote? I hold a few dozen proxies, too, so it may take a while."

"The line seems to be short for the moment. Why don't you go now, and I'll watch Ercy."

As he turned his attention to his daughter, Digen saw that she was in a rapidly progressing stage four. He also noted a debilitating vibration in her faint nager.

"Let me see, Ercy," said Digen, extending his tentacles to examine her arms, her neck, her body. "Hal." The Gen moved closer to Ercy, dividing his attention smoothly so that while he was still controlling Digen's need so that he could concentrate on Ercy, he was also affecting Ercy's nager. The odd oscillations damped down and disappeared. Never in Digen's long career in changeover pathology had he seen such a textbook-perfect changeover—except for those odd vibrations. *Which could be perfectly normal for her,* he reminded himself.

When Im'ran came back, Hal carefully relinquished his place and focused on Digen.

As they talked, Digen watched Ercy and noted just when the vibrations resumed. She fought that battle repeatedly, her defense

100 JACQUELINE LICHTENBERG

ever weaker and shorter-lived. Digen couldn't imagine what was causing her distress.

Ercy screamed.

Eyes widening as if seeing the inside of terror itself, she screamed again, rending the ambient nager of the pavilion, leaving every Sime there in shock. Im'ran and Digen held her as she struggled against invisible horrors.

To Ercy, it seemed she was transported into the middle of hell itself. Before her a wall of searing orange flame engulfed a building. In that building her best friend was burning to death, and they wouldn't let her go to rescue her. She struggled, augmenting with all her might, heedless of the cost in selyn, and screamed, "Let me go! It's all my fault! Save her! Save her!"

Suddenly, the searing heat, the deafening roar, were gone. Only an immense burden of guilt remained. *I've killed my best friend*. She collapsed sobbing into an enormous, cool fog that enveloped her inside and out, damping all the flames, soaking into her bones.

"Hal, don't—" started Digen, before it became apparent that Grant's grip on her shoulders was working. As he grabbed her eyes with his own, and began talking at her, low words nobody could hear above the murmur of the crowd about them, Ercy stopped screeching fragmented nonsense about a fire and a best friend, and relaxed into Grant's arms.

On the other side of the pavilion, someone else—a Gen—was also yelling, sounding more outraged than terrified, capturing Grant's attention.

All around them people were muttering, and Digen caught the word "hallucinations" several times. Many aberrations were common in changeover, but hallucinations were not. "Ercy, Im'ran, come with us to the— Hal? Hal!"

"What?" said the Donor, turning toward Digen. "I'm sorry, did you say something?" He'd been staring at the bandstand.

Digen quelled his annoyance at Grant for becoming distracted—after all, the Gen had been working straight through without sleep.

"They just had a little accident over there," said Digen. "The tall-pipe fell off the bandstand and nearly hit a Gen."

He took Ercy and the two Donors up to the transfer room he'd had equipped for this occasion and, in the insulated nageric stillness, took all his usual readings and got just what he'd expected from monitoring her downstairs. Normal—normal—perfect—and normal.

While he worked, Hal napped and Im'ran hovered anxiously. It was a relief when Ercy went into stage five transition and he could put Im'ran to work on her again.

Ercy fell asleep and Digen sat watching the two Gens and his daughter sleeping. He could not understand what had caused Ercy's fit. One more problem to add to the already existing ones.

Chapter 9

Ninety minutes later, they all strode back to the pavilion. Mora met them breathlessly. "I think they've just finished counting the ballots."

Her mother held Ercy at arm's length, zlinning her condition, examining her swollen arms. Ercy couldn't look directly at her forearms without nausea. The whitening, stretched blisters, six of them around each wrist and streaking up her arms toward the elbow, looked like some contagious horror. It was different from looking at pictures in a book. These were her own arms.

"Digen, there you are—Ercy, Im', Mora," called Sarton. They all turned as he approached, flanked by Kfarlin and Yniss, members of the vote-counting committee. "You're wanted up on stage, for the verdict."

As they all began working their way toward the stage, Sarton said, "She lost it in the proxies, Digen." He cast a duoconscious glance at Ercy. "You're going to have to deal with this matter of the breakstep—and quickly."

Lost? The whoosh of emptiness in him told Digen that he had never really considered that possibility. *Lost!*

Behind him, Im'ran's arm tightened around Ercy's shoulders. Only Hal seemed unaffected. By the time they'd reached the dais, though, they had absorbed the initial shock.

As Digen began to mount the steps, his eye lit on the fallen tallpipe, and he stopped to examine it closely. Beside him, Hal's nager pulsed with surprise. The owner of the tallpipe came up as Digen touched the deep dent in the instrument. "Sectuib, my instrument is ruined! It sounds like—"

Digen waved that aside. "Zeor will stand good for the damages. How could it have been bent like that?" It looked as if the huge metal cylinder had been hurled onto the ground with great force.

And then they were on the stage and the tally committee was reporting the results of the vote. Two hundred seventeen votes to

MAHOGANY TRINROSE 103

accept Ercy now as Sectuib; one hundred ninety-three votes to delay acceptance until the end of her First Year. One vote to disqualify her from Householding office. There was an aborted cheer for Ercy, and the announcement went on.

By proxy, one thousand seven hundred ninety-three votes to accept Ercy now. One thousand eight hundred twenty-three votes to delay decision. Totals, two thousand ten for; two thousand sixteen against—four thousand twenty-seven total votes cast.

She had lost by six votes.

As Digen took the microphone, a question came from the floor. "Sectuib Farris—are you going to continue with the planned breakstep?"

Without thinking, Digen said, "Yes." *If I were dead, they'd rally around Ercy without argument.* "I will accept Ercy's pledge to Zeor as planned. However, I will honor your wishes and not resign my position to her at this time. I hope you all realize that this puts me in a very awkward spot."

There was a rush of sympathy in the ambient nager, and also some consternation and surprise. Apparently, some people hadn't considered the situation from Digen's point of view. Digen smiled. "I will carry the title for Ercy awhile yet, but I no longer consider myself Sectuib in Zeor." *And I haven't since the day Ercy was born.*

"Dad, I don't feel too well."

"Small wonder," said Digen, finding an encouraging smile for her. "You've been in stage six transition for the last five minutes and you hardly noticed."

Digen turned to the microphone again. "Ercy is in stage six transition. Anyone who doesn't belong to the House, please leave the pledge area. Marshals, check the perimeter and secure the tent flaps. Those in need, sort yourselves out with your assigned Companions and approach the front to experience Ercy's breakout. Please, those of you who had normal breakouts, allow those who have never had the experience to take front positions. Make it quick. Stage six is also short for a Farris. Mora ambrov Zeor, please come up front—Mora's the one who has been keeping food on the tables here and seeing that things run smoothly. She deserves honors for heroism under battle conditions—after all, she is Ercy's mother!"

There was a flurry of laughter and a stirring excitement as people rearranged themselves, each checking the identity of the one next to him to be sure that only Zeor members were present. Suddenly, Digen noticed Hal, a pastry in one hand, a glass of tea

104 JACQUELINE LICHTENBERG

in the other, being escorted away. He jumped down and stopped him. "I didn't mean you. As soon as Ercy and Im' are squared away, you and I have an appointment. You belong here."

During Grant's inevitable pause, one of the marshals, a Sime woman, objected, "But Sectuib—"

Digen said, "You should have seen the way he was handling those reporters trying to pump him about our proceedings! We can trust him—and—Hal," said Digen, in sudden decision, "I extend to you the invitation to pledge Zeor tonight—I mean today—Ercy was right. You are one of us."

"I—am—truly honored, Hajene Farris. But I can't take on such an obligation at this time."

Digen was astonished. Never had anyone turned down his invitation to join Zeor. But Digen had no arguments ready to offer. "We'll talk about it another time. Meanwhile—" He turned to the marshal. "One of the advantages of being Sectuib is the authority to break rules."

The marshals went about their business and Digen took Grant up onto the stage, saying, "Finish your pastry and set your tea down over there. I must check Ercy and you have to keep me steady."

As he moved to Ercy's side, he felt the ghostly threads of Grant's nager enveloping him. His breathing steadied, his mind cleared, and he was focused wholly on Ercy. He had time only for one stray thought that Im'ran and Grant were two polar opposites. Im'ran's nager was strong, commanding, dominant. Grant was a ghost—a chameleon who somehow disappeared when working.

As Digen approached, Ercy was cringing away from Im'ran, fretting whenever he tried to touch her. "Please don't. I just want to be left alone." Stage six was progressing rapidly, the membranes at the wrist orifices stretched to transparency.

"Of course you feel like crawling into a hole," said Digen. "That's a normal instinct so that even Simes who don't know what's happening will not expose themselves during the helpless phase."

Ercy knew all that. She shuddered against the strength of the instinct for solitude. "I don't know if I can really do this."

"The hardest part is over. We're here to help you. Try your relaxation drill now."

As he spoke, she managed again to relax the muscles of her hands and arms so as not to trigger the breakout reflexes too soon.

MAHOGANY TRINROSE 105

Digen said, "Now remember, we're doing a no-flow pledge exchange because you're not to be exposed to my juncted condition."

"I remember. I remember. Stay relaxed and there's no trick to it."

Digen felt in his own arms the stinging of stretched skin ready to burst, the tingling tickle of selyn activating the entire dual nerve system in her body—primary system that the ordinary Sime had, and the channel's secondary system ready now to function. He began to feel sympathetic need, and he was sure his own need was affecting her. He stepped aside, letting Im'ran get in closer. And then he was enveloped again in Grant's field.

"Here," said Im'ran. "Sit down, Ercy." They had brought some comfortable lounges onstage, but Ercy twisted fretfully away from them.

"I can't. I want to—to move."

And then a gasping shudder went through Ercy and danced about the Simes in the pavilion, attuned in sympathy with her. For them it was a delicious anticipation, but for Ercy it was the unknown. Im'ran glanced over his shoulder at Digen. "Time it for me."

Digen nodded, concentrating on Ercy. He could trust Im'ran. "Take her hands," suggested Digen.

Ercy was deep in the grip of breakout, her world narrowing to the rich and deep sensations in her body. Her hands and fingers dug satisfyingly into Gen muscle. *It's supposed to feel good. It's not supposed to hurt.* And it did feel good. There was a sharp, tearing sting in her arms, the ache of tissues squeezed aside to accommodate new organs, and the ever-present queasy flutter in her middle. But one could hardly call any of that pain. The good feeling, though, was impossible to describe. It was unique in all her experience, a culminating drive for—*something.*

It was good. And then, suddenly, she was seized with muscle-knotting contractions.

"Now, Ercy! Im'!"

She couldn't help herself. Her fingers dug deeply into Im'ran's arm and she gasped as the contraction forced all air from her lungs. Twice more that happened, leaving her only a second to draw breath. Sweat poured from her and she went weak all over save for the straining muscles.

"Relax, Ercy. Down and down, as deep as you can." Though her muscles were hard as knots and she couldn't breathe, still mentally she floated into the deepest state she had yet achieved.

106 JACQUELINE LICHTENBERG

The sensations that flooded her body were rapture times ecstasy squared. She wanted it to last forever.

The sense of suffocation vanished as she concentrated on the contracting muscles fighting to break the wrist-orifice membranes and release her tentacles. *My tentacles!*

Once more and yet again the contractions came, and then, in a bittersweet crescendo, the membranes tore and the tentacles sprang free, dripping fluids. They felt raw in the air, cold fire outlining them.

She was unable to hold her relaxation under the bombardment of new sensations. Her arms and trunk were a tracery of lines of fire—*selyn transport nerves,* her textbook knowledge said. She felt one of her own tentacles, still not under her control, touch the skin on the back of one finger. The pure sensation made her hair stand on end. And suddenly she knew, with an indescribable ache: *I am beautiful.*

Every Sime in the room picked up that vibration and gloried in it.

She could feel the fluid squeezed out of her tentacle sheaths running down her hands, her arms, her legs and feet—her shoes, too, but Mother wouldn't care.

With her second breath after breakout, Ercy was plunged into a kaleidoscope of wild colored, pulsing zones of brilliance. She opened her eyes after a blink, and knew a moment of panic when she couldn't see—until she noticed she couldn't hear either. *I'm zlinning! Oh, God, it's beautiful!*

In front of her she recognized Im'ran—an etched grid pattern in black and white, a fanir's nager. Behind him, perceptible through him, was her father, a dark aching need, laced with conflicting and tangled webs. Behind her father, the pearlescent swirl could only be Halimer Grant. He was a wisp of fog, glowing with selyn.

With her third breath of recovery, she found the fields outside of her setting up vibrations in her systems. At first she could not perceive within herself two separate systems, but knowing the physiology, she was able to separate the sensations she felt tearing her apart, so that, by her fourth full breath, she could almost control herself.

And then she felt herself slipping, falling away from the world. It felt as if the floor had suddenly dropped from beneath her. She lunged, grabbing on to something to stop her fall. It was Im'ran. The sickly quiver in her middle blossomed again.

Suddenly, she was standing on the stage, clutching Im'ran

MAHOGANY TRINROSE 107

around the waist. She opened her eyes to see the channels and Companions arranged before the stage, looking up at her in hushed awe.

Her father's hand came onto her fingers, her tentacles going out to his fingers seemingly of their own volition. There was a confusing, multi-textured caress inside her—*fields?* Slowly, Im'ran eased her away and her father took his place. The sick flutter receded again as he said, "Now, Ercy."

He took the Zeor crest ring off his finger and held it out to her. As they had rehearsed it, she placed her hands over the ring, and Im'ran covered their hands with the shiny Zeor blue cloth, cutting the crazy confusion of fields to bearable limits for her.

"Unto the House of Zeor," said Ercy, in what she hoped was a clear voice, "I pledge my heart, my hand, my substance. And unto Digen Farris, Sectuib in Zeor, I pledge my life, my trust, my undying loyalty—as from death I am born, Unto Zeor, Forever."

Digen said, his voice as hoarse as Ercy's, "Unto Aild Ercy Farris ambrov Zeor, I pledge my substance, my trust, my undying loyalty, in my own name, born from death, Unto Zeor, Forever."

Then Im'ran was back and the pavilion was gone from around her, leaving only the infinite black and white checkered squares of his nager. She knew from the way the squares seemed to be superimposed on her insides that she must have made the four-point lateral contact.

All at once, the hot, sick quiver she'd been ignoring burst into a firestorm, sending sparks of agony throughout her body. Paralyzed by the shock, she lost her grip on Im'ran and fell away again, panic blooming.

Try as she would, she could not induce the state of calm in which she could think. She grabbed for the security of selyn-presence, and the checkered structure entered her body again. This time, she found the place where it seemed to be wrenching and tearing at her and she realized with horror that the squares of the checkerboard weren't all the same size. It was like looking through a distortion lens, violently sickening. She couldn't keep from thrusting that grid pattern away from her with all her strength.

Each time it invaded her person was worse, as if each time scraped away some protective layer inside her, leaving her raw and—too sensitive! *Oh, no, I don't want to die! Wyner died because he was too sensitive.*

108 JACQUELINE LICHTENBERG

Digen watched Im'ran try repeatedly to make a support contact and gain control of Ercy's need. After the third failure, apprehension eating at him, Digen moved closer to monitor. Ercy, eyes closed, was nearly unconscious, whimpering with pain, shock, confusion, and the ultimate frustration.

"Digen, don't," warned Im'ran over his shoulder. "Her need will wreck your control."

Digen reached out one hand and drew Grant closer. "You can hold me on this." The Gen positioned himself, and Digen felt the cool fog blowing through his body, helping keep his attitude distant and clinical. From this closer vantage, he could feel the painful grating screech in Ercy's systems as contact with Im'ran maximized, and the sheer drop in that irritation the moment Im'ran relinquished his hold.

After the fourth abort, he said, "Hold it, Im'."

"Digen, I'd swear it's me she's reacting to!"

"I'm very much afraid you've been right all along. To her, that tiny increment off-true is a major dissonance too painful to bear, Hal. Change places with Im'—as quickly as you can."

Im'ran flashed a piercing glance at Digen as Hal began shifting places. "That's right, Im', we're abandoning the breakstep plan. Hal, we discussed this once—can you do it?"

"Yes."

Im'ran carefully relinquished his position to Hal and came to Digen's side. Digen worked to shield Ercy from Im'ran's field as Hal took her into transfer position.

Ercy felt the painfully distorted checkerboard recede into the far distance. The shrieking panic of need bloomed. And then she was enveloped in a sweet smoke that cut off awareness of the distant checkerboard. Though she was lost, and still falling, she felt safe.

She floated down onto a thick, comfortable supporting cloud that conformed to her shape and solidified about her. Her world was lit by a frosted glow. She breathed the glowing fog into herself, each tiny droplet nourishing one cell of her body. She wanted more—and there was more—and more—it came into her without any sensation of movement—of *transfer*—as if she had let herself become one with the universe.

There was none of the euphoria, or ecstasy, or rapture she had been warned to expect, but only a sober acceptance of glory.

She opened her eyes, and found Halimer Grant's startling blue eyes engaging her own, his face transforming before her gaze from concentrated inward pleasure to a stricken awe as he focused

MAHOGANY TRINROSE 109

on her. In a moment hung from a silken thread of eternity, Ercy was aware that her second wish had come true not by magic but by the simple fact that she couldn't tolerate Im'ran's nager. Her father had given up everything that mattered to him for her sake: the breakstep, the disjunction, everything. She had failed him.

Grant waited patiently. Her tentacles were still coiled tightly about his arms, her laterals against his skin. As she relaxed, her laterals withdrew across the lightly haired arms, sending prickly shivers all through her. She wanted to retract the handling tentacles, too, feeling sticky and messy now that it was all over, but she didn't know how. Yet, when she thought of it, the tentacles loosed and retracted of their own accord.

She heard a massive intake of breath from her left. All around the stage, channel and Companion pairs were also relinquishing transfer contacts, having shared with her the full cycle of breakout, first need, and First Transfer. She had succeeded in presenting the Sectuib's gift to her House, even though she had not yet been recognized.

Digen and Im'ran had delayed retiring for transfer until the guests left the pavilion. Now, sleeping for the last time in her own room, Ercy dreamed one of those all too vivid dreams, seeing again the look on Im'ran's face.

She was sitting on the same stool from which she had observed Mora's transfer. Im'ran was reclining on the contour lounge while Digen sat beside him, saying, ". . . owe it to ourselves to try. If I can't do Ercy's conditioning transfers, who can we get?"

"Sels can do it, if the Tecton will let him stay here."

"His response times are low for a Farris four-plus."

"The worst that could happen would be that the conditioning might not take."

"With her capacity, speed, and sensitivity, she could, without conditioning, end up killing a First Order Donor, which would instill such fear in her next Donor that she'd surely kill again. Im', she's as much your daughter as she is mine. Help me."

"All right. We'll give it a try." He rolled to his feet and went to the window, shoving the heavy drape aside. The spotlights outside splashed over his thin, craggy features. She watched an odd change working there, almost as if another person now inhabited his body, a distant, uninvolved person she didn't want to know. Her father, too, sitting with closed eyes, was subtly transformed into a stranger. He stretched out on the lounge, melting into full relaxation as Im'ran came to sit beside him. .

110   JACQUELINE LICHTENBERG

Their arms met in transfer grip, her father's need manifested in the eager quivering of his laterals as they made contact. Tension wrinkles melted out of Im'ran's face as he bent to make the formal lip-lip contact. Then, in dreamlike slow motion, she saw her father's tentacles clench tight on Im'ran's arms as he strained up off the lounge, his eyes coming open though starkly unfocused, and a mask of ravening greed twisted his features.

Im'ran's serenity shattered into momentary confusion, and then he did something that terminated the contact. Gasping, her father fell back onto the lounge, shuddering, his legs twitching uncontrollably. "Im', I couldn't hold it! I'm sorry."

"I shouldn't have shenned you. You can't take any more of this," said Im'ran, reaching for a breathing mask. "Come, we'll do the full transfer."

Her father batted aside the mask, but she could see he couldn't control his arms. They twitched, wandering randomly, and Im'ran brought the mask into position, triggering a valve that hissed medication to her father. The random twitching subsided, but Im'ran still had to struggle to capture both Digen's arms in transfer position.

And then he made the fifth contact, Digen rising off the lounge into a sitting position, forcing Im'ran awkwardly back. In a flash, it was over, but Ercy would never forget the gargoyle mask of maniacal ego-bliss suffusing her father's face. *Junct.*

Nor would she forget the horror-stricken realization that overcame him just as the contact dismantled. When the tears coursed down his cheeks, and he wrenched away from Im'ran to curl, sobbing, in the corner, she could only think: *I've never seen him cry.*

She woke with tears flooding her own eyes.

It's just a stupid dream! But she couldn't get rid of the echoes of desperation and failure.

Chapter 10

It was almost noon when Ercy, a sheaf of enrollment documents in one hand and a small case with her personal belongings in the other, opened the door to her new room. Across from the door, the window shade was hanging askew, the curtains in a heap on the floor. Paper streamers drooped from the the light fixture, and the entire room was strewn with blue, black, and white confetti.

Her changeover party had been a big success—at least here.

The train was due within the hour. The departing class was already at graduation, receiving their Tecton rings. The arriving class would probably find every room in this same condition. *Oh, they're going to love me!*

She threw her case on the bed near the window and set to cleaning up.

By the time the train came in, Ercy was standing at the window, watching, confident the room behind her could pass inspection. She could see part of the pavilion the workers were dismantling. In the distance, the train station was filled with graduating students, departing faculty, guests, departing news teams, and no doubt somewhere on the platform, her father.

She watched the scene below, but her mind was on Halimer Grant—his strange touch and the odd things it seemed to do to her.

She stretched experimentally, extending her new tentacles, wondering at how they seemed to do her bidding just as her fingers did. A baby had to learn to use its fingers. Tentacles seemed to come with the learning built in. But there was still a marvelous newness that made her want to watch them, touch them with her fingers or to each other for the strange sensation it produced all over her body.

Something caught her attention. Out in the hall?

It took a conscious effort to focus on the selyn fields, but with that effort, she was zlinning the hallway, dimly because of the

111

112   JACQUELINE LICHTENBERG

heavy insulation in the walls and doors. Coming toward her room, a Sime—a channel—Farris? She opened the door.

"Uncle Sels?" said Ercy, struggling now to see his face visually. When she had him in focus, she suddenly remembered she was a First Year student. "I mean, Hajene Farris!"

He chuckled. "Why don't you just invite me in, Ercy? This is a family visit."

Passing her, he said, "Let me just put this tray down. I brought it for you. You never did have a chance to sample the buffet at your own party—and it was terrific."

She managed a "Thank you" from some automatic brain circuit. Then she noticed she was still holding the door open. But she couldn't keep her mind on the business of closing it.

Sels turned and took the door from her, shutting it gently. The glowing fields in the room shifted fascinatingly as he held out his hands to her. Her hands went to his. The multiplex fields between them meshed perfectly. Then, without transition, she was hypoconscious, the world appearing solid to sight, taste, touch, smell, and sound. It was such a relief she didn't question what he'd done to her.

"Ercy, you're less than twenty-four hours old. Don't worry, you'll learn to handle duoconsciousness and carry on a conversation at the same time, while moving around doing things."

Ercy essayed a smile, letting loose a deep breath. "Oh, hey, that smells delicious."

He took her over to the desk, holding the chair out for her and taking the other chair from her roommate's desk. "Come on," he said, "let's eat up before it spoils." He poured tea for both of them.

Once more, she became aware of the fields between them. She sensed that through the fields, he was sharing her newborn senses discovering the world. She came out of it to find his hand on hers, the tip of one of his laterals just brushing her skin.

"I came here, Ercy, not only to bring you something to eat, but also because I wanted to talk to you. Digen has asked me to stay to do your conditioning transfers. I wanted to be sure— before I accepted—that we could work together."

"I've been brought up to do what I'm told." But she remembered her dream.

"Of course. So was I. But there's a matter of channel's professional judgment here, Ercy. Digen was wrong about you once—once out of thousands of crucial decisions he had to make

MAHOGANY TRINROSE 113

for you. That's not a bad score. But—well, I make my own judgments when it's my life on the line.''

Ercy froze. *No! It was only a nightmare.*

"I didn't mean that quite the way it sounded," Sels responded. "In a few months, you'll begin to appreciate the myriad possibilities a channel has to consider before taking any action. The things that can go wrong always outnumber the acceptable outcomes. But nobody could have predicted what happened to you and Im'." He broke off, taking her hands firmly in his again. "Let's try a few seconds in duoconsciousness—like this."

Ercy felt the world half dissolve into shifting gossamer fields. She could still see, feel, hear, smell, taste, and at the same time, she was zlinning. It felt like the first time she'd ever been on ice skates—wobbly but fun.

"I want to thank you, Ercy, for the beautiful changeover you gave the House. We all know the years of hard work that are behind the Sectuib's Gift. You gave me something I'd never had before—the breakout experience at its very best. That's almost a—a sacred thing. In that experience, Ercy, you became my Sectuib. The rest is only formality. We all—all the Firsts who were there—we all feel the same way. For us, you *are* Zeor."

Then Sels did something and abruptly the world became normal again. Ercy shook her head, dazed. He said, "I'm sorry, it's too soon to burden you with all this."

"It's just that—that I can't seem to pay attention to anything. I get fascinated by something and can't tear myself away to other things that are more important."

"That's normal. Everything—every little thing—requires your complete attention now. It's just like a second infancy. But it will pass very quickly. Your learning rate is soaring—I think Digen said a factor of nine immediately. You may be the first in history to hit a full factor of eleven."

"I don't want to be first. I don't want to be exceptional. I just want to be me."

"Don't we all?" He sighed, letting go of her hands and standing up to walk around the room. "I'm going to tell Digen we'll be staying."

At first, Ercy didn't understand the change of subject. "We?"

"Bett, of course, stays where I stay; Landar may stay as well. It's been a long time since this family has been together."

"Bett." There was so much to think about.

"You've lived with Digen and Im' all your life; you know

114 JACQUELINE LICHTENBERG

what an orhuen is like. Lortuen is even a bit stronger, you know.''

Lortuen. Yes, she remembered now. Sels and Bett shared the same kind of transfer dependency as her father and Im'ran, only with Bett being a woman, there was the added dimension of sexual love. With a recorded lortuen, the Tecton could never assign them to work in separate places—just as they could never separate her father and Im'.

She dragged her attention back to what Sels was saying. He was gesturing toward the hallway. ''Zlin that?''

There were more people in the building now. The whole structure seemed to glow. Two nageric centers separated out, heading for her door. One she recognized immediately had to be Halimer Grant. The other was a little like a child's scribble, a black knot of chaos—with the feel of a Sime's nager.

The door opened without hesitation, and Grant started to usher the Sime into the room. ''This will be your . . . oh, I apologize. I didn't know you'd moved in already, Ercy. Hajene Farris.''

''I was just about to leave,'' said Sels.

Drawing the young Sime into the room, Grant said, ''This is Joeslee Teel, QN-3. She's been assigned as Ercy's roommate.''

Ercy looked at the girl with interest. She had long, blond hair with a dark, outdoors complexion. Dressed in the ragtag gypsy style, she was large-boned, but already Sime-slender, and as Ercy inspected her, she raised her deep, dark blue eyes to stare back with a beaten, sullen look that bespoke much fear endured. Out-Territory changeover victim? Ercy was instantly overcome with sympathy—yet at the same time, she felt her future change again.

Sels and Grant were discussing the assignment in highly technical terms from which all Ercy gleaned was that Faron Mandrel, Grant's Co-Dean at the college of channels, had also agreed, so there was no appeal.

Joeslee was edging slowly away from Grant, like a wily animal trying to escape. Ercy watched her, but didn't draw anyone's attention to her. *Why is she so frightened of Hal?*

Grant set down the sheaf of papers he was carrying and said to Sels, ''So her whole tribe was killed in that witch-hunt. She was saved from the stake by a troop of Tecton marshals—flames already burning her feet as she was in the last stages of changeover. Since then, she's been whisked around from Center to Center until today they took her off the train here—like this. I don't think she really understands where she is or why she's here.''

MAHOGANY TRINROSE 115

Joeslee's lips compressed slightly. Ercy had the impression she understood what was said.

Before Ercy could sort out some appropriate words, Sels was gone. The nager in the room descended on her with a crash. She hadn't realized the channel had been managing the fields.

"Ercy?" Grant said her name, moving between the two channels, his nager almost as calming as Sels's.

"Yes," said Ercy, trying to get a grip on herself. "Umm—does Joeslee speak Simelan?"

"Well, her tribe was from in-Territory, but apparently all she knew when she arrived at Hilaski was a gypsy dialect or two. They tried to teach her Simelan—with some success, it says there." He indicated her papers.

To Joeslee, he said, "Ercy completed changeover less than a day ago, so you're older than she is by a week. She's still disoriented, so we thought you might be able to help her. I'm going to leave you to that, now."

At the angry crackle in the room, Ercy lost track of the conversation to examine the pyrotechnic effects with wonderment. As the door closed behind Grant, she snapped out of it, suddenly realizing she was alone with this angry stranger.

Comparing her nager with the Farris feel of Sels, Ercy began to understand a lot about her new senses. The Farris was light, with inertialess response to every changing input, drifting slowly back to dead center without overshooting. Joeslee's nager was heavy, maintaining its state with a massive inertia. Any impulse strong enough to move Joeslee the least bit off-center caused short, sharp vibration back and forth around that center. Instinctively, Ercy felt that any input strong enough to knock this channel into a Farris-magnitude reaction would be enough to shatter that nager and kill the poor girl.

Ercy picked up Joeslee's bag and put it on the bed, trying to smile. "Well, the Tecton strikes again," she said, "and this time you and I are the victims. I guess we'll just have to live with it."

Joeslee grabbed the bag out of Ercy's hands as if Ercy's touch were contaminating. Holding her arms around it protectively, she backed against the wall.

The girl remained glued to the wall, studying Ercy. Ercy didn't know what to do. She took a deep breath and deliberately relaxed. Gradually, Joeslee responded, relaxing too. She set the battered case on her bed, and one hand still on it, she said, "He looked too old to be your father."

116 JACQUELINE LICHTENBERG

"Sels? He's my uncle. He's been assigned to do my conditioning transfers. He is several years older than my father."

"Your father runs this place."

Ercy had the sudden impression that Joeslee was gathering information as a survival exercise. She nodded cautiously. "Yes, but that won't get me any special treatment. If anything, it will make it harder for me. Say—did you just learn Simelan this week?"

"They made me."

"Well, I don't speak any other languages, yet. And Simelan is what they teach channeling in."

Joeslee shrugged, her tentacles moving with the gesture naturally, but without the fluidity of an older adult's movements. *Yes, she's young, like me.*

Before Ercy could think of something else to say, the intercom speaker over the beds called out, "Ercy Farris."

"Yes, I'm here," she answered in the speaker's direction.

"Report to Faron Mandrel's office for schedule counseling."

"I'll be right there."

When the speaker had clicked off, Ercy rose.

"I'll be back, Joeslee. We have a lot to talk about."

Ercy shoved that from her mind as she strode the long, curved hallways of the student dormitory. She went outside, along the familiar paths among the lawns, flower beds, and shade trees.

As she passed over a little arched bridge beneath which was a fishpond, she noticed the fish lurking under lily pads. Then she realized she had zlinned them by the wispy ambient nager of all the Gens who lived at Rialite. She became acutely conscious of those faint fields shifting across her body as she walked through them.

By the time she entered the administration building, she was walking slowly, concentrating on the symphony of new senses that seemed to intrude only when her attention lighted on them. As she waited for the elevator she wondered if she was late. And then it occurred to her that Simes have an inbuilt elapsed-time sense, connected, she'd been told, with the selyn consumption rate and psychospatial orientation, two awarenesses she had not yet found in herself.

On the way up in the elevator, she searched inwardly for awareness. Halfway down the hallway to the Dean's offices, it hit her.

It was as if she'd been standing on well-packed beach sand, and suddenly the tide had swept that illusion of solidity out from

MAHOGANY TRINROSE 117

under her, pitching her backward into the air. Simultaneously, her head seemed to explode into a cloud of dispersing vapor in which sparks whirled round and round in illusive patterns.

For one terrifying moment she didn't know who she was.

Then her throat was raw from screaming. There was an arm around her shoulders supporting her in a sitting position. Another arm in front of her, she clutched with her fingers and tentacles in a fierce, bruising grip. Male arms. Gen arms. Transparent nager—glittering hard nager, like glass—"Hal?"

Her eyes fully focused on his face. She let go her death grip and curled into the protection of his broad chest.

Grant's nager faded from glittering hard to virtually imperceptible. "It's all right, Ercy, it's over."

Faron Mandrel, Dean of the college, and sub-Controller of Rialite under Digen, knelt beside her, inspecting her with channel's senses. He smiled, the warm, friendly, fatherly smile she'd grown up with, and said, "Yes, you're fine now. But I'll have to report this to Digen. He's still your physician of record. Come on, let's see if you can stand up without vertigo."

Ercy let him help her to her feet. There was a sense of vast distances with whirling sparks embedded in haze. Reality was transparent underneath its painted surfaces. But the painted shells were only barely sturdy enough to hold her. Panic grabbed at her again. In that moment, there was a wild scream from the office next door, and the strangest sound erupted there. Mandrel started to his feet, attention riveted on the wall. He lunged through the door.

Grant stood holding Ercy's shoulders, no sign of shock or disturbance in his nager, though he was poised to react instantly. Ercy was studying this strange effect in Grant and wondering how it was possible to be keyed up and prepared without the slightest hint of tension.

Mandrel came back into the hallway.

Grant asked, "What was that?"

"Apparently, a water main broke in the wall of the Science Office and a piece of it came right through the wall, hitting one of the Gen secretaries. She's not hurt. They've got it shut off now. The duty janitor is Sime, or we might still be running around searching for the right valve!"

Ercy let her new senses penetrate the walls, until she found the shutoff valve on the floor below them, inside an access panel. The janitor in question was sitting on the floor beside the open panel, zlinning the water pipes in the building warily.

118   JACQUELINE LICHTENBERG

Mandrel shook himself down out of augmentation mode, and that attracted Ercy's attention back to the hall as she wondered how he did that. "I'll order everything triple-checked," said Mandrel. "It isn't a new building, you know." Leading the way into his office, he went to a sideboard, saying, "Ercy, would you care for some tea? It's not as good as Im' makes, but—"

"Anything trin suits me fine," said Ercy. A hot drink would soothe her throat.

The tea had already been steeping in a tall pot with a long curved spout. As Mandrel poured for them all, Grant watched Ercy. She felt his attention as a tangible thing. Searching for a metaphor, she decided it was like her mother's fur coat, soft, silk-satin.

As he handed her the tea, the sensual delight of the aroma claimed all her attention. A sip sent shivers down to her toes. The warmth mellowed the knot of jumping nerves in her middle and laved her throat soothingly.

She noticed Grant's attention on her again. It was heavy, pondering. He was thinking lonely, frightening thoughts. She wondered how she knew that, and in the same breath, wished she could read those thoughts, and then quickly wished the wish away. She didn't want to read thoughts—she already had more senses than she could handle.

"Well, Ercy, since all our crises are under control for the moment," said Mandrel, "I think we'd better get some work done before the next one hits. We're on a tight crisis schedule around here, you know."

"Yes, I know," said Ercy, smiling at his joke.

Mandrel rattled off a whole list of courses Ercy would be expected to master: there were over fifteen. Any spare time would be spent with either Hal or Sels.

Ercy was appalled.

"Your father," said Mandrel, "wanted you to get a good general education this month and begin to specialize next month. He specifically recommended that one of your advanced degrees should be in Inter-Territorial Law. It's more or less the same course he sets up for every Householding Heir-Apparent."

Law?! I don't have time for . . . "He never told me . . ."

"I suppose he just assumed . . ."

"Assumed."

"Ercy, I've caught you at a bad time, haven't I? You're not really tracking this conversation. Do you suppose we should skip over choosing your electives until tomorrow?"

MAHOGANY TRINROSE 119

"Faron," said Grant quietly. "I don't think you should worry which electives she chooses. She's industrious and self-motivated. Why not see how she goes about training herself?"

Mandrel looked at Grant, and nodded. "You might well have a point there. Ercy, this is a very soft schedule, I know. You'll probably have quite a lot of free time toward the end of the month. If you don't use it to advantage, next month we'll schedule you a lot tighter."

"Yes, Hajene, I know I'll keep busy." *Oh, boy, will I!* She would now be allowed to audit the courses leading to plant genetics, and the garden would take time. . . .

"One more thing. I know I don't have to warn you, but it's imperative you get a regular three hours' sleep every night, even if you're not tired. The mind simply can't assimilate at this rate without adequate rest. You understand?"

"Yes, Hajene!" Insanity and even suicide had resulted when channels didn't get enough dreaming sleep during the first three or four months of First Year.

"The Controller has left time in Hal's schedule for you. I want you to be sure to call on him if you have the slightest trouble sleeping." Mandrel closed the folder with finality. He looked up at her with his eyes. "It isn't all grim drudgery, Ercy. This is going to be the best year of your life. You'll find in a day or two that the work load is really mimimal and what there is of it is fun."

Dismissed, she rose to go toward the door, holding the stack of papers and the schedule he had filled in while he talked. "Thank you, Hajene Mandrel." *Next time I'll come prepared!* Next time she would get *all* courses *she* chose.

Chapter 11

When Ercy woke, it was still dark. From the portion of the sky she could see from her bed, she knew it was nearly dawn, her favorite hour for gardening.

She started to sit up, her mind already planning the garden work, when an eerie shifting feeling made her think she was fighting awake from a nightmare. It was the wrong window—the wrong angle on a patch of sky.

In the room, someone groaned and stirred.

Ercy's senses riveted on the bed beside hers, the Sime sleeping there. It all came back to her. She was zlinning the room. She was Sime. First Year. Joeslee. It was no nightmare.

As she searched her mind, her orientation cleared. She could zlin every detail around her. She knew precisely to the second what time it was, and where she was. She had a shadowy impression of people, mostly Sime, dispersed through the building, some moving around already.

Wonderingly, she raised her arms and studied the thin threads of circulating selyn outlining her laterals, the wispy haze of dissipating selyn each cell of her body was using. In one glance, it was all relegated to the automatic part of her mind.

She extended her tentacles one at a time. First the right dorsals, sheathed along the top of her right arm as she held it up, palm down. She tickled the end of her thumb with the inner one, and wrapped the outer one around the end of her longest finger—it just barely stretched that far. Then she made all four handling tentacles of her right arm, dorsals and ventrals, touch the tips of her fingers and then each other. The sensation made her suppress a gasp, her hair standing on end as her whole body tingled. *Am I going to be ticklish?*

She tried extending just one of the sensitive lateral tentacles, the right inner one that normally lay sheathed along the thumb side of her hand. Even in the privacy of darkness, she felt exposed—naked and, yes, frightened, as the dry air touched the

120

MAHOGANY TRINROSE 121

moist skin of the lateral. She had to grit her teeth as it slid along the rough skin of her thumb, and she found she had little deliberate control of its movements.

I'm lying in bed playing with my tentacles! she thought, a sudden image of a gurgling infant flashing through her mind. She got up and went to shower and dress. Halfway through this process, she noticed that without even thinking about it she had moved through and around the room with the total silence of a Sime. *How did Mom and Dad ever endure having me around?*

And when she'd finished showering, marveling along the way at the myriad new sensations the water produced, the tactile awareness of her clothing, smells, shapes, colors, she noticed that though she had seemed to dwell on each new experience for hours, scarcely minutes had elapsed since she had wakened.

Her hand on the door, she paused to zlin Joeslee, sleeping curled around herself. Joeslee stirred again in her sleep, reacting unconsciously to Ercy's attention.

Ercy knew that, as a channel, she should have the ability to keep her inner reactions from showing in her external field, her show-field. But though she carried some selyn in her secondary system from her First Transfer, she had as yet no conscious control of her vriamic node, the nerve ganglion connecting her primary selyn transport system, which fed the need of her own body, with her secondary selyn transport system, with which she would perform services for Simes and Gens.

As Ercy watched, Joeslee stirred again and came awake, sitting up and looking at—no, zlinning in the dark—Ercy's form by the door.

"What's wrong?" asked Joeslee.

Ercy noted the gypsy accent had faded markedly overnight. "Nothing," she replied. "I was just going out. Sorry I woke you."

"It's all right. I can't seem to sleep much anyway."

"Say, did they ever call you for counseling?" Ercy had just realized she had slept nearly twelve hours, a record. She imagined it was to be the last such sleep of her lifetime.

"They did."

"What are you taking? Did you get what you wanted?"

"It's not important—" answered Joeslee.

Ercy took her hand off the door and folded her arms across her chest, an old habit. It made her dizzy, so she hastily unfolded them. "What do you mean, it's not important? It's only your whole life."

122   JACQUELINE LICHTENBERG

"If you say so."

Ercy was curious—here was a girl who had been through things you only read about in newspapers. She knew she should try to help her adjust to Rialite, but she couldn't seem to communicate with her.

Ercy went out, saying over her shoulder, "I'll see you later and we'll talk if you like."

Ercy's trip across the grounds didn't seem as strange as the day before. A hazy glow wrapped all Rialite, the ambient selyn field. There were vital centers of selyn glow—in residence buildings and in some of the class buildings. Classes ran twenty-four hours a day, as did most of the recreations. But there was still a pre-dawn hush over everything, the same as there had been when she was a child.

There was a big yellow circle on the grass where the pavilion had been, and surrounding it, a trampled area. She came to her garden, and at first thought that the manure odor had indeed protected it. But as she knelt, dawn lightening the sky, she could make out marks where people had walked. There were heavy heel and scuff marks where somebody had lost balance, and a few branches on a white rose bush were broken.

She set to work to repair the damage, reveling in the garden through all her new senses. She put her hand behind a leaf to watch the selyn field shine through it, illuminating the tracery of veins, and wondered what it would zlin like with a Gen hand behind it. She worked her way across the garden to the trin bushes. The new annuals were just peeping above the soil. In one place, a shoeprint mashed down one of the new shoots.

It was as if she could see the heavy brown shoe descending on the helpless shoot—*Rellow!* No—that made no sense. If he'd meant to destroy, he'd have destroyed all . . . unless someone had stopped him. *Ramirze.* She could almost see them.

Then the image was gone and she found herself staring emptily at the plants. In a fit of temper that surprised her, she flung down the trowel with all her might. It buried itself in the loose soil a full blade length deep. Only dimly aware that she had augmented, Ercy stared numbly at the mashed trin plant. Suppose it had been the one mahogany bloom? Killed.

Junct.

On every side, junctedness, closing in around her. Her father, unable to disjunct. Some nameless foot that killed plants as a junct killed Gens. She made herself say it aloud. "Junct." And again. "Junct." How many Gens were there in the world who

MAHOGANY TRINROSE 123

could stand up to her if she attacked in killmode? How many *channels* were there who could withstand her attack? Precious few. And the number would shrink with every day that she grew in speed and capacity, under the forced growth of the First Year regimen.

Through gritted teeth, eyes screwed closed, fist clenched over the handle of the trowel, she forced herself to say it again. "Junct."

There was nothing between her and the kill except her naked will. *This is what I've been trained for. Why does it frighten me so much?*

She pried the trowel out of the dirt, tugging with all her unaugmented might until it suddenly came loose. Without conscious effort, she zlinned the trowel beginning to break loose and diminished the force she was using, so she didn't overbalance and sit down hard in the dirt.

She loosened the dirt around the mashed shoot, tenderly tying it to a stake. She was crying openly by the time she finished. *Maybe it will survive. Shen! Oh, Shen!*

"Ercy?"

She became aware of a commotion in the barns, horses screaming, people running, a bright plume of alarm rising from the building as Simes and Gens scurried to the emergency.

"Ercy?"

It was Halimer Grant, standing behind her.

She couldn't turn. She just knelt there in the dirt, shaking. His huge Gen hands came to her shoulders, and it suddenly occurred to her that she had only to survive until her second transfer—her anti-kill conditioning transfer with Sels—and she'd be safe from ever going junct.

"I didn't expect to see you here," said Grant. "I thought you'd sleep another hour or two at least. Perhaps—perhaps you should have."

"Oh, I'm all right," she replied, putting the trowel down. At least she hadn't broken it. "What do you suppose is happening down there?" she asked, looking toward the barn.

"I can't imagine," said Grant. "Can you zlin that far?"

"No detail. But everybody is running around all excited."

"With practice, it should come well within your range." He examined the hole the trowel had made, but all he said was "Have you had anything to eat this morning?"

"No. Hadn't thought of it."

124 JACQUELINE LICHTENBERG

"You have, as I recall, a class in less than an hour. I don't think you should start your first day without breakfast."

"Did I ever tell you you sound like my father?"

"Yes, many times."

"Hal, I never really knew what a Gen was before our transfer. I just thought I did."

He squatted down on his heels beside Ercy and said, "Before our transfer, I never knew what a Sime was. I'm looking forward to the next time."

Ercy was almost overwhelmed with tears. He handed her a handkerchief. "You're just a little post, that's all. Tomorrow, you'll be able to work out your problems almost effortlessly—at least most problems. There are always those that nobody and nothing can help you with." He glanced toward the barn again.

"Do you have any like that?" Ercy asked.

"Yes, of course, doesn't everybody?" There was a distant look in his eyes, a cloudy swirl in his nager that sent an indefinable ache all the way through her.

With sudden insight, Ercy said, "You're lonely here, aren't you?"

"After the transfer we shared, how could I ever be lonely again?" He drew a finger across her face where the dirt had crusted with her tears. "Go get ready for class."

The first lessons of her new life were vocabulary and adult syntax. It was a large class conducted by two channels and two Gens, who demonstrated the meaning of each word or phrase flashed on a screen before the class. The students, arranged in two rows around them, had nothing to do but watch.

By the time she was out of there, Ercy had the vocabulary to discuss seventy-five new perceptual experiences, some of which she hadn't even heard of before. She had to put it all to use in her next class, Primary System Anatomy. It was conducted by two channels with a class of only ten students. There were nine students present.

The channel in charge glanced down the roll and said, "Does anybody know where—Joeslee Teel is?"

The other channel was passing out textbooks. Ercy said, "Hajene?"

"Trainee Farris," said the instructor.

"I'm rooming with Joeslee. I haven't seen her since she woke up this morning, but she seemed well then."

The instructor made a note, and then launched directly into a demonstration in which he required each student to zlin the

MAHOGANY TRINROSE 125

primary and secondary system of his assistant, pointing out the different structures in each of the channel's two separate selyn transport systems.

Searching for her next class, Ercy found it in a small room, hardly more than a booth, which had once been used as a transfer room. Sels was there waiting for her with her Aunt Bett. Ercy threw her arms around her aunt, a gaunt but startlingly beautiful woman a little older than her father. Her Gen nager was a whirling vortex of brightness linked in some dizzying fashion to that of Sels.

Ercy pulled away and said, "Thank you for what you did for me at the party!"

"We all have faith in you, Ercy. You're looking better, now, too."

"I feel a lot better than I did yesterday. How's Dad?"

Husband and wife looked at each other.

"It's bad, isn't it?" asked Ercy. *It was only a dream!*

"Im' and Mora are taking care of him. He'll be all right in a few weeks."

"I knew he'd have come to see me if . . ."

"I doubt that," said Sels, businesslike.

"Parents aren't allowed visiting privileges," said Bett.

"This isn't supposed to be a Householding reunion," said Sels. "It's a class. Where's Joeslee?"

Ercy sighed. "She wasn't in Anatomy, either. Did they put her in *all* my classes?"

"As many as possible. They expect she'll fall behind you, but in the beginning, you might help her get oriented."

Ercy chewed her lip, worried. "Nobody told me I was supposed to escort her."

"You weren't. Bett, go see if the page can locate Joeslee. Ercy, we'll start with simple augmentation control. Have you discovered how to augment yet?"

"I think I did this morning, but I'm not sure how I did it."

Sels laughed. "Lost your temper, huh? We're going to require finer control than that from you, Ercy. And you'll find that a mild first-level augmentation helps you get through an assignment like reading a book and retaining enough of it so you can integrate it when you sleep. Tomorrow," continued Sels, "I'll begin feeding your system extra selyn as we explore transfer mechanics. But I can't do that until you've read and absorbed the textbook."

126   JACQUELINE LICHTENBERG

"I'll do my best," said Ercy, eager to get started on the beginning of her career as a channel.

"Now zlin this carefully." Sels picked up a large stone from a table filled with stones of various sizes.

"The rock?" asked Ercy, zlinning it. He couldn't get his hands around it.

"No—*me*. Zlin what I'm doing."

Now that she knew how to distinguish between the channel's primary and secondary systems, and how the two systems interacted, she was able to zlin exactly what he did to summon a very low level of augmentation.

He tossed the rock into the air. "Ercy, catch!"

Without thinking, Ercy reached out and stopped the rock in mid-arc. It weighed more than her biggest watermelon, but to her utter amazement, she found she'd shifted into that same low level of augmentation, and could handle it easily.

Sels picked up a larger rock. "Now second-level augmentation!" And he threw it at her.

She caught it, throwing the first rock back at him. "Hey, stop it!" she said. "Or two can play that game."

Sels laughed again. "Only a Farris would think to throw it back at me! Everyone else drops the rock, usually having to scramble to get their toes out of the way."

Ercy set the bigger rock down, gently.

"Now, let's go up to first level and quell back to normal, then to second, to first and base. Then we'll try third, and so forth, and see how far you can go."

Ercy laughed, feeling light-headed. "I'm game. This is fun."

Ercy made it all the way to tenth-level augmentation, learning the transitions, juggling rocks with Sels and simultaneously holding casual conversation. By the time they were finished, she was giddy. On the final quell, she caught her breath, laughing. "I haven't had so much fun since the Union Day when House of Imil invited us to an open party!"

Sels also sat down, laughing. "Augmentation goes to your head. I've been doing this all day, and—where do you suppose Bett is?"

"Hey, it's been twenty-five minutes. It doesn't take that long to page one student."

"I'd better go look for her. You stay and study." He got to his feet, straightening his hair by running his tentacles through it. "You may feel very tired after all that. Just lie down for a few minutes. If you feel any discomfort, use the emergency page to

MAHOGANY TRINROSE 127

get Grant. Bett was supposed to be here for you . . . I'll be right back.''

Ercy couldn't imagine feeling tired. She was floating. She sat down with her text on transfer mechanics and began to read. After two chapters, though, she noticed a heaviness in her head and hands. Two more chapters and she stretched out on the contour lounge, propping the book against her knees. Slowly, her knees sank and the book slid to the floor as she drifted into a light doze.

She came to with black panic closing in from every side. *Need.* Then she remembered she was supposed to use the page to get Hal. But before she could decide if she ought to bother him, Bett was in the room, and suddenly everything was all right again.

Bett took a seat opposite Ercy, her attention trained on her. Engulfed in the fabulous Farris Gen nager, Ercy compared her aunt to Halimer Grant. There was the same strength, but where Grant made her feel disembodied, the Farris Gen made her feel as if *she* were Gen.

"Ease off, Bett. She's all right now."

The sense of the Farris Gen presence seemed to fade out of her awareness. Ercy asked, "Did you find Joeslee?"

"Nobody's seen her all day," said Bett. "The staff is searching."

"Oh, no," said Ercy. "Do you suppose she's run away?"

Bett said, "Don't worry. There's no place to run to. It's all barren hills and desert out there."

Ercy thought that wouldn't deter a gypsy.

"Time's almost up, Ercy," said Sels in his instructor's voice. "How much did you get read?"

"Only five chapters," admitted Ercy.

"Only five?" asked Sels with a chuckle. "That's twice what I'd expected. But, Ercy, you've got to have it finished by tomorrow. What's your next class?"

"Uh," said Ercy, scrambling for her notebook. "—Sensory Discrimination. Just upstairs from here."

Sels nodded. "We'll have to do something about your memory, too, or you're likely to augment yourself into attrition. Well, get going, and no more augmentation until tomorrow—understand?"

"Yes, Hajene."

As Ercy went to her next class, she could not get her mind off Joeslee. The class itself was a large lecture in the vocabulary of

128 JACQUELINE LICHTENBERG

Sime sensory distinctions. After that, she had a smaller laboratory course in how to correlate her inner sense of elapsed time with the standard clock time. Working with her time sense against inaccurate mechanical clocks made her sick to her stomach. She decided to skip lunch.

When she got to Science History her interest was caught by the idea that the Ancients, whose civilization had reached great heights before the Sime/Gen mutation, actually knew more biological science than modern man did. Householding Frihill had recently uncovered hints that the Ancients had understood the complex nucleus of the living cell right down to the structure of the genes themselves.

The Sime/Gen mutation could have arisen because of tampering with the cell nucleus—on purpose. Ercy could barely contain herself. If the Ancients could manipulate genes, then surely they could have grown a mahogany trinrose—and if they could, then she could. More than that—if the Sime/Gen mutation could be proved to have been the result of genetic tampering, then all the superstitious nonsense about magic and the supernatural would be swept away and her experimental goals would become acceptable.

She walked out of class, her mind whirling, just moving with the crowd, not paying attention to her surroundings. But she stopped dead in her tracks when it struck her that she was hoping for proof that science had caused the mutation—which could easily create a frenzied, superstitious reaction against science.

She let the flow of the crowd carry her toward the main dining hall for Muir faculty and students, thinking, *The key is the mahogany trinrose, I know it is. Suppose the Ancients had both the Sime mutation and the mahogany trinrose for kerduvon, but somehow the mahogany trinrose deteriorated into other kinds of trin plants. It wasn't the Sime mutation that proved lethal—it was the loss of the mahogany trinrose. If I can make kerduvon, then it won't matter to anyone how the Sime/Gen mutation occurred, because the mutation itself won't have been the destroyer of civilization!*

Ercy found that she had stopped outside the dining hall. The sun was lowering in the sky, the intense summer heat easing off. Her brain just didn't want to think anymore, no matter how excited she was.

The scene around her came into a painfully clear focus. Behind her, Halimer Grant said, "And when was the last time you ate anything, Ercy Farris?"

"Hal! I can do it, I really can!"

MAHOGANY TRINROSE 129

"Of course you can. Now, I asked you a question."

How did he know what I meant? "Uh, I had some orange juice and a glass of trin tea this morning before classes."

"No lunch."

"Well—the clocks took away my appetite."

He took her by the elbow on into the spacious, multileveled cafeteria. There were many serving areas operating, some serving dinner and some breakfast. As they took dinner trays to a table, Ercy noticed most of the Simes were with Gens, which made the ambient nager bearably well balanced.

When they were settled, she asked, "How did you know what I meant?"

"By what?" asked Grant.

Ercy unwrapped her silverware. "Uh, I said something like that I could do it, and you said of course I could. How did you know I meant I could grow a mahogany trinrose?"

"Is that what you meant?" asked Grant. "I assumed you meant you were able to keep up with your courses. That usually astonishes the new students."

Ercy nodded. "I can't believe all I've done today. I can't even remember it all. What if I can't remember it tomorrow?"

"Eat, Ercy, eat. You're more tired than you know and in a while it's going to catch up to you. I'll put you to sleep and when you wake up, it will be just like this morning—only better. Sels says your learning rate is still increasing."

"He does? He would know." Ercy picked up her spoon and set it down again, staring at the soup. All of a sudden she was achingly homesick for Im'ran's scrap soup, the Controller's Residence dining room, her father. Would he really live through it this time, too? What was going on that they weren't telling her about? *Shen, what a dream can do!*

Grant was eating with the gusto of a ravenous Gen. "What are you so frustrated about, Ercy?"

"Knowledge," said Ercy. "Who has the right to withhold knowledge? Who's the judge whether a person—or people—should have knowledge or not?"

"Censorship."

"Yes! What if somebody knew what really caused the Sime/Gen mutation? And told the world. It would cause worse trouble than we've got now."

"Reading the papers lately, I've come to think that it surely would."

Ercy shoved her tray aside and leaned on the table. "Does that

130 JACQUELINE LICHTENBERG

mean that the person who knows shouldn't tell or should be forced not to?''

"That's an age-old question, Ercy. I think the senior philosophy course gets into questions like that.''

"Oh, I'm so sick of being told I'm too young to think the thoughts I think!''

Grant reached over and moved her tray back in front of her. "Eat." It was a firm command.

She picked up her spoon and began on the soup. After the first few mouthfuls, it wasn't bad.

"Before I came to Rialite,'' said Grant, "I had always felt that it was wrong to keep any knowledge secret. But I'm no longer sure where I stand on the issue. So I can't answer your question.'' Grant's nager seemed to quiver, and Ercy thought the issue must be important to him.

"I'll bet that's because you required some bit of knowledge that somebody has and won't give,'' she guessed.

"I rather doubt that. Has it ever occurred to you to wonder if knowledge *can* be given?''

" 'You can't give knowledge as a gift.' My father always says that. He says a lot of things I can't make sense out of.''

"Have you thought that in those moments he's trying to give you a gift of knowledge?''

Ercy let the spoon clink into her empty bowl. "It's possible.''

Grant reached over and put her dish of casserole in front of her, propping the fork in her fingers. Mechanically, she ate.

"Try another word, Ercy. Understanding.''

"Science is the process of collecting and organizing knowledge to reach understanding.''

"So I used to think. But lately, it occurs to me to wonder if such a goal is attainable.'' Again the nageric quiver. It was rare that Grant ever revealed anything so personal.

But he said no more. Ercy was crunching cookies with her tea when she suddenly remembered the morning. "Hal? Did you ever find out what happened in the barn?''

There was one of those long pauses characteristic of Grant. "Yes—I did,'' he said. "Wind knocked one of the hanging lamps down. It shattered, exposing the wires and igniting some straw. By luck, all the grooms on duty were Sime. They managed to get the fire out before it could get started.''

"But there was no wind this morning! Not a breath.''

"That did occur to me,'' said Grant, and Ercy felt his attention on her intensify. "But what else could it have been?'' His pale

MAHOGANY TRINROSE 131

eyes almost glowed as they fixed on her. It seemed for an instant that what he felt was fear.

She wanted to ask what he was thinking. But his nager resumed the sheer crystal clarity that distinguished him. It made the world so beautiful around her that she was bemused by the effect. She felt content, languorously content and very, very tired.

It wasn't a physical depletion, though, she realized as they walked toward her residence building in the twilight. Her mind was simply unable to accept one more new thought.

She was opening the door to her room when she gathered her last energy and said, "I'm not going to bed until we find Joeslee. I'm really worried about her—what's that?"

As Ercy walked into the room, despite Grant's nager, she had the vague impression there was somebody else here. The impression led her to the bathroom door, which was also heavily insulated. "Hal, there's somebody in there . . ."

There were no locks at Rialite. It was a custom handed down from the days of Klyd Farris that, as in the householdings themselves, respect for privacy was so absolute no locks or keys were necessary.

Ercy knew that hers and Grant's combined nager was surely perceptible on the other side of the bathroom door. She strained to identify the Sime nager she was reading, employing what she'd learned that day. "Joeslee? Is that you in there? Are you all right?"

There was no answer, though a faint shimmer might indicate the other had heard her. Well, thought Ercy, it's my bathroom, and if that's not Joeslee, then that person has no right in here. And if it is Joeslee . . .

Ercy opened the bathroom door.

Grant, standing right behind her, laid his big Gen hands on her shoulders as they gazed at Joeslee Teel, still in her pajamas, curled up on top of the hamper and staring at them round-eyed.

Her eyes shifted to Grant. She blurted, "What are you going to do with me?"

There was one of Grant's long pauses in which the nager in the room seemed to grow cool and misty, making everything transparent. "Is it up to me to do anything with you, Joeslee?"

"What else are you here for?" It was a sullen accusation.

"Hal's an instructor, so naturally he has disciplinary powers." It was the wrong thing to say. Joeslee's nager tightened with fear of Grant. Then she said, "Sosu Grant, why don't you call the page and have them turn off the search for Joeslee? I'll stay with her."

Grant nodded, leaving them alone in the bathroom. Ercy took Joeslee by the hands, lightly grazing her arms with her own handling tentacles. It was still new and strange enough to Ercy to make such a contact that she got a deeper reading of Joeslee's nager than she really wanted, and she knew Joeslee got more than she wanted, too. Ercy pulled her out into the room and made her sit down on the bed.

"Have you been here all day, Joeslee?" asked Ercy. When she didn't answer, Ercy went on, "Everyone has been frantic looking for you. If you didn't feel well, you should have called for a Donor Therapist. Joeslee?"

She was sitting staring dully at her hands on Ercy's arms, but inside, she was strung to high tension. She flinched when Grant put down the phone.

Ercy said to Grant, trying to stay between them, "Be careful. I don't know what's the matter with her." She felt, irrationally enough, as if she were the only thing keeping the gypsy girl from attacking Hal. But that was impossible.

Out in the hallway, passing among the people there, came a Farris channel's nager. She said, "Here comes Hajene Sels."

Chapter 12

All eyes were on the door as Sels approached, paused to note the anticipatory attention from within the room, and entered.

With the door closed behind him, Sels blended his nager into the room's ambient with Farris delicacy and moved toward Joeslee.

Now that the senior channel was handling the fields, Ercy could let go, and she felt herself shaking all over, as if an overstrained muscle was now being relaxed.

Grant made her sit down on the bed as her uncle continued to watch Joeslee. Finally, the elder Farris said, "Joeslee, have you been in this room all day?"

She seemed to withdraw more into herself if that were possible. Sels said, "Joeslee, I asked you a question. You will answer."

Nobody defied a Farris who spoke in such a tone, but Joeslee clamped her mouth shut and averted her eyes. Sels reached out one tentacle and moved her face back toward him. "Answer civilly!"

Grant took one step toward Sels. "Hajene—by her customs it is not civil to look at you directly. Don't touch her. You're only making it worse."

Sels glanced at the Gen. "I'm not a student of the gypsies. If you can get through to her, go ahead."

"I know little of her people," said Grant, "but I think it's obvious she's taken all the pushing around she's going to take."

Ercy said, "I think she's been here all day, hiding in the bathroom."

The smoldering eyes came to Ercy, but Sels's field made a barrier between them.

"All right," said Sels. "Assuming you've been here all day, then you're guilty of not answering your page—every five minutes for hours on end. You've not attended any of your classes or made your Gen therapy contacts. You've not even eaten today . . ."

133

134 JACQUELINE LICHTENBERG

"Slow down," suggested Grant. "Her Simelan wasn't very good yesterday."

Sels added more slowly, "You've risked your sanity by remaining in this understimulating environment."

Joeslee spat at Sels. He moved so it went by the edge of his sleeve. Ercy was stunned. She never guessed that people did that outside of stories.

Grant laughed, his powerful mirth brightening the room, every color painfully vivid and every shape a sensory delight. It made Ercy feel flushed and warm all over, a completely new sensation.

Grant said, "Well, Joeslee, you've broken your silence. You may as well talk to Hajene Sels—or have you nothing of interest to add to that comment?"

"So that's what you're going to do to me—solitary. Well, you can do your worst. You can't break me."

"No, Joeslee, the Tecton's only method of discipline is the simple withholding of transfer into attrition, if necessary."

"Shidoni?" whispered Joeslee—death by attrition.

The horror in the girl was palpable enough to waken in Ercy the memory of her four aborted transfer attempts.

"No, no," said Ercy. "The Tecton will never let you die— certainly not like that." She reached out to touch her fellow student, trying to be reassuring. "The rule here is one hour transfer delay per penalty point earned. It's a punishment that strengthens your ability to withstand deprivations and makes you a better channel."

The inchoate fear was overwhelming to Ercy. She tried again. "Joeslee, you're stuck here. There's nothing at all you can do about it. Defying the rules will only make life difficult for you."

While she'd been talking, Sels was backing away. The roiling mass of defiance, fear, and contempt swelled in the gypsy girl with every breath she drew. It all seemed to be focused on Halimer Grant.

Joeslee, Ercy reminded herself, had almost been burned alive as a witch while she was in changeover. Ercy's accusers hadn't even believed there could be such a thing as a witch. Driven by an inarticulate sense of identification with Joeslee, Ercy reached out for nageric contact.

Joeslee screamed.

In high augmentation, the gypsy girl leaped at Halimer Grant, the only Gen in the room. Ercy had time for just one thought: *Not Hal!* And she leaped in front of Joeslee, receiving the girl's attack.

MAHOGANY TRINROSE 135

Her lateral tentacles twined around Joeslee's laterals, the other channel's body already committed to a savage draw. Reflex caused Ercy to draw against the void into which her substance was draining. A flash of pain, an adjustment, and on another level there was a return flow into her, complementing the outward flow.

For one split instant, it was blessed relief, and then all at once her spine was on fire, her mind engulfed in bright green light. The pain rose and rose in pitch until she couldn't feel it anymore. In that new peace, every part of her tingled with a new glow, and in its light, the universe was open, nothing hidden from her. Everyone she had ever known was afflicted with mental blinders preventing them from seeing what her mind saw.

She stood in trembling awe of the searing scope of her knowing. It came to her that only she herself was strong enough to withstand this power; it was up to her to protect others from its destructiveness.

And then the light went out.

The pain swooped down her spine in one flashing wave. A sudden cool mist invaded her being. The room emerged around her, etched everywhere in green fire. Her throat was open, every breath expelled a scream of pain that died to a whimper in the focused stillness she now recognized as Grant's nager.

Sels was bending over Joeslee on the floor.

Grant had wrapped a heavy blanket around Ercy and his huge Gen hands engulfed her shoulders protectively—strange, there weren't any heavy blankets in the room—and he whispered in her ear, "Relinquish to me, Ercy. Total relaxation."

Who is he to tell me what to do? What does he know?

Ercy stood horrified by that within her which produced that thought. She remembered the infinite awareness she had felt, and even now it had an allure of transcendent truth to it that frightened her beyond all words.

He spun her around to face him, the room whirling dizzily about her. A flash of indignation consumed her mind, and then she heard him say again, "Relax, Ercy. You can do it. I know you can."

She was burning up with fever, and the pain was eating her inside out. "Help me . . ."

His hands were nestled among her tentacles, naturally drawing her laterals into a transfer grip. He leaned forward, placing his cool Gen lips in contact with her forehead, right between her eyes. The five-point contact opened a primary transfer potential

136 JACQUELINE LICHTENBERG

between them, but the Gen was refusing her selyn. At first she was incensed at this affront, but she recognized that as another reaction not really her own. By tremendous effort she denied herself the impulse to hurt him for his arrogance. This was Hal, her Qualifying Donor.

As she made that effort to grasp her real self, she found his cool nager seeping through her, and in that new peace, she lost touch with the room again.

When it swam back into focus, the pain was gone, and so was the fever. She was still standing, supported against Hal's chest, her head on his shoulder. The blanket about her shoulders wasn't heavy anymore. The carpet all about them was soaking wet, and a trail of water led to the bathroom. She could feel the stiffness and ache in the Gen from holding her unmoving for so long.

The moment his attention wavered from her as he said, "Sels?" Ercy fell whirling into fierce need.

Tentacles grasped her, seizing her in lateral-lateral contact, and then all she knew was the rich selyn field and a golden stream of warmth and light flowing into her. Soon, it was more than she could take, and still the flow came. She began to ache.

The flow fell off to nothing, his lips leaving hers with the lightest of impressions, his laterals sliding away with a tiny shock.

Sels sat on the bed beside her, one arm around her shoulders, and she felt him on the verge of tears. "Ercy, baby, Ercy, baby," he said over and over. "It's too soon for you to fight your way into this grown-up world. Ercy, promise me, from now on, leave the problems of your fellow students to the staff."

Across on the other bed, Joeslee lay under the care of Bett. The ambient nager was quiet except for the angry knot of conflicting fields around Joeslee.

"Is she dying?" asked Ercy.

Sels looked up. "No. You saved her life—and her chance at anti-kill conditioning, too, by keeping her from Grant. But when she attacked, you should have let me intercept. You nearly got yourself killed. I still don't quite understand what happened—" He broke off, looking to Grant.

"Neither do I," said Grant, "but I think it was her relaxation drill that saved her life."

Sels glanced at the water marks on the carpet and fingered the dry blanket. "Well, the wet blanket was a brilliant improvisation. I never would have thought of it." He gathered up the fuzzy blanket, folding it. "Digen will want the lab to test how much water it holds to determine the amount of waste heat Ercy's body generated. You'll have to write a complete report, too, Ercy. Oh, you haven't had report-writing yet, have you? Well, use Form 1076 and do the best you can.''

"I think," said Grant, "that Ercy is due for a long sleep."

"Overdue," said Sels. "Bett, can you handle Joeslee?"

Bett nodded, her concentration focused on the other channel trainee. Ercy felt Grant's attention again. At first, it summoned echoes of that hideous moment when she'd been so drunk on green pain that she'd gone out of her head. Was that what it was like to be junct?

Grant's nager enveloped her. "Sleep now, Ercy. Tomorrow you'll be older and stronger."

She let herself be tilted over to lie on the bed, Grant seated behind her with one hand on the back of her neck where the ache centered at the base of her skull. His attention came totally to focus on her. The rest of the room disappeared to Ercy's Sime senses.

It was a vivid dream. Her coarse spun clothing itched from stale sweat. The army encampment spread out about her, acre by acre, as far as she could see; frozen ground, trees stripped nude by the long, harsh winter, and row after row of patched, muddy tents. She was a perimeter guard; pacing, pacing, turn and pace back. Sweep the adjacent camp of Simes for any hint of movement.

Simes?

She was Gen, a soldier camped by a wide strip of nearly frozen river. On the other side, the rooftops of a large town fringed the ashen winter sky. The wind was cold.

But the Gens about her, huddled by their fires—she was not one of them. She belonged over there—among the Simes. *Householder*. It was almost sundown; her watch almost up.

In the sudden, crazy way of dreams, a figure loomed before her. Her rifle was wrenched aside, flung away into the snow. It was a Sime—scarecrow thin, lackluster hair, filthy crusted sores all over him—Freeband Raider; the Enemy. From across the river, occupying the town. Whole band of them; locusts.

She faced the Sime, seeing his raw need in bulging glands and restless tentacles. "You can't kill me," she told him. "And I'm not going to let you kill any of *them*." The vulnerable Gens she guarded.

He moved, studying her stance. She rotated, keeping him in front of her. She had the odd impression she knew this Sime.

138   JACQUELINE LICHTENBERG

"Come with me, and I'll take you to someone who can teach you not to kill."

"Pervert!" he spat and leaped to seize her for the kill.

Confidently, she yielded selyn to him. When he had drawn all he could, he thrust her away, eyes wild with horror that still she lived.

"You see," she said kindly. "I've proved you don't have to kill to live. Come and join us."

But he drew a long knife and came at her, face twisted into a mindless, feral threat. In the instant before she died, she knew him. *Halimer Grant.*

"Paging Ercy Farris. Paging Ercy Farris."

The window was open, letting in the bright morning sunshine. The damp spot on the carpet was gone. She wasn't dead. And Halimer Grant wasn't there. *Shen! What a nightmare!* And she wasn't even in need yet. After what she'd heard about need nightmares, she was now ready to swear off sleeping for life.

"Paging Ercy Farris."

"Hhhh," said Ercy, trying to find her voice somewhere in her raw throat. "Ummm, Ercy Farris, here, Ginny."

"About time. How are you feeling this morning?" said Ginny through her page system, more than her customary sunny smile in her voice.

"Uh, I'm not supposed to feel all right?"

"Well," chuckled Ginny, "you may if you want to. But you've already missed two classes, you know."

"I have? Oh, no!" She leaped out of bed, and then clung to the bedpost as the room spun alarmingly.

"I have a medical dispensation here for you, Ercy, if you want it," said Ginny. "Of course, if you feel . . ."

"I'll take it. I'll take it. I just discovered how lousy I feel."

"That's good," said Ginny, "because your therapist and your conditioning channel will be waiting for you in clinic six-oh-two in an hour."

"I'll be there. Thank you."

The page clicked off. Ercy examined the sour cotton feeling in her mouth, the burning acid in her stomach, and general used feeling. Maybe a shower?

"Ercy?" Joeslee was climbing out of bed, offering a steadying hand to Ercy. Ercy drew back, remembering everything that had happened the previous evening.

"Ercy," said Joeslee again, pleading. "I meant you no harm."

"No harm? Going after my Donor—my therapist? You're

MAHOGANY TRINROSE 139

kidding. How would you expect any Sime to react?'' And with that, for the first time, Ercy realized she had reacted like a Sime—a channel whose own Companion was threatened. Maybe that was why Sels hadn't even slapped her with a penalty?

"Look, Joeslee, I'm sorry. I didn't mean to hurt you, either. I'm sorry I said—all those things that made you angry. I'm sorry I intercepted you—I should have let Sels handle it, then nobody would be hurt.''

Ercy turned toward the bathroom, contemplating the long, long walk across the room. She clung to the bedpost, waiting for a dizzy spell to pass. Joeslee swung around in front of her.

"I'm sorry about the Heil'ro. I didn't know there were any in the Tecton—I just couldn't stand it anymore. I had to make him try to kill me and get it over with.''

She spent that whole day alone in the bathroom—no wonder she went crazy! Ercy felt compelled to try to understand, and said, "Halero? You mean Hal—it's Halimer. Sosu Grant to us.''

"Yes. The Heil'ro—our word for the ghost people.''

"Ghost people?''

"How do you call them?''

"Ghost people,'' repeated Ercy. Yes, if there were more Gens with transparent nager, surely they would be called the ghost people.

Joeslee nodded, seemingly satisfied her language problem was under control. "I am sorry my plan did not work. I am sorry you got hurt. I wished you no bad.'' She put out her hand again, saying, "I will help.''

Ercy let herself be helped into the bathroom, where she found a note from Hal in his oddly disciplined script, propped up against a tea glass with some white powder in the bottom. Next to it was a glass for Joeslee with a note from Bett.

"What does the writing say?'' asked Joeslee.

"Well,'' said Ercy, filling the glasses and stirring with one tentacle. "It says to drink this stuff whether we want to or not.'' Handing one glass to Joeslee, she said, "Don't taste it. Just take a deep breath and gulp it all down at once.'' Ercy demonstrated.

Lips compressed, Joeslee poured the medication down the sink. Ercy was too stunned to think of stopping her. *How am I going to handle this? Leave the problems of the students to the staff?* But something in her went out to the lost gypsy girl. "Joeslee, this isn't a prison. Nobody here means you any harm.''

With a dark, calculating look, Joeslee turned and left the bathroom. Ercy forced herself to turn on the shower and proceed

140 JACQUELINE LICHTENBERG

as if nothing were amiss. Toweling herself dry, she came back into the room to find Joeslee sitting dejectedly on the end of her bed, still clad in yesterday's grungy pajamas, her hair a matted mess. She sat with her feet turned inward, soles facing each other, and for the first time, Ercy saw the scars. *They tried to burn her—in changeover.*

Suppressing a shudder, Ercy drew her bathrobe around her shoulders and sat cross-legged on the floor at Joeslee's feet. "It must have been horrible."

"I just wish it were over."

"It is," assured Ercy, touching the scarred feet with one handling tentacle. "They're healed now; you're safe."

Joeslee gave her a sharp look, zlinning. "You—you could lie to me and I would never know."

"I wouldn't lie to you, Joeslee."

"Then he hasn't told you. But he'll find a way—they know how to do ma—accidents."

Ercy had such a distinct impression that Joeslee had started to say "magic" that she almost laughed. But the girl's pullback from that word held a texture of awe that made Ercy ask, "Who could possibly have any reason to harm you here?"

Joeslee snapped, "Why else would a Heil'ro be here? They don't work for the Tecton!"

"Hal!?" She didn't dare laugh. She cast frantically for some counter-argument. "He's been here almost a year!"

"They have a way of placing themselves conveniently among events."

Hal does have that knack, all right.

"Joeslee—" *You can't tell a paranoid she's being ridiculous.* "Joeslee, what possible reason could Halimer Grant have to want to do you harm?"

"Harm? He will murder me!" And then she fell silent as if regretting what she'd said.

Ercy took a deep breath, trying to stay calm. Her father would have to know about this. "But *why?*"

Holding back tears, she said, "It is between my tribe and the Heil'ro. B-but I am the last of my people—" Tears spilled down her cheeks though her features remained wooden.

The radiating loneliness wrenched at Ercy until she couldn't stand it another moment. She sat on the bed beside Joeslee and circled her with her arms. The girl resisted. Then in total despair, she melted against Ercy, crying openly.

When it abated slightly, Ercy made a dangerous decision.

MAHOGANY TRINROSE 141

"Joeslee—will you swear to keep a secret if I tell you something of the very—very—very private business of Zeor?"

Her face in her hands, Joeslee zlinned Ercy, gradual calm coming into her nager. Almost hungrily, Joeslee nodded. "I promise never to tell anyone—even if they torture me."

"No one will torture you—but—Joeslee, I—I would be Sectuib in Zeor now, except that they—they accused me of witchcraft for trying to grow a mahogany trinrose."

"You mean you summoned the Heil'ro to help you grow the magic flower?"

"No—no!" said Ercy before she thought about it.

"Then he *is* here after me! But why would you tell me this?"

"I—"

"You will help me with your magic?" asked Joeslee.

"I have no magic! There's no such thing as magic!"

"You have shared your secret with me," said Joeslee, hardly seeming to hear Ercy. "I will share our secret with you—because I am the last." And as she spoke, there was such a lifting of an intolerable burden that Ercy just let her go on. "We had two Heil'ro with us, claiming travel shelter. It was ours to protect them. But where we camped, far from here, but also desert like this, there was a storm, and a flash flood came, breaking houses in town but not the small land on which we camped. The Heil'ro magic, you see. The town people saw, too, and came to kill us all. We failed to protect the Heil'ro. And since I am the last, he is here to take my life because we failed our obligation."

"No, Joeslee, Hal came here to work—he gave me First Transfer—he—he—"

"Then you will be able to protect me. You have given me your secret—I have given you mine. Tell me what to do, and I will do it," she said in serene capitulation.

Oh, no, now what? "Well, the first thing is to get cleaned up and dressed and start attending classes. We're going to have to talk about this, but there's no time now."

Chapter 13

"Digen," said Sels, "I tell you, that man handled Ercy as if it were a standard emergency drill he'd been trained to." He stretched out his tentacles, making an emphatic grasping gesture. "I'd like to know what you intend to do about him. His papers still haven't come through, have they?"

Digen, Sels, and Bett were waiting in Digen's office for Im'ran. Digen shuffled through the newest stack of papers on his desk. "Hal's papers don't seem to be here yet. I can't put Ercy's qualification papers through until I have the serial numbers on Grant to validate her as a First. I'd like to get my tentacles on the lorsh who misfiled . . ."

"Digen, suppose his papers weren't misfiled? Suppose he's not a Tecton Donor at all?"

Digen stopped his shuffling to stare at Sels. The hypothesis had been dormant in Digen's mind for months, but only now did he realize it. "If he isn't Tecton," said Digen, "then what is he?"

"I thought *you* might know," said Sels flatly.

"He's not Distect," said Digen. "There's nobody alive who could say that as positively as I can."

"But if he's not in fact Tecton," said Bett, "then he's here under false pretenses."

Digen looked at his Gen sister and chuckled. "There's no way anyone could *pretend* to be a Donor—let alone a Tecton Donor. Just zlin the man," he said to Sels, "and tell me you have any real doubts."

Sels nodded, conceding that point. "We were all there when he gave Ercy First Transfer—but, Digen, it wasn't just perfect. It was too perfect—somehow."

"Several people have mentioned that to me," said Bett. "People who had normal experiences in changeover were hit just as hard by Ercy's experience as those who had never had the benefit of a normal breakout and transfer."

MAHOGANY TRINROSE 143

"Nobody who witnessed her changeover," said Digen, "will ever deny that this is her House."

"Maybe," said Bett. "But just try to pin Grant down on anything having to do with Ercy or Zeor!"

"Try to pin him down on anything having to do with himself!" added Sels. "Why won't he talk about his training?"

"Isn't that nager of his enough?" asked Digen. "Have you ever seen a Sime walk by him without a second glance? The Tecton prohibits personal attachments between channel and Donor. If I were a Donor with that kind of attraction for Simes, I wouldn't dare say anything about myself for fear of triggering a personal interest I couldn't handle."

Bett said, "Digen's right. All that should be known of any Donor is name, order, and Proficiency Rating. That Tecton custom has saved me from some nasty situations."

That was true, thought Digen, zlinning her. She had provided First Transfer for Digen, qualifying him, so he knew her characteristics very well.

"It makes me uncomfortable when you zlin her like that," said Sels. "Shouldn't Im' be here by now?"

"I'm sorry," answered Digen, turning his attention from his sister. "Actually, it isn't the same between Bett and me since you came along, Sels. I don't know if it's your lortuen or my orhuen—or both—that's changed it. We were a lot closer when Bett was my First Companion, only then we had to be so fanatically careful not to create a dependency. . . . I think now, without that tension, it's easier between us."

Bett said, "Sels is getting too frantically possessive even for a lortuen mate. Just ignore it, Digen. You and I know where we stand."

At that point, Digen and Sels turned toward the door, zlinning Im'ran's approach. As the other Gen opened the door, Bett said, "It's about time, Im'. Where have you been?"

Im'ran just shook his head, going to Digen. "You shouldn't be out of bed, Digen. Mora is having fits . . ."

"I'm sick of being sick," said Digen. "I'm not going to lie down and turn senile waiting to be declared well. Let's get to work."

Im'ran took a chair beside Digen, adding his steady nager to the crosshatched interference patterns in the room. Soon, even Sels was steadier, and Digen found the nagging pain in his head was gone.

"All right," said Im'ran, "what's this about Ercy?"

144 JACQUELINE LICHTENBERG

Digen gave Im'ran the new, slender file on Ercy, flipping it open to Sels's report on the previous night's happenings. "And they did a thorough scan on her this morning in the clinic. She's fine, except for some stress signs."

"Stress?" muttered Im'ran, reading through the report. They all waited while he absorbed it and looked through the lab reports. "I don't understand. What did happen between Ercy and Joeslee? I thought I'd seen almost everything connected with transfer, but this . . ."

Bett said, "I didn't get there until after the excitement was all over, but I did see Ercy burning up with fever and twenty minutes later almost normal. You tell me what happened, Digen."

"I wasn't even there," said Digen, looking at Sels.

"I put all the facts down on paper."

"The facts don't seem to tell us much, do they? I called this conference because I don't know what to make of them. Sels, let's have some impressions, intuitions, feelings, anything you can add to the facts."

Sels looked around at the three others in the room. "We're all Zeor, and Firsts. Shen, we all have four-plus Proficiency Ratings. I don't think I'd say this where anyone else could hear. Digen, I don't think it was entirely a selyn transport phenomenon. While it was happening, I was in augmented motion, intent on getting them apart. But for just those few instants, Digen, that room became cold. Then Ercy's body produced more waste heat than the selyn consumption could account for. Now you name a selyn transport effect that can explain it."

Digen shook his head. "We have to have more than this to go on if we're going to ask the theoreticians about it."

Sels shrugged. "You asked for impressions. Here's one for you. *I* haven't the vaguest idea what happened to Ercy. But I'm convinced Halimer Grant knows."

"We'll ask him," said Bett.

"I did," said Sels. "Flat out. He evaded so smoothly I don't even recall his exact words."

"Maybe if I ask him," said Bett, "Gen to Gen, as it were, he'd be more willing to give of himself."

"I doubt that," said Sels, "but you can try. I'll tell you one thing: he's disturbed. I've never seen him so—"

Digen and Sels simultaneously zlinned the approach of the crystal nager of Halimer Grant. Digen motioned Bett to open the door and Sels to move aside so he could get a direct reading on Grant.

MAHOGANY TRINROSE   145

"Come in, Hal," called Digen. "Perhaps you can help us."

"Help you?" asked Grant, closing the door behind him. Sels shoved a chair out for the new Gen.

Grant sat, his nager blending lucidly into the room. "I'm always glad to help," he said, "but I came to ask a favor."

"Oh?" said Digen. Grant had never asked for anything before. "Ask ahead, I owe you a few."

Grant looked toward Sels. "I'm glad you're here because it concerns Ercy." He turned back to Digen. "Controller Farris, I want to be removed from Ercy's case."

Digen zlinned Sels, his eyes on Bett. Im'ran asked, "Why?"

"I would have come this morning," said Grant, "but I couldn't think of an acceptable answer to that question." He lowered his gaze, his nager closing up around him until he was in the room, but not of it. Digen hadn't zlinned that effect since he'd first met the man.

"I did say I owed you a few—and I meant it. I suppose I could assign Bett to Ercy—"

"Digen!" said Sels. But Digen held up two tentacles, gesturing for silence.

"Ercy's had what amounts to a Householding upbringing, hardly knowing anyone but relatives. If she's to be prepared for Tecton work, she should have some early training from outsiders."

"I have sincerely done my best," said Grant. "But—"

"What's changed? As far as I can see," said Digen, tapping one tentacle on Ercy's file as he held it in his fingers, "she has recovered completely from last night's incident. It was a curious business, but essentially trivial."

Grant looked him in the eye, his nager unreadable even to Digen, and said, "You understand what happened?"

The question was so neutrally inflected, Digen couldn't divine any implication from it.

Bett said, "We want to know how much you understand of this."

Grant said, "I was hoping you would explain it to me. If it's something known in Zeor but not for outsiders . . ."

Shen! thought Digen. The man was diabolical.

Sels said, "When we were talking to Joeslee, you indicated some knowledge of the gypsies. How did you come by that?"

"I only know what I've read. They have a closed society and don't tolerate strangers. Joeslee is distressed at being immersed in a strange culture. It's best not to call her down for bad

146 JACQUELINE LICHTENBERG

manners when she's actually displaying good manners by her own customs.''

''Would you say,'' asked Digen, ''the gypsies are a hobby of yours?''

''No.''

''Do you have any hobbies?'' asked Bett.

''I am a Donor Therapist,'' answered Grant as if that were his hobby.

''Your knowledge of the gypsies,'' said Digen, ''may contain a clue to tell us something more of exactly what happened last night.''

''My knowledge, such as it is, is superficial and general, only from books.''

Sels said, ''Joeslee's emotional state at the time she attacked you was a mass of contradictions. Today, she seems perfectly rational. And this morning, when we went over her in the clinic, she showed no stress to her selyn systems from her contact with Ercy. Whatever happened, she gave worse than she got—and to a Farris channel, too.''

''Can you account for that?'' asked Bett.

''No.''

''I have a theory,'' said Digen. ''Ercy is a known quantity. I have sixteen years of detailed records on her, and she's a Farris. Between the three of us, we've quite a bit of personal expertise on what can be expected from the Farrises. None of this knowledge seems to apply to this situation. Joeslee, however, is an unknown quantity . . .''

Sels picked that up. ''The gypsies keep pretty much to themselves. Nobody even knows where they came from. I vaguely recall hearing they have a social structure resembling the early Householdings, but I also read somewhere that nothing anthropologists have recorded about them is really valid, because they shun all outsiders.''

''I don't remember,'' said Im'ran, ''that I ever met a channel of gypsy stock working for the Tecton. They must be awfully rare.''

''Or,'' added Bett, ''a Companion of the gypsies. There are all manner of legends about the power of the gypsy Companions over ordinary mortals.''

Come to think of it, thought Digen, both Grant and Joeslee did have blond hair, though Grant's was a painful white-blond that made Joeslee seem dark by comparison. Other than that, they didn't look anything alike. Digen realized that he rarely focused

MAHOGANY TRINROSE   147

on Grant's physical features. It was the nager that captured the attention—a white-blond nager, transparent as a ghost. A nager like that would surely have created legends back in the old days.

When Grant didn't seem motivated to comment, Digen asked, "What do you know of the gypsy Companions?" This time, Digen focused on Grant's nager with all his sensitivity.

Grant said, "I've read that, in most tribes, the channels and Companions both remain in virtual seclusion."

Digen concluded that if Grant was lying, he was too skillful for detection. But he suspected that Grant was merely sticking scrupulously to the truth while being deliberately uninformative.

"I think," said Digen, "for the moment, we'll go with the theory that the odd occurrence was caused by Joeslee, though it affected Ercy. On that theory, there'd be no reason to remove you from Ercy's case, Hal. Unless, of course, you had some other reason for asking?"

"Are you going to separate her from Joeslee?"

"I think we'll wait awhile and see what happens. Faron and I considered very carefully, and we think Ercy is best for Joeslee. And Joeslee should be a good, sharp example to Ercy of what she's going to face in the outside world. If it's going to cause her problems—well, she'll have to learn to cope with problems."

"You could be risking her life," said Grant.

"Being born is a risk, and we take further risks every day. Or do you mean something more specific?"

Grant's eyes focused on Digen during one of those long pauses of his. "I—understand that Zeor encourages the cultivation of hunches. In respect of the hunch of a non-member, could you possibly reassign me just until after her conditioning transfers?"

"You're so good at the Donor's craft," said Digen, "you've never had the injuries and accidents other Donors consider all in a day's work. Now you're getting a touch of what it's like to work with a channel who could hurt you. If you're going to continue to be of use to the Tecton—and to yourself—then you've got to make a stand of it."

Again Grant regarded him for seconds before responding. He did that, Digen realized, when he had to think something over, and he felt he had the right to take his time about it. Wasn't that a gypsy attitude toward time?

"As usual, Controller Farris," said Grant, "your words contain a certain wisdom I can't fail to recognize." He rose and went to the door. "Forgive me for taking up so much of your time when you have not been well."

148   JACQUELINE LICHTENBERG

Digen smiled. "Reports of my frailty are usually exaggerated—I hope."

"Then may I perhaps tell Ercy that you are well and again working toward the disjunction you so desire?"

"You may tell her that I am well enough. As for other plans—it's best she not be involved. Her mind should be on her schooling now."

Grant's exit plunged the room into a gray twilight. It was fully two minutes before their senses adjusted to the new ambient. *Shuven!* thought Digen, *and that man gave Ercy First Transfer just a few days ago!*

Digen drew a shuddering breath as Im'ran placed a hand on his left arm, saying, "I told you that you shouldn't be out of bed." And Digen realized he was shaking all over.

Sels was zlinning him alertly. Digen drew himself to his feet and put some water on for tea. "I didn't realize I was working so hard just to penetrate his nager. But if I don't work, my insides will turn to jelly! So stop trying to put me back to bed."

"Here, let me do that," said Sels, taking the pot from Digen.

Digen let him take over and went to where Bett was sitting, watching. Im'ran began to follow him, but Digen motioned him away. "Wait. I want to try something." He sat down next to his sister, zlinning her nager carefully.

Sels turned from the tea glasses.

Digen said, "I'm just trying the discernment I was using on Grant. Say something, Bett, anything."

"Two and two is five? All gypsies are junct."

"Was that the best you could do?"

She laughed. "Brother, you think I'm going to demonstrate how I get around you when I want to?"

"You don't!" declared Digen. "Never once."

"What about the time—oh, no, you don't." She clamped her expressive Farris lips shut and Digen knew he'd get not another word. He turned his attention to Im'ran again, waiting to see if the shaking would start up again. He did feel a little weak flutter, but it was gone quickly as he moved to stand. He'd had to work a lot harder on Grant. He turned around, eyeing Bett speculatively, zlinning her deeply.

"Digen!" complained Sels, one hand on his shoulder. "How would you like it if I zlinned Im'ran that way?"

Digen turned to Sels, leashing back his sudden excitement. "I don't know. Try it." He remembered the exultation he'd felt piloting the chopper to rescue Grant. *Maybe Grant is right; we*

MAHOGANY TRINROSE 149

should start working on it again. The freedom to be young, healthy, and involved again, instead of a perpetual invalid, would be worth it.

Sels broke away, extremely discomfited.

Digen said, "Can you sense him as off-true?"

"Is that what you want to know? Actually, I can—just barely. I don't think I could put a number on it, though."

Digen stepped behind Im'ran, propelling him toward Sels with both hands. "Come on, let me zlin what you're like together. Humor me."

Im'ran looked around at Digen to see if he'd really gone crazy. But then the long years they'd spent together cued him in. He smiled, brushing Digen's hands off. "All right, Sectuib, you asked for it."

Im'ran turned his full fanir's attention onto Sels, taking the other channel's hands in his own, stepping between Sels and Bett to cut out her influence and drag Sels into his rhythm. Bett said, "Digen, you're not thinking what I think you're thinking, are you?"

"Probably," answered Digen, watching his experiment. It did give him a crawling sensation all over. Sels was infernally close to him in Proficiency Rating, but he wasn't matchmate to Im'ran any more than Digen himself was matchmate to Bett. There was enough discrepancy between them to make it feasible.

He interposed Bett between himself and Im'ran. Kneeling, he offered her his hands, handling tentacles spread wide for her Gen arms to find. She hesitated, and then turned her attention onto Digen as Im'ran was doing with Sels.

Digen could feel the unsteady shiver that ran through her. The discords from the competing lortuen/orhuen bonds were enormous. Yet—

"That's enough," said Digen. "I think it could work."

Im'ran relinquished Sels's grip as Digen got up. Digen was barely upright when his knees began to sag. All three of them lunged at him to keep him from falling. Bett was closest, but Sels got to him first, scooping him into a chair, where Im'ran picked up the contact and supported Digen. "Digen, if you insist on trying to use your secondary system like that, one day you are going to faint."

"The water is boiling," said Bett.

Sels went to the sideboard, saying, "Digen, do you mind telling me what this was all about?"

"I don't think I want to hear this," said Bett.

150 JACQUELINE LICHTENBERG

"Well," said Sels, "we can't argue against a plan that hasn't been put on the table yet."

Im'ran said, "I'm beginning to wish fervently that Ercy was Sectuib already."

"She will be ready for that by the time this plan comes to fruition," said Digen. "I figure Im' and I can stay in step with her transfers, and you and Sels can work around into sync with us. If we spend the intervening months working with each other, there's no reason we can't make a double-breakstep work for us, just as Ercy assumes office, so there's no risk to the House."

Bett swung around to face Digen, and he saw her suddenly as older—a brief echo of his mother's image. Were they really all getting old?

"Digen," she said, "Ercy's first act as Sectuib would be to forbid any such thing."

"I don't think so," said Digen. "She might want to—for personal and selfish reasons—but by then she'll be able to put aside such considerations and think of the welfare of her members— namely, us. Being Sectuib changes your perspective."

"You never did want to be Sectuib, did you?" said Bett, as if it were a completely new thought. "When Mom and Dad and Vira and Nigel and Wyner—died—the House was dumped in your lap."

Digen remembered that day as if it were only weeks ago. He had been on the critical list under the care of two teams of physicians because of the injury that had left one lateral tentacle scarred and barely functional. At that time, they'd expected him to die any day—and he'd been eager for the release. Then suddenly he was Sectuib, and the House depended on his survival. He didn't even have time to mourn. His business became survival, the running of the House, the production of an heir.

And all those years he hadn't really let himself know how very much he didn't want to be Sectuib. Now, with the end in sight, the weight of the burden was almost intolerable. *I've done what I had to do.*

"Digen," said Sels, bringing the glasses of steaming trin tea, "I can't let Bett try that again. It almost killed her fifteen years ago."

Digen took one glass and, savoring the aroma of fresh-brewed trin as it soothed him inside and out, looked to Bett. "As I recall, you as much as said it was time and past time for you and Sels to go through a breakstep."

"I did?"

MAHOGANY TRINROSE   151

"Some comment about him getting fanatically possessive, even for a lortuen mate?"

"I said that, didn't I?" She sighed.

"And, Sels, you know as well as I do that your sensitivity when I so much as glance at Bett is almost paranoid. Get too possessive, and you'll begin to hate each other. That's why Zeor developed the breakstep techniques into an obligatory practice."

It was mainly the higher-order Farrises who tended to become insanely possessive like that. But the syndrome appeared in milder form, even between two perfectly average people involved in nothing stronger than a transfer dependency. In the past, such relationships had been the root of violence, even generations-long blood feuds. The Tecton survived only because it strictly outlawed all such relationships on every level with the exception of the locked dependencies such as orhuen and lortuen—because the partners could not usually survive the breaking of such bonds.

"Look, Digen, I know you don't intend to try to take Bett away from me. It just makes me uncomfortable because you and I are so close. You feel it, too."

"The reason I can tolerate your attention on Im'ran," said Digen, "is that we've gone through the pre-breakstep conditioning routine. It helps, Sels, truly it does. In the end, it even strengthens your relationship."

Bett, sipping her tea, seemed to be adjusting to the idea. "You know," she said, "Digen has a point. It's been a long time since we attempted transfer with anyone else. It might well do us both good."

"Bett!" protested Sels.

"No, listen. Fifteen years ago, when we had to do it so that I could try to give Zeor an heir who wasn't too Farris-inbred, it went wrong because you really didn't want to do it. I think if you decided you wanted to do it, you could—now."

Im'ran said, "Assume for a moment that it is time for you to attempt another breakstep. You hold an unusually strong lortuen, Farris to Farris. How would you go about choosing your out-transfers?"

Sels's eyes went to Im'ran, but he was zlinning Digen and Bett. Then he shifted his Sime senses to Im'ran, appraising the Gen anew.

"You'd want to make it easy on Bett," continued Im'ran. "Who could be easier for her than Digen? You'd want the minimal risk for yourself. You said yourself, you and Digen are so close it takes a high Farris to discern the difference. You can't

152 JACQUELINE LICHTENBERG

quite measure my nageric distortion. To you, I'm almost as good as any dead-true fanir with a four-plus rating. And I'm just a hair faster than you require, so I could keep ahead of your abort reflex. And to tell the truth, if I have to do this for my Sectuib, I'd rather do it with a Farris channel.''

Im'ran fell silent and Sels picked up his tea glass, gazing at his reflection in the surface of the dark liquid. Then he looked up at Digen. After a long time, he raised the glass in salute, conceding to his Sectuib.

"Unto Zeor, Forever!"

Chapter 14

The hectic first few days faded as Ercy threw herself into the whirlwind of learning, adjusting, and growing. Every day was like a week of her prior life. When she had a moment between activities, a creeping exhaustion would claim her mind, but she was sleeping less and less as she adjusted to being Sime. Most often she would wake burning with a renewed curiosity, which had to be fed with more and more information.

She couldn't sit still. Everywhere she went, like all the other new students, she would jog or run in augmentation, using as much selyn as she could, forcing her systems to mature at a phenomenal rate, producing a heady exhilaration.

With all of this came the dreams. She'd been warned to expect nightmares. Almost all of her sleeping time was spent in the dreaming state, and her altered perceptions were bound to produce some real nightmares. She found she could combat them best by regular stints in her garden. Her trinroses were thriving, and she tended them with suppressed excitement, remembering that two of her three wishes had already come true. Although when she worked in the garden the nightmarish quality of her dreams faded, one in particular haunted her.

She was standing in a valley, surrounded by acres and acres of trin plants. The area where she stood was a large, flat stone table. Overhead, the stars had been rearranged to form a flaming starred cross, the symbol of the old escape routes children had followed out of Sime Territory when they discovered they had established as Gens.

Dark, hooded figures stood in a circle, silently waiting. Whispery shapes rustled in and out of the center of the circle while she stood outside and watched. As night drew to a close, Halimer Grant flickered into the center of the circle, and this time she heard what transpired.

"Two of the Company have died," one of the shapes told

153

154 JACQUELINE LICHTENBERG

Grant. "The tribe that protected them was wiped out. Decision has been taken to call in all our travelers, and even you."

"I cannot return now," answered Grant. He was dressed in the long emerald robe with the flashing jewel on the breast. "I have acquired obligations. And I may have found the true reason I had to be exiled from the Company."

"We would know more of this."

"I have no pattern yet. As I told you before, I have caused events and so am responsible. Since you have refused help, I must do what I can—alone."

"What must you do?"

"I don't know yet. But one more piece has come to me. I am bound to her because once I took her life. I owe her a life. I cannot—you cannot ask me to refuse that debt."

And Ercy woke in the midst of a falling nightmare. She was used to that nightmare, and just sat up to rub the sleep out of her eyes and suppress a giggle. *Serial dreams, now. I could write a book!*

As the days passed, Joeslee applied herself doggedly to her course work, but she was losing ground in her studies, daily. Every time she had to repeat a segment of a course, she withdrew a little further into herself.

This left Ercy more alone than she'd thought it possible to be. Halimer Grant seemed to be avoiding her. Her relationship with Sels had fallen into a surface professionalism. The other students had little time for socializing, and what little time they did have was not spent with Ercy Farris, Sectuib-Apparent in Zeor and daughter of the head of Rialite.

On Joeslee's turnover day—halfway to her second transfer— Ercy met Joeslee on the stairs heading back to their room.

"Come on," said Ercy, wanting to be friendly, "I'll race you to our room. Last one in cleans the bathroom."

Joeslee looked at her, then turned, trudging up the stairs wearily. "Never mind, I'll clean the bathroom."

"Come on, where's your spirit! There's always a chance to win any race!"

Joeslee looked at Ercy, a slight smile rising to the surface. "All right, race."

Ercy let the other girl get five steps ahead of her so she could watch her shift into augmentation. It was awkward, like a beginner, and altogether she cut a lumbering, clumsy figure. *Is there something wrong with her?* thought Ercy.

Ercy shifted into augmentation and flitted around Joeslee and

MAHOGANY TRINROSE 155

then held herself back, letting Joeslee catch up. As it appeared that she might actually win the race, Joeslee put a mighty effort into it and by the time they were dodging down their own corridor, she was beginning to function more smoothly in the augmented mode.

At the crucial moment, Ercy held back a step or two, letting Joeslee take the door first. Laughing, the two girls shifted out of augmented mode, dropping their books and flinging themselves on the beds. Ercy bounced to her feet, saying, "Well, I guess it's latrine duty for me."

But Joeslee had sobered. "You let me win," she accused.

"It was a fair win," said Ercy.

"I may be slow, Ercy Farris, but even you can't lie to me!"

"All right, so I could have run rings around you—but that wouldn't have been fair. I can make tenth-level augmentation. You can barely make third. So I raced at third level—and you won. Fairly."

Joeslee picked up a science textbook and flung it savagely at the desk, where it broke off a corner of the molding and fell with pages crumpled. Ercy stared at it, horrified. Nobody treated books like that. She picked it up, straightening the pages. "I guess I said the wrong thing again."

"Ercy, zlin me."

Ercy turned her whole attention to Joeslee, surprised, for the gypsy girl always seemed to resent her attention.

"Ercy, I swear I'm doing my best to do the course work so that you will be able to protect me from him. But I can't do it. I'm constantly losing things, which just makes me late for class. And every time I turn around, somebody is handing me demerit slips. Today I got demerited twice because I folded an accounting paper wrong! And then the instructor looked through my notebook and poured on another three demerits for sloppiness, even though I thought it was neat."

Ercy looked now around the room. Gradually, Joeslee's side of the room had become a disaster zone. The bed, though "made," had the spread on slantwise. There was a heap of laundry on the floor of the closet, and the door wouldn't close because Joeslee liked to throw her things across the top. There wasn't a drawer that didn't have some wisp of clothing jamming it and hanging out.

The desk was in worse shape. Brand-new books already looked as if they'd been used for ten years. The notebooks were dog-eared and dirty.

156 JACQUELINE LICHTENBERG

"You're not the only one who gets demerits," said Ercy. "This morning I got three because I forgot to eat breakfast again."

"They didn't catch me," said Joeslee. "If they had, I'd probably have told them off, and gotten ten more for insubordination. I think the worst of it is," she added, "that the harder I try, the worse it gets. If I were really a witch, I could make them not-notice."

Ercy looked at Joeslee slumped with her hands between her knees, her ankles bent inward, one shoe on top of the other. Her hair looked as if it hadn't been combed in a week, and there was a looseness about her.

"Joeslee, do you know why Rialite puts such an emphasis on cleanliness, neatness, and posture?"

Curiosity was the primary trait of the First Year student, and Joeslee was burning up with curiosity now, but she said, "You're going to tell me whether I want to hear it or not."

"It's an old theory," said Ercy, hoping she could make it sound as reasonable as her father had when he'd explained it to her. "We can affect our thinking processes by controlling the environment we live in. If we deliberately surround ourselves with order, our thinking processes eventually will become orderly and thus more efficient. It is this precise, orderly, efficient thinking which is the mark of the Rialite-trained channel."

Glumly, Joeslee said, "That sounds like something the Sosu Grant would say. He's always talking about discipline." She straightened, clamping her lips shut as if the words had escaped her accidentally. And then she looked at Ercy and relaxed. "No, you will protect me. He won't come after me here, even if we speak of him."

"Joeslee—" started Ercy, feeling she should put a stop to this nonsense. "I'm not a witch—there are no witches."

"Your cousin Rellow knows better and admits it; why do you keep insisting? You were even selected by the Heil'ro in First Transfer and bear his mark within you."

"What do you mean, Rellow admits there are witches?" *He wouldn't—he doesn't believe any such thing!*

"He teaches the course in Channel's Deportment they keep making me repeat, and he makes a point of saying channels should be very careful when speaking to the press never to say anything about witches. The Tecton does science, not witchcraft, he keeps saying—and—it is all very funny, because here we are! Don't worry, I will not tell the Tecton's secret."

MAHOGANY TRINROSE   157

"Joeslee," said Ercy, controlling her exasperation, "there *is* no secret. Rellow didn't mean—"

"—that science and magic are one and the same thing? Ercy, I *know*. You don't have to pretend with me. I can't pass the courses. But I'm not stupid. Anyone can see they teach magic here—and the Heil'ro, he trains those who will become the Tecton's true magicians. Soon the time will be up and he will not have made his claim on me, so it will be permitted to resist. You will have protected—"

"Joeslee Teel," came Grant's voice from the page.

She turned to Ercy, eyes wide with sudden dread.

On impulse, Ercy said, "Ercy Farris. Can I take a message for Joeslee, Hal?"

"Wouldn't do much good," replied Grant. "I wouldn't have expected her to miss our appointment on her turnover day. I hope she isn't in trouble somewhere on the grounds. If you see her, Ercy, will you call it in to Ginny?"

"Sure." She didn't say immediately.

The page clicked off. "I shouldn't be arguing with you like this on your turnover day," said Ercy. "But we really must get this straightened out before you take your anti-kill conditioning transfer. Sels is your conditioning channel, too, isn't he?"

Joeslee nodded, but said, "I'm not going to take his conditioning, though, even if he tortures me."

Ercy said quickly, "I've known him all my life. Joeslee, don't be afraid, he's going to make it as easy for us as anyone could. Hal's job is to help prepare us to take the conditioning easily and seat it deeply so it will never fail us."

As she spoke, Joeslee's frown deepened. "You mean," she said, "you plan to take this—anti-kill conditioning?"

"Yes—of course—it's what we're all waiting for. It means you're safe—you'll never have to worry again about what you might do if provoked by a careless Gen—" *Or even what you might do by accident to your own Donor.*

"I have learned about this—anti-kill conditioning. It is what my mother called the Tecton Brand. It takes away your free will. But you already carry the mark of the Heil'ro. How could he let you take both? So you can't protect me from him?"

"I can't protect you from him," said Ercy. "There's nothing to protect you *from*."

"Then I'll have to protect myself," said Joeslee grimly.

At that point, Ercy noticed that the room had gone crystal clear—Grant's nager. A moment later, Joeslee noticed, and as

158 JACQUELINE LICHTENBERG

Grant approached, she turned a feral gaze onto Ercy—her nager showing an angry disappointment and even real fear.

Oh, no, thought Ercy, opening the door to Grant, *I try to explain and I just make matters worse.* As he entered, she was very glad that he couldn't zlin.

"Hal, guess who's here!" she said brightly. "I didn't get around to telling Ginny yet, and now I suppose I don't have to."

"No, Ercy, you don't have to tell Ginny." He advanced into the room. "Joeslee, Hajene Sels wishes to see you, and I've been instructed to attend to your comfort beforehand."

Joeslee stood her ground, eyes wide, hardly breathing. "I won't require your assistance, Sosu Grant."

"In that case," said Grant, "allow me to escort you to Hajene Sels."

"Go ahead, Joeslee," said Ercy. "He'll just want to talk about the pre-conditioning routines. Nobody's going to hurt you."

There was an opaque shadow of nervousness at the center of Grant's nager, just barely perceptible to her—she knew by now that it would be indiscernible to any other channel. But she ached for Grant—having to face an unconditioned channel who has tried to kill him.

Joeslee donned her sullen prisoner's attitude and went with Grant. The last Ercy zlinned as they entered the elevator was a clearing of Grant's nager as the door closed, as if he'd left the source of his discomfort behind. But that couldn't be. She shrugged it off, thinking that she'd have to practice reading Gen nager some more.

Over the next few days, all the others in her class went into turnover. The shadow of approaching need eclipsed every nager, bringing out the worst in each new channel's temperament.

Ercy, the youngest of them, avoided her classmates as much as she could. Their resentment of the way she had soared past them in so many subjects only led to unpleasant scenes.

But Joeslee displayed no such temperament. As need clamped down on all of them, Joeslee began to come into her own. Her slow progress remained steady. She caught up to the rear of the class in academics, though not in physical development, and remained the class leader in demerits earned. Since her accrued punishments already exceeded her life expectancy under attrition, she had nothing to lose and deliberately flouted all discipline. In a way, she became the class hero as the others secretly envied her while they shunned her.

MAHOGANY TRINROSE 159

Ercy couldn't decide which of them was more lonely, Joeslee or herself.

The day of Ercy's first turnover, she was more nervous than she wanted to admit. She kept remembering the few minutes of real need she'd felt just after breakout. She knew it wouldn't be that bad—but still, she had a few nightmares of disgracing herself and her House.

She arrived for her appointment at Grant's office half an hour early, not knowing what to expect of him. He'd been avoiding her at dawn in the garden and no longer took time to eat with her.

The attendant in the outer office told her to wait in Grant's office. She went in, noting it was furnished in the style she called Tecton standard.

Grant had come to them owning nothing but the clothes on his back, and even those had been thoroughly ruined. Yet he'd done wonders personalizing his office. One bookshelf was devoted to a collection of rocks, some of which Ercy thought must be semi-precious gemstones. Each had a special shape or texture, and the whole arrangement seemed endlessly intriguing both to the eye and to the Sime senses. Some ivy hung in a planter made from a trin tea jar suspended by decoratively knotted colored strings, which Ercy recognized as standard office packaging materials. On the desk where neat stacks of charts and routine forms had been moved aside was a soup plate in which Grant was building a cactus garden.

Curious, Ercy set her books down and sat in the desk chair to examine the cactuses. Each had been carefully transplanted from the wilds around Rialite. Some were planted in colored sands matching the colors of their blooms. At least she now knew what Hal did on his mysterious walks.

She had nearly half an hour to wait. Deciding not to waste it, she pulled out the side leaf on the desk and dug into her bag for notebook and pen. Her fountain pen was out of ink. In despair she just stared at it.

Oh, come on, she thought, annoyed. Surely it couldn't be beyond her ability to find something to write with.

Her gaze rested on the stack of files and it was only with an effort that she realized there was no ink on the desk. It was as if her mind simply refused to apply itself to the subject. When she thought of Grant, or Sels, or her anti-kill conditioning transfer, she could think as swiftly as ever. But study for Political Science— no.

Ercy had never had such an experience before. After a moment

160   JACQUELINE LICHTENBERG

or two of struggle, it began to frighten her. And then she recognized it. Turnover. Need. Gradually, over the next two weeks, transfer would become the only subject of any interest.

She summoned herself to work it out logically. In a Tecton standard office, there ought to be a supply of Tecton standard pens in the middle desk drawer. She opened the drawer but all she found was an array of rubber stamps and colored paper, some memo forms, and a jar of sand. The memo forms belonged in the lower right-hand drawer and the stamps in the upper left.

Where were the pens? With just a twist of attention, the desk became translucent to her senses and something in the lower right-hand drawer caught her attention. She opened the drawer and found a box full of new pencils, but nestled under the pencils was a metal object—no, not a pencil sharpener—a starred cross.

As her hand closed over it, Ercy marveled. In outline, it was ordinary enough—two equal bars crossed in the middle, with a five-pointed star superimposed. But it seemed to be made of solid silver, engraved all over with intricate designs picked out with precious gems—ruby, emerald, diamond—a fortune if they were real.

This, Ercy realized, was an art treasure that belonged in a museum, not a pencil box. She could feel the age of it as a kind of vibration in her bones.

She knew, as every child did, the story of the Shrines of the Starred Cross. Centuries ago, even before Rimon Farris started the first Householding, the troubled world had resolved itself into islands of Sime Territories surrounded by land held by the Gens. Any Sime going through changeover outside of Sime Territory was doomed unless he could make his way to the safe haven carved out by his fellow Simes. Likewise, any Gen establishing selyn production in Sime Territory was doomed to be stripped of selyn in the kill.

The only hope for such a Gen fleeing Sime Territory had been the secret routes leading out of Sime Territory, along which were the Shrines of the Starred Cross.

Children in-Territory swiftly learned they could run for their lives, finding food and shelter in the shrines. They would also find there a little starred-cross medallion—wood, or sometimes ivory, but plain and simple, not like this heirloom she held. There was always the admonition to trust in the starred cross and it would protect the Gen from the killer Sime's attack. It actually worked, too, because trust removed the beacon of fear that made every fugitive Gen a perceptible target for a Sime in need.

MAHOGANY TRINROSE 161

To this day, nobody knew who had established the shrines, or who had maintained them all those years. Perhaps Joeslee and her people had simply misunderstood the secrecy of the Heil'ro. Perhaps the Heil'ro traveled with the gypsies to found and maintain the shrines—and they had to do it in secret because such activity had been a crime against society—denying people their just kills.

Ercy caressed the object she held, turning it so that it caught the light, and suddenly what she held in her hand became a brilliant fire which she recognized—too bright to look at, against an emerald background—Grant's robe, Grant's jewel.

That's just a dream.

She had an impulse to search the closets and drawers for the emerald robe—but no, Grant had come to them possessing nothing. He had probably worn the heirloom starred cross under his shirt. She zlinned the jewels, trying to discern if they were real or just colored glass, totally bemused by the interlocking patterns at the center of the cross. They formed some kind of illusion leading down into the metal of the cross, down and away.

Bright golden sunshine from a crisp blue sky over a waving field of trinroses—rich, dark, mahogany trinroses. The air was cold despite the bright sun. The trinrose field was a jewel in the center of the surrounding crops. People worked barefoot, in shorts and shirts, cultivating the trinroses.

She was working beside them, the starred cross on her breast marking her as one of them. They worked down the rows, concentrating on each plant they tended, just like Donors attending a channel. And she knew what she was doing—to the rhythm of the waxing moon, she was coaxing the blooms to maturity for harvest. On one of her plants, she found a pink blossom, and knew that she had not compounded the lumpy white fertilizer correctly last time. Now she applied a correct mixture to the roots. She repaired a splice binding and knew how the grafting had been done. With the right graft, the right fertilizer, under a favorable moon, people were growing mahogany trinroses for kerduvon.

As she worked down her row of plants, she was aware of the pastel-washed stone block buildings clustered under a deep overhang on the side of the valley, little curls of smoke rising from chimneys. At the end of her row, she stood up, and there before her was an open space in which a huge, flat rock surface lay swept clean and waiting.

162 JACQUELINE LICHTENBERG

With a rush of shock, she recognized it from a dream—the place where Grant had been warned and called home.

One point of the starred cross was biting into her hand as she clutched it, the office snapping into focus around her. It was all very well to dream. Imagination was a scientist's greatest asset. But this wasn't the first time Ercy had found herself literally transported *elsewhere*, almost against her will.

Serial dreams—escape fantasies. *What's the matter with me?* But as she thought about it, she realized that the dream had told her how to grow a mahogany trinrose. *It's just a dream. I'm not getting enough dreaming sleep, so my brain is playing tricks on me*. How many times had she been warned of that? Yet what harm would it do to try out the method? She often got her best ideas in dreams.

She had no time to pursue the thought, however. Grant arrived and Ercy just managed to put the starred cross back into place before he opened the door. Without conversation, he put her to work.

Chapter 15

Ercy knew something was wrong.

She fought her way out of the groggy haze of sleep, in panic. Since her turnover, Hal had always been there through her sleep period, waking her gently without nightmares.

"I'm sorry, Ercy."

She got herself awake, leaning now on his returning attention. It was six and a half minutes after midnight, she knew without thinking about it. Hal was across the room, holding the telephone to his ear with one hunched shoulder as he scribbled on a notepad.

"Joeslee's disappeared again," said Grant over his shoulder.

She rolled to her feet, grabbing a fresh jumper and shoving her feet into her shoes. "Today's her anti-kill conditioning transfer!"

"Right," said Grant, but he was talking to the phone, not her. "Right. I'll be there. Don't worry. Right." He dropped the phone back on its pins, shoving the notebook into a pocket. "Bett will put you back to sleep. Why don't you take a shower or something until she gets here . . . ?"

"Oh, no. I'm going with you."

He stopped, one hand on the door. "Your father wants you to stay here and call in if Joeslee shows up."

"She won't come back here," said Ercy, remembering Joeslee's determination to "protect" herself. "She sees you—I mean, all of us as a threat. She thinks she's fighting for her life."

"You could be right. I've got to go." He pulled the door open and made for the stairs. Ercy followed him, fastening her coverall at the shoulder with two tentacles while the other two yanked a comb through her hair. By the time they emerged from the building, she was presentable.

She was sure Grant's talent for turning up at fortuitous moments would lead them right to Joeslee.

Striding down the moonlit walk, Grant said, "Ercy, you can't go with me. It could be dangerous for you."

163

164 JACQUELINE LICHTENBERG

"A berserker Sime is dangerous to me but not to you?"

"I can manage Joeslee."

The floodlights were on full all over the campus, cloaking Grant in sharp shadows, his face unreadable. But Ercy felt the serene confidence in his nager.

As they sped across the campus, Ercy realized they were heading for the garage. She could get wherever they were going faster if she ran under augmentation, but she was determined to stick with Grant. As they neared the building, several cars whipped by them, filled with Sime/Gen teams spreading out to search.

"Ercy!" said Manny, the head Sime mechanic of the motor pool. "First Year students aren't allowed in here!"

As two more cars loaded and left, she got into the backseat of the last one.

Grant slid in beside her. "Your father is going to hold me responsible for this."

"Where to?" asked Manny.

"Digen assigned me to the Folsom College grounds. Try the Spook Rock bridge first. What do you think, Manny?"

"Don't know what to think," said Manny, taking a sharp right as they emerged from the garage. "Last time we ran around like crazy for hours, only to find her in her room!"

As they climbed the rolling hills toward the college where Rialite trained its Donors, Ercy suddenly found the need she had been able to ignore thrusting itself into her awareness again. *Oh, is life always going to be like this?*

"You should have gotten more sleep," said Grant. "Here, let me help." He slipped his hand behind her head, resting cool Gen fingers along her spine. The other hand went to her forehead, gently massaging her temples. As he worked, the tension drained out of her. She sat up, taking an interest in things again.

Manny said, "There's Spook Rock. How close do you want to get?"

"What's Joeslee's range now, Ercy?"

"About a third of mine, but increasing every day. Need would sharpen everything, too."

The darkness was thick in the gully.

"I can't see a thing," said Grant. "Manny, you zlinning the Rock?"

"Easily," said the renSime.

"Then this is close enough."

Manny stopped the car and Grant got out, blocking Ercy's exit. "You stay here with Manny. You've done your part."

MAHOGANY TRINROSE 165

Ercy said, scrambling after him, "Hal, I've got to go with you—I can zlin her for you."

He stopped, his nager searingly intense. "Ercy, we have orders not to let her kill under any circumstances. The Folsom Gens have to be protected. One kill could demoralize the whole school."

He didn't say it, but Ercy knew she was classed with Joeslee—preconditioning channel in need. She was as vulnerable as Joeslee to Gen panic.

Grant's nager made the rocky terraced hillside above them clearly zlinnable—almost as if the sun had come up. Stubby little trees clung to sheer rocks, and paths wound from little formal garden to fountain to picnic areas set aside for the use of the Folsom Gens.

As Grant again turned to climb the trail, leaving her behind, Ercy zlinned Joeslee's lackluster nager.

On the road high above them, winding upward to the astronomical observatory above Folsom, Ercy perceived a car stopping, and two channel/Donor teams fanning out from it, working down the mountainside trails. But they were far away, moving obliquely.

And then she zlinned the Gen. It was a high-field Gen nager unlike any Ercy had yet zlinned. It had to be a student. Joeslee was closing on the Gen rapidly—*she'll scare him!* Ercy had lost track of the channel/Donor teams as the channels masked their fields.

Wishing she knew how to do that, she started after Grant under augmentation until she caught up to him and slowed to a walk, taking his hand. "This way," she said. "She's over here. Hurry. There's a Gen—"

"Ercy, you're not to be involved in this."

She dropped his hand and took off through the rocks, dodging cactuses and chuckholes by the brilliance of Grant's nager. Joeslee was talking to the Gen now. Ercy felt the moment the Gen recoiled in denial, trembling fear rising in that potent nager. Her own need responded, and she paused to fight it down by relaxation drill. Then she was running again, under augmentation, finding it helped release her tensions.

As she came into the cleared area—automatically noting the tumbled mass of boulders above them, the graded, crushed-gravel picnic area with a small waterfall on a terrace between two cliffs—Joeslee reached for the retreating Gen. Ercy zlinned the exact moment when the gypsy girl lost restraint, her killust triggered by the Gen's fear.

166 JACQUELINE LICHTENBERG

Without thinking, Ercy leaped toward them, arms and tentacles out to force them apart. She had barely made contact when, behind her, the intense beam of Grant's nager burst onto the scene. He paused a moment, and then everything went stark white for Ercy.

The next thing she knew, Joeslee was shaking her frantically where she lay on the ground beside the unconscious Gen. Grant was approaching across the crushed gravel, and Joeslee seemed to be trying to hide behind Ercy while at the same time dragging Ercy to safety—away from Grant.

Ercy struggled up just as Digen and Im'ran arrived along another hiking trail. As Grant closed the distance, Joeslee crouched and sprang at Grant, all tentacles spread for a killing grip. Grant received her, backing a step or two to absorb momentum. Joeslee was nothing more than a raging animal—and Ercy found her own system deeply resonating to that primal need, echoed in her father's system, too.

Selyn flowed.

Hyperconscious, Ercy found herself at one and the same time above and outside the scene, and yet also at the center of a unified energy flow with Joeslee and Grant on one side and Digen and Im'ran on the other, herself somehow connecting the five of them into a webwork of eight selyn systems. There was a quick upsurge, as if the pattern of fields had unlocked a spillway from another dimension. She found herself zlinning the gravel under her feet.

As she shifted to duoconsciousness, the gravel bed was oozing down the hillside, the overhang of boulders leaning downward in a stately bow as support collapsed.

"Rockslide!" shouted somebody.

The unconscious Gen student beside her was sliding with her as the whole area, picnic table, waterfall, and all, flowed down the hill. She scooped up the Gen, a dull throbbing nager that barely plucked at the edge of the need in her, and under full ninth-level augmentation, she ran for solid ground.

The crashing rumble grew deafening. Sels whipped into view, tilted Grant across his shoulders, and dragged Joeslee by one hand until they all came to a halt on level ground—and Ercy quelled her augmentation. The weight of the Gen over her shoulder drove her to her knees, her ankle twisting painfully under her as she tried to lower the limp body carefully to the ground.

Before she passed out, one image was etched searingly into her brain. Her father, standing bolt upright—Im'ran with one hand reaching out to him—and then her father's knees giving way, his face going utterly blank as he dropped to the ground as limp as a dead body. But his nager still throbbed as Im'ran, breaking his fall, brought all his skill to bear.

Through her own shock, she noted how unconsciousness stripped him of his tightly controlled show-field. For the first time, she zlinned the faint scintillation forming a pattern in his nager—the junct's pattern—that she had been taught should not be there. He had never killed—but he had lost his anti-kill conditioning.

When her head cleared again, Bett's nager was focused on her, Gen hands on her ankle. Two Simes were taking the Gen student away on a stretcher, and Joeslee was plastered against a rock face, wide-eyed. There was the smell of dust in the air. Joeslee was saying, "—not!"

Her nager was a throbbing bruise of terror. Coughing, Ercy struggled to sit up. "It's all right, Joeslee. Nothing so awful happened." *Nothing? She lost her chance at a good anti-kill conditioning, that's all.*

Her father was on his feet, seemingly unaffected, though Im'ran hovered protectively at his left side, and she could sense his worry.

"Ercy!" said Joeslee.

"Just be still, Ercy," said her father, "and let Bett tend that ankle."

Grant stood to one side, his nager hardly reduced by having given Joeslee her fill of selyn. "Joeslee, listen to me," said Digen. "We never did want to break your spirit. The Tecton wants allies, not slaves. And nobody can make a slave out of a Tigue."

She looked at him blankly.

"That explains everything!" said Sels. "So she's a Tigue! I should have seen it!"

Digen said, "The Tigue mutation isn't that common—especially the channels. We haven't had one at Rialite in five years. I only caught on yesterday, going over her test scores."

Joeslee remained tense, struggling to understand. Digen dug into his shirt pocket and brought out a little folder. Holding it out to Joeslee, he said, "This is your ticket to Ipsilante Crossing. You can draw on the Tecton credit line for the next three months. You can go anywhere in-Territory that you want to—build yourself a new life."

She took the ticket and credit pass. "You mean—I'm free—free to go?"

168   JACQUELINE LICHTENBERG

Digen nodded. "If that's what you want, Joeslee. We can flag down the morning train for you. But before you go, there are a few things I have to tell you. It's still possible for you to become a Tecton channel—we can implant the anti-kill conditioning with your third transfer, and I think we can manage to give you all the abort conditioning you'll require with your fourth transfer.

"You've been having a hard time with your courses because the Tigue normally takes two years to complete the post-changeover adjustment that others do in a year. So your systems will still be malleable enough to accept conditioning during your next two transfers. If you stay with us, we'll bring in some Tigue instructors and adjust the speed of your curriculum so that life here won't drive you crazy."

Joeslee's gaze slid past Digen to Ercy. "*He* is your father? He has the power to do all this?"

Ercy nodded, beginning to understand what her father was up to.

"One other thing," said Digen. "I think you should know. The Tigue is the only sex-linked channel mutation. Any boy child you give birth to will be Gen, potentially a First Order Donor. Any girl child of yours, by any man, will be a channel, a Tigue channel, and should be raised and trained for changeover. The Tigues are almost always First Order. Joeslee, you can't expect to survive on transfers from just any Donor." He gestured to the papers he had given her. "That will get you a proper transfer at any Tecton Center. You don't have to go junct, Joeslee. You're free."

Ercy could zlin the conflict in Joeslee. Though she had hated life at Rialite, she literally had no place else to go. The gypsy's gaze slid to Grant, dark with superstitious awe. "How can I take your—conditioning—now that the Heil'ro has set his mark in me?"

"The Heil'ro?" said Digen.

Grant met Digen's eyes. His nager was crystal again, flawless in its brilliance. "That is what the gypsies call my people."

Joeslee asked in frantic anguish, "Why did you let me live? What are you going to do to me?"

Digen asked, "Yes, Hal, what indeed?"

Sels said, "You told us you knew nothing of her people."

Grant looked about at Sels and Bett, then Digen and Im'ran, finally resting his gaze on Ercy for a moment, his nager taking on a preternatural clarity.

"I spoke the truth," answered Grant. "All I know of the

MAHOGANY TRINROSE   169

gypsy tribes comes from reading about them. Since I spoke with you, I have learned that her people all died trying to protect two of the Company traveling with them.''

He turned to Joeslee. ''I am not what you think I am, Joeslee. I bear the mark of my training, but I have left the Company.''

''Then why are you here? Except to come after me—''

''I did not come to avenge those who died. Your people are credited with a valiant battle. There is no blame in their failure— the contrary. The two lives lost have caused the Company to withdraw all travelers from the roads.''

''Then why are you here? Why have you not left?''

''How can I convince you? You know how the Heil'ro set obligations. A life binds me here, Joeslee.'' His eye strayed to Ercy.

How does he know? How could anyone know her dreams? The starred cross of her dream had turned out to be real.

Joeslee became darkly suspicious again. ''They teach magic here.''

''No, Joeslee,'' answered Grant. ''They teach science here. It is the opposite of magic.''

She seemed about to argue, but then she nodded as a new thought occurred to her. ''The complement that completes. Of course.'' Slowly, she looked around at all of them, then back to Grant. ''I am free?''

He nodded.

''Then I choose to stay. For a while.''

Chapter 16

"All right, Hal," said Digen, closing the insulated conference room door behind them. "After your cryptic exchange with Joeslee out there, I have the impression you've been lying to me since the day you arrived here—without a single Tecton identification on you." He glanced pointedly at the Tecton ring he had given Grant some months ago.

"Controller Farris, I have never once lied to you. You will note that Joeslee accepted my word—without question. She knows that the Heil'ro and the gypsy share an ethic of truth."

"But you claim you have left this—these Heil'ro."

"The ghost people," said Grant, seating himself at the table. "That is what the gypsies call us—for obvious reasons—but I have never been Heil'ro. I have never traveled among the gypsies to earn that title. I was once a student among the Company. I left before completing my training. I can't help but carry the mark of that training wherever I go."

"But you're still in contact with them?"

Grant looked up at Digen questioningly.

"How else would you know that your people don't blame the tribe for failing to protect them—that your people are withdrawing from the roads?"

Grant sighed, his nager clearing as if the room had suddenly become embedded in a diamond. Digen ignored the spectacular effect. "Withdrawing to where?" he continued. "Not any place that the Tecton knows about. A lot of things about you are beginning to add up for me. You say you don't lie, but you've lied to me about your Tecton credentials."

"Never," protested Grant. "I never *said* that I hold the rank of TN-1, four-plus, in the Tecton."

"You let me assume it."

"I have the right to give you permission to use your mind? Or not to use it?"

MAHOGANY TRINROSE   171

Stunned, Digen sat down. It was true the evidence had been there. "But your nager—"

"I have more than the necessary training and talent to do the work of the Tecton Donors of the highest rank. I have demonstrated that—many times."

Digen couldn't deny that. "But, Hal, that's just not the way the world runs. If you're not properly credentialed, you can't sign Ercy's credentials and *she's* not able to draw on her legal rights—" The snarls of paperwork rose in his imagination.

Grant said, "Will it help if I make out a formal application for Tecton certification?"

Digen sighed. "*Why* wouldn't you pledge to Zeor?!"

"I am already dedicated to excellence as the highest virtue. I cannot transfer that dedication to an individual and exalt that individual to the position of Sectuib over me."

"We've been around this circle before," said Digen. "It's clear that you grasp the nature of a Householding as nobody but a Householder could. Is your 'Company' a Household?"

"No. As I once told you, it is a small town."

"But unknown to the Tecton—unaffiliated, like the gypsies?" And then a sudden, horrible thought. "Hal, is it a junct town?"

"Zlin me deeply, and know the truth of this. I was not raised or trained by Simes who kill Gens."

Evasion. Digen, alert now to Grant's method of misdirected half-truths, said, "Answer the question, yes or no, is it a junct town?"

"Not in any sense you mean."

"In what sense would it be junct, then?" And suddenly, pieces of the confrontation with Joeslee fell into place. "Does this Company of yours practice witchcraft? Is that the hold you have over the gypsies?"

"I don't believe in the existence of supernatural powers, and it is against my principles to manipulate another person's conscience through his ignorance."

"Sosu Grant, why is it you won't give me a straight answer?"

His nager as limpidly clear as a flash-frozen ice cube, Grant turned from the window, bringing his full Donor's attention to bear on Digen. "I am doing my best to provide you with the information you require of me."

"We seem to be holding a conversation, Hal—but I can't see that we're communicating. It's a little like talking to—" Digen had a sudden thought. "Hal, have your people lived in isolation from the Tecton for very long?"

172 JACQUELINE LICHTENBERG

Grant nodded. "You're right, part of the problem is that there is an immense cultural gulf between us that prevents communication."

Digen took a pad of paper and began listing questions. "I am concerned with your Tecton status mainly because it affects Ercy's status, but also because I am Controller here and responsible for any irregularities."

"I offered to fill out the papers."

"I'll take you up on that—pick them up in my office in the morning. Now, second—if you're not a Tecton Donor, what are you? Two concerns: You might, through lack of training, undermine a Tecton channel's anti-kill or abort conditioning. Second, if you're mixed up in anything that people would take as 'magic,' your presence here could cause a riot that would incapacitate Rialite."

"I have two suggestions," replied Grant. "Test the channels I've had transfer with to determine if their conditioning is in any way impaired. You will find that it is not. Second, I have left the Company. Joeslee is the only one who would connect my nageric peculiarities with the Heil'ro. She is now at peace over this matter and won't mention it to anyone, especially if I ask her not to."

Digen listened, nodding. He was beginning to catch on to the way Grant's mind worked.

"So what does the Company do that gypsies assume to be magic?"

"Science."

Digen could believe that. He himself was an initiate of a secret lodge of surgeons—a secret lodge that had lived as an isolated community for centuries, preserving the knowledge of medicine through the long chaos following the collapse of Ancient civilization.

Digen said as much, asking, "Is your Company one of these preserving towns?"

"When you entered the lodge of surgeons, were you not made aware of their old oath of secrecy, which was all that saved them during the long centuries of danger?"

"Yes," said Digen. "Is that why I can't get a straight answer out of you—an oath of secrecy?"

Grant just looked at him, his nager turning the room into a bright, sharp blankness.

"Aren't you already in violation of that oath, just by being here—by all you've told me about the Company, the Heil'ro—"

MAHOGANY TRINROSE   173

Grant's silence took on a heavy aspect.

"Being Sectuib in Zeor, I can't press you to violate an oath."

"Zeor's ethic—as I have said before—is very close to my personal ethic."

"There is more in common than just an ethic. Despite everything—I trust you, Hal. And so does Ercy."

"It's mutual. So I tend to say more than I should."

Digen consulted his notes. "You say that because of what happened to Joeslee's tribe, your people are not traveling now— presumably, you've been called home, too. But you're not leaving—and that has something to do with Ercy. I feel that I must know what the connection between you two is. If she can't be your Sectuib—what is she to you?"

"A person to whom I owe a profound obligation."

"But you just met her—what could she have done to obligate you to her?"

"Suppose I put it this way: Sometimes one comes upon things in life that one must do. The compulsion to do these things is not imposed from without—it comes up from inside, a recognition akin to that accorded a Sectuib assuming a House. Ercy says that Zeor teaches the cultivation of hunches. This is a discipline that I have been taught also, and Ercy is the focus of a—hunch—of mine. I don't know yet what it's going to mean to me—but I know that I can't leave until I find out."

"What if the Tecton sends you elsewhere?"

"Then I will go."

"I'm not comfortable with this, and I won't be until I understand it."

"I can sympathize."

"Don't," said Digen dryly. "Your nager is so powerful that if you did feed that emotion back at me, I couldn't stand it."

For a moment, Grant didn't follow the joking tone, and there was the beginning of real offense in his nager. But then he said, "Will it help if I promise that if it ever seems to me that you must make a life-or-death decision with regard to Ercy, and I have knowledge that you must have to decide rightly, then I will lay that knowledge at your disposal without hesitation?"

"In violation of your secrecy oath?"

"I pray that I will not be presented with that decision."

"It was just a dream," insisted Joeslee.

"But about what that it could make you act like this?" For ever since the night Joeslee had run away and Grant had given

174   JACQUELINE LICHTENBERG

her second transfer, Joeslee had been acting toward Ercy like a newly pledged member of her House, overly impressed with the oath of loyalty to her Sectuib. As the hour of her own second transfer approached, Ercy found it getting on her nerves.

"Well, I dreamed I was hiding in a tent camp," answered Joeslee with reluctance. "It was winter, and bitterly cold. I was Gen, and so were you, but you were guarding me. As I watched, Sosu Grant came—as a Sime—and attacked you. I didn't try to help you because I was frightened. But you didn't die when he killed you. Then, as I watched, he drew a knife and slew you—"

She stopped as Ercy stared at her, losing all control of her show-field. Joeslee flinched as the ambient nager in their room went wild—Ercy was carrying more selyn than she ever had before, but she was still deep into need and within hours of her anti-kill conditioning transfer. For a few moments, Ercy fought to regain control, then muttered, "I'm sorry. But how could you possibly dream my dream, Joeslee?"

"You had it, too? Then it is true—the three of us, we are bound by a life."

"What are you talking about?"

"The Heil'ro—he knows it, too. It wasn't just a dream. It was a memory of a past life—and death. I've never had one before. It's frightening, isn't it?"

A memory of a past life? Ercy knew of the superstition that people lived many lives, and bad deeds of past lives could come back to haunt you in this life. The idea had always struck her as silly. *Yet—we all had the same dream. And two of my three impossible wishes have come true.*

"Joeslee, I'm a scientist. I can't discard the evidence set before me, even though it doesn't make any sense to me. But I can't just take it at face value, either. I have to be able to fit it all together into a theory, and I won't believe that theory until I can get it to predict events reliably."

"I have always thought you were a seer." Joeslee nodded. "Will you counsel me on my future?"

Ercy groaned. "I'll try to explain it to you tomorrow, all right?"

Joeslee nodded. "But you should learn to cope with need a little better. It really isn't that bad, Ercy."

Tigue! thought Ercy, through gritted teeth, and swallowed a retort.

"Look, Joeslee, I'm going to do a little research on my own. We have one of the very finest libraries in the world. When I was

MAHOGANY TRINROSE 175

a kid, they issued me a stack pass so I'd stop bothering the librarians whenever my father sent me after something. Maybe nobody will notice if I sort of float in there after stuff that's not in the catalogue."

"What are you going to research?"

"I'm going to find out how a magician thinks the world works. I'm going to find out why people believe in all that stuff. I'm going to find the explanation for, oh, all kinds of things that have been happening to me. And I'm going to find out where Halimer Grant fits into all this. Are you with me, Joeslee, will you help?"

"I don't like the idea of mixing into the affairs of the Heil'ro."

"It will do you good, Joeslee. You'll learn something of the scientific method of inquiry."

"Science is the opposite of magic. Yes—I will learn science. You will learn magic is real—I just hope you learn to respect its power before you learn how real it is."

Ercy spent the rest of that afternoon too restless to study, and too much in need to find relief in physical exertion. She visited the Memorial to the One Billion, where she'd received Zeor, and there she was finally able to relax before her preparatory appointment with Grant.

Several times as Grant worked over her, she saw him crumpling to the floor, drained wholly of selyn by her attack. The visions didn't have the clarity and power of the ones that had actually materialized, but she couldn't forget the dream of her father risking his life to be able to give her the conditioning transfers.

By the time he turned her over to Sels, she was counting the seconds to safety, and regretting a little the three hours' penalty she had incurred for disobeying Hal during the search for Joeslee.

The transfer room was the same as always—small, lined with cabinets stuffed with medications and instruments. Two contour lounges, a couple of stools, and a desk, all in Tecton standard. There was a sink with a hot plate for tea, and a little shower room opening off at one side. On a wheeled cart sat the hulking shape of a selyn battery, indicators on "empty." It was a huge old thing, roughly worn from student use. The sight of it made Ercy shudder. She had been training on the batteries for the last two weeks, learning how to absorb selyn from battery storage and how to void selyn into it.

Sels came in after her, puttering about the sink, arranging things to suit himself. He saw her contemplating the battery and

176 JACQUELINE LICHTENBERG

said, "It will go easily enough, Ercy, if you can hold your relaxation."

"I held it through changeover, I suppose I can hold it through this."

He picked up her chart from the tiny desk in the corner, zlinning her to compare her field with the figures entered there. "You haven't used much selyn today."

"I just feel terrible. Let's get this over with."

"Well—" He checked the plate riveted to the side of the black battery casing. "They sent us the largest one they had—hmmm, I guess it will hold what you're carrying. You know you must go all the way into attrition if the conditioning is going to take."

Ercy nodded. "I'll do it." *I don't care what it takes, I'll do it. I'm going to be safe after this.*

Sels zlinned her, his field a super-bright beacon sweeping through her as his attention came to focus on her.

He adjusted the battery controls and called her to stand over it and prepare herself. Nobody really understood exactly how this procedure created the conditioning, but she knew she had to void her secondary and primary systems to as nearly empty as possible, and then draw her transfer, holding to her refusal to kill, letting Sels control.

She gazed at the raised red terminals, four sockets to fit her laterals, and the plate she'd have to touch with her lips. Closing her eyes, she gritted her teeth and went hyperconscious. Sels pulled her back—reminding, "You're too tense."

She cued herself into the state of relaxation, then, hyperconscious, made contact with the battery terminals, thinking: *Out of Death Was I Born, Unto Zeor, Forever.*

The vast, black deadness of empty space billowed into her. She fell into it, quelling the screaming terror that threatened to overwhelm her determination. *It's only need again, silly.* Using all of her training, she flattened all her internal barriers and expelled every bit of selyn in her, disregarding all survival reflexes.

When it was all gone, she locked herself against the backrush and knew a moment's peace as she floated disembodied in nowhere. *Attrition—this is nothing to be afraid of.*

Dimly, she felt live selyn fields engage her systems and, floating outside the scene, she seemed to be watching Sels prying her laterals from contact with the battery, taking her into transfer position.

With a slam, selyn rushed into her. When she thought she

MAHOGANY TRINROSE 177

couldn't stand the flow an instant longer, it stopped. Her systems were wholly and completely open even to the junct pathways that had never been touched before. The selyn flow suspended, seeming to hold those virgin pathways open by some profound kind of suction, sensitizing those pathways so they would reject any selyn flow. The weird pause became a wave of euphoria carrying her into a boundless realm that held no fear.

And then it was over. Selyn began to move, and in desperation Ercy drew selyn at her full capacity and full speed. But it wasn't enough to satisfy the cell-deep yearning for a real Gen.

She came down to ordinary duoconsciousness as if this had been just another functional exercise, not a real transfer. She felt Sels's grip on her laterals loosen and fall away. Her eyes focused just in time to see him wilt and crumple to the floor at her feet.

She stared, uncomprehending, and then in growing horror as she realized she had hurt him. *I will not kill—he can't be dead!*

Kneeling, she touched him, and only then realized he was still alive. She grabbed for the emergency signal, knowing Bett was on call.

She waited in a darkening nightmare of anxiety as Bett came and grabbed for the phone, talking into it in rapid technicalese, then falling to her knees beside her husband, with only a half-smile for Ercy and then total concentration on Sels.

"He's all right, Ercy," said her father.

"She doesn't hear you," said Grant.

"She's in shock," said her father. "I was afraid of this."

"Let me handle her," said Grant.

"Don't you touch her!" said Joeslee, running into the room and seizing Ercy away from them.

Jolted, Ercy shook off the strange paralysis of will, clinging to Joeslee. *One real friend is worth anything.*

"I wouldn't harm her, Joeslee. Please accept that."

And Grant's hands soothed her knotted tentacles. Suddenly she was crying, clinging to Joeslee, her head on Grant's chest, the two of them blocking the rest of the room out of her senses. Quietly, Grant urged her to give herself up to the hysterical weeping, and she did, until she could get out a few words.

"Not—for me—for Uncle Sels. For—what—I did to him. He was afraid of me from the first!"

"No, Ercy," said her father, coming to ease her down onto the contour lounge. Sels was being taken out on a bubble-enclosed stretcher with Bett at his side. "He was apprehensive at first, but

178 JACQUELINE LICHTENBERG

he judged he could handle you, and the truth of the matter is, he *did* handle you! He's not badly hurt.''

And then she did dissolve into mindless weeping as all the unfelt, unrealized feelings of the last two weeks of need clamored for discharge, her mind offering only the label *post-syndrome*. There was nothing they could do to get Joeslee to leave her, and at last it was just the three of them alone in the transfer cubicle, until Ercy cried herself into a stupor from which she drifted into a foggy sleep.

Some time after Joeslee had gone, Ercy woke screaming.

Chapter 17

Emergency sirens wailed in the distance, coming out of the confused dream sounds of fire, sirens, and terror.

Grant was seated beside her, his eyes and attention fixed on some distant scene, and she thought she heard him mutter, "I thought this would stop it."

"Stop what?"

He looked at her, startled—a tiny prickle of alarm flashing through his nager. "I didn't say anything."

Aloud.

She hadn't heard that word. It was only an echo in her mind. Fully awake, she said, "I must have been dreaming." She sat up on the contour lounge, looking around at the transfer cubicle. They had also removed the huge, ugly battery. And remembered— "Uncle Sels! Hal, how is he?"

"He's all right. Digen and Bett and Im' are with him now."

Then it was worse than he'd told her. "I've got to go . . ."

"No!" said Grant, restraining her.

Ercy sank back on the lounge, suddenly remembering. "Of course, he wouldn't want to see me—of all people—I hurt him."

"No, Ercy, no. He allowed himself to get hurt—that's all. It's just the hazards of the trade, nothing more."

Ercy made herself sit quietly, act professional about the whole thing. *Hazards of the trade.* How often had Im' used that expression? But she knew she wouldn't rest easy until she saw Sels working again. The noise outside caught her attention. "What *is* that?"

"I'm not sure," said Grant. "There was a huge crash that must have wakened you."

Ercy got up and opened the door. The noise from outside increased. Grant followed her out into the sitting room of the transfer suite. There were several people clustered near the windows on the far side of the room. Another group was talking excitedly near the door. Ercy asked, "What's going on?"

179

180   JACQUELINE LICHTENBERG

"A building collapsed—the new Howard Hall."

"It just flew apart!" said a young secretary. "It was as if a bomb went off and knocked the construction props right out from under it!"

"Oh, no!" said Ercy. "Was anybody hurt?"

"We don't know yet . . ."

Ercy turned to where Grant had been standing. "Do—" He was gone. She saw him duck into a transfer room, fumbling the door hastily shut behind him. Just as the door sealed, she felt the briefest flare of—something. Fear? Panic? Terror? But it was so brief she wasn't sure afterward if she'd really zlinned it at all.

On her way back to her room, Ercy walked by the site of the disaster and found out that nobody had been killed, but the infirmary was flooded with injured.

Despite her increasing course load, Ercy found she still had unexpected amounts of free time for her private interests. The conditioning transfer had left her in a state of limbo—not in need, but not not-in-need either. The next two months would be the hardest of her life, she knew, because her next transfer would also be a conditioning transfer from a channel, again leaving her in limbo. After that, her fourth transfer would be with a good Donor, and the worst would be over. Everyone in her group was going through the same thing, and she was determined not to complain.

Meanwhile, she got many of the courses she had wanted, which opened whole new vistas of research for her. She began working on the ideas she had gleaned in Grant's office when she'd found his starred cross, but she had no opportunity yet to get into her library research on magic.

She saw little of Halimer Grant, as Bett substituted for him most of the time, and he no longer stopped to talk with her in the mornings. But her aunt wouldn't talk of family affairs, and the first Ercy knew that Sels was recovered was when she saw him strolling into the Controller's Residence at dinnertime with Rellow and Im'ran. As she watched, she was overcome with a pang of jealousy of Rellow—casually taking a place at the family dinner table from which she was now excluded.

I'm homesick! The thought jarred her out of the pain, and she suddenly realized that if the no-family-visiting rules were designed to make students confront homesickness preparatory to being cast out into the flow of Tecton service around the world, she wasn't

MAHOGANY TRINROSE 181

missing out on her training by staying at Rialite—to the contrary, being within sight of home was worse.

Digen looked up as Rellow came into the dining room. Beside Digen, Bett said, "Bad news, Rellow. Landar won't be coming back to be your Donor this month."

Rellow paused as Im'ran and Sels followed him into the room. He turned to Digen. "Does that mean that I have Grant this month?"

Rellow seemed a little too eager to Digen. *No—not eager—thoughtless.* "There are others in line ahead of you," said Digen. "But if I can get a couple of mid-Firsts for them, I'll put you on Grant's schedule. Stop into the office tomorrow and I'll show you how to juggle the factors from the Controller's seat."

"Thank you, Uncle Digen," said Rellow, taking Ercy's place at the table as if he'd always been there. Digen had long since given up wondering why every word the boy said made him want to banish him.

As the dinner cart was rolled in, Sels took his place and said, "How did you lose Landar? Or is that too complicated for now?"

"Oh, the wire I got only said his service was more urgently required in Farwheeling, which was on the way to Rialite, so he's being delayed. I'll put through a request to the Farwheeling Controller in the morning. I'm sure we'll have Landar for Ercy's fourth transfer."

"I certainly hope so," said Sels. "After two months of conditioning deprivation, I wouldn't want to turn her loose on anyone but Landar."

"Or Grant," added Rellow.

"That could produce complications," said Digen, helping himself to the soup. "Her fourth has to be someone else—Landar would be perfect. I think I can convince Farwheeling of that."

"I think," said Bett, "it's more than a case of 'perfect.' After what she did to Sels, you'd better have some new lab studies made on her."

"I just picked up the results on those," said Im'ran, reaching into a pocket to hand Digen a little folder. As Digen looked over the figures, Im'ran said, "As I read it, it's the deepest and strongest anti-kill conditioning ever recorded."

Digen handed the report to Sels. "What do you make of it?" Bett looked over his shoulder at the forms, frowning.

"Looks like a hair-trigger reflex to me," answered Sels.

182   JACQUELINE LICHTENBERG

Bett said, "Suicide-abort is supposed to be an act of will, Digen. Could she be triggered involuntarily?"

"May I see that?" asked Rellow, taking the folder.

Sels stared at his soup. "It's that sensitivity of hers, isn't it?"

"I don't think it's anything to worry about," said Digen, "because I don't think Ercy will ever encounter someone who could hit that trigger point against her will. I'll flag her chart to be sure it's double-checked from now on."

Sels looked up. "Digen, are you sure you want me to do her abort conditioning?"

"Yes, I'm sure. This wasn't your fault, Sels. You told me yourself how she voided too deep into attrition."

"This school isn't geared for the likes of Ercy," said Im'ran. "The instructors will always say, 'Now do this as best you can' or 'as hard as you can,' and Ercy *will* give it all she has, only her all is too much."

"That's a good point," said Digen. "I think I'll call a meeting of Ercy's instructors tomorrow."

"Am I invited?" asked Rellow. "I'm the only high First on staff who hasn't been teaching Ercy. I'd like to know what you're saving me for."

Digen looked at him, zlinning him, too. He wasn't unaware of the status Ercy's instructors had acquired among the general staff. "I don't think I'll be assigning you to Ercy, Rellow. I've got everyone else working overtime for her, so who's left to pay any attention to the rest of the school?"

Rellow rose, balling up his napkin. "You all hold it against me, don't you? It's that Grant character who's been poisoning my reputation! Well, don't think you can get away with this forever. There's something going on around here, and I'm going to find out what it is."

"Grant has nothing to do with this—" said Bett.

"Well, then why are you putting through new papers on him?" Rellow asked Digen. "I saw them on your desk. And why all of a sudden is Bett substituting for Grant on Ercy's service? Why am I kept off Ercy's service while you use every incompetent lorsh around? And why won't you give me a transfer with Grant?"

Before Digen could find something constructive to say, Rellow had hurled his napkin down and departed.

Gradually, Ercy's regimen was changed, de-emphasizing her physical development, since she'd already gone off the measur-

MAHOGANY TRINROSE 183

ing scales. She was allowed more and more free time, so she was able to begin her research into the history and theory of phenomena classically labeled magic.

She soon read through the library's meager catalogue of books and went down into the storage rooms with her pass, searching through unsorted boxes of books, some of them very old. She found references to many magical practices, but nowhere did she find what she was looking for—the magician's own account of what he did and why he did it, and how it worked. She couldn't disprove it if she couldn't find it.

At the same time, though, she was beginning to assemble a notebook—hesitating to commit some of her ideas to paper after what had happened with her garden notebooks, but unable to conceive of doing science without records. She wrote down the strange things that had happened so far, and began keeping a log of her dreams together with a daily account of events to compare the dreams with.

One day, she was sitting on the floor of the library basement, digging through a box of moldering books, when a nageric disturbance flickered at the edge of her awareness. Someone had come in. Sime. She heard the distant fire door thud shut. There were rows of standing shelves solidly packed with books between her and the Sime, but still she knew that nager. Farris—Rellow! She froze, controlling her show-field as best she could.

But he went away from her, toward the farthest end of the basement where the oldest, untouched boxes resided in heaps stacked to the ceiling. For a good twenty minutes she listened to the thuds and scrapes as he poked through the books on the shelves, sneezed repeatedly, and then began to cough and wheeze until the musty dampness finally drove him away, searching his pockets for his allergy medicines.

When the fire door thudded shut behind him, Ercy went to see what he had been doing. Near a leaning pile of boxes, she found a slip of new white paper. In fresh purple ink was scrawled: *Gypsy Conspiracy, by F'delyor Apodrinyin*. She looked around at the books on the shelves with renewed interest.

She spent the next few days' free time at that end of the basement, uncovering nothing of interest. But one night, when she was about to give up and go back to what she had been doing, a stack of boxes toppled over by themselves.

Sorting through the tangle of old books, sincerely glad that she had not yet developed any of the debilitating Farris allergies, she

184 JACQUELINE LICHTENBERG

found an old wooden trunk with an antique puzzle lock made of intricate ivory carvings:

The stenciled lettering on the outside of the trunk was illegible, but it was repeated on the inside of the lid, still dry and readable: HOUSEHOLDING INVOR ENDOWMENT TO RIALITE, and a date indicating this must have been one of the original shipments of materials to the Rialite library.

The volumes were the large, old wood-bound ones that must have been printed on a press using carved wooden type. But they were legible—and they were what Ercy had been searching for. Instructions in magic.

Ercy emptied the trunk and put everything back the way she had found it, carting the heavy books to her end of the basement where she had arranged a small study nook for herself.

She had to puzzle at the language, inferring much of the terminology from context. Her mind was always busy with these new puzzles as the days passed, mounting into weeks.

But occasionally, she would be working in her garden, thinking of Grant's starred cross, and suddenly she'd find herself working in the mountain valley on the mahogany trin plants, or standing on the huge flat rock looking up at the pastel-painted buildings nestled under the deep overhang.

She found the daydreams an effective cure for her attacks of homesickness at dinnertime, and she began to indulge them deliberately.

Now that she was taking lab science courses, she had access to all the chemicals and had no trouble compounding some of the lumpy fertilizer she was sure would be the key to her mahogany flower. She picked a midnight when the moon was right, and hoped the grafts would take.

The job went much faster than the last time she'd attempted grafting—before she had tentacles. It was only after she'd finished that she thought of trying a magical wish.

She stared at her handiwork, and couldn't make herself add a magical wish. *It's too silly*.

It was some days later that she found a tiny footnote that referred to kerduvon in a text on alchemy which had seemed to be pure rubbish. The book seemed to imply that the making of kerduvon—or several other kinds of chemical mixtures—was all that was required to change attitudes and personality, or even to disjunct a Sime. The kerduvon was described as a heavy brown oil, and she made note of the instructions for extracting it from the mahogany trinrose.

MAHOGANY TRINROSE   185

As she got into her study of magic, witches, gypsies, and other superstitions, her awareness of the passage of time dimmed. Her second conditioning transfer went without incident, leaving her again in a limbo which didn't begin to irritate her until the week before her fourth transfer.

At the same time that Joeslee went for fourth transfer, Ercy was assigned to her cousin Landar, Rellow's brother. She had hardly known Landar over the years, and now he worked with her without letting his individuality intrude.

Two incidents stood out clearly from those early weeks. One whole night, Joeslee wept inconsolably because she had welcomed and enjoyed the sexual advances of her first assignee, a man Ercy had never met. Mystified, Ercy had held Joeslee through that long ordeal, unable to respond to her friend's odd gypsy emotions. Her own need was too acute, and Landar's attentions had begun to waken her to an eagerness for transfer she had never known before. Toward morning, Joeslee had calmed enough to talk it out, and though Ercy never understood Joeslee's upset, they shared their dreams and hopes.

And a few days later, it had been Ercy's turn for fourth transfer. Landar had exceeded her wildest expectations. It was a transfer to rival her First. She'd been warned that few transfers would ever come up to such a standard, and she let herself indulge in it with total abandon. Afterward, with her own assignee her sexual initiation had been so satisfying that she had no post-transfer hysterics.

That was the last event that made a distinct impression on her consciousness for many months. Winter set in with days of overcast, and days of bright crisp winds, nights of real chill. Her fifth transfer was given by Halimer Grant, inaugurating a series of unspectacular routine transfers rotating between Landar, Grant, and two fairly competent Firsts who always left her in a mild discomfort she had to learn to ignore.

She had become totally absorbed in her studies when one day she discovered a box of textbooks for a course in dead languages Rialite had once offered. She found the real keys to some of the old books she was studying, and gradually found she had had flashes of what had once been known as clairvoyance, and once or twice had the eerie experience of precognition, though she couldn't seem to do it on purpose. Little by little, she was able to entertain the notion that her dream of Halimer Grant—shared with Joeslee, and with Grant as well—was not just a dream but an actual memory of a past life.

186 JACQUELINE LICHTENBERG

Then one day she found herself devising an experiment to test one of her new hypotheses. In her chemistry lab, she tried to use her imagination to influence the course of an organic reaction. But afterward, when she got the most minuscule yield of her expected product, she wasn't satisfied with her experimental technique. She might easily have been so busy imagining that she'd just not done the work correctly.

She dove again into her library basement, searching for some way to set up a real experiment.

The only one she could talk to was Joeslee, even if the gypsy girl rarely answered. Ercy was pleased that Joeslee, now that she was being treated as a Tigue, was making normal progress in her studies and growing into a fine professional channel, though her side of the room never looked neat.

Around midwinter, Ercy had worked out a regimen of exercises compiled from a number of different books purporting to help develop what the Ancients called ESP. Many of them were common practices in Zeor, including relaxation. She was fairly certain that during the few days just after a transfer, when she could stay hypoconscious without effort, she could actually see the body aura visually. It was quite different from the selyn fields, but she knew no way to prove what she was doing was not zlinning.

Clairvoyance was just as useless—either her Sime senses *were* what the Ancients called clairvoyance or they were indistinguishable from it.

Next she tackled telepathy—but soon decided that she had already become so skilled at deducing thoughts from emotional nager that she couldn't get reliable data.

Pre-transfer, and somewhat despondent over her failure to design an experiment, Ercy took the matter up with Joeslee.

"If you *could* do any of those things," said Joeslee, stuffing dirty laundry into a pillowcase, "you would simply be proving my point—magic is real."

"But I'm only doing science—"

Joeslee said to Ercy, who was sprawled on her bed watching Joeslee's weekly attempt to clean up her side of the room, "That magic is real does not imply that Science is unreal. I know, I was very confused when I came here. It was Hal who explained it to me. Science and magic are opposites!"

"That's what I've been trying to tell you—I'm doing science, not magic! There's nothing to be afraid of."

Joeslee raised one incredulous eyebrow, then gave a short,

MAHOGANY TRINROSE   187

sarcastic chuckle. "No, just being burned alive as a witch—or burning yourself up with forces you don't understand."

"But nothing is beyond scientific understanding, and I'm doing science, not magic."

Joeslee set the laundry aside and sat down facing Ercy.

"Ercy—science and magic are opposites. That means that you must do science from a magical standpoint, and magic from a scientific standpoint, in order for your operation to come out safely. That is why I must learn science. Hal has put his mark in me, but I am no good to him until I learn science so that he can teach me to do magic."

You expect Hal to make you a witch? But Ercy didn't say it aloud. "Look, I still haven't figured out what magic really *is*. But this much I know. If it works, it's not supernatural. Joeslee, you're a very intelligent person. How can you fear something simply because you don't understand it? All I want you to do is help me run a few experiments."

"To do what?"

"Well, as I see it, the field of magic is divided into two main parts—phenomena they call ESP that I've been talking about, and other things which involve the manipulation of imaginary, invisible beings. None of that makes any sense to me, but this ESP stuff was once a science of sorts. Now, I have a hypothesis for a way to get physical science to prove that the phenomena exist. I've been trying for days to do it by myself, but I can't—so I want you to try with me."

"Try what?"

Ercy bounced off the bed and pulled the blinds and drapes closed, took a candle out of her underwear drawer, and set it up on a dish on the floor at the end of her bed. Then she filled a soup plate with water and put it beside the candle. She carefully set an ordinary sewing needle on the surface of the water.

"This is how you start to learn telekinesis—if it can be done at all, that is."

"What's the candle for?"

"I don't know. That's just the way it says to do it in the book. You see, you're supposed to concentrate on the needle and make it move to the edge of the soup plate."

"If you're not going to invoke and control a demon, then it can't be evil magic. But I still don't think you know what you're doing."

"Will you help, though?"

188 JACQUELINE LICHTENBERG

"All right," Joeslee agreed, looking at Ercy and zlinning her at the same time. "I trust you."

Ercy was more touched than she wanted to admit by that.

Holding hands with Joeslee, Ercy used the mental focusing skills she'd learned to survive changeover. But Joeslee beside her became more and more tense, her muscles knotting as her mind instructed the needle to move.

"No, not like that," said Ercy. "Zlin this!" And Ercy demonstrated her relaxation drill.

"How do you do that?" asked Joeslee. So Ercy spent the rest of that day teaching Joeslee the elements of relaxation. It took several days, but zlinning Ercy and other classmates, Joeslee began to grasp it. Her Gen instructors saw what she was attempting and began to help. Within the week, Joeslee was able to trigger her own relaxation response, and their experiment continued.

Lying prone on the floor of their room, chins propped on their hands, the only light coming from a single candle, they concentrated on the needle. Ercy felt Joeslee's nager as solid as if it were a thrustblock behind her.

Abruptly, the needle skimmed across the bowl and hit the ceramic rim with an audible *tink*. The bowl tipped and then flipped up and over, splashing the water all over the carpet.

As this happened, Ercy felt a prickly tingling explode through her chest and etch dotted lines out to her fingers and toes. The world became dotted, like a newspaper photograph seen too close, then snapped back to normal, leaving her whole body feeling light and porous.

"Ercy?"

Joeslee was leaning over her as she lay sprawled on the carpet. "I'm all right," protested Ercy as Joeslee zlinned her.

"You're sure?"

Ercy struggled up, ordering her systems and wondering how she'd come to faint. "Yeah, I'm sure."

"Good," said Joeslee with genuine relief. "Ever since that Farris kid in my battery-packing class just up and died over nothing, I get nervous when you go off like that."

Then Ercy's eye fell on the upended soup plate. Joeslee followed her glance, eyes wide. "Ercy—you have the power!"

Ercy picked the bowl up and dropped the needle back into it with a tiny *clink*. "Joeslee, we've discovered a new channel's functional mode!"

Joeslee shook her head. "I should never have gotten involved in this."

MAHOGANY TRINROSE 189

"Just zlin our selyn expenditure! There's nothing supernatural about what we did. We moved the needle—*shen!*—the whole plate!—by applying selyn. That must be what the Ancients called telekinesis, though how they could apply selyn to move things when they weren't even Simes, I don't know."

"Maybe that's not what really happened . . ."

"Snap out of it! Zlin me! Compare my field before and after."

"I don't zlin any difference."

"Well, it is small," admitted Ercy. She picked up her notebook and wrote out her observations of the fields, did some quick arithmetic, and thrust the book at Joeslee. "See, it's a very tiny amount but it is very definitely expended, though it cost me lots more selyn than it did you."

As the gypsy looked at the numbers, Ercy went on. "We'll have to experiment with larger objects so we get larger expenditures—something you can measure yourself."

"Ercy, I don't want to do this. We could hurt someone, or ourselves. If you have the power—"

"Together, we have power, Joeslee. But it's nothing to be frightened about. If we can prove that the mind affects the material world, we prove the reality of the mind, and of wishes as a causative factor in the universe. The implications are endless!"

In the end, Joeslee's First Year student curiosity, coupled with her trust of Ercy, brought her into the program of experiments Ercy constructed.

As they worked together, the two girls became closer and closer friends. Ercy no longer fainted after moving an object, but it always left her feeling strange. When they couldn't work at moving objects, Ercy found she became increasingly nervous and tense, desiring the peculiar sensations that flushed through her after each telekinetic event. It crossed her mind that perhaps this work was addictive, because the moment they resumed moving objects about the room all the tension left her.

But she had little time to dwell on this. Her studies mushroomed. She hardly had time to notice that she'd never felt so happy in her life. And then the day came which drove the reality deep into her consciousness.

She was kneeling in her garden, turning the soil and pulling weeds, as the sun came up, the short winter giving way to early spring. She glanced up, and there before her, atop one of her grafts on which she'd been using her experimental fertilizer, a tiny bud had unfurled—mahogany. She cupped her hands behind it, almost unable to breathe.

190   JACQUELINE LICHTENBERG

It was a small, limp little bud, and it was more a deep red than it was brown—but it was certainly not an ordinary trinrose.

She stayed there enrapt while the sun rose and the tiny flower unfurled, her mind filled with the old picture from her fairy-tale book, the rippling satin background and the graceful Sime hand holding the trinrose. But now, shimmering in the back of her mind was the antique starred cross, the true meaning of the mahogany trinrose—harmony and understanding between Sime and Gen—opposites that were complements.

Now her life had begun at last.

The days ticked by, and the spring winds came. All over Rialite, the little weighted stands with the warning signs—DO NOT UNSHEATH TENTACLES OUTDOORS DURING SANDSTORM—sprang up like daffodils to herald spring as they did every year. The warning signs were so much a part of her world that she, unlike the other students, could walk among them without noticing them at all except as the happy harbinger of springtime. And during the second, and most severe, blow of the season, she made a careless gesture while walking with Joeslee, exposing three tentacles, two on one arm and one on the other.

She spent two days in the infirmary with inflamed arms.

When she got out, she went immediately to her garden, hoping against hope that the rest of the grafts would have produced mahogany trinroses. But no, they weren't in bloom yet. And the single stem which had sported a dark flower was bare.

The storm! she thought, cupping her hands about the empty stem. A scene flashed through her mind—Rellow fighting the winds, clipping the tiny flower. No—she was imagining things. He had stayed carefully out of her way all these months. But the stem *had* been cut, not broken off.

Her dismay was short-lived, however, for during the next few days, the warming sun urged forth a glory of buds from her trinroses, and a goodly portion of them were what she came to call near-mahogany. Her third wish had come true.

Her father was still alive, and now she would be able to produce the kerduvon to disjunct him safely.

Following the instructions in the book she'd found, she harvested the flowers.

She hid her kerduvon experiment among the equipment deployed for several textbook experiments she was running. Inside two weeks, she had produced a small vial of heavy brown oil which looked and smelled as if it might indeed contain kerduvon. But was it pure enough to use as a drug? She ran four different types

MAHOGANY TRINROSE 191

of chromatography on her specimen without finding any toxic chemicals as constituents.

She collected her reams of graphs, notes, and charts into a respectable notebook, which she kept with her other schoolbooks, on the theory that nobody, even Rellow, would expect her to keep anything private out in plain sight. She wanted to wait for the rest of her crop to mature before announcing her discovery. The late bloomers might be true mahogany, and might produce a better grade of kerduvon.

In moments of pre-transfer depression, she wondered if she wasn't simply delaying her moment of reckoning. How would she get her father to use the kerduvon? Was the world ready for such a gift? What if people thought it the product of magic?

And so her explorations of the entire realm of magical philosophy went on. She began to grasp the implications of the immortal soul stripping off personalities at death and gaining new ones with each rebirth; she thought she could feel within herself the part that was her real self and the part that was just her personality.

She began to explore the mechanism of the human mind and how it could block off inner awarenesses. She found some forgotten memories of her early childhood, found that when she evaluated them from adulthood, she became much more at peace with herself, able to exceed her own marks in her channel's functions.

One day when a late-spring deluge was threatening to wash Rialite away in an ooze of mud, classes were canceled because of severe thunderstorm warnings. Ercy and Joeslee spent the day in their room, studying by artificial light.

Finally, Ercy tossed her pharmacology text on top of her Tecton Law books and got up to pace restlessly around the room. Joeslee ignored her, reading an economist's study of the House of Keon's financial empire. After nearly twenty minutes, Joeslee said without looking up, "Ercy, you're hatching a plan."

"No," said Ercy. "I've hatched the plan, and I'm wondering where we'll get the courage to try it."

"Count me out," said Joeslee, still turning pages. "It says here the Tigue Sectuib in Keon has been known to pretend to cowardice when it suits her purposes. If she can do it, so can I." She turned another page.

Ercy suddenly realized she was being teased and retaliated by snatching the book out of Joeslee's tentacles. "Will you be serious!"

"I'm always serious—it says so right in that book."

192 JACQUELINE LICHTENBERG

Her mind told her she was still being teased, but she couldn't zlin it in Joeslee's nager.

"You know, you're getting good at that," said Ercy.

"At what?" asked Joeslee innocently. But she overdid the innocence and Ercy finally zlinned the gleam of humor she was hiding at the core of her nager. The two laughed together, and then Joeslee said, "Come on, Ercy, give the book back. It was just getting to the good part where Keon took Zeor to the cleaner's."

Ercy flipped the book open, searching for the account, sure *that* had never been written up in any book.

Zlinning her, Joeslee sat up straight, unable to control her display of shock. "You mean there really was one? Come on, tell me about it. I'm not in Keon—you can trust me."

"If there's anything to find out, you'll be told after you've pledged Keon—that is, if they'll invite you to pledge when they find out you don't consider members of Keon trustworthy!"

Ercy suddenly realized she'd been sidetracked. A deep rumble of thunder rattled windows as far as she could zlin.

"Come on, Joeslee, we've got work to do. Remember I said we could do this telekinesis thing because you took my 'speed' factor and stepped it down to a lower 'gear' ratio where my speed was turned into power? Well, I did some computer work with our data, and I proved that equation I wrote—you know, the one I concocted in differential analysis the day we—"

"I don't want to hear about that equation."

Joeslee's only interest in mathematics had to do with compound interest or currency conversions.

"Look," Ercy said, picking up her notebook, "to prove the equation, I have to have some data on what happens when you and I lift a mass exactly equal to our combined mass. You said you'd help me finish my experiments. This has got to be the last one. Honest, I mean it this time."

Joeslee gave in, mumbling something about rainstorms being bad luck. "So where are we going to find a mass exactly equal to the sum of our masses? Do you know how big a pile of sand that would be?"

"I think if we take the mattress off my bed and take the frame apart, we can make it into a bundle that would do. Then all we'd have to do would be to add—"

"Oh, no . . . what if there's an inspection while we're dismantling the furniture?"

This from Joeslee, who had never cared about rules or demer-

MAHOGANY TRINROSE 193

its, startled Ercy. But then she realized Joeslee was right. It had been a long time since an inspection, and today would certainly be the logical day for one.

Joeslee had risen and was now pacing around the bed, zlinning it. "Suppose we pile all our books on—no, it wouldn't even take all of them. We could just pile books on your bed until it equals the mass of the two of us."

They couldn't get in much trouble if they were found with books on the bed. She grabbed an armload off Joeslee's stack and said, "Here, spread these out evenly." Then she added her own books, until she thought she had it right. She rarely missed estimating mass by more than fifteen percent—which ought to be close enough for her purposes.

There was a click, and the intercom speaker came to life. "Due to the inclement weather, afternoon classes are suspended. However, the faculty flyball team is staging a special Sime vs. Gen match in the main stadium in fifteen minutes. All students are invited to observe. The Hiroam Quartet is performing in Gredding Hall now. And the large faculty pool is open to students for the afternoon."

"Ercy, let's get this over with. I want to see that flyball match—Sime against Gen, by the faculty! That has to be the match of the century!"

As Ercy went to pull the shades and curtains closed, she saw a stream of people leaving the dorm, heading for the main stadium. What Joeslee didn't know was that the faculty did the Sime/Gen thing every spring during the most threatening storms to get people up to the main stadium—on the highest ground and most solid rock foundation in the valley.

Ercy had never seen the water come as high as the dorm she was in—and besides they were well up off the ground floor. Gredding Hall was the only place in Rialite safer than where she was now. She closed the drapes, putting the outside world out of her mind.

As she set up the candle on the dresser, she said, "You ought to stop playing difficult, Joeslee. This is a lot of fun, and I can't wait until we can teach others to do it."

"Well, I suppose it would be fun if you were doing it with someone who knew how to have fun—instead of making everything into mathematics and experiments and such."

Ercy shook her head. "I suppose one day I'll get used to you. They say First Year students are adaptable." She lit the candle, aware that this was a very important moment.

194   JACQUELINE LICHTENBERG

Oh, I hope—I wish—this will somehow lead to getting Dad to accept the kerduvon and disjunct safely. To her surprise, she found tears streaming down her cheeks.

"What's the matter, Ercy? I didn't really mean—look, you're my only friend—the best friend I ever had. And you're right—this is fun."

Ercy sniffed her tears away, and made the preliminary observations in her notebook. Then they joined hands, handling tentacles twined, but without actual lateral contact. Ercy led the way into deep relaxation, trying with every breath to get Joeslee deeper than they had ever been before.

"Now, Joeslee, together."

Ercy felt the selyn fields building between them.

Behind them, the candle flame seemed to loom larger, throwing their shadows onto the bed and the wall behind it. Ercy, duoconscious, could see the shadow waving about liquidly.

The bed had not so much as trembled as they willed it to lift straight up. Ercy emptied her lungs, drew a deep breath, and tried to lead Joeslee a little deeper into relaxation. It was like dragging her own weight behind her. She could now sense the currents of tension in her partner—a prismatic pattern through which selyn drained down and away like the swirling pool of water sucked out into—where?

Ercy felt suddenly giddy. It was as if she were looking through Joeslee—a billion-faceted prism throwing her attention into high focus in hundreds of directions at once. Peripherally, she sensed only two other people in the building, both Gens. One in the lunchroom doing some bookkeeping, and the other at the front door looking out at the rain.

Ercy, while holding the bed at the center of her concentration, was still aware that her mind was wandering. She should not be aware of anything but the bed. With the effort of learned discipline, she brought herself back to that focus, imagining it floating up off the floor.

Something broke.

There was a dizzy, draining moment, a surge of selyn, the world dissolved into a matrix of dots of which she was also a part, expanding and expanding to encompass all.

With a rush, it was over, and she was on her knees on the floor, faint and panting. There was still that odd awareness of the entire building—and with a shock, Ercy zlinned blooming fans of flame erupting from the walls, the floors, the furniture, all over the building.

Joeslee, clinging weakly to the bedpost, said, "Ercy, it didn't move. I don't know what happened."

Ercy picked herself up. "Can't you zlin it? The building's on fire!"

Just then, flame erupted from their light fixture and the ceiling began to blacken.

"Let's get out of here!" said Ercy, grabbing up her notebooks. She blew the candle out and raced for the door, pulling Joeslee behind her by the shirt sleeve, thinking crazily that she shouldn't have wasted time blowing out the little candle. She pulled the door firmly shut behind her.

Together, they leaped gouts of flame just licking at the stairwell, which was supposed to be fireproof, and Ercy was glad she could zlin her way through the fire to safe footing. Then suddenly she remembered the Gens she'd zlinned.

On the landing, Ercy flipped the alarm switch. "There's a Gen trapped in the lunchroom. You get that one—I'll search for the other one I zlinned up front. There's nobody else in the building."

Chapter 18

Digen was in his office with Im'ran, Sels, and Bett when the fire alarm sounded. From the window, Sels said, "It's the east dorm—Ercy!"

Im'ran started out of his chair. "She knew what the flyball announcement meant."

Bett was already flinging the door open, grabbing her raincoat. "Ercy has an invincibility complex as big as Digen's. She'd sit down to lunch on a dry streambed in this weather without a second thought."

They followed her out into the rain as the clanging fire trucks converged. At the path near Ercy's garden, Halimer Grant joined them without a word. By now they could see gouts of flame sprouting from the dorm roof.

Digen and Sels drew ahead of the Gens, zlinning the building anxiously as they ran. Visually, the bright red flames made a dramatic contrast to the rolling black thunderclouds that hung low over the valley, boiling eastward on a raging wind. As they reached the building, the fire trucks drew up, Simes jumping off in every direction. Meanwhile, cars full of volunteer fire fighters spilled more Simes into the confusion. Slickers and helmets, hatchets and breathing masks, were handed out from the big pumper truck while another crew deployed the hoses. With a roar, the pumper started up and pairs of Simes pulled spewing hoses toward the inferno.

The fire chief came over to Digen. "Hajene Farris, I don't have to tell you the building is a total loss. My sensitives tell me there's nobody inside as far as they can zlin." She shook her head and wiped soot from her face with one handling tentacle. "I'm not going to risk any lives fighting this one."

Digen took several steps closer to the building, zlinning keenly.

"Hajene," said the fire chief, putting her hand on Digen's elbow. "This is what you pay me to be expert in. Please, don't risk your life for nothing."

MAHOGANY TRINROSE   197

Behind them the hospital truck drew up and deployed equipment, volunteer Gens converging on the field hospital that blossomed in the middle of the lawn. Digen shook off his fire chief's restraining hand and made his way closer. There was a commotion behind him, but he ignored it. At her changeover party, Ercy had had a vision of a fire . . .

Behind him, he heard tatters of Grant's voice borne on the wind. ". . . -en who . . . in the . . . alarm?" Grant followed Digen, with Sels, Bett, and Im'ran right behind him. But it was Grant who was at Digen's side when the basement door of the building flew open and Ercy staggered up the steps, carrying a Gen man whose clothes were on fire. Her hair was smoldering, and one shoe was badly blackened.

Digen surged forward, catching up her burden and rolling the unconscious Gen on the ground to smother the flames, yelling over the roar of the fire and the wind, "Down, Ercy! Your skirt's on fire! Sels!"

Grant moved in, scooped Ercy to the grass, and rolled her in his slicker. Sels came up, kneeling beside the burned Gen to examine him. Bett took her place across the patient from him, saying, "See to Ercy, Digen."

As Digen turned, the fire chief ran to them, yelling, "Get out of here! That wall's coming down!"

They could barely hear the words over the roaring fire, but Digen zlinned the wall above them and motioned Sels to move his patient back while he picked Ercy up and together they all ran. Somehow, the structure held.

Sels took the Gen right into the field hospital. Digen stopped with Ercy as she squirmed around to look at the building. He set her on her feet, letting her lean on him as she coughed smoke out of her lungs. She showed no signs of shock, and as far as he could tell, she wasn't burned anywhere, though it had been awfully close.

"Aild Ercy Farris, don't you have the sense you were born with!"

But Grant stepped between them. "Not now, Digen." He took her by the shoulders. "Is there anybody else in there?"

Ercy looked about her, shaking off the dazed expression. "Where's Joeslee?" Then her head whipped around and her gaze centered on the blazing building. Her hands flew to her face, tentacles extended, mouth open in a soundless scream. This was the scene of her vision come alive.

Suddenly, Ercy broke free of Grant's hands and ran toward the

198 JACQUELINE LICHTENBERG

building. Caught off guard, Digen couldn't catch up to her until she was stopped by Mora, coming around from the other direction, Im'ran right behind her. Digen joined Mora in holding the struggling Ercy, who was yelling something incoherent about the lunchroom.

Panting, Im'ran said, "They've located another selyn field in there, Digen, and the hoses are concentrating on the area."

Grant joined them, also panting. Digen said, "Have they got a rescue team in there yet?"

Im'ran shook his head. "No way in—or out again. There's just that one pocket—the lunchroom, somebody said."

"Joeslee!" screamed Ercy, fighting madly to get loose as Mora and Digen hugged her tightly between them. "Let me go!" she screamed. "Let me go! It's my fault! Save her! Save her!"

Digen shifted his grip to her hands, his handling tentacles urging her laterals out of their sheaths so he could make a full channel-to-channel contact while Mora held her. "Ercy—listen to me. Listen! It's not possible. Nobody could get out of there alive—nobody!"

He commanded her attention through the selyn flows, attempting to impose a druglike calm on her hysteria. Reason returned to her gaze, though she was still wild. "It's all my fault. I set the fire. I did it. Let me go!"

Grant moved in then, spreading his hands over the lateral contact Digen was holding with Ercy. "Let me, Hajene."

Digen looked at him over his shoulder. The Gen's nager was preternaturally calm, painfully lucid. Digen found himself trusting the Gen's control even more than his own. He dismantled the lateral contact, releasing Ercy into that bubble of Gen clarity.

She's not hurt, Digen told himself. Then the enormity struck him. Ercy had foreseen this moment—her best friend burned to death in a fire she feels responsible for. And Joeslee had nearly been burned to death at her changeover—Ercy would know how the gypsy girl felt about fire.

Im'ran came up on his left, one fine Gen hand finding its welcome place on his arm.

Once more, Ercy began to scream and struggle to get loose, her panic now shifting to a purposefulness Digen didn't like at all. He caught her back, restraining her in Grant's hold as she began to scream again, "She's not dead yet! Let me go! The ceiling's going to collapse! Let me go! Let me go!"

Another large hose was dragged around to the side of the building, playing on the general area of the lunchroom. A rescue

MAHOGANY TRINROSE 199

squad was poised at the edge of the heat, but there was no way for them to get in.

Ercy began screaming inarticulately, eyes peeled wide in utter panic as if she were the one in the burning room, looking up at a flaming ceiling. And then an odd thing happened. Digen saw the same look of terror reflected on Grant's face as the Gen hugged Ercy close as if protecting her with his own body from falling debris. His nager fragmented under a surge of pure adrenaline, Ercy's fields welded to his as if they were in transfer.

Three things happened simultaneously.

There was a grinding crash as the building's roof collapsed, sending towers of flame upward and spraying flaming debris in every direction. Barely audible beneath that, Digen felt an odd whooshing pop that was both audible and nageric, and in the fractional second afterward, he saw Joeslee crouched on the ground before Ercy, clothes blackened. She was coughing, fighting to draw air into her smoke-seared lungs. In that same fractional second, Ercy stiffened in Grant's arms and her selyn fields collapsed inward as all selyn in her body ceased circulating.

Joeslee emitted an involuntary croaking scream as disorientation hit her. Grant finally registered Joeslee's presence, and then Ercy's collapse, and his grip on Ercy tightened. Digen slid his own hands up under Grant's and probed through the lax wrist orifices with his laterals until he could just make contact with her laterals. *Suicide-abort.* The diagnostic computer in his mind rendered a calm verdict while the trained channel simply acted.

He threw a surge of selyn into her systems, attempting to shock her to awareness. He waited on the black edge of hysteria. Three beats, and he reversed the polarity, pulling selyn out of her systems, hope sinking under him.

Grant's focus inside Ercy seemed to bend around some inconceivable corner and disappear. In the instant Digen sensed this strange thing, Ercy's heart resumed beating, driven by a rising pulse of selyn circulation. And then all her cells were throbbing with returning life.

As Digen began to dismantle the forced lateral contact, he realized what he'd just done was technically illegal. He was junct—barred from any and all channel's functionals lest those he helped find themselves unable to resist the temptation to kill.

The strain of using his secondary system had Digen trembling, but he hung on, grimly.

Im'ran was bending over Joeslee as she fought to get to her feet, croaking hoarsely, "I'm all right, I tell you! It just surprised

200 JACQUELINE LICHTENBERG

me, that's all.'' With a resigned shrug, he helped her up, and then let her lean on him as she fought off a wave of dizziness and an urgent desire to vomit.

The last pieces of flaming debris were just landing around them. Everyone's attention had been on the collapsing building. Only Digen, Im'ran, and Grant had seen Joeslee materialize out of thin air. Only they, Mora, Bett, and Sels knew that Ercy had named Joeslee as being inside the burning building.

Just then Mora drove up in an open cart. "Get in! You, too, Joeslee! That wall's about to go—and the flood is coming!"

All around them the fire brigade was pulling out in a well-coordinated pandemonium. The front wall of the building leaned majestically toward the skirling flood waters encroaching across the lawn. As Digen helped Grant lift Ercy into the cart, the water had already reached his toes. He said, "It's never come this far before!"

"The retaining wall went," said Mora. "We couldn't hold it."

Digen gave her a quick hug.

As Im'ran climbed onto the front seat between Mora and Joeslee, Mora set the cart in motion toward the Controller's Residence, and said tightly, "I don't think Rellow saw Joeslee appear out of nothing. As soon as the sparks stopped flying, I diverted everyone's attention to the flood."

Joeslee coughed, a long and racking sound. Ercy was half lying between Digen and Grant in the backseat, limp and barely breathing. Digen said, "Im', those oxygen tanks we stored in Ercy's room—they fully charged?"

"Yes, I attended to that the day you decided you weren't sick anymore and went back to work."

"Mora, drop us off at the back door, and go over to the infirmary and get two oxygen masks. And pick up a field burn kit. I think we have everything else."

Glancing toward Joeslee, Mora said, "All right, but what are we going to do—about what—happened?"

"Don't think about it—not yet. One thing at a time."

Two hours later, recovered, Digen joined Grant in the sitting room of the family apartment. Ercy and Joeslee had been put to bed in Ercy's room under oxygen with Bett attending. Mora was busy with her staff finding temporary domicile for the displaced students. His own staff was busy drafting clean-up plans for tomorrow.

MAHOGANY TRINROSE   201

So at last, Digen could address himself to the real problem. "A fireproof building going up like a torch; Joeslee appearing like some sort of special effect in a film; and Ercy going into suicide-abort when she wasn't even in transfer."

Grant, who had been slumped dejectedly in a chair, looked up with a haunted expression. "And a man died in that fire."

"Yes." And he began at last to come to grips with it all. "Wasn't there a flood the day of Joeslee's changeover—and that's when they tried to burn her alive as a witch? And you arrived in a flood very much like this one. Hal—is it possible that Joeslee really is a witch? That's what they call someone who can violate natural law."

He was saying the words, but inside he shrank from the thought. *If that happened, nothing is real.*

Sensitive to Digen's horror, Grant sat up straight, his nager clearing until the room was crystalline. "If what we saw happen—really happened—then it wasn't in violation of natural law, it was the operation of some principle we don't understand."

Digen sat down across from Grant, knees suddenly weak. "Whatever's going on, Ercy's at the center of it. And you know a lot more about this than you're letting on."

"If I gave you some advice—based on information not available to you—would you take it?"

"Let's hear it."

"You'll have to remove Ercy's anti-kill conditioning. And it will have to be done before her next transfer or she'll suicide-abort again—and die."

"What!" said Digen in utter dismay. "That conditioning is permanent. Sometimes it fails—but nobody knows how to remove it."

Grant looked at him as if confronting his own executioner.

Digen said, "It's your oath of secrecy, isn't it?"

Grant nodded, tension drawn out to a singing note. The inward conflict wrenched at Digen until suddenly something gave way. Crystalline peace again filled the room, and there wasn't a trace of guilt as the Gen said, "I've handled this badly. I thought it would all stop with her conditioning, but it didn't. I was sure it was over when things quieted down after her fourth transfer and I finally got you to take me off her service. But that was a mistake, too. I cut off communication with her, and now because of that, a man is dead. I can't let this go on."

"I don't understand," said Digen. "I can see why you might think transfer will trigger that abort reflex again. As we saw

202 JACQUELINE LICHTENBERG

today, that conditioning is so sensitive that strong emotion alone triggered it.''

Grant shook his head. "The suicide-abort was triggered by the flow of selyn into what you call her junct pathways.''

"Transfer pathology is one of my specialties,'' answered Digen. "I think there's at least a good chance I can prevent Ercy from dying in suicide-abort if this incident has sensitized her.''

Grant had a hunted look about him, and then the peaceful resignation was back again. "With all respect, Sectuib Farris, she almost killed you when she grabbed on to your systems, accidentally causing that rockslide. If you try to override her abort reflex now, you'll both die, leaving Zeor without Sectuib and heir.''

"That's important to you?''

"Yes.''

"Why?''

"Because the Householdings preserve an ideal which is closer to my own than the Tecton's.''

Digen said, "I swear I will not discuss what you may reveal to me with anyone who is not a channel or Companion in Zeor, and I will use this information only as a last resort to save a life. This I swear Unto Zeor, Forever.''

"Considering the terms of my oath, that is no help at all. But I accept it. The moment I have dreaded has come. You must make a life-or-death decision for Ercy—and you will act mistakenly unless I can convince you.''

"To remove her anti-kill conditioning? Hal, that's just not possible.''

"It *is* possible. Let me do it for her,'' pleaded Grant.

"I wish I could trust you to do that, but, Hal, you've said yourself your training is incomplete. It's my daughter's life at stake.''

"More than that,'' said Grant, the hunted look back again.

"Let me get us some trin tea,'' offered Digen. When he returned, the Gen had collected himself, ready to talk.

Speaking in that slow manner that characterized him, Grant said, "It has been theorized that eventually, among channels, there would emerge those who have the selyn field control and perceptivity of the channel together with the talent for—controlling selyn flux through the 'junct pathways' to do the kinds of things you attribute to witchcraft. Seeing the future. Seeing and knowing things happening far away. Moving objects by thought alone.

MAHOGANY TRINROSE 203

Setting fires by thought alone. We call the channel who has all these talents the Fully Endowed.

"As far as I know, until Ercy, such a person has never appeared, unless they, like she, were lost to the Tecton's anti-kill conditioning—as we saw today."

"Wait a minute. She never did anything—supernatural—before today!"

"How could you have missed the poltergeist! It wasn't serious until she destroyed Howard Hall. That was the biggest, except for the rockslide—I should have done something then—and now that Gen is dead, and it's my responsibility."

"You didn't set that fire."

"But I cut myself off from Ercy, so I didn't realize she was still dangerously active. Now she's discovered some of the esper functionals she can do using Joeslee. She lost control of the experiment she was doing, probably because of her anti-kill conditioning, and *whoof!* up went the fireproof building.

"When she teleported Joeslee out of the building, she used me. I've been trained for it, but I couldn't prevent her abort. And there's only one thing I know for sure. There's a big difference between doing sensory-mode things like she was doing before, unconscious poltergeist functions, and deliberate power functionals like teleportation, telekinesis, and pyrotics. Those require the full controlled use of what you term the junct pathways. Only channels can develop such control."

"Why can't we explain this to her, teach her to control it?"

"We can—after the anti-kill conditioning is removed."

Digen wasn't sure he believed any of this. But he wondered if he dared disbelieve it. "You said you know a way to remove her conditioning."

Grant sighed, sipping his tea. "This is the issue over which I left the Company. You see, there is a medication which we make and use which would radically transform the Tecton in a decade— if the Company let it be known to you. I thought you should not be treated as children, protected from dangerous knowledge for your own good.

"Only now that I've seen more of the Tecton—I've decided the Company may have been right to withhold the knowledge of this drug. So just let me use it on Ercy. I know how to manage it safely."

Digen shook his head. "There's no drug that can affect a channel's conditioning. I know what I'm talking about—it's my field. Only one thing I know of can actually break the conditioning—what happened with me when I was doing surgery—repeated exposure to Gen pain coupled with extreme transfer deprivation and an irresistible offer of a junct transfer. You'll have to go some to convince me that any drug can possibly obliterate the conditioning.''

''We call it moondrop. You know it under the gypsy name—kerduvon.''

Chapter 19

Erasure, Hal had called it.

Ercy stood by her window, looking down at her garden. Soon they'd be coming for her. Below, the bare stems of the grafted perennial trinroses held her gaze. They had bloomed mahogany. She would have cut them herself, would have processed them clumsily according to her own theories. Instead, while she was still bleary from the aftereffects of the fire, she had given Hal permission to cut them and make kerduvon—to be used on her, not on her father.

So much for wishes.

Hal had refused to verify her own theory of how the flowers should be processed. Her notes had been burned up with the dorm building. She had sacrificed them to save a man's life. Now she wondered if she'd done the right thing.

They're going to make me junct.

She tore herself from the window and paced the room. Need grabbed at the edges of her control. But another sensation demanded even more urgently that she do something—anything. She knew it now for the—need—there was no other word—to use her endowment, as Hal termed it.

They had made Joeslee leave her during this time, afraid perhaps that they'd succumb to the lure of their new functional and kill themselves or destroy all of Rialite by accident.

She paced for a while, feeling a growing desire to talk to someone—anyone. *I won't do this—I can't—I won't.*

Grant's crystal nager filled the room, and after a silent pause, the door opened.

"It's time?" asked Ercy.

"Not until you're ready. This can't be done Tecton style, by the clock."

Bitterly, Ercy spat words she regretted as she said them. "Doesn't the exact position of the moon count?"

"Not as much as your condition."

206 JACQUELINE LICHTENBERG

"I'm not ready. And I never will be." She flung herself down on her bed. Grant started toward her, and she said, "No! Don't!"

Grant sat down on Joeslee's bed, deliberately keeping his distance. His nager closed up around him like a glass cocoon. It was almost like talking over the intercom instead of in person.

"You're right to have misgivings, Ercy. This will be permanent. You will have to learn to live with it."

She looked him in the eye. "I refuse to learn to live with it. I choose to die—now—instead."

"In suicide-abort?"

"I've nothing to live for—have I?"

"Zeor," he said quietly.

"It's for Zeor I'm doing it. And for the Tecton. What could we do with another juncted Sectuib?"

"You mean what would your life be worth to you—as a junct?" She flinched at that, and he added, "Perhaps I'm wrong—but I thought Zeor still practiced the Reception."

Ercy started. "How do you know about—"

"History shows that in those Houses which practice Reception, the death of the Sectuib without heir is invariably followed within twenty years by the dissolution of the House. Ercy, if you have Received this House, then its life depends on you. Perhaps the time is right for the value of excellence to perish from human awareness. It's not my responsibility to judge that. Nor, I think, is it yours, despite your being the Sectuib of the House of Excellence."

Ercy sighed heavily. "Now I know what House you belong to—the House of Responsibility."

Grant laughed—the spontaneous and uninhibited laughter of his carefree moments. Ercy watched him, bewildered.

"No," said Grant. "I belong to no House. It's true, though, responsibility does seem to dominate my every move and thought lately."

Ercy remembered her father's guess that Hal was saving her life by violating an oath that could cost him his life. She felt her resolve to die slipping away.

"How did you get Dad to agree to this? He's always been so fanatical about Tecton law—ever since—since Ilyana."

"I don't know—Ercy, we talked for nearly five hours, ranged through all of philosophy. He simply came to the realization that this was something he had to do—regardless of the consequences. There are things like that in life, you know."

MAHOGANY TRINROSE 207

"What would you and he have done if I'd refused to let you use my trinroses?"

"I don't know. But I wouldn't have taken them without your consent, whatever the consequences."

"And it would all be on my conscience—even into my next life."

Grant looked at her, startled.

Ercy shrugged. "It's just a theory I stumbled across. I thought you'd know all about it—it explains an awful lot with one elegant postulate called karma. It explains how come good people suffer and bad people get rich. It even explains how some people are born with a sort of compelling knowledge—like me and the mahogany trinrose. I have a new theory—want to hear it?"

"Why not?"

"I had a dream—one of *those* dreams—like the one Joeslee says is a memory of a past life where you stabbed me to death and she just watched. I dreamed I was Wyner, holding my father's hand—I mean, my little brother Digen's hand—as he was about to receive Zeor as I had, only from my father Orim. I dreamed it was my fault Digen had gone junct with Ilyana. Then the dream ended, and I never figured out how it could be my fault."

"And your theory?"

"I think I was Wyner Liu Farris, in my last life."

"Even if it's true—it doesn't matter."

"I think it matters. All my life I've been dedicated to saving my father, to preserving Zeor and the Tecton. If that is from a decision made in a past life, according to the theory of karma I can still unmake that decision now. But, Hal, I'd rather die than go junct. And without the conditioning, there's nothing to prevent the kill."

"Ercy, your free will is your only protection against—anything—and if it's not exercised daily, it won't be strong on your day of trial and it will fail you. Tecton conditioning cripples the will. And some say the honing of the will is the purpose of life."

At that point, Ercy was struck by how terrified she was of going junct—killing. *I believe that I really want to kill!*

The mystique of the kill was an incredible lure to any Sime—but especially to the channel, the only Sime in modern civilization who was permitted to feel need and to know Gen transfer.

"Ercy, what's the matter?" Grant had moved to sit beside her, one Gen hand resting across her wrists, fingertips just grazing her lateral orifices.

Trembling, she rested against him until her heart stopped

208 JACQUELINE LICHTENBERG

pounding. "I'm just so scared, Hal, scared I'm going to go junct killing you. What's to keep me from it?"

"Your naked will—and mine." His hand found its place across her wrists again, his fingers gentle on her lateral orifices, which were damp with ronaplin as her need grew under his touch.

With his other hand, Grant pulled a thong over his head and extracted a medallion from where it nestled inside his shirt. It was the starred cross Ercy had found in his desk. He looped it around her neck. "I want you to have this, Ercy. It belonged to my many-times-great-grandmother."

"Oh, Hal, no . . ."

"I should have given it to you a long time ago."

As she touched it, a hazy vision of the valley rose around her. She could shut it aside now, though. That much control she had learned. But even so, the feel of the valley was with her, a whole chord of orchestrated feelings that said: *home*.

"This," said Grant, touching the starred cross with its gleaming jewels, "can help you not-kill, just as it can protect a Gen, because it stands for the human will united to the balance of nature which is the harmony between Sime and Gen."

They sat silently for a while, and then Ercy found herself walking with Grant, out of her room and across the private apartment to the room rigged for this special transfer with heavy black curtains and layers and layers of foam-rubber baffles until it was anechoic and dark as well as selyn-insulated.

She roused only when Grant brought the little vial of the drug, kerduvon, or moondrop as he called it. It was a lighter brown oil than she had produced. But it smelled the same and had the same oily consistency. It even tasted the same. *They could have used mine*.

She had meant to make kerduvon for her father—to *dis*junct him. And here she was about to use it to become junct. There was hysterical laughter somewhere inside her, but humorless need commanded her now.

Grant handed her a small glass of liquid, holding one for himself, motioning for her to swallow the dose. She upended the glass and drained it, feeling a languid warmth spread over her need.

Draining his own glass, he said, "We'll share this experience— as we did at First Transfer—and afterward, we'll both return to our ground state—perfect normal health. You'll find that you'll be able to take your transfers without difficulty, and all of your

MAHOGANY TRINROSE 209

selyn flows will be smooth and unobstructed and will remain that way, perfectly balanced, and responsive to your will. You may dream—but nothing will happen in your dreams that you do not desire to happen. You are safe. I am safe. We are safe.'' His voice trailed off.

The lights went off and silence descended. In the absolute dark, there was only Grant's quiet nager, all cascading rainbows of crystal dancing in the mists. They filtered into her cells and dissolved her in stillness.

In the distance, behind transparent satin, Grant's starred cross caught the ruddy light of the rising sun. Closer to her, her own tentacles held the graceful stem of a mahogany trinrose while the tips of her fingers caressed the velvet brown petals.

With the glowing mahogany rose held up before her like a candle, she advanced through a door and stood in a field of blooming clover, confronting her mother, who sat on the bank of a stream, her nager a flaming emerald calix about her whole body, which was swollen in pregnancy, rippling in labor.

A glittering green translucent wall framed another doorway, through which Ercy passed. She was naked, her bare feet on a glassy green flooring. At the top of a waterfall, her father and Im'ran stood back to back, carved out of solid nager, two pillars supporting a chain of circular emerald links.

She knew she would stop between the two pillars, raise her arms, and take down that chain—and she was pierced with shattering terror.

But she did not want to resist the playing out of the inevitable. Only this time—she knew what it meant.

She moved between the pillars, feeling the nageric tension ripping at her.

With the greatest effort she had ever put forth, she lifted down the chain, which had the inertia of thousands of tons of matter— the substance of the entire universe. She expended every last dynopter of selyn in her nerves to find the strength to complete her task of dragging that chain down from its place. She wrapped it about her waist, and suddenly the tension field that had held her broke open, spilling her into a rose arbor bridging a lake.

Overhead, the night sky was lit by a green sliver of moon, but she was not cold, nor—despite her depleted state—was she in need. Her chain belt protected and strengthened her. Across the lake, Joeslee beckoned. Joeslee, too, showed selyn depletion. She carried a heavily carved staff made of opal surmounted by a

210 JACQUELINE LICHTENBERG

globe of pure yellow light that attracted the mahogany trinrose Ercy still held raised before her like a candle.

Ercy advanced, and perceived within the yellow globe of Joeslee's staff an image—her mother left far behind in the clover, giving birth—*to me,* Ercy thought.

She reached upward and touched her rose to the globe of pale yellow light. The globe burst open like a doorway, and she was swept into it by the rose she held. From her feet, stretching out in every direction, rays of rainbow light formed a fan. She chose the central, green ray at her feet and walked it.

It narrowed rapidly until she walked a spun emerald wire across a black abyss. Above her, a shadowy blue moon cast a spot of light onto the emerald thread she balanced on. As the blue light fell upon her, she felt for an instant that she stood at the apex of the universe.

All about her stretched sand dunes, of transparent yellow satin. To her left, in the distance, was an oasis. Between two palm trees hung a shimmering blue veil decorated with scintillating starred crosses. Before the veil sat a woman shrouded in blue robes, decorated with the stylized Zeor symbol that looked so much like a dagger. She held a laboratory notebook out to Ercy, beckoning and saying, "Here. This way. It's a shortcut."

Ercy looked at the narrowing emerald thread under her feet, the abyss beneath. The thread sagged under the weight of the belt she wore. It stretched into the distance with no end in sight. The shortcut looked so tempting. She could go that way.

To her right appeared a high range of mountains. A well-trodden path led off into the mountains, a wide, secure path.

Guarding the path, facing away from each other, stood the ebony figures of her fathers, forming the gateway to safety. She could put her emerald belt back upon their heads and go home to become Sectuib.

And in sudden déjà vu, she knew that once she had come out on that wide path and leaped over the green thread to attempt the shortcut. She had failed. Hurt and suffering, she had returned in anguish along the safe road. She had never before attempted the green road. There was only one way onto the green road—the way she had come. There was only one way off—straight ahead.

She took another step forward, edging out of the shadow-blue circle of light from above and losing the clarity of her knowledge. The green thread sagged under her, stretching. Gripping her courage, she took another step, plunging at once into darkness.

Alarmed, she stood still, but she could feel the thread beneath

MAHOGANY TRINROSE   211

her stretching and sagging, letting her down, down into alone-
ness. Behind her, she heard Joeslee yelling, "Run, Ercy, run!
Hurry!"

She could not see. She could not zlin. But she could feel the
thread cutting into the soles of her feet, and she edged another bit
forward, telling herself that her trained relaxation was her only
weapon here. She advanced, her breath steady, relaxed.

And suddenly, the sun rose.

Before her, in a halo of bright pearl sunlight, stood Halimer
Grant. He wore a pearl-white robe, too bright to look at, and had
grown a beard, but she knew him.

"Stop!" he called to her. "You must cast off your belt or the
weight will break the strand. This is your last chance. Cast off
the chain, Ercy."

She dropped her hand to the belt, feeling its glassy substance.
She could not cast off the belt. It was her protection against need;
it was her strength; it was her life. She—could—not . . . To
keep her balance, she had to edge forward a little, and the thread
sagged alarmingly.

"Cast it off, Ercy, and come to me . . ."

The brightness ahead hurt her eyes, but it warmed her, and she
felt herself pulled onward.

"Ercy, no! You can't come like that. Bring no protection here,
for you are your own protection."

She held the mahogany trinrose tightly clutched in one tentacle
and bent both hands to the belt. But the rings would not part and
free her for the long journey ahead.

Defeated by her fears, she raised her eyes to where Grant stood
beckoning her onward. All at once, as her eyes came to the
brightness behind him, she was filled with a paralyzing wave of
pure awe. She could not breathe.

And then Grant's shadow fell over her, cutting off the impossible radiance, and she could breathe. Through a hidden door,
opened within her by the shock of awe, came a goldenness that
spread outward all around, even a little way into the darkness
beneath her feet, and everywhere it touched there was beauty.
She was the gateway through which poured a golden current of
high-voltage love.

She started to turn to look back, to see if the beauty also
existed behind her, if perhaps she had come far enough and could
now go safely back.

"Ercy, no! You can't go back. Trust me. Cast off the belt and
come to me."

212 JACQUELINE LICHTENBERG

Of all the paths open to her, only the one straight ahead held any hope. She ripped apart the linked circles and cast the belt aside.

In two secure steps she flung herself into Grant's arms, relief and exultation, triumph and a trembling awe, all seizing her at once.

Free.

Great golden rushing currents suffused her cold, aching blackness in perfect flowing streams. Satisfied. Safe.

The fifth contact point, lip to lip, parted. At first she thought that hours and hours had passed, but her time sense telescoped into focus under Grant's sure touch and she knew it had been less than an hour. She lay back and let herself come to. The silent, black room around her was filled with Grant's now subdued crystal nager, her own blazing forth over his.

She said, "You didn't tell me what hallucinations that stuff causes!" But it came out a weak, trembling whisper.

"How do you feel?" he asked, in a similar whisper.

There was a sharp, strong current in what she had come to know as her junct pathways, and the ever-nagging itch to do power functionals was gone. "Junct," she answered. "I guess I'm junct." It still held a horror for her, but she thought she might learn to live with it.

"Well," he said, "I'm alive." He seemed only a little surprised. "You didn't kill, Ercy, and you never will unless you choose to."

She thought of the stretching green thread over the black canyon and raised one hand to his face. "You have no beard."

He avoided her touch. "I'll get Tziel."

She sat up as he moved. "Who's he?"

"Your assignee. You're still a student, Ercy, in spite of everything, and Rialite does have its rules."

She came down to reality with a thud.

Chapter 20

"Ercy?"

Joeslee was sitting up, sleepily spilling a newspaper onto the floor, as Ercy came into the room they shared once again. "Yes, it's me."

From her bed, Joeslee asked, "They did it to you?"

"Can't you tell?" She couldn't keep the bitterness out of her voice.

"You know I'm not very sensitive, Ercy. You seem the same to me."

"It feels like a huge, ugly scar disfiguring my whole body."

Joeslee came over to her on bare feet. "But your transfer went all right?"

"Sure, no trouble. Hal is always perfect."

"But now you're disqualified as a Tecton channel."

Ercy turned away. "That was cruel."

"I didn't mean it to be. It's just that now," she said, grabbing up a folded page of the paper, "they'll surely brand us witches or worse and kill us." She handed the article to Ercy. Ercy read the article. The gypsies her father had rescued and been forced to turn over to the Gens in Carlston for trial had been convicted and executed.

Ercy shook her head, wiping away tears. "I'd like to think we could run away but we've got to face reality."

Joeslee said, "Whatever you decide, I'll stay with you." Joeslee's quiet statement of loyalty relaxed the last knot of tension in her. She had one friend, anyway. No matter what.

As Joeslee curled up to sleep—she always seemed to sleep well—Ercy propped herself up in one corner of her bed to try to do some hard thinking. But it wasn't long before she slid down and drifted into a light doze, the starred cross Grant had given her caught in her fingers and tentacles.

* * *

214 JACQUELINE LICHTENBERG

"Events have now converged. One way or another you must be out of there before Rellow gets to Digen. Now, are you prepared to show cause why you should not be put to the test for betraying your obligation of secrecy?"

She was seated against a rough old tree trunk, her legs stretched out into soft grass. The trees formed a dark wall, an unnaturally perfect circle. In the center of the circle was a round pond edged with a perfectly circular mound of earth. The water was mirror smooth, reflecting the man who stood on a tiny pedestal in the center of the pond, barely room for his feet to find purchase.

He stood perfectly balanced while before him, arrayed in a semicircle, were nine heavily robed men and women, Sime and Gen. All were dressed in the emerald-green robes, the flashing jewels on their chests. Lazily, Ercy recognized Halimer Grant on the pedestal.

"I did not tell Ercy Farris how to grow the mahogany trinroses. I will admit I did nothing to lead her away from the method. I did not want to be a causative factor in her life, but that may have been my mistake.

"Events converged to lead me to break my obligation of secrecy, but I did so with great care, having learned from Ercy Farris and Joeslee Teel Tigue that our secrets keep themselves.

"Our oath of secrecy is not the vow to prevent a natural course of events. It does not dam up the stream of truth, as I once thought. Rather it impels us to respond when someone comes to us, seeking the answers we have formulated and tested. The teacher does not choose the student; the student chooses the teacher, and the oath of secrecy obligates the teacher so petitioned to respond as best he can.

"This is what I could not grasp until Ercy, experimenting with the power functionals—and as I demonstrated earlier, she is the Fully Endowed—burned down a building, causing a man's death and nearly killing herself, merely because I had not responded when she came to me seeking knowledge about the strange things that were happening to her. I thought the obligation of secrecy prevented me from answering, forever.

"Now I know that had I completed my training before setting forth, I would have been free to give her the theory that would have prevented her from attempting that power functional during such a storm. So I respectfully petition to return to the School of Rathor, renewing my vow of secrecy, to complete my training."

The robed figures murmured among themselves, Ercy catching only a phrase or two. Her eyes were riveted on Grant's figure,

MAHOGANY TRINROSE 215

poised in perfect balance, his feet bound to the pedestal by chains circling his ankles.

"Are you prepared for the test?" asked one of the judges.

"I forfeit this life to the holder of my oath without regret. If my forfeit should be accepted, please remember I consider it a lesser price than I would have paid had I failed to provide kerduvon for the Fully Endowed."

One of the robed figures bent for a moment, and suddenly the pedestal plunged straight down into the water, pulling Grant under so swiftly he was gone before she could blink. She lunged to her feet, rushing to the pond to stare into its dark surface. But there was no sign whatever of Grant or the pedestal.

She turned on the executioners. "You've murdered him!" And at that moment, she would gladly have murdered them.

"It's Ercy Farris!"

"But I set the wards myself!"

"Who could ward the Endowed?"

"You've got to stop this!" cried Ercy. "Get him out of there. Take me instead. It was all my fault—I'm the one who should die."

"How long has she been here?"

In anguished frustration, Ercy turned toward the well, searching for sign of Grant, but there wasn't even a bubble to show where he'd been. She would have to dive in after him.

"Stop her!"

Suddenly the robed figures stood arrayed before her, blocking her path to the well.

"You have seen, but you have not understood. We have not harmed Halimer Grant."

"You mean none of this is real?" *Then I've got to wake up and find Hal.*

"She's fading!"

"Don't let her go . . ."

On the other side of the clearing, behind where the executioners had been standing, there was a watery noise, and Ercy turned to see Grant shooting up out of the ground, borne on a plume of water. Then he fell back with a splash. Running toward him, Ercy realized this must be another well connected by an underground tunnel to the one they had tried to drown him in.

As two of the robed figures reached to pull Grant out of the water, he scrambled to his feet. "Ercy!"

"She broke through the wards."

Grant placed his fingers around the base of her neck and lifted

216 JACQUELINE LICHTENBERG

the starred cross he had given her for all to see. "It's my fault. This was mine—I gave it to her." He let it fall, gave her one last squeeze, and set her aside.

One of the heavily cowled figures stepped forward. "Incidentally, Hal, welcome back to Rathor—to stay, I hope."

"Thank you, Dad." He looked at Ercy, his pale hair plastered around his skull, his pants and shirt dripping. "I'll stay—if Ercy will. You'll come home with me, won't you?"

"Will you teach me not to do any more harm with my—endowment?"

Grant looked at those around them. "I can't yet—but there are those among us who can."

"We would treasure the opportunity," said one of the women.

Another said, "The Tecton believes you're now junct, and a witch, but we know your condition is the normal one for a channel. And there are Gens here who can match you and work with your endowment. Let us welcome you—come to us, Ercy."

"I can't go without Joeslee!"

"The gypsy whose tribe died protecting our travelers? We owe her a place among us."

"Then bring her, too, and be welcome to the Company."

Ercy looked about in sudden confusion. "I'm not really here . . . how am I going to get here?" Her positional sense told her she was still on her bed—*here* was at her bed, but it wasn't. "Where are we?" And panic blossomed. "Hal! Hal?"

He took her by the shoulders, and she felt safer even though she couldn't zlin his nager. "Ercy, this is a real place. But physically, you and I are still at Rialite. To come here, we must go back to Rialite and take horses to ride out into the desert and up into the mountains. There, people will meet us and return the horses to Rialite. But we'll have to make it on our own that far—the three of us."

Chapter 21

"After what she went through, she must still be sleeping, Digen," said Sels, his tense frustration evident.

"If we're going to stay in step with her," said Im'ran, "we'd better get on with this transfer."

Digen paced up and down the center of the transfer suite. "I don't like being way over here while she's at the Controller's Residence."

"Well, then, let's get this over with and go back there," suggested Bett.

Digen paced. "I don't want a Big Sister just now." It came out a little more tartly than he'd meant, and he added, "I know you're right, of course." *Ercy's junct. Where in all the world can she find a place? And who will be Sectuib in her House?* He halted and looked at Bett, then went hyperconscious to zlin her speculatively, letting his need rise into his awareness as her replete selyn fields penetrated him.

Perhaps they could try the double-breakstep now?

Digen drifted toward Bett, aware at the same time of the cautious way Im'ran approached Sels. They'd been working toward this for months, conditioning themselves to endure it even during the hysteria of hard need. They had had the largest transfer room appointed to accommodate the four of them in comfort so they could take their transfers together.

As Digen focused deep into Bett's fields, drawn to her despite his trembling awareness of Im'ran, he found he could keep his reflexes from closing him away from her. Even when he knew her hands were on his arms, his laterals tentatively flicking into contact with her skin, he was able to hold to her. *I could do it with her. I can.*

Sels jerked away from Im'ran with a cry.

Searing pain ripped through Digen, flinging him away from the promise of selyn. Gasping, he curled in on himself, rolling on

218 JACQUELINE LICHTENBERG

the floor until he fetched up against a chair leg. Then Im'ran was there, cooling, soothing, calming.

"I couldn't hold to him, Digen. It was my fault. Here, come on, let me . . ."

But Digen was still fighting for inner equilibrium, half aware of Sels and Bett poised at the brink of transfer.

"I'm sorry, Digen," said Sels, relinquishing contact with Bett, without taking the transfer he craved.

"My fault," said Digen, letting Im'ran help him to his feet. But he couldn't stand long, and sought the contour lounge, Im'ran sinking down to sit beside him. "Bett, do something for Sels!"

Bett guided Sels firmly to their own lounge and made him sit while she ran her fingertips expertly over his face and neck, down his back and arms, until the vibrant tension drained away.

"We got closer that time than ever before," said Im'ran.

"But it's too soon," said Digen.

"You almost made it that time, Digen," said Sels. "If Im' and I hadn't broken, it would have worked. You two are ready—we're not."

Im'ran sat silently, but he made no effort to hide his sense of inadequacy. "You're good," said Sels to Im'ran. "It's no disgrace not to be able to compete with Bett for me."

"I think that's the problem," said Im'ran. "I'd still rather compete with Bett for *Digen,* while competing with any Donor goes so much against my early training . . ."

"Im'," Digen said, "it's not just you. We're all having the same problem. Let's not give up in sight of our goal. Now, let's go find out what's been happening this last half hour, and when we've collected our wits, we'll do the transfer the way we did last month. We're trying to build endurance, remember, not destroy our will to live."

As they crossed the rotunda toward the Controller's Residence, a helicopter circled into the landing pad, triggering the automatic lights and alarms. Zlinning, Digen said, "It can't be Rellow! He's supposed to be teaching with Landar—"

Sels said, "But it is him, and with five—no, six—"

"Seven, counting the pilot," concluded Digen.

As the copter touched down, Rellow leaped from the door and trotted toward Digen's little group followed by several other Simes and Gens.

Digen waited for Rellow's group to gather themselves. He recognized several of them as members of the World Controller's

MAHOGANY TRINROSE   219

staff. At least one of the Gens was a First Companion in another Householding, but Digen couldn't remember which one.

When the group had gathered, Rellow said, "Controller Farris, perhaps we should step into your office."

Controller Farris? Has he resigned from Zeor?

"I didn't notice your appointment on my calendar," said Digen formally. "My secretary should be able to arrange a comfortable place for you to wait. I may have some time free around midnight."

Digen began to turn away, leaving Rellow speechless, when one of the Simes stepped forward to walk beside Digen, speaking softly and politely.

"Sectuib Farris, we have come on a matter of such grave consequence that none of us will rest a moment until we hear your refutations."

Digen didn't slow his step. "If it's such an important matter, it should wait until I've had my transfer and can devote my whole attention to it."

The Sime's attention darted to Im'ran for a moment. "I believe you'd prefer to sweep this matter aside so that you'll have the whole night clear before you. I assure you, we don't seek to place you at an intolerable disadvantage . . ."

But Rellow does . . . There was something familiar about this very persuasive gentleman. "May I ask your name?"

As if surprised at the question, the Sime replied, "Destar Jiplain."

First Assistant World Controller! Now Digen recognized him from hundreds of magazine photographs and speeches. Inwardly, he groaned. There was no way he could put this off.

"My apologies. Your pictures don't do your nager justice, Hajene Jiplain." Digen singled out Sels from the crowd. "Would you have conference room four readied immediately, Sels, and join us there. Bett, please show our guests to the visitors' lounge, where they can refresh themselves. I see that some of you carry recording equipment . . ."

"Yes," said Rellow, "this is being covered by Foresearch Media and Two Territories Intercontinental. Everything—"

"Yes, Rellow has been quite efficient," said Jiplain, cutting smoothly across the younger channel's belligerent tone. "But it shouldn't take long to dispense with the whole affair."

"I confess I'm very curious, Hajene Jiplain," said Digen, noticing the long microphones now pointing in his direction. "However, I do require at least a few moments with my Donor,

220 JACQUELINE LICHTENBERG

and then I'll join you all in conference room four. Rellow knows the way.''

When Digen arrived at the conference room, the microphones had been placed in the center of the long table and the cameras were on tripods in opposite corners of the room.

Digen took his place at one end of the table. Bett came up beside him as Sels arrived, followed by the rest of the delegation, and Im'ran.

Rellow began to take the chair at the other end of the table, but Jiplain smoothly diverted him into a conversation and assumed the other high-backed seat, opposite Digen. Rellow chose not to contest and took the next chair, zipping open his briefcase. He extracted a sheaf of papers resplendent with official seals.

"Now, I think we can get started," said Rellow.

Digen cut him off with a quick gesture as the cameras began to whir. "One moment, Hajene Farris. If you will all please introduce yourselves for my records, we can then proceed." He pressed a switch set into the tabletop before him and a camera descended from the ceiling and began rotating to pick up each place around the table. Digen nodded to Im'ran on his left, who said, "I am Imrahan ambrov Zeor, First Companion in Zeor and Chief Donor of Rialite."

Cooperatively, the man to Im'ran's left, the Gen reporter from TTI Digen had spotted as a Householder, said, "Adenire ambrov Imokalee, First Companion in Imokalee and currently employed by Two Territories Intercontinental. Respect, Sectuib, from House of Imokalee."

Imokalee? Ah, the citrus growers! "House of Zeor offers respect to House of Imokalee."

To Adenire's left sat a short, blond Sime woman who said, "I'm Inia ambrov Narthex, Associate Secretary of the Householding Board of Governors. Respect, Sectuib."

But Digen wasn't too sure to whom she had said it, himself or Rellow. He didn't want to imagine why she was here.

"House of Zeor extends respect to House of Narthex," said Digen.

"Destar Jiplain, First Assistant World Controller, no affiliation."

"House of Zeor offers full respect to the Tecton, Hajene Jiplain." Digen tried to make it sound casual, wondering if he'd done the right thing to put this on a formal Householding basis. He hadn't realized the others were all Householders.

"Rellow Farris, third channel in Zeor."

But Rellow wasn't third in Zeor anymore. He was fourth.

MAHOGANY TRINROSE 221

Digen passed his attention to the other Sime woman at the table, seated to Rellow's left.

"Nohevia ambrov Lizrin, Foresearch Media representative. Respect, Sectuib."

"House of Zeor extends respect to House of Lizrin."

"Sels Farris, channel in Zeor and the new Co-Dean of the college of channels here in Rialite."

"Bett Farris, Second Companion in Zeor, Assistant to the Chief Donor of Rialite."

Digen met Jiplain's eyes, and the other Sime took up the proceeding smoothly. "It's difficult to know how to conduct this interview since I believe it will come as a shock to you."

Rellow cut in. "It's not really news to him. Digen Ryan Farris, I have here a fully processed warrant for your recall as Sectuib in Zeor."

The words made no sense to Digen at first. The office of Sectuib was a matter internal to the Householding. But then he remembered some of the new laws that had recently been passed providing for the displacement of a Sectuib who was proven incompetent to manage the affairs of the House. As far as Digen knew, the law had never been invoked before and had never been tested in court.

"That," said Sels ferociously, "is utterly absurd."

His own son! "Take it easy, Sels."

Rellow again made as if to rise, but Jiplain abruptly took the document from Rellow and went toward Digen's end of the table. "As the only unaffiliated Tecton representative here, allow me to summarize the charges.

"Digen Farris has not taken a pledge transfer in well over twenty years and is therefore not an acting Sectuib.

"Under Section twenty-three of the Tecton Code, his junct condition makes him unfit to manage the affairs of a House.

"Digen Farris has no heir. His ex-heir is junct and proved to be a witch, meddling with forces which have once toppled civilization on this planet. Because of physical illness, Digen Farris is not likely ever to have another heir."

Digen listened in growing shock matched by the heavy grief in Jiplain's voice. How did Rellow know what they had just done to Ercy? He must have been preparing this for weeks—months . . .

". . . Farris has violated Tecton law and thus placed all of Zeor and everyone who depends on Zeor in jeopardy by:

"A. Employing at Rialite a Donor who is not pledged to the Tecton, Halimer Grant.

222 JACQUELINE LICHTENBERG

"B. Fostering and sheltering and encouraging witchcraft; documentation appended includes pictures and one example of a mahogany trinrose together with notebooks in Ercy Farris's handwriting delineating the particular witchery used to produce the flowers. These notebooks were exposed in Zeor private session and ignored by the membership hypnotized by Ercy Farris's unnatural persuasion.

"C. Allowing a continued rash of inexplicable happenings to plague Rialite even though they could be traced directly to Ercy Farris and the illegal employee, Halimer Grant. A list of seventeen fires, disappearances, accidents, and strange occurrences is appended with signed affidavits.

"D. Deliberately allowing Halimer Grant to remove the witch Ercy Farris's anti-kill conditioning with a drug made from the conjured blossoms.

"There's more, but if you can dispense with this, the rest of it won't stand up."

"These sweeping, complex charges," said Digen, "can't be dismissed with the wave of a tentacle. The list is so long that my need-fogged brain can't hold it all at once. Ercy and Halimer Grant should be brought in to confront the charges against them. And as for the list of strange fires and other occurrences, Hajene Mora ambrov Zeor, our Engineer, will have to advise me as to the facts of each case. This all will take some time—"

"You're not going to squirm out of this that easily!" shouted Rellow from the other end of the table. "And what about Joeslee's appearance—"

"Hajene, please," Jiplain interrupted him.

Digen replied, "I'd like to dispense with your charges in as orderly a fashion as they have been presented to me. Unfortunately, I've just been through an abort, and you caught me just minutes before we were scheduled for transfer.

"I beg your indulgence, and offer you all hospitality of Rialite while we attend to our necessities and assemble the involved parties."

Digen rose and, followed by Im'ran, Sels, and Bett, left the conference room via the private door to his own offices. The staff escorted the others to guest quarters in another wing of the building. Digen slammed the door of his office, shutting them off from the clamoring nager, and said, "Tell me it's just need—tell me it isn't as bad as it seems."

Bett sighed, clinging to Sels. "It's bad. That's why it seems bad, because it's bad. My own son . . ."

MAHOGANY TRINROSE   223

"He's my son, too," added Sels.

"If he gains control of Zeor, he could do a lot of damage to this world before the House dies."

"Yes," agreed Bett. "Digen, I've never seen you use need as an excuse before. Not ever."

"I couldn't think of any other legitimate way to gain some time," replied Digen, reaching for his phone. "Zeor has some good lawyers among the membership. I've got to find out whether Rellow can really do this."

"If Rellow is organizing it," said Sels, "you can bet it will be legal enough."

As he was waiting for the connection, Digen said, "Im'ran, go see if Ercy can come down and confront these people. If not, check her into the infirmary. I wouldn't want those reporters at her. Then find Hal and get him over here even if you have to drag him out of bed."

Im'ran started to go, but hesitated, frowning at Digen. "I don't want to leave you like this."

"I'm stable for the moment," said Digen, a little more briskly than he intended. "You've seen me do this for days on end when I had to. And I wouldn't send anyone else to Ercy now . . ."

Reluctantly, he left.

"Why doesn't she answer this phone!" said Digen. Then, leashing back his need-fueled temper, he said, "Sels, take Bett and find Mora. She went for transfer when we did. Don't page her, whatever you do. Maybe we can dispense with this whole thing quietly."

"I can't imagine how," said Sels, "but we'll try. Bett, you want to stay here with Digen?"

"No," said Digen as Bett began to nod. "Go on with Sels. Im'ran will be back soon, or Hal will show up."

Reluctantly, the two of them left just as someone answered the ringing at the other end of the phone. Digen turned his whole attention to the Gen woman who was Zeor's best lawyer.

Before long, Digen had set up a four-way conference call with two other law specialists of the House, and the argument was raging fiercely while Digen listened without real comprehension.

Suddenly, all the outside lights went on and loudspeakers called for the emergency squads to form at the motor pool garage for a desert search. *Not Joeslee again!* Then he remembered she had not willingly left Ercy's side for five minutes since the fire.

Hastily, he told the lawyers to continue their deliberations and

224 JACQUELINE LICHTENBERG

he'd call them back. Then he headed for Ercy's room. But he got as far as his office door and met Im'ran.

"What's going on?" demanded Digen.

"Ercy's *gone,* and so are Joeslee and Hal. Sels and Bett and Mora and I have checked all the likely places, even the Memorial. They aren't here, and three horses are missing from the stables. Ercy's desert gear is gone, and—"

"Gone?" Cold black shock washed through Digen for the second time that night, and a moment later he found himself sitting in his desk chair, Im'ran bent over him, worried.

"Digen, you ought to have transfer before tackling this."

"Not *now,*" said Digen. "We've got to find them before sunrise."

"I don't think any harm will come to them. Hal has spent a lot of time out in the desert, and Ercy was raised here. Joeslee isn't your average city-bred girl, either. Mora is supervising the dispersal of the search teams, and Sels and Bett have flown out to coordinate the desert search. I have your large copter on standby alert, and we'll fly right out when they locate them."

The phone rang, and Digen snatched it up. "Controller," Jiplain asked quietly, "could you perhaps tell us what the commotion is all about?"

"I would have thought Rellow would tell you. It's the Rialite Rescue Service assembling a search for lost faculty or students."

"I see," said Jiplain. "May I inquire who's lost?"

"Two students and one faculty member—it appears they've ridden horses out into the desert."

"Oh." Then Jiplain said in closing, "I hope the commotion didn't shen your transfer again, Hajene. I expect you'll have the situation under control soon. Shall we set our meeting time for nine in the morning?"

Six hours. Joeslee has managed to stay lost longer than that. "Could we make it ten, Hajene? My Engineer won't have time to pull those files for us until the search is concluded."

"I think that should be reasonable enough. Some of our party are Gen, after all, and do require a little more sleep. Do you suppose you could turn the loudspeakers off?"

"I'll see to it," promised Digen, and with all courtesy, cut the connection. He had no sooner set the phone down than it rang again. This time it was the TTI man asking permission to send his Sime cameraman along with one of the search copters.

"One moment," said Digen, and to Im'ran he said, with his hand over the phone, "Did you brief Mora on this situation?"

MAHOGANY TRINROSE   225

"Yes," answered Im'ran.

Digen went back to the phone. "Have your man ask for Hajene Mora ambrov Zeor. She'll find a copter for him to ride with."

A moment later, the Foresearch people called in with the same request, only it was the Sime woman reporter who wanted to go along with the search teams.

Digen replaced the phone. "If those reporters get with the lucky team—"

"They're responsible journalists, Digen. They won't jump to unwarranted conclusions."

"Ah, but the warranted conclusions are bad enough!" *Why are they running away?*

When Im'ran began nervously and insistently to press for transfer, Digen said, "All right, Im'. Call Mora and get her to tell Sels and Bett we're going, so they can come in as soon as possible."

By the time he and Im'ran had made their way back to the transfer suite, Digen was convinced that Im'ran was concealing from him the fact that Ercy had indeed been kidnapped. *By whom, how, and why?* It was a possibility every prominent family lived with. But it would take a very unusual kidnapper to be able to hold Ercy Farris for long. *Hal? Nonsense.*

He let the niggling thought surface. *Suppose she's dead. Suppose the kidnappers have killed her? Then what of Zeor?* So many years he had been counting on Ercy to get him out of the job he'd never wanted in the first place that he found it impossible to consider a world without Ercy. If she were dead, a great hunk of himself would go black and never light up again. As a youth, he had fathered several children who had died young, and the loss, though far away in time, was still an ever-present pain. Yet he had hardly known those children.

When Im'ran finally settled down next to him, Digen asked, "What do you know about Ercy that you haven't told me?"

"Digen—"

"Was she kidnapped? Was there a ransom note?"

"No, Digen, nothing like that."

"Im', if Ercy's dead—then you and I must complete this disjunction now—tonight—if it kills me. Zeor depends on it. Zeor must have a proper—functioning—legal Sectuib. The lawyers all agreed that was the only serious charge Rellow had. Without that, my actions regarding the rest would be above

226 JACQUELINE LICHTENBERG

reproach. My condition casts doubt on my judgment about everything—''

Tense and grave, Im'ran sat with his hands between his knees, inspecting the floor. ''Ercy is junct, too, but without the option of ever disjuncting. ''

''According to Hal—but we don't know that for sure. Everything depends on me now—I've got to be able to hold Zeor for her until she can serve, or until another heir can be found to displace Rellow. Either way—it all depends on me—and it has to be done tonight.''

''What if it does kill you?''

''Zeor won't be any worse off. Im', don't you realize I'm about to become the first Sectuib ever to be deposed by a non-Householding law? What of Zeor if I should fight it in the courts—a junct fighting to be Sectuib? Better to die in a disjunction attempt.''

''The House will never accept Rellow, no matter what. But they accept you, Digen. The membership won't let this happen.''

''I don't think they'll be able to stop it short of disbanding the House. My physicians may not understand what's kept me alive all these years—but I do. Im', I must—and I will—preserve Zeor to give it to Ercy.''

''Yes—I guess so.''

''Now, will you tell me—whatever it is?''

''Ercy didn't just leave, Digen, she left a note, on your bed where no one else would find it. I saw it when I was looking for Mora, after I couldn't find Ercy.''

He pulled a much-folded piece of notebook paper out of his back pocket and handed it to Digen.

Dear Mom, Dad, and Im',

I'm not running away. I don't think you'll understand or believe this, but I've come to know that I've finished here at Rialite. Zeor will always remain the central point of my existence, but I am content to remain second under the rightful Sectuib, Digen Ryan Farris.

There's no place for me now in the Tecton, and I'm just a liability to Zeor. So I'm going where I have things to learn and things to do. Think of it the way out-Territory families think of their children who turn out Sime and have to go live in-Territory.

Unto Zeor, Forever
Aild Ercy Farris

MAHOGANY TRINROSE 227

P.S.: Here is all the rest of the kerduvon. Hal says if Dad and Im'ran use it together, they should be able to complete the disjunction without any trouble. Don't be afraid—the dreams may be kinda wild under kerduvon, but the transfer afterwards is great!

Digen read it over and over. Her childish scrawl had become a rounded, disciplined handwriting. It seemed she had not been under undue stress while writing the note, but it didn't make much sense.

"Where in the world does she think she can go where the Tecton isn't?"

"Wherever it was Hal came from, maybe?"

Digen thought: *Yes, off to learn his secrets. She'll come back. I did.* "Kerduvon?" asked Digen, aloud.

"There was a little bottle of it with the note. I put it in a safe place."

Digen thought of all the things Hal had told him about the drug. "It would increase the odds in our favor."

"Digen, you aren't thinking seriously of . . ."

"Ercy survived it."

"Hal knew what he was doing. I don't."

Digen put one hand over Im'ran's fingers, the contact opening his need afresh. "You have all the skills I've ever needed. All right, it's a nasty thing to do to you—asking you to perform the act that may kill your own orhuen mate. Making it your Sectuib's order just makes it worse—but we're going to do this tonight, and we're going to succeed or die trying. Or isn't your House worth your life?"

"But it wouldn't be worth surviving your death."

"Neither of us will survive the other by long. We've known that for years and years."

They went back to the darkened chamber in the Controller's Residence and Im'ran produced the vial of kerduvon that Ercy had left. It had her laboratory label on it. It was just enough for two doses, according to what Digen remembered.

With great, long hesitations and a sense of a deliberate choice, the kind a junct had to make in order to disjunct, Digen took the dose.

Waiting for the drug to act, Digen was aware of Im'ran beside him in the utter darkness, the total silence. The last waking awareness Digen had was of Im'ran downing the drug with an aura of heavy fatalism masking a very real dread.

228 JACQUELINE LICHTENBERG

Digen's whole body came apart into tiny hard bits of spinning awareness; one at each shoulder, one at each knee, one outside each ear, one between his heels, one at the groin, one centered at the vriamic node, and one which was his eyes, though it seemed to float several inches beyond the top of his skull.

Well, this wasn't such a terrible dream, he thought fuzzily, and decided just to wait. Before long, the spinning bits began to expand, rising like yeast bread. He was a pan of baking rolls in an oven, rising, rising. His substance became spongy, filled with myriads of little holes through which hot air (selyn?) circulated and expanded, driving him to expand even further. The rolls joined into one mass, forming a complex loaf of bread, spongy and light.

Somebody turned on the light in the oven, and it was orange. Pure, clean orange—the purest, unmixed orange color he had ever experienced.

Then softly he became aware of something above him. It was a huge, curved fire ax made of gleaming gold, with two tiny wings at the handle that whirred like a hummingbird's as they worked the ax toward him. There were two eyes in the blade blinking at him speculatively.

With two swift chops, the gleaming blade cut him into four neat pieces. Sharp as surgical steel, the blade did not hurt him at all, but suddenly he was aware of a manifold reality and could give each one his undivided attention.

He was riding in a helicopter, leaving his life of exile at Rialite behind him with mixed emotions. He had lost much, but now he was free.

He was sitting in the World Controller's office planning to redecorate the place in orange and brown.

He was examining his emotions from a whole new understanding.

He was apportioning all the material wealth of Zeor among its members.

It is the end.

Naked, he stood in a burning forest, flaming trees like huge torches all about him, but he did not burn.

The forest was on the side of a mountain. As long as he kept trudging upward, he would not burn. The path wound before him, paved with glowing gold. Each tree flamed higher as he passed, and as if in salute gave out a pure musical tone that seemed to strengthen him for the onward journey through the burning forest.

MAHOGANY TRINROSE 229

Once, as the cliffs rose higher before him, he took a few hesitant steps downward, but as he did, all the energy he had absorbed from the burning trees on the way up flamed from his surface—and hurt. He had soaked up too much fire. He could not go back.

He went ever higher until each burning tree of the flaming forest was an evergreen.

Above the timberline, he left the flaming forest behind and trudged into snow up to his knees. To either side of his path the snow was white, gleaming yellow from the glowing moon overhead. The rocks were purple shadows.

He scaled the heights with dogged determination to get to the top so he could end this insane trip.

Bruised and bleeding, naked in the snow, he clawed his way up the last cliff face and rolled onto the summit.

There, framed by two huge antique dueling swords larger than herself, stood his beloved Ilyana, naked in the snow, Gen nager a glowing promise. As he watched, the snow melted from around her feet, so that she stood on blue water as deep as the ocean. All about sounded the drip and clatter of melting snow.

He looked upon her, every cell of his being hungering with all the ache and longing of a thousand years of need.

And he also was surprised and even shocked at the intensity of this buried emotion he now knew had been there all along. *Ilyana*.

But as he slogged another step closer, it was Ercy who stood there, and then Im'ran, only he was chained by huge golden links to the twin swords that seemed to grow out of the bedrock beneath them. And then it was Ilyana again. He stood in the blue waters that circled her feet, as naked as she. Only she stood between the swords voluntarily. Their eyes met.

He came closer to her.

She had already made her choice. She was at peace. But she could not help him make the same choice she had made. He had to do that himself. *I can't.*

Within her eyes, he saw himself reflected, recognized himself, and knew himself. And in the eyes of the tiny figure that was himself, he saw reflected—himself—and in those eyes there was an ocean whipped to stormy foam waves higher than any mountain. The waves crashed down on themselves, whipping themselves to torment in anger and unresolved conflict. They were blown about by every force—because they were formless.

He rode that stormy sea until he was exhausted enough to decide he must do something. He became the sun, driving the

230 JACQUELINE LICHTENBERG

dark storm clouds away and evaporating the stormy seas. He became the air, carrying the dispersed moisture high into the mountains over the flaming forest, and there he became the moisture itself, climbing high into the sky where it was cold. He froze.

Each piece of him was a dainty snowflake floating down onto the mountain, burying the two naked figures there between their gleaming swords. His emotions had taken on form through the imposition of his conscious intellect. *I can take whatever form I desire.*

Darkness descended around him; soft, peaceful darkness. *Oh, yes, this is what it's like to be a snowflake buried miles deep in snowflakes.*

Then he looked into two familiar eyes and saw himself, and felt he was about to be sliced in two. *I will do it to myself. None other should have such a privilege over me. And it must be done.*

"This is insane," he heard himself say out loud.

"What is?" the eyes asked, hovering. Nageric eyes?

He was in the insulated room. "The drug must be wearing off," he said to Im'ran.

Im'ran bent close, his gentle hands sliding into transfer position as he made the fifth contact neatly. The golden fire poured through Digen, surging up his arms, plunging down through his chest, and radiating warmth and life through his whole body. But, by deliberate choice, he pulled no selyn into his junct pathways.

And then it was over; easy and without anguish.

"That," said Digen as they dismantled the contact, "was the most peaceful transfer I've had since I injured that lateral!"

"You're all right?"

Digen took a deep breath, testing himself throughout. "Not a bit of turbulence anywhere." And then he remembered. "Im', we did it! It's gone! I'm not junct! I'm free!" In his jubilation, he reached out and seized Im'ran's hands. "We did it!"

Im'ran's hands rested still in his grip. It was several seconds before either of them realized that no sharp burst of static had driven them apart as it always did with orhuen mates after a transfer.

Digen's grip tightened with that awareness. "Im', what—Im'?"

The Gen's surprise wiped aside their growing realization of what they had just accomplished. *The orhuen is gone.*

Together, they fell into empty shock.

Digen sat up. He was alive, his mind told him. Im'ran was

MAHOGANY TRINROSE 231

alive, his flesh told him in no uncertain terms. He wasn't dreaming now. There were no searing nerves, no bleeding edges where the intertwined systems of orhuen mates had been joined. Neither of them was suffering.

What have we done? What have we discovered?

With a quaver of fear, Im'ran asked, "Digen, what's happening?"

"Give me transfer position again. I want to check something."

And after a momentary contact, Digen took the Gen by the shoulders to steady him. "Prepare for another shock, Im'. You're back on true. The Tecton can calibrate its instruments by you—just like before you had the shaking plague."

And that was a shock.

"We're not matchmates any more?"

"No, not any more."

"Digen—what have we lost? What have we lost that we never really knew how precious it was?"

"It's going to be all right," said Digen, trying dully to gather some shred of optimism. "We survived it, and we're not hurt. We can get used to this—like we got used to everything else."

Chapter 22

Several days later, Digen was called to the horse barn.

He had spent most of his time in his office or Mora's, pressing the search. In off moments, or when Im'ran came around, it was driven home to him that his old life was now over. He would have to start anew—learn a whole new world that had grown out there while he hid at Rialite. Intellectually, he knew his obsession with the search was a defense against facing what was already cold fact. *Give me time. I'll find the strength.*

He got to the barn when the early-afternoon sun was slanting through loft doors, illuminating the three horses that the grooms were rubbing down. These were the horses that had been missing.

"Yes, it's them all right, Hajene Farris," said the stablemaster, an old Gen woman.

"There was no sign—of the riders?"

"None. We backtracked them and scoured the area for a day's ride in every direction. Not a sign. And I'll tell you, these horses have been running—days, I'd think. They're in bad shape."

Digen went up to the animals, running one hand over a quivering flank, feeling the sweat-matted hair full of dust and weeds. The stablemaster was saying nothing but the obvious.

Mora came up behind him, her transceiver on her hip. Every once in a while, a tiny voice could be heard reporting from the search parties. Her nager was quivering on the brink of utter despair. Digen turned and put his arm about her, the only woman to give him a child who survived to adulthood. Now, belatedly, he realized how very much of Mora's fierce independence was in Ercy. Mora went her own way, managing and organizing and accomplishing, and mostly you never knew she was there—because she never failed. Never, until now.

As her nager crumpled, he gathered her in and offered what silent strength he could. It was then and there he came to the clear confrontation. *We're going to leave Rialite. But not together.*

A few hours later, as the search parties came in for the night,

MAHOGANY TRINROSE 233

Digen gathered Mora and Im', Sels and Bett, into his office. Digen said, "Don't dispatch the night patrols, Mora. Call everybody in. We'll never find them." *Could anything be more final?*

Mora had been sitting in the chair beside the lamp table, where she had set her transceiver. She picked it up. There was no quiver in her voice as she called off the search and sent her people off to rest.

The Simes in the room turned toward the door a moment before the intercom on Digen's desk chimed. "Sectuib Farris, the First Assistant World Controller to see you."

"Send him in," said Digen. The secretary ushered Jiplain into the room, followed by Rellow.

Jiplain took the remaining chair at Digen's invitation and Rellow was left standing beside him. "I'll come right to the point," said Jiplain. "I know this is a difficult moment, but it will be better for you when I can pull my committee out of here and grant you at least that much privacy. Have you heard the evening news?"

"No," said Sels.

"I'm just as glad," said Jiplain. "I'd rather you heard it from me, in person." He was holding his slender briefcase between his hands. "I've been empowered—I suppose that's the right word—to declare Aild Ercy Farris, heir to Zeor, legally dead. With Zeor at stake, we can't wait for the normal procedures to cycle through. A new heir has to be chosen."

Digen had seen some of the articles and news items detailing what the public and several prominent economists believed would happen if Zeor were suddenly to be thrown into the legal no-man's-land of not having a Sectuib.

"Suppose Ercy turns up again, alive?" asked Sels.

"We'll cope with that when it happens—perhaps by then there will be some proper legal mechanism standardizing the lines of succession within the Householdings. For now, though, we must have these papers signed and on file." Jiplain handed Digen a sheaf of papers.

On top was Ercy's death certificate—signed by a court of law but unwitnessed. Digen realized *he* was being required to witness that death—who else but her Sectuib? Under that was a long printed document—with his name neatly typed in at the top, it became his will, naming his heirs and beneficiaries—the heir to Zeor.

"It's not my place," said Digen, "to name an heir arbitrarily."

"I don't think you fully appreciate what we're offering you,

234 JACQUELINE LICHTENBERG

Sectuib Farris. My committee has met and agreed to drop the charges against you since they all leaned heavily on the fact that you were—and had been for some time—junct. That situation no longer exists. Your judgment—presumably—has returned to its former trustworthiness. Now, you have only one small act to perform which will establish that our faith in your judgment is justified—name Zeor's heir so that in the event of your death Zeor Industries will not collapse, taking our entire economy with them.''

Digen glanced at Rellow, who stood silently, face expressionless. Then he took his time examining the document he had been handed.

It was, as far as he could see, his own will with not one comma changed except that where he had named Ercy, Rellow's name had been neatly typed in. *If Rellow should ever get his tentacles on this House,* thought Digen, *he surely would bring the world economy down around our ears.*

With sudden decision, calm settled over Digen. He called for his secretary and dictated: ''I do hereby recommend to Zeor that, in the event of my death without a direct-descended heir for prior consideration, Zeor should consider Rellow Gishrun Farris for the position of Sectuib ambrov Zeor to serve under the Regency of Sels Herum Farris and/or Liam Bett Farris, his parents, so long as either Sels Herum or Liam Bett shall live. In the event of the death of Sels Herum Farris and Liam Bett Farris, Rellow Gishrun Farris will stand for Sectuib along with every other able-bodied channel in Zeor according to Zeor custom. In no event will Rellow Gishrun Farris be allowed to serve in violation of Zeor custom.''

Maybe by the time this is invoked, Landar or Rellow will have fathered a child who can become Sectuib.

Digen handed the folded will to his secretary. ''Type that up and attach it here, crossing out the provision for the heir. Then have the lawyer check it over, and I'll sign it in the morning.'' When she had gone, he said to the very silent Jiplain, wondering how Rellow had managed to keep still, ''That's the best I can do. It honestly is. Sels here is third in Zeor, and would be in line after me except that he's older than I am.''

''I will have our experts look it over. Perhaps it will suffice.''

Digen looked down at the death certificate, the only thing left on his desk. ''If you don't mind, I'll sign this in the morning, too. I don't have the heart for it right now.''

My last child. How can she be dead, too?

MAHOGANY TRINROSE   235

*   *   *

The next morning, Digen signed the papers, and the committee, along with Rellow and the news teams, left Rialite.

A few days later, they held a funeral, erecting a formal monument for Ercy, even though Digen at first objected. Mora, ever practical, had pointed out that the Rialite staff had known and loved Ercy—and Halimer Grant, and even Joeslee after she got over her wild stage. So beside Ercy's monument, they placed a tall white marble one that reminded every Sime of Grant's nager, and forming a triangle, they put up one for Joslee Teel Tigue.

Sentiment ran high during the week all of this was going on, and after Digen conceded, they persuaded him that Ercy's and Grant's and Joeslee's names should be entered in the Memorial to the One Billion, and in Zeor's roll of martyrs. And so he presided over that very final ceremony. During those days, they all cried until there were no more tears in them.

Digen was in need again by the time they unveiled the monument stones with great and solemn ceremony. And despite the need, a few tears pooled in the corners of his eyes and he had to turn away from the news cameras. When it was over, looking down on the little garden from the window that had been Ercy's, Digen thought the monuments stood on the exact spot where Grant had first met Ercy.

He looked around the empty, echoing apartment. All their things had been packed for the move back into the city. The painters were already spreading drop cloths and bringing in ladders. Sels and Bett would be taking over Rialite, occupying these apartments.

Im'ran came in, not seeing Digen where he stood half behind a painter's ladder festooned with canvas. Digen watched the Gen's nager flick through anxiety, curiosity, a tinge of nostalgia, and an impatient shrug. Then he said over his shoulder to another figure, a Sime, obscured behind Im'ran's ripe nager, "I honestly don't know where he could be then, but he'll turn up soon. We're scheduled for transfer."

"Isn't that—?" gently inquired the visitor, indicating Digen's direction.

Digen stepped out where Im'ran could see him. "Were you looking for me?"

Gypsy? thought Digen, examining the visitor.

"I was, Sectuib Farris," said the gypsy. "Could I have a word with you in private? I can wait if necessary."

236 JACQUELINE LICHTENBERG

"Come into the kitchen," suggested Digen. "The painters aren't in there yet."

When Im'ran followed them into the kitchen, which was bare already, awaiting its paint, the Sime gypsy turned to the Gen questioningly. *That's right,* thought Digen, *we're not orhuen mates any more—no privacy privileges with each other now.*

He could feel Im'ran going through the same thought.

"I'll be waiting," Im'ran said, and left them.

"Well, I presume it was something important," said Digen, and then regretted his sharp tone. "I'm sorry—"

"I have been entrusted with a message for you, Sectuib Farris—from your daughter."

Digen gasped, glad he was in need, all his emotions bound up in that perfectly normal obsession and unable to respond even to this.

"When—when did you get this message? Is she all right? Where is she? Is she coming back?"

"Please allow me to repeat the message. She says she is fine. She will keep Zeor's ways, but she will not come home. She says to be sure to tell you she loves you. She asks only that you keep the fact that she is alive a secret."

"But where is she? I have to see her!"

"The message was passed to me by another gypsy who got it from another. I have no idea where your daughter could be, or how far the message traveled to reach you. I must go now. My apologies for disturbing you at this time."

"No—wait!" said Digen.

"I know nothing else."

"Can you take a message back to her?"

"I don't know—I can try. I doubt if I will see the one who gave me this message for a year or maybe more. And—you are leaving here—"

"My sister and brother-in-law will be here. Any message for me can always be given to them, and it will reach me—confidentially. Please, try to get word to Ercy—Aild Ercy Farris—I love her well enough to want her content and happy—but Zeor must have an heir or her cousin Rellow will become Sectuib when I die. She'll know what that means."

Digen offered the gypsy the customary fee for his services, but the man unaccountably refused, and left after emphatic promises to try to get the message through.

Before he went to Im'ran for his first transfer to this phase of his life, Digen went down into the Memorial to the One Billion.

MAHOGANY TRINROSE   237

He stood where Ercy had stood to Receive Zeor, joy and grief mingled with the need in him. *If she gets the message—she'll give Zeor an heir. She'll come home. When she can.*

And when he turned to go, he knew that at last he was finished at Rialite.

He had a new future in which to rebuild his life. And he knew he could do it. The dedication of his young years was alive in him again. The world could yet be changed—perhaps to be a safe place for Ercy.

ACE ANNOUNCES A NEW DIMENSION IN SCIENCE FICTION AND FANTASY PUBLISHING

ACE HARDCOVERS

The #1 publisher of paperback science fiction and fantasy proudly announces the launch of a new hardcover line. Featuring the finest quality fiction by top, award-winning authors, and striking cover designs by today's most respected cover artists, ACE HARDCOVERS will make an impressive addition to your science fiction and fantasy collection.

COMING IN SEPTEMBER 1986

THE DRAGON IN THE SWORD by Michael Moorcock. *The first new novel in fifteen years in the classic Eternal Champion epic. This swords-and-sorcery adventure takes the Eternal Champion to an alternate world and a confrontation with the heart of evil itself.*

THE FOREVER MAN by Gordon R. Dickson. *The author of the Childe Cycle explores an exciting future where scientists are trying to solve the puzzle of a man who disappeared two centuries before—and has returned with his mind and soul merged with the circuitry of his ship.*

And look for more Ace hardcovers by Steven Brust, Clive Barker, Alan Dean Foster, Patricia A. McKillip, and Jerry Pournelle!

Ace Science Fiction and Fantasy

THE BERKLEY PUBLISHING GROUP
Berkley • Jove • Charter • Ace

SCIENCE FICTION AT ITS BEST!

____ **THE MOON IS A HARSH MISTRESS**
Robert A. Heinlein   08899-5 — $3.50

____ **MILLENNIUM**
John Varley   08991-6 — $2.95

____ **DUNE**
Frank Herbert   08002-1 — $3.95

____ **HERETICS OF DUNE**
Frank Herbert   08732-8 — $4.50

____ **INTERPLANETARY FLIGHT**
Arthur C. Clarke   06448-4 — $2.95

____ **THE GREEN PEARL** (Trade ed.)
Jack Vance   08746-8 — $6.95

____ **GODS OF RIVERWORLD**
Philip José Farmer   09170-8 — $3.50

____ **THE MAN IN THE HIGH CASTLE**
Philip K. Dick   08656-9 — $2.95

____ **HELLICONIA SUMMER**
Brian W. Aldiss   08650-X — $3.95

Available at your local bookstore or return this form to:

B **BERKLEY**
THE BERKLEY PUBLISHING GROUP, Dept. B
390 Murray Hill Parkway, East Rutherford, NJ 07073

Please send me the titles checked above. I enclose _____. Include $1.00 for postage and handling if one book is ordered; 25¢ per book for two or more not to exceed $1.75. California, Illinois, New Jersey and Tennessee residents please add sales tax. Prices subject to change without notice and may be higher in Canada.

NAME_____

ADDRESS_____

CITY_____STATE/ZIP_____

(Allow six weeks for delivery.)